# STAR CROSSED

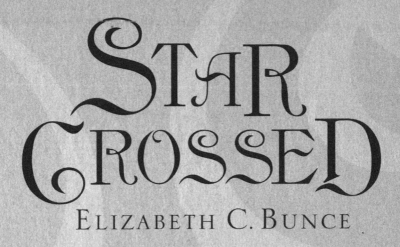

# STAR CROSSED

## Elizabeth C. Bunce

# ARTHUR A. LEVINE BOOKS

An Imprint of Scholastic Inc.

Library of Congress Cataloging-in-Publication Data
Bunce, Elizabeth C.
    Starcrossed / by Elizabeth C. Bunce. — 1st ed.
        p. cm.
    Summary: In a kingdom dominated by religious intolerance, sixteen-year-old Digger, a street thief, has always avoided attention, but when she learns that her friends are plotting against the throne she must decide whether to join them or turn them in.
    ISBN 978-0-545-13605-1 (hardcover : alk. paper) [1. Fantasy — Fiction. 2. Religion — Fiction. 3. Kings, queens, rulers, etc. — Fiction. 4. Social classes — Fiction. 5. Magic — Fiction. 6. Robbers and outlaws — Fiction.] I. Title.
    PZ7.B91505St 2010
    [Fic] — dc22

                                                                            2010000730


Book design by Phil Falco

10 9 8 7 6 5 4 3 2 1      10 11 12 13 14

Printed in the U.S.A.      23
First edition, October 2010

For Christopher,
my staunchest ally

*8 -056*

PART I

# STAY ALIVE

# CHAPTER ONE

I couldn't think. My chest hurt from running, and I wasn't even sure I was in the right place. Tegen had given me directions to a tavern on the river — was this where he'd told me to go, if things went wrong?

It didn't matter. I had to get off the streets. Behind me, the Oss splashed moonslight over a row of riverside storefronts, bright enough for me to make out the sign of a blue wine bottle and the short flight of stairs down into the alley. Down was shadows and safety. I took it.

*You'll know the place,* he'd said — and there, under my fingers as I felt for the door latch, sparked a tiny, wavering star, carved into the wood so faintly it was nearly invisible. Its odd smoky light faded when I moved my hand away. I tumbled the lock (Tegen had the keys) but had to bang the door open with my hip. I left a smear of blood on the frame as I wrestled it shut again.

Breathing heavily, I took stock. Shelves, barrels, damp stone floor. It was dank and musty, as if the river crept in on rainy days. All good, for me. Must and stuck doors meant neglect, and neglect meant nobody was likely to find me here, no matter how busy the tavern got. The only door was the one I came in. A single window at street side, too low for moonslight. Except for the occasional passing light of a boat overhead, it should stay dark here all night. Still, I kept to the shadows. Eyes could look into windows as well as out.

*How long should I wait?* At least until Tegen came — or Hass showed up with our pay.

Or until the Greenmen got here.

I choked back that thought, my throat tight. I leaned against one of the barrels and peeled back my sleeve, hissing as the cloth pulled away from dried blood. Not as bad as it felt — the point had just grazed my skin. And if I hadn't blocked that blow, I probably would have lost an eye.

Or worse. I took a shaky breath. Bandages. A safe house for thieves should have bandages, right?

The safe house was very much wine cellar and much less hideout, but a bench under the window held spare clothes, at least. I dug out a rumpled green gown like nobs wear, a doxie's split silk knickers, and a screaming-pink doublet and trunk hose. The hidden mark I'd found on the door meant this place had refuged Sarists during the war, but now it looked more like a hangout for bawds and their bucks. No bandages.

I sacrificed the knickers. Using my teeth, I tore them into ragged strips and tried to concentrate on the work and calm my hammering heartbeat. I uncorked a bottle of wine and went to pour some over the wound, but my hands were jouncing so badly I dumped half the contents on my skirts, dousing the strips of cloth. Cursing every god I knew, I mopped up as much blood as I could, pinning the wet cloth in the crook of my arm to hold it there.

*What happened?* I couldn't slow the images spinning in my mind enough to make sense of them. We'd finished the job; we should have been safe. Tegen had thrown an arm around me and kissed me. I had laughed, the blood rushing in my veins. Hass's client would have the letters, I'd have fifteen crowns, and Tegen would have me. Everything had gone perfectly.

Until the men in green slammed through the street-side doors and wrenched Tegen off me, a flashing silver blade easing the separation. A bloom of red sprang up on Tegen's knife — the guard's blood — a burst of blackness blinded me, and for a moment I couldn't breathe. And then, cutting through the chaos, Tegen's voice: *Digger, run!*

And I ran. Like I'd never run in my life, crossing what felt like half the city. All the way here, I'd heard their pounding footsteps behind me, but didn't dare look back. At least one of the Greenmen had to have gotten a good look at me — the one who'd cracked my skull against the wall. Or the one who'd grabbed Tegen.

Panic seized my belly and I fought back nausea. *You got away. You got away.* I repeated the words silently until I no longer felt like gagging.

Bruises would heal. But Tegen . . . I swallowed back another wave of panic.

*Get hold of yourself if you want to live through the night.*

Where was he? He must have gone to Hass first, to deliver the letters. He'd shake the Greenmen, drop the cargo and get our pay, then circle back here when things were safe. It might take a while. That was why he'd sent me here, to wait for him. I closed my eyes for a moment, but I still saw Tegen, bloody knife in hand, kicking and slashing as I ran away.

I checked the window, although there wasn't much to be seen from down here. My knee almost buckled under me when I slid off the barrel, but I couldn't sit still. The grille on the window made the room feel like a cell, and the smell of my own blood was starting to make me light-headed.

Food. I needed food, and sleep, and a plan. I probably also needed medical attention, but it wasn't like I ever had access to that. Food could wait; I'd spent more than one night hungry — though not lately — another wouldn't kill me. Dry clothes, however . . .

The guards were looking for a girl in black wool. As a boy I'd be less conspicuous — but *not* in that ridiculous pink costume. The green then, wrinkled as it was. It was safest, anyway. Guards were less likely to stop someone in green to check papers. I clawed the pins from my hair with one hand and twisted my laces free with the other, but as the kirtle loosened, I felt the crinkle of paper between the wool and my corset.

Everything in me sank again. Tegen must have slipped Chavel's letters into my bodice when he kissed me. The pins scattered to the floor as I dipped a hand into my dress to pull the packet of letters free.

They were spotted with blood.

Tegen wasn't coming.

I stood there, half undone, staring at the folded papers in my trembling fingers. I hadn't let myself believe he wouldn't get away. He was *Tegen*. But my bruised knee, my cracked skull, and my bloody arm told the truth. If Tegen hadn't stabbed that guard — stupid, reckless, deadly thing to do — the Greenmen would just have arrested two thieves. Searched us, branded us, maybe even let us go, if Hass coughed up our bounty. But instead they got one heretic: It was a sin to strike the servants of the Goddess, even her pox-ridden temple guards. And heresy was the only crime those men in green really cared about.

I wanted to charge straight back there and drag him away, but at the thought of those hands on him — on *me* again — I sank to the floor. I knew what every thief knew, what every citizen of Gerse knew, these days: Nobody gets away from Greenmen.

I sat there all night, even as my leg stiffened up, even as I knew I had to get out of there and move. A safe house was temporary; someone was bound to come down here eventually, and I had the evidence of my crime all over me.

I should get rid of the letters. I should get them to Hass, get paid for them.

But Hass hadn't been there. He hadn't seen the men in green melt out of the woodwork and seize Tegen —

A sickening idea stopped that thought cold. *Had he set us up?*

I didn't know what to do next. This was Tegen's job, and Hass was Tegen's contact; I'd just been along to make sure we lifted the right documents. Tegen didn't read — he couldn't tell one language from another, couldn't distinguish a symbol that might be charmed from something commonplace. I possessed that unique skill, and it had made me a valuable partner. *Valuable enough to trust with the prize?* I turned the letters over, rubbed their folded edges, but stopped short of opening them. They were written in Corles, a language I could recognize but not read. Hass had given specific instructions about what to look for — the language, the mark of the king's private secretary. There was nothing . . . special about these papers. They lay cold and dead and ordinary in my hands.

The smart thing would be to toss them into a hearth or the river. But I didn't have anything else. If they were worth Tegen's life, then they were worth a damn sight more than fifteen crowns. There was no reason to carry a full purse on a job; whatever money I had was safely stashed away in my rooms, which was the last place I could go right now. If I couldn't go home, and I couldn't get to Hass to get rid of the letters and get paid, that didn't leave a lot of options open.

City, royal, and temple guards patrolled the streets at all hours of the day, and they spread news among each other like a plague. An injured Greenman would have the whole lot of them on the hunt for the attacker's accomplice. There wasn't anybody I trusted enough not to give me up for that kind of crime. I had to get out of Gerse.

Finally, a pale, uneven light filtered through the narrow window. Night was fading, and with it, the last of my cover.

I hauled my sore body up from the floor and tested my leg. It would hold me, without limping, but wasn't any too happy about it. I could creep upstairs and help myself to something from the tavern kitchen, or the tavern strongbox, or the tavern patrons . . . but a sudden jostle of voices from the river walk quenched that notion. I had to get moving.

I had to get *dressed*. I tucked the letters into my corset and pulled on the green dress, doing my best with the inconveniently placed laces and my inconveniently placed wound, then hoisted myself onto one of the barrels and watched through the ironwork. Richly shod feet passed by, inches from my nose. I was nothing more than a mouse in the corner, a pigeon on a windowsill.

When the walk was clear, I eased off the barrel and shook myself tidy. There wasn't so much blood — only a smear on the inside of my sleeve and a few drops on my skirt, not that noticeable on the dark silk. I bundled my black dress around a loose brick I found on the floor, strode out onto the wharf as if I belonged there, and pitched the clothes into the water, for the mudlarks to find at low tide.

I needed a lady's maid, a snub-nosed little dog, a *basket*, for gods' sake! I was too exposed out here alone. I kept wanting to slink back into the shadows, but shadows were scarce in the morning on the river. Oss Harborway was bustling this late in the season, the river walk busy with fishermen, merchants, and Nob Circle servants stocking up on the morning's provisions. I cast about for where to turn next, but it was nothing but tall white houses to my left, and clear gray water to my right. Boats crowded the harbor, a tangle of hulls and masts and the sleek black bodies of swift little river cruisers.

The river was my best hope, but how was I going to sneak onto a boat looking like a lost nob?

I swept my skirts out in a wide arc, giving me room in all that fabric to move along at a pretty good clip, up out of the tavern's neighborhood, toward the busier section of the city. It wasn't much past dawn, and sunlight bounced off the green-tiled roof of the Celystra, making the temple complex glitter in the morning like a field of emeralds. It was only the roof; the temple and its guards were safely behind a wall three streets away, but my gut clenched as I hurried past, ready to get as far as possible from the goddess Celys and her dogs.

"Hey, greensleeves!"

I didn't hear him at first. I was looking over a merchant trader, trying to decide if I could get hired on as a boy-of-all-work. I'd have to waylay a *real* boy, and shake him down for his clothes, of course —

"Milady! You there — greensleeves."

This time my attention snapped to the bank, as I realized that comment was directed at me. I hammered down the jolt in my throat and forced myself to look down calmly.

A long, gaily painted pleasure skiff had drawn up beside me, and a young nob in an absurd hat was leaning over the side, waving at me. The amber of his ring sparked like a flame in the sunlight. I took an involuntary half step backward, but he didn't *look* like a Greenman. . . .

"Milady greensleeves, pray tell us, do you know how much farther to the city gates? I promised my companion here that I'd get him out of Gerse. There'll be a copper in it for you."

I hesitated, glanced across the riverway. How could anyone not know where the gates were? I straightened my shoulders and kept walking.

"All right, a silver." The nob dipped his oar into the water, pushing the boat a few yards forward — following me. This time I stopped and looked his way. He wasn't alone; there were two girls and another young man in the boat with him. They reeked of money, but looked like they'd all slept in their clothes. Or hadn't slept at all, maybe.

The young nob fished inside his slops and withdrew a coin, which he held out to me, like baiting a shy dog. My frown deepened. The longer I stood here in the sun, the better the chances somebody would see me.

"Take me aboard and I'll show you," I said.

A grin spread across the young nob's face. "Ah, a counteroffer! But democracy reigns in this boat; we'll have to take a vote. What say you all?" He turned to his companions with a wave of his arm.

I didn't have time for this. I shrugged and started down the pier again.

"No, milady, wait — you have a deal." He rose up with exaggerated grace and offered me his hand, the silver coin still glinting in his palm. Suddenly suspicious, I drew back and glared at him.

"I'm not a prostitute."

"Of course you're not," Absurd Hat said with a soothing smile. "Still, I thought you might be able to cheer my friend up." He gestured toward the other young man, who sat hunched and sour-faced, as if he'd spent a hard night.

"He looks like he's had plenty of good spirits already," I retorted. The girl beside Absurd Hat, a thin beauty with the requisite vast green eyes and light brown hair, gave an unbecoming snort. The other girl, a plump brunette crammed into her high-waisted velvet gown, watched me with worried eyes.

"Leave her alone, Raffin," she said.

"Shut up, Merista," said Beautiful. "You — what's your name?" Her voice fairly dripped with snobbery. Nobs.

"Don't be scared," Raffin said. "You can tell us. What are you doing on the docks all alone, in that *stunning* gown?"

Beautiful snickered.

"Flown your fetters, have you?" he continued. "Well, us too. I'm Raffin Taradyce — you may have heard of me — and my companions are the

Lady Phandre Séthe, Durrel of Decath, and the very proper Merista Nemair."

My empty belly tightened. Taradyce — of course I'd heard of him. I'd done work for his father, but I'd never met the son. Sons. I racked my brain, trying to remember — was this the heir? No, he couldn't be. Not gadding about on the river all night with a son of Decath and two noble girls.

"Where are you going?" I said, not sure how to pitch my voice. Who did they take me for? Who *might* they take me for?

"Nowhere," said Durrel, the first word he'd spoken. "Raff, would you turn the damn boat around? The sun's in my eyes."

"Oh, the gratitude!" cried Raffin. "After all I've done for you! And look, I've practically plucked you the finest fruit this side of Gerse town. The least you could do is be a bit welcoming. We're Dur's bachelor party," he added confidingly to me.

"You're his what?"

Raffin threw an extravagant arm around his friend, who looked like he'd punch him if he could only summon the energy. "Milord Durrel has just had the exquisite good fortune of meeting his betrothed. So we had to cheer him up."

"You seem to have done a fine job," I said, and immediately cursed my loose tongue. *Careful, Digger, careful. You are* not *their class; you can't just speak to them like that.*

"That's why we need you," Raffin said, climbing out of the boat. I forced myself to hold my ground. I had a knife in my boot — I could use it, if I had to. Although stabbing a son of Taradyce in broad daylight in Nob Circle . . . not the way to go undetected. "To round out the numbers," he continued.

"Hey!" Lady Phandre squawked. "How does five round anything out?"

"Fetch your mind from the gutter, milady — Meri's his sister! Or near enough. What say you, Lady? Join our little party?"

"Where are you going?" I asked again, glancing toward the shoreline.

"Anywhere! Downriver, certainly. It's a day's sail to Favom Court — Decath lands. Dur has a whole day and a night to decide just how far he wants to run."

At least a day outside the city, a whole day to decide what to do with myself. A day away from Greenmen — but a day between me and my pay. I pinched my finger. Better to just abandon the dream of those fifteen crowns; fat good they'd do me in the dungeons. The sharply angled sunlight was softening to dawn now, the moons fading from the sky, all but Tiboran, ever visible day and night, both constant and inconstant. Was this boatful of drunken strangers the fickle god's idea of a gift? An apology?

Half a moon now: even chances. I fingered the silk of my skirts, trying to think. And the sun rose higher, and the Greenmen would be changing shifts . . .

*Don't trust anybody.*

"Why me?"

"You're pretty," I heard Raffin say, just as Phandre said, "He's bored."

That I believed. I wasn't that pretty: A year ago, I'd still been able to pass as a boy.

The merchant trader had hauled anchor, and was pushing away from the docks.

I looked around carefully. Still no sign of Greenmen. Yet.

"Do you have any food?"

# CHAPTER TWO

They had food, and plenty of it — the remains of a lavish feast, abandoned halfway through when thirst overtook their appetites. Once I was settled in the boat, Raffin pushed me a tray laden with the carcass of a peacock (I think), and Durrel blanched as it passed over him. I tore a piece of cold meat from the bird and shoved it in my mouth, as much to stop myself from screaming, "Row! Row!" as to quiet the roaring hunger in my belly.

Merista sat across from me as I ate, looking worried. She was obviously the reluctant party in this outing. Raffin had said she was Durrel's sister, or near enough. Cousins, raised together? The Decath were like that, intertwined with every noble family in Llyvraneth, and probably beyond. It was impossible to tell how important these two were. People said the Decath were ciphers; nobody could pin them down politically. That could be useful — or it could be dangerous. I had no idea who Merista's family was, but the plump little pussycat didn't seem like much of a threat.

"What's your name?" Phandre demanded again. This time I was prepared to answer.

"Celyn."

"Of course it is," said Raffin, pinching off a bit of my meat. The Taradyce were minor nobles, but they owned half the riverfront in Gerse, and court circles in town were overrun with Taradyce brats and Taradyce bastards. He didn't wear the round green brooch the nobs affected to show their loyalty to Bardolph, and he didn't strike me as a rat who'd lark out strangers to the guards for a handful of gold marks. Not that I was ready to wager my life on that yet.

"Your *family* name," Phandre said impatiently. Hers — Séthe, he'd said? — meant nothing to me, but she obviously thought herself something special. Clad all in green, the only one of the lot, besides me. No brooch either — and if she'd had one, I'd have lifted it. She reminded me of a kestrel, the beautiful but temperamental hunting birds flown by the nobs. You never knew whether they would nibble sweetly from your fingers, or lash out and nip a chunk of flesh from your hand.

"Contrare," I said, hoping somebody would remember that.

"Never heard of them."

"I have," came an unexpected voice. Durrel slid upward in his seat. His doublet — neutrally gray and broochless — was much the worse for a night in a boat, and he tugged unconsciously on its hem. He had a boyish face and a shock of mousy hair, untidily smashed by his soft cap. "Jewelers, right? Up in the Third Circle?"

"I — yes." Why had he said that? Durrel watched me evenly, an unreadable expression in his dark eyes. This was just as likely to be a trap as it was to be helpful, but for now it was all I had. At least he'd picked something I actually *knew* about.

"Merchants." I could *hear* the sneer, even if she hadn't made it plain on her face.

"Oh, Phandre, leave her alone." This from Merista. "What happened to you? Did you run away?"

Better and better. I nodded faintly, glancing to shore. Where were they? You couldn't go an hour in the city without seeing one on the nearest street corner —

"Indeed?" Raffin said. "Here, have some grapes. Tell us, what circumstances did the merchant's daughter find so intolerable?"

"What?" I hadn't been listening.

"Yes, do tell. Who were you running away from? Arranged marriage? Overbearing nurse? This should be amusing." Phandre gave a barely disguised yawn, then broke into a grin. "I know — you're a Sarist!" She shrieked with laughter, much too loud.

"Phandre, that's *enough*." Raffin's voice had turned abruptly hard, and he grabbed her wrist. Phandre yanked her arm away, but seemed to realize she'd gone too far. She sank a little lower in her seat.

"Ignore her, Celyn," Raffin said. "I don't know why we let her out of her cage."

He plunged the oars into the Oss and pushed off again. I didn't realize I'd been holding my breath until we were back in the water and I felt the pressure on my chest lifting. I could almost let myself relax. Almost.

"Go ahead, Celyn, give us your tale," Durrel said.

Apparently, my presence here depended on an entertaining — and convincing — account of my history. Well, I didn't worship at Tiboran's table for nothing, did I? I said a quick prayer to the god of liars and took a long swig of the wine to fortify myself. I looked my audience over.

"First of all, I am *not* a Sarist," I began, trying to sound light. The others gave that the laughter it deserved. "My parents are dead." That was all true enough, but Merista gave a mew of sympathy that made it seem like tragedy anew. I turned to her. "Since then it's been just me and —" I paused. Tegen's advice: *Tell the truth; it's easy to remember.* Luckily, my companions took my hesitation for a clench of grief, nothing more. "My brother. He couldn't stand that I'd come of age before him, and was already eligible for my inheritance." That was reasonable: Girls came of age at fourteen, but boys not until twenty-one. My "brother" wouldn't be the first man galled by that.

"How old are you?" Phandre demanded.

"Sixteen," I continued. "So —"

"You look like a ten-year-old!"

That was an exaggeration. I couldn't help being tiny, but I had all the right parts, and this stupid gown was supposed to show off my assets. I held my arm out toward Phandre.

"Here. Why don't you cut off my hand and count my growth rings?"

Raffin laughed, but Phandre turned scarlet. "How — how *dare* you, you city brat! I'll have you flogged for speaking to me like that!"

I tensed, the platter of fowl balanced on my knees. I could reach my dagger. I could cause a scene. I could climb ashore and forget them. But I would *rather* go to Favom Court — and beyond. I took a deep breath. "Your pardon, milady."

Durrel held up a warning hand to Phandre. "Please go on."

"So . . . my brother finally came up with a plan to get rid of me."

"Murder you?" Merista cried, fingers pressed to her lips.

I closed my open mouth. "No."

A soft voice suggested, "Marry you off?" Durrel was watching me intently now, but it was impossible to tell what that look held. He seemed kind enough, but I wouldn't be the first girl led to ruin for trusting the pretty gazes of a nobbish boy.

I turned my eyes to shore instead, where the green domes of the Celystra loomed over the city — and here my god Tiboran betrayed me. "No. He sent me to the Daughters of Celys."

Pox and hells! Why *not* claim to be a Sarist? Why not just tell them the truth? Greenmen paid dearly for errant Aspirants; why should I suspect these nobs were immune to temptation — or fear? People sold out their loved ones all the time, and I was nothing to these people.

Durrel exchanged one long silent look with his cousin, and I wondered desperately what shared thought was in that grim gaze. But Raffin leaned back and regarded me with something like respect, a lazy smile on his languid face. Finally, though, Phandre broke the silence.

"Convent school!" she said. "I'd've run away too. Gods, *imagine* it! No clothes, no maids, and the *food!*" She shuddered.

I didn't have to imagine it.

"Well, clearly you never made it to the school," Raffin said, taking a handful of my silk skirts.

"No, I *did*," I said, catching up again. "And had Tiboran's own time getting out again, let me tell you! It took months of planning — just to get the clothes alone. . . ."

"Weren't you scared?" Merista broke in, her voice small and breathy. "Out on the streets alone? Where were you going to go?"

"I — I hadn't thought that far."

She folded her hands in her lap and looked at her cousin. "I think we should take her home. Her brother — not to mention everyone at the Celystra — must be worried sick!"

I sat very still. If Tiboran ever loved me . . .

"Now, now, cousin," Raffin said, "don't be fobbing off your own feel-ings on our fair guest here. You seemed perfectly willing to come yesterday afternoon."

"Well, I didn't know you were planning on sailing out of the *city*. And besides, I only came along to keep an eye on Durrel. I don't trust you, Raffin Taradyce."

"Don't I know it," he said, toasting her with the wine bottle. "Come on, Meri. You'd not condemn our lovely friend to a life as a convent sis-ter! Not even you could be so dull. Little Celyn here obviously wanted an adventure, and I think we'd be failing in our duties as her hosts if we didn't provide one. Besides, you know what they'd do to her." His voice had grown solemn.

Merista, eyes wide, shook her head.

"Probably shave her head and hang her for a Sarist," Phandre said quietly.

Merista looked stubbornly unconvinced. "Durrel —" she pleaded.

Raffin looked between us all. Finally he turned to Durrel. "This is your voyage, brother. What say you?"

Durrel looked straight at me. "Celyn?"

"I am at your mercy," I said. And that, at least, was the honest truth.

Durrel leaned back in his seat. He seemed to be reviving some, now that the sun was higher in the sky.

"I knew your father a little," he said, startling me. "Janos, right?"

I nodded jerkily. It was extraordinary, really, considering I had only just invented the man.

"He was a good man," he continued. "Steady. I don't think he'd want to see his daughter in a convent. Celyn Contrare, will you accept my per-sonal welcome as my guest aboard the *Taradyce Swan*?"

I stared at him, my heart a cold knot in my throat. Was this nobleman offering me his protection? That was almost as good as money. Hastily I shifted the platter of meat to the cushioned bench and knelt before him on the floor of the skiff.

"Milord, I do most humbly accept your offer of hospitality. May the gods find me worthy."

"Get up, girl!" Raffin cried. "He's not making himself your liege lord!" He yanked me back to my seat. "But I think I speak for us all — except our tedious cousin there, who is not yet of age and who therefore does not get a vote anyway, when I say: Bugger the convent!"

I hooked the wine out of his fingers. "I'll drink to that."

The bottle made its rounds once again, but the night was catching up to all of us.

"Pass me that, Raff. My head is splitting." Durrel hunched forward, rubbing his eyes.

"It serves you right," Merista said.

"Scold me later?"

Merista softened and slid toward him. "Here." She pushed her heavy sleeves back and slipped a silver bracelet off into her skirts, where there was no way I could retrieve it without being seen. She tugged off her cousin's hat and pressed her hands against his temples, fingertips on his eyelids, stroking gently. A moment later, Durrel sighed deeply and leaned his head back against Merista's chest.

"Thank you," he breathed. She shrugged — but something pricked at the edges of my thoughts. I hate that.

"Neat trick," I said.

"I just know where to push hard," she said, slipping her bracelet back on.

Raffin was cozying up to Merista. "Give us all a little love, won't you?" She just scowled and shoved him away.

I faded in and out of the conversation after that, watching the city change shape around me. The tall houses along the river cast shimmering shadows on the water; green flags and banners rippled from every window and rooftop, concealing any other green shapes that might be lurking there. Once the riverway would have been a riot of color — not just Mother Celys's green, but colors flown for all the gods, showing each home's allegiance: Tiboran's turquoise at a vintner's house. Brown for Mend-kaal over the shop of a smith or a baker. Sometimes even Sar's violet, for healers and mages. But that was years ago, long before anyone in this boat was born. It wasn't exactly illegal, of course, but these days the only acceptable color was green. Or white — for a house in mourning.

Any other color would have your neighbors asking questions or men in green uniforms knocking in the middle of the night.

A movement on shore caught my eye, and I clenched my fingers on the rail as two bulky figures in identical green-and-gold livery emerged from the shadows, strolling the river walk as if it had been given to them by Celys herself. Their breeches, boots, gloves, and tunics were the bright crisp color of new-mown grass; the tree silhouetted against the golden circle of the moon emblazoned on the chest and back was the only embellishment. Unless you counted the nightstick.

Greenmen. Or more properly, the Acolyte Guard. Not King Bardolph's secret police *precisely*; officially they were in the service of the Celyst temples. But everyone knew they reported directly to the king and to his left hand, Lord High Inquisitor Werne Nebraut, seeking out signs, hints — even mere rumors — of heresy. A blue flag or a hearth statue of Mend-kaal earned a smack on the wrist and a brand of the full moon on the back of the hand. But anything that hinted at Sar, goddess of magic — well. Shaved heads were the least of an accused Sarist's worries. Fire, flayings, bodies suspended above public circles to bleed to death . . . these were the marks of the Inquisitor's affections.

I tried to stay out of it — *well* out of it. Politics was a game for the rich; street thieves like me didn't choose sides if we could help it. I was just as happy picking a Celyst's pocket as I was rifling a Sarist's desk. But word was that Bardolph had lost control of the Inquisition, and now nobody was safe from his men in green — not even his own nephews, princes Wierolf and Astilan. I gripped the side of the boat, so tense and stiff I hardly needed my corset to keep me upright, and tried to look invisible.

The men in green walked the shore, cudgels swinging as they peered over the passing boats.

I heard a creak of the skiff's polished wood, a faint rippling splash of the oars, and realized that my party had gone silent. Merista sat still and pale, Durrel clasping her hand. Raffin's expression was unreadable, but Phandre —

"Bastard pigs!" she cried, flinging the empty wine bottle into the water hard enough to make me flinch. The Greenmen lifted their faces, and one of them gestured toward us.

"Raffin — *row!*" I lunged for one of the oars. But Durrel was faster, and together the boys turned the skiff into a black knife slicing through the water. Merista skillfully loosed one of the smaller sails, and the *Swan* picked up speed. As we cruised out of Nob Circle, Phandre lurched up on shaky legs and made a rude gesture to the pursuing Greenmen. Raffin reached out a long velvet arm and pulled her roughly down again.

Finally we rounded the wide swath of the Oss that swept through the Third Circle, Gerse's busy merchant district. Raffin and Durrel relaxed their pace, but I watched the shore long after we'd left the Greenmen behind. I expected some sort of dressing-down of Phandre, who sulked in a frothy green heap, but Raffin burst out laughing, and even Merista looked exhilarated.

"Don't get too cozy there," Raffin said. "We still have to make it out of the gates, and it's going to take some diplomacy, if the Greenpigs alert their friends at the checking station."

Durrel straightened, tugging on his doublet. "Right. Well, the last I heard, insulting the Guard wasn't a hanging offense, but we don't need to make enemies. Meri, raise the sails. Phandre, do — what you do." He gave a vague wave in the direction of Phandre's bosom. Obligingly, she adjusted the fit of her bodice and gave her hair a tumble. "Celyn, try not to look terrified, all right?"

He laid a reassuring hand on my sore knee, but I flinched away. "What if they won't let us through?"

"Don't worry. Raffin and I are the sons of lords, and Phandre is . . . persuasive. They'll let us through."

I dropped my eyes, smoothed the folds of my skirts, and nodded. But I was calculating the distance from the guards' station to shore — and whether it was something I could jump.

Eventually we pulled in sight of the city gates and the great sandstone arch that could — at one quick word from the guards — cut off our exit from Gerse. I had only seen the iron bars lowered over the Oss Gate once, for nine days the previous winter, when Bardolph ordered a crackdown on foreigners in Gerse, and the Guard swept through the city, burning out immigrants and traders. The city had smelled of smoke for weeks afterward, and ash had coated the Oss, sometimes inches deep. *We should have gotten out then,* Tegen had said more than once in the last year, fled through the gates the instant the king lifted the restrictions.

But we were city brats; neither of us had been able to imagine a life outside of Gerse. The spiraling streets, the crowded squares, the tumble-down buildings of the Seventh Circle — that was home in all its squalid glory. Tegen had always said we'd still be there when Marau sent his crows for us.

And he'd turned out to be right. I pressed my eyes closed, blinking away the vision of blood coating his beard, the last taste of his lips on my mouth.

Raffin skillfully steered the *Swan* into the queue of merchant vessels, liveried barges, and water transports ferrying citizens out of the city. As we waited, my companions fished about for their documentation — municipal papers or house seals that would allow them free passage past the gates, onto the King's Waterway. I froze. What was I supposed to offer up — Chavel's letters?

I grabbed Durrel's arm. "My papers — I don't have —"

Raffin turned his head back and grinned. "Peace, sweetling. I've got you covered."

"This should be interesting," Durrel said under his breath.

At the checkpoint, a young Greenman leaned out over the water for our passports. He barely looked at us, but I found myself studying his face for anything familiar. It had been dark and confused at Chavel's, but I should recognize *something*; one of the Greenmen who'd grabbed me would have a swollen jaw, at least. If not a couple of missing teeth.

"What about her?" the guard said.

"She's our spiritual advisor," Raffin said. "Don't you recognize the colors of the Divine Mother?"

Horrified, I glanced at him — then somehow heard my *own* voice saying, "Peace and plenty to you, brother. Praise Celys."

"*She's* a holy sister." The guardsman's voice was flat with disbelief. "Prove it."

"My good man," Raffin said, sounding affronted. "Surely you know the Daughters of Celys are not required to carry documentation when traveling abroad. The Divine Mother's aura *is* her identification."

"I don't care if she's the Matriarch at the Celystra. I still need her passage licenses."

Next he'd be asking to see my earthstones and my lunaria. I thought frantically, scrambling for ideas — but apparently I'd drained my well of lies for one morning. Raffin was starting to get flustered. This scheme was moments from collapse.

And then, who should pipe to our rescue but . . . *Merista?*

"Oh, please," she said, her soft voice pleading. "Can't you see she's just an Aspirant? They haven't issued her robes yet, but she had to give up her papers when she joined the order. We're taking her to visit her family before she takes her vows and enters the Celystra forever."

Merista's eyes were shining and sincere as she leaned toward the guard. I grabbed her lead. "Oh, sir, please — this may be the last time I ever see my . . . grandmother. She was so proud when I decided to take orders, but she's been so frail lately —" I broke off as something sharp jammed into my foot.

"*Don't overdo it,*" I heard Durrel's faint murmur.

We must have looked ridiculous, the lot of us, smiling stupidly up at the guardsman, in our rumpled clothing, reeking of wine and flesh. But after one last suspicious glance, the Greenman handed back their papers, and I'm pretty sure I saw the glint of silver move from Raffin's hand to his. I wondered if he'd bribed the guard with the money that he'd offered to me, or if he had just an endless supply of coins at the ready.

"Fine. Just see to it that she stays out of trouble."

Raffin and Durrel hauled us past the gates and into open water. "My dear man," Raffin murmured as we left the city behind, "I have no intention of it."

# CHAPTER THREE

We sailed in silence after that, as the broad highways and crowded river of Gerse gave way to farmland and open waters, leaving me to watch the endless water and reflect upon my own situation. And fortify myself a little for the journey ahead. Raffin Taradyce, at least, had a purse bulging with silver marks. He wouldn't miss a few.

Had it been a wise move, throwing my lot in with these people? I was completely at their mercy. They'd been nice enough so far, but once they slept off the drink and came to their senses, who could tell what they were planning? All right, maybe they weren't going to turn me over to Greenmen, but there were other dangers in the world. Raffin had picked me up for some reason, and I wanted to be ready when I figured out what that was.

I studied them. If I had to, I could probably take *one* of them out. But which one? I could summon the initiative to stab Phandre — but sweet, nervous Merista? Durrel? I'd thought my days of defending myself that way were far behind me. But what happened to Tegen showed me how naive I'd been.

And even if the Pleasure Boat Four truly had no dark designs on me, what was I going to do once we reached this Favom Court?

As the sun rose higher, chasing off the moons, the fields and pastures were replaced by more and more trees. I had never seen such trees — vast, haunting things, stretched up into the heavens, reaching their branches over the water as if they would snatch me from the boat. Was this Celys's land, then? In the chill air from the water, I shivered.

I couldn't go back. With Tegen gone, and Hass missing, there wasn't anyone in the city I trusted enough to take me in. My rooms, such as they were, had surely already been searched, if not planted with Greenmen lying in wait. How long would they look for the girl that had been with Tegen? Hass was connected; he knew people at all levels of society, from street scum like me, to men like Lord Taradyce. I had no illusions about who he'd side with, when pressed.

And — *be honest, Digger* — there was no reason to suspect Tegen hadn't given me up.

They wouldn't have killed him outright; that wasn't the Greenmen's way. Sometimes people just . . . disappeared. We all knew what that meant.

Dungeons.

Torture.

The Inquisition.

I pulled my knees into my chest and pressed my cheek to my skirts. I knew what could happen. I had always known it *could* happen, but that was worlds away from the men in green stepping out of the shadows and drawing their swords in your face, jamming their hands up your skirts as you twisted and screamed, kicked and bit —

I rubbed my wrist, where the short one almost had me. I'd have pulled hard enough to break my wrist, I think, if I'd needed to. I'd gotten a good kick in. Tegen could have that to remember, as they bent his beautiful fingers back, one by one, waiting for him to scream.

"What's the matter?" said a soft voice beside me. Durrel.

I sniffed and lifted my head, hoping my face didn't betray too much. "I think I'm just tired."

He reached for my hand but recoiled as I snatched my arm back and pulled my sleeve down over the wound.

"You're injured." There were all kinds of questions in that brief sentence.

"It's nothing. I — fell, going over the temple wall. On the roses." I met his even gaze, willing him to ask me nothing else.

Finally his set jaw relaxed and he sat back. "You're freezing. Here." He pulled a damask robe from the bench and draped it around my shoulders. "Why don't you rest a while? We won't be at Favom for a few hours."

I heard another sentence beneath the words: *Nothing can happen to you out here.*

I wasn't safe, but I was safe enough, for the moment. As I lay back into the bench, my head cradled on Durrel's balled-up cloak, I wondered at him. Raffin Taradyce's boat, but I was here at Durrel's whim.

Before I could give that any more thought, I saw something in the distance and shot upright, my eyes locked on the shoreline.

"What — what is it?" Durrel frowned and turned his head to follow my gaze. "Gods," he swore, and lunged for Merista.

"What are you doing?" she cried, but he held her tight, pressing her face into his shoulder.

"Don't look, don't look, don't look, don't look," he repeated over and over.

Phandre and Raffin had stirred as well, and were silent as we sailed past. There on the northern bank stood the Adonia Laia, one of the royal palaces that had been converted to gaols during Bardolph's reign. But it wasn't the golden sandstone towers or the glint of the famous colored-glass windows that had snagged my attention.

It was the row of spikes lined up before it, thrust into the earth like a grisly fence line. Eleven of the spikes bore the severed and rotting heads of those who'd died in the Inquisition, victims of Werne the Bloodletter. I could not stop myself from counting, from searching for . . . Some were bare skulls, bleached white in the sun; some still had ribbons of flesh and hair clinging to bone. Some were hideously recognizable, if they had been your friends or loved ones. All of them topped spikes hung with shredded violet banners — a warning to anyone who might even sympathize with those who followed the goddess Sar.

Not seeing Tegen didn't make me feel any better. It only meant they hadn't gotten him up there *yet*.

A little apart from the row of heads stood a gruesome scarecrow, something white and tattered fluttering in the breeze behind its broken body. I pressed a hand to my mouth, feeling sick. A magic user — or one so accused, flayed and put on display. Beheading was too good for anyone with the gall to claim mysterious powers from Sar.

Something caught me by the arm, and I jumped, my hand flying to my boot cuff. My fingers found — nothing. My ankle sheath was empty, and suddenly I felt naked. I must have lost the knife during the fight. I didn't even remember drawing it.

The grip on my arm got my attention. It was Durrel, still clutching Merista. I read his message clear enough. *This* girl was important to him. So far, he had acted to protect me, but only so long as I was not a danger to anyone on board. If it came to a choice between Merista, or Raffin, or Phandre — and me . . . If it came to a confrontation with the Greenmen . . .

I nodded my understanding and dropped my hem, easing back against the cushioned seat.

"Gods, what a world we live in," Raffin said.

"What was it?" Merista asked, rubbing her face as she sat up from Durrel's crushing embrace. She looked us over and went sober. "Oh. Did we go through Traitors' Pass?" There was nothing to see now except pallid blots against a wall of gold. "It's so awful," she said. "How can the Inquisition do that?"

"They're savages," Phandre said with surprising bitterness. "And you, Celyn Contrare, or whoever you are, had better be grateful you didn't let those Little Daughters of Celys get their filthy hands on you!"

At long last, the wine and the sleepless night caught up with them and, one by one, my companions dozed off. I took swift advantage of the moment. It was easy enough lifting Raffin's purse, even with Phandre draped all over him, but Phandre, oddly enough, wore no jewelry. Disappointing — I'd have enjoyed stripping her of some of those fine feathers.

I found myself reluctant to steal from Durrel, but Merista wore two long strands of silver necklaces, tucked deep into her bodice. One silver link was worth a week's food, five could buy passage on a vessel sailing to Talanca. As she slept on her cousin's shoulder, I carefully worked the clasp and slid the chain free of her hair and dress, coiling it down my sleeve.

But as the silver snaked away, Merista's pale skin seemed to give off a strange, ethereal light of its own. As she breathed, a wavering, misty haze swirled across her neck, lifted her dark hair with colorless luminescence, spun like dust motes across her bare cheek and plump fingers. I yanked my hand back like I'd been burned. The silver gone, it was as clear to me as moonslight in a dark room.

Merista Nemair had magic.

Marau's *balls*.

Two thoughts bound themselves together in my mind: Did the others know? Did they *see*? The first was dangerous for Merista — but the second put *me* at risk. By some twisted humor of the gods, I'd been born with the cursed skill to see the Mark of Sar, wherever that goddess had touched — the faintest traces of magic, eddying swirls of power that were invisible to everyone else. *I* wasn't Sar-touched; I had no magic of my own. But for whatever reason, for me, magic gave off a kind of glow, which lit up the user or the object like sunlight on water.

The silver chains — and now I realized the bracelet she wore, as well — must be used to bind Merista's powers. Somehow the silver worked against the magic, the way water doused a fire, keeping it suppressed and invisible. Normal people couldn't see the haze of power given off by the magical, but that didn't stop suspicious neighbors from pointing fingers, or Greenmen from stopping you on the street. It was safer just to keep that little spark buried deep where it could not escape. But Merista wore so much of it — I'd seen her cure Durrel's headache with a touch, and she'd only had to doff the bracelet to do it. How *much* power was coursing under all that silver?

Cursing myself for a softhearted fool, I poured the chain from my sleeve into my cupped hand and pooled it carefully on the floor of the boat, just behind her slippered foot.

"Lady Merista," I whispered, trying to nudge her without actually *touching* her — I hated the way magic sparked and flared under my fingertips, even if I *felt* nothing. "Milady —"

She mumbled and shifted in her sleep, blinking awake.

"You've lost a necklace, I think." I grated out the words with effort, and showed her.

"Oh." Merista leaned down to retrieve the chain, and I saw that Durrel had woken up and was watching me again. By the gods, but those intense eyes were unsettling! Back home I'd smack him for it, but here I let my own gaze drop, wondering what he might have seen.

Eventually the rocking boat and my own rough night caught up with me, and the next thing I knew, Durrel was shaking me awake under four full moons. I jumped up, knocking his hand away. It was dark, I was stiff, and for a heartbeat I couldn't remember where I was.

"Easy there," Durrel said.

All my muscles tense, I glanced around, the day filling in its details in my memory. "I can't believe I slept so long," I said, surreptitiously examining myself. Bruised and thirsty, but I seemed to be all here — and the letters were still tucked inside my bodice. Strangely, though, I had a soft dark hat in my lap.

"You must have been exhausted." Durrel retrieved the hat and perched it on his head. "Meri was afraid you'd burn."

I glanced between him and Merista, who smiled faintly at me. Who were these people? This was not the behavior I'd been led to expect from nobs. But they'd saved my life, smuggled me past the Acolyte Guard, fed me, watched over me while I slept, and protected my delicate skin to boot. So far I hadn't done too badly in their company.

"We're almost to Favom," Merista said, pointing downriver, to where a pale shape hulked on the left bank. Favom Court. By night, there was little to see, and my small party grew quiet as we approached Durrel's home.

"It's not too late to keep on sailing, old boy," Raffin said, but Durrel shook his head.

"We need to get the girls in." He grinned and clapped Raffin on the shoulder. "Might as well take our medicine like men, eh? Pull to the left

here. The mooring's under that big oak. Don't look so surprised, Raff —
this is the real country, boyo."

We tumbled onto the dock in a shivering heap of wrinkled court
clothes. Phandre fished a pocket mirror from somewhere — I had a sudden desperate longing for the thing, all gold and enamel, with a massive
green carnelian on its back — and examined herself. She gave her mane
of tawny hair a violent shake that somehow managed to make her look
even *more* polished, and, bowing low, reached deep inside her bodice to
arrange her bosom. I thought Raffin's eyes would fall out of his skull.

Merista turned to me. "Here, let's get you tidied up a bit, Celyn." And
under the bright light of the moons, she seized the laces of my bodice
and undid me almost to my waist. I scrambled frantically for the letters and managed to slip them into the lining of my sleeves before anyone
noticed. She pinned up my tangled hair in her own gold fillet, brushed
down my skirts, and finally pronounced me "quite seemly."

"Dear Meri," Phandre said. "You were born to be a lady's maid."

And even in the moonlight, I saw Merista's pale face flush as she
turned away from us.

Durrel glared at Phandre, and even Raffin noticed. "Oh, very nice,
Phandre."

"What?" she said. "What'd I say?"

Durrel led us through the scrabbly undergrowth between the lap-
ping water and the cold stone walls of the keep, into a walled paddock
and the stables beyond. As he pushed the door aside, the smells of
hay and horseflesh rose in the cold clear air. Durrel motioned us to wait
and stepped inside.

He returned a moment later, his face grim.

"Well, they got here before us."

"Who?" I said. Greenmen — *here*?

Durrel glanced at Raffin. "Our parents."

# CHAPTER FOUR

Raffin swore. "Not *all* of them?"

Never having contended with parents, I had a little trouble grasping the gravity of the situation, but Merista looked close to tears, Raffin had an expression on his face I can't begin to describe, and even Phandre was subdued. Well, for fat or lean, I had thrown my lot in with these people, and irritated parents seemed a mild alternative to what awaited me back in Gerse.

"There's nothing for it, I'm afraid," Durrel finally said. "The faster we get this over with, the faster it's over with." He ushered us all inside. Something rustled in the pungent darkness, too close to my head, and I jumped.

"Easy, Celyn," Durrel said. "It's just the horses."

"Horses," I echoed faintly. "Right."

"What will they do to us?" Merista whimpered, but Phandre was calm.

"You don't seem worried," I said.

She turned slowly to gaze down her perfect nose at me. "My father died in exile."

"Oh." Bastard pigs, indeed.

"What are we going to tell them about Celyn?" Merista said.

"Don't worry," said Raffin, reviving a bit. "We'll say she's Phandre's maid."

And in the darkness, it was really impossible to tell who found *that* idea more offensive.

It was not until we had crossed the threshold that I remembered something critical: I *knew* Raffin's father.

The recollection brought me up short, and Phandre stumbled into me and swore. I felt like swearing myself. After that long day of flinging myself blindly between danger and opportunity, I wasn't sure which this was. It had been a long time since I'd seen Lord Taradyce; would he recognize me? Would he *help* me? Have me seized for the thief I was and thrown into whatever served Favom as a dungeon?

I had no idea.

The jobs I'd done for Taradyce had been simple things — a councilman's incriminating love letters, a doctored accounts book for a shipping firm — your basic fodder for blackmail, and the kind of things noblemen did to their enemies all the time. Only Taradyce made a career of spying on his *friends* as well.

The stables opened out onto wide, moonslit gardens, herby and fragrant and ridiculously tidy. Durrel marshaled us through a narrow, low-arched doorway — obviously a back way; I approved — and into a shadowed service corridor.

"Easy here," he said, one arm raised to hold us back as he glanced down the passage. From my position between Phandre and Raffin, I could hardly see anything but age-darkened stone and rumpled damask. The same sleepy quiet of the gardens, a smell of river and damp, and behind it — something cooking. If Tiboran truly loved me, we would head in that direction. Nobs might live off wine alone, but I required actual sustenance.

"We need an ally," Durrel said, and I detected a trace of mischief in his voice. He waved us across the corridor and toward the roasting chicken. Or was that rabbit? Rabbit was rare enough in the city; most establishments were likely to serve up an alley cat and — *concentrate, Digger!* This was no moment to let my guard down.

Round a corner and under another arch, and the five of us slinked into a warm, glowing kitchen — and nearly into a wide-eyed serving maid clutching a pot of grease. Immediately Durrel had his arm around her, one soft hand clamped against her mouth. He held his other finger to his lips. The corner of her mouth lifted in a smile behind her lord's hand. She gave us a wink and ducked out of our way. Nice. I would have found a less . . . charming way to silence her.

The stealth of our approach did not last long, however; once inside the kitchen, Merista gave a cry.

"Morva!" She flung herself headlong across the ruddy tiled floor, into the arms of a squat woman swathed head to foot in aprons and kerchiefs and veils.

The woman gathered Merista to her bosom and glared at the rest of us. "Ach, seedling, you're all right now. You, young master — your lord father will have words about this, mark me!"

I looked around the kitchen, realizing with devastation that all the work was being done for the wrong end of the meal. The fire had been tamped down, the spit was bereft of meat, and Morva shifted Merista aside just in time to avoid a splash of water cast on the floor from a scrub bucket. I tried hard not to moan.

Merista was pouring out the woeful account of her kidnapping and torture by the roguish knavery of her cousin and his friend, when Durrel's voice broke in. "Lady Morva, please get the girls some food. And make sure Celyn gets seconds. She missed breakfast."

When Morva's gaze came to me, her eyes grew shrewd, and for a moment I was sure I'd been caught out. "And what in Her holy name have you lot done to this poor girl, then? She's a fair mess!"

"We found her like that," Raffin put in cheerfully, and Phandre snickered.

"You! Do not speak in this kitchen if you don't wish to know what I think of Taradyce manners. Why, you'll have the —"

Before Morva could finish, Raffin swooped down and kissed her squarely on the lips. Her already scarlet face turned purple, but she grinned. "Get on, then. Lord Durrel, what would your lady mother say, I wonder?"

"I think she'd ask you to please get Phandre, Celyn, and Lady Merista something to eat," Durrel said patiently.

The kitchen woman fed us, tut-tutting all the while over the state of our clothes, our hair, our appetites, and my size. "A mousy thing like you, even your clothes don't fit proper. We'll find you something else, pet. Lord Ragn don't let his guests go hungry or cold."

I ate in silence, taking in the noisy room as servants bustled about. The food was simple and good, obviously the servants' portion, but I would have eaten cat stew and liked it at that point. They only gave me a clay bowl and a hunk of bread to mop up the broth; hadn't these people heard of spoons? They hadn't heard of much that was grand or valuable, apparently. In all that great room, aside from Merista's silver and Raffin's amber ring — which I *would* have, by the end of this — the only things of value appeared to be the roasting spit (too big to carry), the stone statue of Mend-kaal on the hearth (impossible to sell these days), and a couple of books on cookery. Not even worth it.

As I absorbed my surroundings and my meal, Morva filled the others in on just how much trouble they were in. "You've done it now, then, Master. Don't you know they've been at hounds and pitchforks looking for you both? The night of your own betrothal, and the very day Lady Meri's parents sail back to Llyvraneth?"

"What?" Merista pulled away from the woman.

The cook held up her left hand and kissed her knuckles. "You didn't hear it from me, but word came this morning. They've landed in Tratua and will be sailing home this week. You were *supposed* to meet them in Gerse, young lady, so that the entire lot of you could be presented before the king. His Majesty won't be pleased. No, not at all."

"But they never wrote," Merista said in a shaky voice. "What happened?"

"Ah, pet, I'm sure they meant to, if it weren't so sudden. Seems His Majesty's decided Llyvraneth no longer needs an emissary in Corlesanne. Or Corlesanne's decided they don't want Llyvrins in their court. Either way, it amounts to the same thing, love: Your lord parents are on their way home even now."

Even I knew that wasn't a good sign. A king recalling his eyes and ears in a foreign court — particularly one that had shown itself sympathetic to Sarists? It could be a prelude to war. The Corles letters in my sleeve didn't seem so cold and dead anymore.

"That's just like Bardolph," Durrel said grimly. "Pick a fight overseas, and ignore the trouble brewing on your own doorstep."

"Take cheer, Lady Meri," said Morva. "It means your lord parents will be here for your *kernja-velde*, and they'll be wanting to take you home with them again."

I perked up. The *kernja-velde* — a girl's passage into adulthood on her fourteenth birthday — was a cause for celebration for any Llyvrin family: fine food and presents for hosts and guests alike, including a traditional gift of seven coins from everyone in attendance to build the girl's dowry. Seventh Circle *kernja-veldes* meant coppers and strikes; a nob's had to be a festival like nothing I'd ever seen. Fountains of gold. I could almost *smell* the coins.

"Where's home?" I interjected.

"Caerellis," Merista said. "But my birthday's not for *months*."

Pox.

"Aye, and you'll spend those months as girls in this family have spent them for generations: in seclusion with your family," said Morva.

"Yes," said Phandre. "They need to turn you into a proper lady."

Merista flushed, and Morva gave Phandre a short, hard look. "As if the likes of you would know anything about being a proper lady."

I *liked* this kitchen drudge.

Merista just poked at her food after that until Durrel finally stood up from the table. "Where's my father now?" he asked.

"Still at table. With the Taradyce, I might add."

I saw Durrel nod. "Fair enough. Come, lad and lasses!" He grabbed a flagon and some goblets from the table. "Let's serve up our own punishment, shall we?"

Merista fell in line easily, but Phandre scowled heavily. I took my cue from her. "Maybe I should just stay here."

"Oh, no, no, no," Raffin said, yanking me to my feet. "In for a finger, in for a fist. You're one of us now, Celyn."

That's what I was afraid of.

We followed Durrel from the kitchens to the dining hall. Torchlight threw leaping shadows against the low stone ceiling, which was black with years of smoke, making the room feel even more closed in. Even I hunched a little.

A handful of men and one or two women looked up at our approach. Seated at the very center of the high table, like a vast golden lion, and holding court as if this was *his* familial manor, was Raffin's father.

"Stop."

We froze in a ragged line at the sound of that voice. It came from a man at Hron Taradyce's left hand. I swallowed hard, sure I had been discovered.

"Lord Durrel."

Durrel stepped forward. "Yes, sir." Somehow, even carrying a silver ewer and goblets like a servant, he managed to look noble. With a slight bow to his head, he set the pitcher on the long table.

The diners seemed to part around the man with the cold voice. He was obviously Durrel's father; the younger Decath would look like that in another twenty-one years or so.

"Lord Durrel, do you care to explain your actions of the last two days?" His voice was like a knife of ice.

Durrel did not move. "No, sir."

"'No, sir'?" Lord Decath echoed. "You removed two girls from the care of their guardians and took them on a drunken orgy in a stolen boat, and all you have is 'no, sir'?"

"Yes, sir."

"Lord Decath, I think I can explain —" Raffin's silver voice cut through, and he stepped toward the table, bowing deeply. "You see —"

"Shut up."

Raffin reeled back as if he'd been struck. Hron Taradyce was leaning his golden bulk over the table toward his son. I could imagine how Raffin felt; Taradyce was like a small sun burning at the center of his own universe — too easy to get singed in his presence.

But I couldn't spare much sympathy for Raffin. I was too busy staring at a small crack in the stone of the floor, letting the dim light of the hall keep my face in shadows. Anyone in this room had the power to send me straight to King Bardolph's gaol, but only Hron Taradyce had a good reason for it. A few forged patents, an incriminating letter or two. This was . . . inconvenient.

"I'm sure you find this all very amusing, boy," Taradyce was saying, as Raffin shrunk a good few inches. "But I'd like to remind you who owns that boat you've been cruising about in. Who owns that wine you reek of."

"You do, milord," Raffin said miserably.

"And then who?"

His head bowed, he spat out the word. "Stolo."

"That's right. Your brother. And *if* you don't manage to get every harbor brat between here and Yeris Volbann with child before you come of age, you miserable waste, then there *might* be something left over for you. But until then, you will not treat my property as if the city is your own personal pleasure garden."

"But, Father —"

"You will address me in public as Lord Taradyce. Do you need another reminder?"

Raffin swayed on his feet. He was still a little drunk, and I hadn't seen him eat anything all day. It would put the cap on his humiliation if he were to spew his gorge right here at his father's feet.

Durrel put a hand on Raffin's arm, but his friend would not look at him. Durrel stepped forward smoothly and cleared his throat.

"My lord Taradyce," he said, and the note of iron was back in his voice. "You and your son are guests in my father's home, and I must insist you show your fellow guests the same courtesy the Decath have always offered you."

After a frozen moment when all the color drained away from Raffin's face, Lord Taradyce roared with laughter. Seated again, he turned to Lord Decath. "Now there," he said loudly, "is a son a man could be proud of."

Raffin turned on his heel and ran out of the room.

Lord Taradyce gave a disgusted sigh and threw his napkin on the table. Decath leaned toward him and murmured something, and a moment later, Taradyce rose and gave the merest hint of a bow to the Decath. "Lord Ragn, Lady Amalle, if you'll excuse me, I believe I have some property to reclaim. I shall see you both back in the city."

"Indeed." Lord Decath's voice was a low, bemused murmur as he watched Lord Taradyce cross the stone floor with clipped, purposeful strides. He turned back to us when Taradyce had gone. "Well, now that that's settled, it appears my son has a tale to tell us. If my understanding of the situation is correct, when you left home, your female companions numbered two. And now I see a third in your party. Step forward, girl."

Durrel stepped aside, and Phandre gave me a brief push forward. I stumbled toward the high table, and leveraged it into a curtsy at the last moment.

"Explain."

Did he mean me?

"I don't care *who*," Lord Decath prompted. "You, girl — look at me."

With a thin breath inward, I tilted my head up into the light, just enough for Decath to make me out. Taradyce might be gone, but that didn't mean I was safe.

"My lord, we, uh —" Durrel gave a chuckle. "Picked up a stray. Please welcome Celyn Contrare, gentlewoman of Gerse."

Lord Decath's mouth quirked. "I see. You know if you feed them, they'll never leave."

"Ah, too late then, I'm afraid. Morva had soup."

"Well, then, Celyn Contrare, it looks like you're ours for keeps. No, no — don't slink away, girl. Give some accounting for yourself, and pray Tiboran made you a more entertaining storyteller than my son. And perhaps we won't make you sleep in the scullery with the rats."

"I've slept with rats before, milord." Which didn't sound *at all* like I'd intended.

Beside me, Phandre stifled a snort, and the woman at Lord Durrel's left said, "How charming. Lord Durrel, your little friends grow more and more amusing every day. But she blushes very prettily, so we may just forgive her."

Lord Decath's eyebrows had quirked upward. "I see," he said. "And just where did my son find you?"

I glanced around, taking in the stage for my second performance as jeweler's daughter Celyn Contrare. "Outside the Celystra, milord. I — escaped."

Lord Decath glanced between me and Durrel, and the corner of his mouth twitched. "Indeed? A runaway nun. That *is* entertaining. Quite a few rats in the Celystra, then, Celyn Contrare?"

"My lord, you have no idea."

Decath gave a loud, choking laugh. "I did ask her to be entertaining," he said. "I suppose I can't fault her for obliging me. Celyn, be you welcome to Favom Keep. Now, it's obvious the poor girl's dead on her feet. Cossum! Find someone to show her and Lady Phandre to their rooms. Lady Merista, you'll remain here for a moment; I have news you'll be interested in. Good night."

And like that, we were dismissed. Phandre grabbed me by the arm and practically dragged me out of there, though flight seemed the sensible next move to me as well. I couldn't help one last look at poor Merista, standing before that panel like the condemned.

# CHAPTER FIVE

We left her there, following on the heels of an efficient manservant. I should have been paying attention, looking for exits or valuables, but I was too busy going over that scene in my mind. I still didn't know whether Taradyce had recognized me. Tiboran watch me, I was racking up too many near escapes for one day.

Phandre dragged me upstairs, to a small firelit bedroom where I was unceremoniously stripped naked by two lady's maids and plunged into a steaming vat of soapy water. Though my bruised knee and filleted arm sang with protest, for a few scalding minutes I felt the day's concerns melt away as I was dunked and lathered and scrubbed like a saucepan. The maids whisked away my bloody clothes, but not before I managed to rescue my corset, with its lock picks hidden in the lining, and the packet of letters I'd stashed in the sleeve.

"Love letters?" Phandre said from the tub. Marau's balls, but those kestrel's eyes were *sharp*. Thankfully she was too wet — and too far away — to lunge for them, though I could see her longing to.

"I wish I knew," I murmured, turning them over in my hands.

So clean I shone, redressed in a hideous gold robe, a soothing salve and neat dressing applied to the cut on my arm, I reflected that I'd managed to get nearly everything I'd wanted that morning. I should count my blessings; how often does *that* happen?

I didn't have a plan, but I knew it wouldn't involve a long-term stay at Favom Court. I needed clothes and money and transportation to a port city like Yeris Volbann or Tratua, where I could hop a ship to Talanca or Brionry. Either city might even be far enough away, if I could snake my way in among the locals. I'd have to prove I was trustworthy, win a couple of fights, and probably perform some outrageous initiation. Pretty much like I'd done in the boat, really.

The bath had made me sleepy, but I had work to do, and Raffin's purse wouldn't get me to Talanca. As soon as Phandre and the maids disappeared, I went to the windows and looked out. We were on the third or fourth floor of the court's central tower, and outside, the moons shone on a series of tidy gardens and beehive-shaped outbuildings.

Naming the seven moons was one of the earliest lessons any Llyvrin child, nob or common, ever learned. Bountiful Celys and black Marau, who held the constant perfect balance of life and death: one bright, the other in shadow, all through the long year. Small, smoky, mysterious Sar, spinning the wrong way in the night. The twins, Mend-kaal and Tiboran, as different as work and play. Bright, fiery Zet, who lit the way for hunters and kings. The Nameless One, a tiny, white hot dot of light coursing at Marau's heels like a relentless hound, dealing out her horrible justice to sinners.

High above a thatched outbuilding, I could just make out a narrow slip of Tiboran's moon. The only reliable thing about Tiboran was his moon's fixed place in the sky, by which you could chart a course or read the hour as easily as by the sun.

Taking the chance that everyone was still roving about on nob or servant-of-nob business, I hiked up the long skirts of the robe and let myself out into the hallway. Some said it was risky to go working by Tiboran's new moon, when the god's back was turned and his eyes looking elsewhere, but that was probably just something somebody made up to discourage thieves.

Castles keep their secrets in the kitchens and the bedrooms, but their valuables can be anywhere. The Favom Court valuables, however, were elusive. I knew this was a working farm, not a palace, but the Decath seemed to live as spare and frugal a life here as any monk.

Not that I ever saw a poor monk.

I did find one silver button beneath a bed, and a pretty glass inkwell that I just liked and was small enough to slip inside my sleeve. With a defeated sigh, I finally decided to have a go at the kitchens. In the absence of treasure, food is a worthy alternative. Besides, I'd liked that kitchen

woman, Morva. She might tell me more about this place and its people —
and maybe the Decath trusted her with their household accounting.

I headed down a wide corridor hung with tapestries of fruit and birds,
trying to look purposeful and deliberate and like I belonged here. Near
the end, I heard someone coming up the stairs — Raffin's voice, turned
curt and sullen, and the low, harsh tones of his father. Pox. I popped the
nearest door and slipped inside, just as the argument carried past me
down the hall.

When the corridor was clear again, I launched myself toward the
stairs and followed the yeasty scent of tomorrow's bread and brewing
down to the kitchens. Shoving my way in ahead of my plan, I found
myself face-to-face with Morva once more.

"Ah, pet, you've not gotten lost?" She grabbed my shoulders with
floury hands and held me steady for her examination. "You're shivering!
Come sit down and I'll fix you a posset."

"I don't know what that is."

She gave me a surprised look. "Hot wine and curdled cream. It never
fails to soothe Lady Meri."

It sounded horrifying, but milk was a luxury in the city; I had rarely
had it before it became cheese. I followed Morva to a long, wiped-down
table near the fire, where the statue of Mend-kaal leaning on his hammer
guarded the hearth. The roomy kitchen was snug and warm, and the
Favom farm seemed prosperous; Mend-kaal certainly seemed to be doing
well by the Decath. Well enough that they could afford whatever bribes
or fines let them keep such a statue on display.

"Here. Drink up. You look half starved."

I tried to drink it slowly, savor the warmth of the clay cup in my
hands, the warm wine, the thick rich milk. It *was* horrifying, but it was
also hot and strangely fortifying, and all the while Morva clucked at me
sympathetically, nursing a heavy mug of her own.

"I'm no friend to Sarists, mind you, but I could teach those holy
daughters a thing or two about caring for wee girls."

I almost smiled. I could believe her.

"Is Du — Lord Durrel in trouble?" I asked instead.

Morva threw up her hands, apron and all. "Ach, aye, that one. No more than usual. We got their rooms ready when we heard the news of the betrothal. Figured the young lord would turn up at Favom sooner or later, probably with Merista in tow. Those two always come here when there's trouble."

"How long have you been with the Decath?"

"Five years, ever since their lordships have been abroad. I was Lady Meri's nurse, before Lady Amalle decided she was too old for one, and Lady Lyllace's too, before her."

This was fascinating, but ultimately unhelpful. "Favom seems like a busy place," I said. "There must be a lot of traffiç in and out."

"You should have been here last month, pet, during the harvest! Barges stopping at our docks for grain, an army of wains rolling out for the city."

"How often do the barges stop?" That question was bordering on suspicious, but Morva seemed happy to talk about anything. Unfortunately all my questions about river traffic and how much travel the Decath did and how often anyone left here for somewhere besides Gerse dried up to nothing. I plunked my empty mug down on the table, and left the conversation to Morva, who was bubbling over with excitement for the arrival of the Nemair.

"Corlesanne! Godless country! I shudder to think what they've been through, living among all those heathen Sarists all these years." The wine had oiled her jaws. "It's that Nemair's doing, you know," she said. "I told my lady she'd come to no good for marrying a rebel. But of course that was His Majesty's decision, not my lady's. She was always loyal, never one to stir up trouble, and what does she get for her pains? Exile and her children taken away." Morva pursed her fleshy lips and looked into her mug. "Well, you're too young, I suppose. You won't be remembering the war."

Remember it? No. But I dodged its aftereffects every day. Eighteen years since Bardolph crushed the Sarist rebellion at the Battle of Kalorjn, when one of the Sarist forces had betrayed their movements to the king. The Sarists had been slaughtered as a result. Anyone still living when the smoke cleared had been thrown in prison or driven into exile, their lands and assets seized. And yet after all that, His Majesty couldn't seem to remember he'd won.

"They're coming back just in time, if you ask me," Morva continued. "I don't like the sound of things at all, these days. But now my Meri and my Lyll will be tucked up safe at Caerellis, right where they should be."

"Caerellis?" Merista had mentioned that earlier, but it hadn't meant anything to me.

"My lady's home. The most beautiful land Celys gave this island. Two days northwest of here, and it's a different world. The rose gardens alone . . ."

I seized on this. "Northwest? Along the Yerin road?" Two days would get me practically to the city. I could make the rest on foot. Could I hold out this masquerade that long? I rubbed at my knee, which was starting to throb again. Every muscle in my body felt heavy, and the wavering firelight made me feel like I was still rocking away in the boat.

"Oh, pet, now look at you. Asleep on your feet, just as his lordship said, and I've kept you up with my nattering. Come, let's get you to bed with my lady."

I flinched awake at that. Sleep — with Merista Nemair? With the thickness of her magic wafting off of her and sparking up against me every time she breathed or stirred? "I —"

"No arguing, lass. You've been through an awful day, and you need a fair rest now."

She had no idea. Finally I let her lead me back upstairs to Merista's room, driven by one clear thought: *I had to get them to take me to Caerellis.*

By all rights, I should have fallen dead asleep the moment I slipped into bed beside Merista. (Phandre, it seemed, had braved Lord Taradyce's wrath and gone off in search of Raffin.) But the strange air around Merista was distracting; I kept opening my eyes to brush it out of my sight, like a fog of imaginary gnats. And I couldn't shake my whirling thoughts out into any kind of order; they just kept twisting in on one another, until I saw a plate of peacock flash by Hron Taradyce's golden head, a laughing Merista slipping into the roiling Oss beside Tegen's bloody body.

Oh, gods. How had I ended up here? I pressed my face into my pillow, but the picture of Tegen's dark, bearded face would not leave me — his hooded eyes wide with surprise, his beautiful mouth gaped open on my name. I sniffed, catching the scent of lavender and linen. He'd have loved this — thought it a great game, a lark on the river and a night in some nob's bed. It was all too much, and suddenly I wanted to scream into that too-soft pillow, until the walls of Favom came crashing down around me.

Merista's eyes opened, a flutter of glitter in the darkness, and I started, pulling away from her.

"What?" I whispered, my voice sounding raw and harsh.

A little furrow creased her forehead, and she reached out her pale fingers to touch my cheek. "You were crying," she said, turning her fingertips to show droplets of water, now sparkling with silver in the moonslight.

I cuffed her hand away from my face. "Good night," I snapped, and turned over in the bed, taking the blankets with me.

# CHAPTER SIX

I spent the next strange day as Merista's shadow. Durrel had gone off with Lord Decath on rounds of the Favom farmsteads, and the Taradyce had departed without ceremony, leaving Merista and Phandre and me to skulk about Favom together. "Like a merry band of sisters," Merista said, over which Phandre and I exchanged a *look*.

The manor by day was no more interesting than it had been overnight, but Merista showed us everything anyway. Apparently she was personal friends with every one of the Favom horses (which were quite valuable, it turned out — making me briefly consider the beasts in a new light), and on speaking terms with the geese and the dogs and all of the servants. Finally, when I began to think taking my chances with Taradyce would have been preferable, she planted us in the kitchens with Morva, who tied us up in aprons and set us to work preparing the feast to welcome Merista's parents. I tried to explain that I didn't *cook*, but Morva thrust a rolling pin into my hands anyway.

"Didn't you learn anything at that convent of yours?" she said, as a mountain of pastry dough was dropped in front of me.

"I worked in the manuscript room!" I squeaked, ducking back from the spray of flour, but nobody was listening.

Merista and Morva chattered happily through meat pies and dressed geese, the kitchen woman once more expounding on her favorite subject: Lady Nemair. I listened intently, hoping to learn something useful, but Morva was all sauce and no meat: heavy on the praise but light on specifics. Lady Lyllace was the kindest lady. Lady Lyllace was the very picture of Meri. Lady Lyllace could shoot out the eye of a sparrow at five hundred paces, blindfolded, with her back turned.

Phandre sulked on a stool, picking feathers from the skirts of her gown. "Can't imagine why they'd come back here," she said. "At least in Gerse there's something to *do*."

"Plenty to do around here, young miss," Morva said, handing Phandre a bowl of dismembered goose parts. "And you'd best learn that, if you know what's good for you."

I punched my fists into my fifth batch of dough. This was madness. How was *pie crust* getting me any closer to Yeris Volbann and safety? I told myself to be patient — it was one more day. All I had to do was hang back in the shadows and hold my tongue, and the Nemair would come and I could slip easily into their party heading north.

I just wasn't sure exactly how I was going to do that, yet.

The Nemair stormed Favom Court the next day, at an ungodly hour of the morning with a godless clatter of carts and horses and appallingly jolly voices. We tumbled out of bed, Phandre and I more subdued than Merista, who was bouncing out of her skin.

Clutching my too-large borrowed smock to my shoulders, I joined them at the window. Below us, wagons and horses and a jumble of bodies swarmed the courtyard like happy flies on a pudding. In among the crowd, two figures stood out like the matching Royals on a chessboard: a massive bearded nob in a black fur mantle, booming his greetings to everyone within earshot; and a tall, plump woman in deep bronze silk, who turned her face to the window and beamed up at us.

Phandre, nearly naked in just her smock, climbed half out the window to wave back. "Lady Lyll!" she shrieked.

Really, I needn't have worried about *my* manners.

Merista shrank back from the window, but I lingered, gazing down at the people from whom without question Merista Nemair had sprung forth. I still hadn't figured out how I was going to attach myself to the party bound for Caerellis, and looking at them now, I was having second thoughts. They kept *hugging* everyone. Maybe there was a village somewhere near Favom. I could learn about pigs.

"I should go," I said, moving vaguely toward the door. Never mind that I wasn't dressed. That was my mistake last time, I decided. I should have forgone clothing and escaped with just my skin.

Merista's hand darted out and grabbed mine like a viper taking down an unsuspecting toad. "No, you can't!" she said. Her eyes were wide and desperate. Phandre shrugged into a peacock-colored dress, deftly pulling her laces taut with one hand snaked up her back, while Merista just stood there like a mousy waiting maid.

"Hurry up, you two dullards!" Phandre bent to scoop her bosom into place, flipping curl into her hair as she rose. Her cheeks were pink from the exertion, and I watched the color drain from Merista's face as Phandre flitted out the door.

"Don't do that," I said. "They've come to see you. You." But I guessed how she felt; Lord and Lady Nemair seemed every bit as grand as Morva had promised, and five years was a long time to build up a picture in your head. I pulled Merista's red velvet dress from the heap of clothes at the foot of the bed and gave it two brutal shakes. "Here."

In the end I helped her into it; she was not so flexible as Phandre or I (and I did not want to know what Phandre had been up to, to work those shoulder joints so easily), and Morva never showed up to do the job properly. Touching Merista was not so bad as I'd feared that first night I climbed beside her into bed. The magic running in currents across her skin merely swirled around my fingers and behaved itself. Eventually she was dressed, her silver necklaces and bracelet firmly in place.

"Now you," Merista said.

"No, wait. Did Phandre take her blue sleeves?" I said, hardly believing the words came out of my mouth. "You look — unfinished."

Slipping the beaded silk over Merista's arm, I had the sudden sensation of Tiboran kicking me in the head. I gripped the sleeve laces hard.

*We'll say she's Phandre's maid.*

Oh, gods. But in its own insane way, it was brilliant.

"Lady Merista, will you have a maid at Caerellis?"

She didn't let me finish tying on the sleeve. She spun on me. "Oh, Celyn, that's perfect!"

And when thirteen-year-old, puppy-eyed nobs and fickle trickster gods are in accord, what can you do?

"What about your parents?"

"I know they'll say yes. They have to."

"I have no training," I warned.

"Don't be silly. You know how to get dressed, and you've had a whole day's practice being my companion already."

I wasn't sure whether the painful twist to my mouth was a smile or a grimace, but Merista gabbled on as she finished dressing me. I didn't need the looking glass to tell me I looked a lot more polished than she did. As we were turning to leave, she caught my hand.

"Celyn, here." She was holding out the silver bracelet.

Every dazed instinct in me froze up. "I don't need that." Of all the things to say! "I mean, you don't need to do that."

She gave me an odd little smile. "It's a present. To seal our arrangement." She held it out, looking so hopeful. Merciful gods — did I really look like a stray dog? But I took Merista Nemair's silver, magic-binding bracelet, wondering what in Sar's name I was getting into.

Downstairs, in the unnaturally tidy Favom courtyard, the entire household had spilled out to greet the returning dignitaries. I spotted Durrel beside his father, smiling easily as he spoke with Merista's father. He turned and saw us, and lifted a hand to wave at Meri. She barely twitched her fingers in response.

Lady Nemair had her hands on Phandre's shoulders, while a stocky woman in a satin kirtle pulled tight across her broad chest looked on disapprovingly. It took me a moment to realize it was Morva, all tarted up like a lady. Someone pushed or pulled Merista forward, and her parents bundled her to them in a fierce embrace. After a moment, she freed her arms and flung them about her mother's neck, squeezing back just as earnestly.

I did not belong here.

I looked up past the courtyard wall. Tiboran's moon was obscured by a brilliant autumn sunrise, and there was a hint of chill in the morning that we hadn't felt in Gerse. The world felt huge and distant, and something was pressing in on my chest, making it hard to breathe. A lady's maid! In some house somewhere I'd never even heard of? Stealing one of those fine Favom horses — even if it ate me — was looking better and better.

"Who's this, then?" a deep, jovial voice rumbled. I'd been bustled to the front of the fold.

"Mother, Father, this is my new friend, Celyn. We met in the city." Two days ago, but who was counting? Merista seemed to have lost her shyness; she pulled close to her mother and murmured something in her ear. Lady Nemair's warm brown eyes sharpened slightly, and she looked me over. *What did Merista say to her?*

I sank low in an affected curtsy. "Lord and Lady Nemair."

"It's good to meet you, Celyn," Lady Nemair said in a voice as warm as her eyes. "We rarely hear about Merista's friends." She took my hands, and I had to stop myself from pulling them away.

"Mother, I want to bring her to Caerellis. As my maid."

Lady Nemair looked from me to her daughter, then back again. "Well, daughter, you will be an adult soon, and you'll need to start building your own household. What say you, milord?"

Lord Nemair regarded me solemnly, fists perched on his wide hips. "I say I know better than to argue with my womenfolk. Come, Lady Celyn, Phandre, Lady Merista, let's all get reacquainted, shall we? Ragn!" The word flung out like a thunderclap. "Have you a feast of welcome prepared for your old friends, or what?"

There was a feast, and it lasted *all day*. It took ages to untangle the knot of welcome, but everyone finally settled into the Favom hall around noon. I was seated beside Merista, who couldn't keep her rapt eyes off her parents, through course after course of food and drink — which at first was entertaining, but after a few hours of it, I got restless. I wasn't used to sitting still this long. If something didn't happen, I was going to have to kick somebody.

The conversation revolved around the Nemair, amusing stories from life at the Corles court, everything they'd missed of their daughter's last five years. After the story about Merista falling into the Favom duck pond when she was ten, and a detailed account of her learning to make eel soup, I let my mind wander. Occasionally Durrel would glance my way, catch my eye, and give me an encouraging nod, which I found completely unsettling.

"What do they say in Corlesanne, then?" Lord Decath asked. "Do things look as tense from afar as they seem here?"

Lady Nemair was solemn. "They are tense. Bardolph is aging, he's sick, and if he doesn't name an heir before he dies, there will be war. I don't see how that can be avoided. And if there's a war . . ."

"Astilan will be king," Lord Decath finished. A heavy silence fell over the hall. This same conversation was held in every taproom in Gerse: Bardolph had no surviving children, and had refused to confirm one of his two nephews as his heir. His obvious favorite was Prince Astilan, an avowed Celyst with a cruel streak who'd served in the royal army and had the backing of the military and the support of the church. But the king had never made it official, and many discontented Llyvrins favored Wierolf, the younger prince, who from all accounts lacked his cousin's convictions and connections. He'd earned the nickname "the Lazy Prince" from his habits of hunting and carousing while Astilan was training for battle.

From where I stood, they looked very much the same: no better and no worse than their uncle. And in the gap left by the quibbling heirs, the Inquisitor slipped right in and cozied up to the king, spreading his malice across Gerse and beyond. I twisted the silver bracelet on my wrist.

"All the same," Lord Decath was saying, "Wierolf does have his supporters. I fear, though, that no matter how devoted they are, they'll still be woefully unprepared. Astilan represents the current regime; he'll have the support of Bardolph's councilors *and* most of the noble houses."

"Yours, milord?" Lady Nemair asked with a smile. Decath just raised his goblet to her and demurred.

"Does anyone even know what Wierolf is up to these days?" Durrel put in. "There are so many rumors, it's hard to know what to believe."

"That young man will have to settle down if he wants to be king," Lord Nemair said. "Thirty-one years old and still can't sit still long enough to attend a privy council."

"Do let's speak of something else," Lady Amalle pleaded. "You must be looking forward to Lady Merista's *kernja-velde*, although we'll hate losing her. She's been such a joy in our household."

"Can't be helped, Lady," Lord Nemair said. "The girl must come home. We need a chance to coddle and spoil her for a few months, before some ambitious young nobleman steals her away again."

Merista blushed furiously, but her eyes shone.

"I'm not sure Celyn understands what she's signing on for," Durrel said, grinning at me from across the hall. "I'll imagine her own *kernja-velde* was not quite such an elaborate affair."

"Oh, you'll love it!" Phandre said to me, and actually managed to sound genuine. "It's a house party — everyone comes and stays with the family, and all the marriage prospects are paraded before the girl and her parents."

Lady Nemair cleared her throat. "While I suppose that's a technically accurate depiction of events, I believe Lady Phandre neglects the point. This is a time for seclusion and study for Lady Merista, when she learns the skills and duties of being a wife" — here Phandre snorted, to a black look from Lady Nemair, who continued — "and reflects upon the childhood she's leaving behind. Your coming-of-age was not like this, Celyn?"

Here I snorted, but I covered it up better. "No, milady." Mine had ended in a brawl, in which Tegen's nose was broken.

"When will Caerellis be ready?" Lady Amalle was saying. "You must stay here while your staff prepares for your arrival."

Lady Lyllace blotted her lips with an embroidered napkin. "We're not returning to Caerellis," she said. Her voice was like low, soft music. "His Majesty, in his infinite royal wisdom, has absorbed that property back into his own royal body."

I tensed. Lady Amalle was confused too. "But where —"

"We've been restoring Bryn Shaer," said Lord Nemair.

"Bryn *Shaer*?" Lady Amalle echoed. "In the Carskadons? That old fortress? Surely it's not habitable, after — how long has it been?"

I looked to Merista for an explanation, but she was just staring, white-faced, at her parents.

"Forty-two years," Nemair said, tearing into some bread. "But we've had our people working on it, off and on, for the last five or six. Cleaning up the place, building a new, modern lodge, fireplaces in all the bedrooms, that sort of thing. Spared no expense. It will be a . . . palace again."

"It will be perfectly habitable. Merista, wait until you've seen the views! It's incredible in the winter." Lady Lyllace smiled at her daughter, who nodded automatically.

"Celyn, have you ever been to the mountains?"

"I — uh, no, milord."

"You're in for a treat, my girl. *Bryn Shaer* means 'Bear's Keep,' and the place is aptly named. Silverback bears come right up to the walls, and —"

"Well, not in the winter, my lord husband."

I didn't hear the rest of the winter marvels Lord Antoch described. The *mountains*? Spend the winter in the Carskadon Mountains? "Doesn't it snow there?" I heard myself ask, and everyone laughed.

"Only a little," Lady Lyllace said, but something in her voice was too merry.

After that, conversation moved on to other topics, but Merista sagged a little beside me. I plied her for more information.

"I don't really know," she said quietly. "Bryn Shaer was closed by the king or something, many years ago. He gave it to my parents as a wedding gift."

I did some swift thinking. The road to the Carskadons would take me halfway toward Yeris Volbann. If we left before winter set in, I could probably make the rest of the trip on foot, maybe hook up with a caravan on the road. . . . I had Merista's silver bracelet, and Raffin's money, and Chavel's letters — it was a good start.

The meal dragged on, until I thought I'd go mad. Every time I was sure it was over, a swarm of servants appeared from the kitchens, laden with yet another course of food and wine. Finally I'd had it. I pulled into the background, keeping my mouth shut until everybody forgot about me, and then slipped out.

I found a door that led out onto the tower roof and stepped outside, crossing to the battlement to look down. Dusk had sped along, a band of pink low along the horizon, closing another day between me and Tegen. Tiboran's moon was round and full, staring at me expectantly. I made a rude gesture at it.

Somewhere in the southern distance was Gerse. Would I be able to see it from up here? I climbed up onto the battlement to get a better look, and had to grip hard to the edge as the wind buffeted me like a banner, whipping strands of hair into my face.

"What in the name of all that is holy are you doing?"

Strong hands seized me about the waist. I tensed and kicked out instinctively, but these stupid nob shoes weren't going to do any damage. I wheeled in the grasp — and saw that it was Durrel.

"Milord! I did not hear you approach." That *sounded* dignified, at least.

"What —" He set me down. "What were you doing?"

I tried a smile. "Would you believe I was looking for a way to escape?"

Durrel looked down over the balcony walls. "I might, at that," he said quietly. "I've contemplated the very thing myself, more than once." Nodding into the sky, he added conversationally, "A liar's moon."

"What?" It came out sharp, my heart banging.

"Tiboran's moon is full," he said, his voice easy. "Isn't that what they call it?"

I let out my breath in a slow hiss. "I don't know, milord."

"Why'd you leave? You missed Morva's famous sloe plum aspic."

"That wasn't my place," I said honestly.

"And climbing castle towers by moonlight?"

I had to grin. "My place."

Durrel raised his eyebrows, but said nothing. He leaned against the round rough battlement wall. A blast of wind howled round the tower and hit me squarely. Shivering, I wavered on my feet.

"Here." Durrel doffed his doublet and draped it around my shoulders. It dwarfed me. Warm from his body, it still reeked of sour wine and river air, and a musky, salty scent that must have been Durrel's own. I took a step away from him. It was too easy to stand here beside him, as if I'd known him for years. As if I were the girl I was pretending to be.

"Why did you help me?" I said abruptly.

"What do you mean?"

I waved an impatient hand at him. "You couldn't possibly have known my father."

He sighed and met my eyes. "I guess . . . you looked a little like I felt."

"Miserable?"

"And scared, and lost, and desperate, like you were running from something and couldn't get far enough away." He looked out over the tangled landscape below us. "I don't think anyone should have to feel that way."

"You don't know anything about me."

A shrug. "I don't have to."

"I could be dangerous." Why was I pressing the point? A conversation like this was likely to get me killed.

A smile played at his lips. "No, you looked more *in* danger, than dangerous."

I turned back to the distant Decath fields, washed with moonslight and shadow. The silence grew too comfortable. "Are you really getting married?"

He barked out a rough, abrupt laugh. "I really am. To the indomitable Talth Ceid — a great wooden block of a woman fourteen years older than I am. With four children."

"That explains the drunken flight from Gerse."

"Yes, yes, it does." He shifted against the cold stone walls. "It's a good match, all things considered. Both families will be strengthened by the alliance. What about you?" he said. "Any prospects? That brother of yours hasn't cast you up on the marriage block yet?"

I coughed back a laugh at the image — then remembered I had invented this persona. "Much cheaper to sell me to Celys, and he gets to look pious. So devoted to the Goddess, he tithed his little sister." There was a strange note in my voice I couldn't quite shake.

Durrel eyed me sidelong. "Do I detect a somewhat less . . . robust devotion in you, Celyn Contrare?"

This time my laugh broke free. "Maybe."

"So, have you really decided to leave us tomorrow, then?"

"What?"

"The caravan to Bryn Shaer leaves in the morning, as you'd have known, if you'd stayed for dessert."

"Tomorrow?" What was wrong with me? Yesterday I couldn't get out of here fast enough. "I guess so," I said.

"I wanted to see you before you left. I have something for you." In a sleight of hand that would have done a thief proud, he produced a slip of night-black, and held it out to me in his open palm. "It's cold in the Carskadons in winter; you'll need these."

Gloves. Almost invisible in the growing darkness, black lambskin with embroidered black vines running along the cuffs and up the thumb. Fitted snugly to my small hands, even the fingertips smooth and supple, they might have been made for me. A thief's gloves. I wanted them. "Thank you," I said before I forgot myself.

As I lifted my arm to admire them, Durrel said, "Meri gave you her bracelet?"

I looked at it, embarrassed. "I couldn't get her not to."

He was nodding. "No, it's good. I'm just surprised. Sometimes I forget she's not a little girl anymore." He looked off into the distance for a long moment. "There's something else." This time there was a strange note in his voice. I'd heard that sort of tone before — just before someone asked me to do a job that might cost me my head.

"This is where I repay you for saving me?"

A laugh. "Something like that. I'm glad you're going home with the Nemair. They'll be sympathetic to your situation. Believe me, my aunt and uncle are the last people who would send you back to that convent."

I eyed him warily. I didn't say I was taking my gloves and running the instant we hit the road to Yeris Volbann.

"But more than that, I'm glad somebody will be there for Meri. She may be legally an adult, almost, but she'll always be like my little sister. She's lived with the Decath since she was eight years old. We're the only family she remembers. I'd be grateful if you'd keep an eye on her — be a friend to her."

"Milord, I — that is not my skill."

"Really?" he said. "Now why do I doubt that? I have a feeling about you." He held out his hand again, this time with a sheathed dagger balanced in the flat of it. The scabbard was ornamented in silver, the hilt a swirl of pearl inlay. I shook my head and took a step back.

"Take it," he urged.

A dagger was valuable. And I needed one, after losing my own blade. I took the weapon from his hands and drew it. The steel glinted in the light of Zet's moon, and I saw the crest of a crowned dog bowing in red enamel on the hilt. This was a Decath weapon. This dagger was *very* valuable. "They'll think I stole it," I said.

"No, they won't."

"Why would you give this to me?"

He gave a little grin. "A stray cat needs her claws." Durrel bent low over me, until his mouth was very near my ear. "Stay with them, Celyn. *Please.*"

I clutched the dagger tight in my gloved fingers. I had a feeling Durrel did not often have to beg a girl for something, and I was starting to feel the weight of all these gifts. Damnation. Every instinct I had was telling me to run, but if there was one thing even a thief believed in, it was that you did not turn your back on someone who'd pulled you out of a scrape. That was a debt you honored. With your life, if need be.

Finally I nodded.

"Are you — a Sarist?" I scarcely whispered the words into the night.

He looked surprised. "Not me. I wish I had their conviction. I'm just a pawn on the vast Decath game board. I'm not allowed to have thoughts of my own. But I have a feeling it took a great deal more courage than I lay claim to, to do whatever you did in the last few days."

*Courage*. To leave Tegen behind in the hands of the Greenmen? "I'm no hero."

"Just staying alive's heroic these days." He drew back and took my shoulders in his hands. They were warm and strong. "Be well, Celyn Contrare."

# CHAPTER SEVEN

*Something was following me. I ducked behind a corner and listened for the footsteps. Light, scuffing — in the dark I couldn't be sure whose. I pulled myself tighter into the shadows and held my breath. The footsteps slowed, turned. Fifteen feet away, maybe closer. Searching.*

*I cast about for an escape. Any move would put me straight in my pursuer's vision, but was I fast enough to scale that wall? Would the trellis hold my weight? Could I make it across the road and into the sewers before he grabbed me?*

*Should I turn and fight?*

*Pale fingers traced along the shadowed walls, searching for gaps. I held my breath until my chest was bursting, counted footsteps, weighed my options.* Stay hidden. Don't call attention to yourself. *But the tension was unbearable. I ran.*

*I was almost at the sewer when fingers brushed my neck, caught my belt. I swallowed a yelp and spun around, jamming the heel of my hand upward. It hit something hard and sharp, sparking pain through my forearm. I struggled, turning left and right, trying to pull free. Finally I ripped my knife from its sheath and sawed at my belt.*

*Too slow. A long arm curved around my face, and I had to bite — hard. My knee jammed upward, and my attacker doubled over in the street. I resisted the urge to kick him while he was sprawled in the gutter, but cut the turquoise scarf from his face with my blade. I shoved my trophy into my sleeve and scrambled up the side of the tavern.*

Wintry sunlight spilled through the leaded glass and throbbed against my aching eyes, and for a moment I couldn't remember where I was; my dream and its memories seemed more real than the last several days had been. I had known I was in trouble as soon as I breezed into the Mask & Barrel that night, brandishing the kerchief.

"Damn it, Digger, you weren't supposed to hurt anybody!" Tegen had said. He held a rag to his chin; his lip was swollen. I might have felt penitent, but not with that crowd assembled.

"You grabbed me! What did you expect?"

"I caught you! You were supposed to surrender! Pox, I think you broke my damn jaw."

I pulled off my cap and shook down my hair, sliding up toward the bar. His strong arm blocked my progress. "If you're caught by the City Guard, do you plan to beat the hell out of them until they let you go?"

I scowled. "I don't understand. Of course. You don't expect me to let them catch me, do you? Isn't that the first rule? Don't get caught? Stay alive, no matter what?"

I pressed my fingers against my eyes, trying to blot out the memory. I was alone in the bed; Meri was in her dressing gown, staring out the tiny window and its view of nothing. The country outside Favom had given way to a dark, forbidding forest, and this roadside inn was apparently the last habitation that dared to push back against Celys's demesne.

Meri turned from the window. "Bad dreams?" she asked.

Her eyes went past me, to the bed. "Oh." The bedclothes were a tangled mess, stripped from the mattress. My pillow looked as though I'd fought a battle with it. I shimmied to the side of the bed and swung my feet to the ground.

"I have bad dreams too, sometimes," she said softly.

I withheld my snort. What kind of nightmares could haunt pretty Meri's sleep? Someone taking away her pony privileges?

I had been included in the party to Bryn Shaer after all. Merista's parents didn't just resemble their daughter physically, they also shared her easy sympathy, and when Meri recounted my harrowing escape from the Celystra, they insisted I stay with them. The only snag had come when Lady Nemair insisted on sending a letter to my "brother."

"The convent will surely have reported you missing by now, dear. We must let him know what's become of you."

I couldn't help protesting. "I'm an adult."

"Well, of course you are, but I'm sure he's still worried about you."

"My brother stopped worrying about me a long time ago. Milady."

She just clucked and petted and wrote the damn letter. I scrambled for an address to send it to, then realized it didn't matter. Deliver a letter to any house on — what was it, Ruby Lane? — and the recipient would merely be perplexed and bemused by the news of Celyn Contrare. Nobody would have any reason to put her together with the thief on the run from Greenmen. And I could manage a man's handwriting well enough, should a return letter ever be required. I finally agreed, inventing a direction. I even consented to put down a few lines of my own, apologizing for my impulsiveness and begging my dear indulgent brother's forgiveness. Marau's balls.

Lady Lyllace briefly glanced over the letter. "Merista tells me you were a manuscript copyist at the Celystra," she'd said. "You have a very pretty hand."

I did, but it wasn't my own. I wasn't sure I'd know what my own handwriting looked like, I'd spent so much time perfecting the script of others.

Now, in the face of our expedition's waning comforts, my promise to Durrel Decath was starting to lose some of its weight. Last night we had managed to find lodging, but the first night we had *camped*. Along the Oss, in a big jolly caravan like a band of Tigas Wanderers. Phandre had seethed until the very roots of her tawny hair turned pink, but Meri had reveled in it, in the breezy night and the lumpy earth and the giant star-lit sky with Celys's moon staring down on us enormously. I had shivered, my back to the dying campfire, and prayed to gods I wasn't sure had ever been listening.

Hopping on the icy inn room floor, I climbed into my borrowed dress and hiked my skirts into my belt. We'd leave the main road today; if I wanted to light out for Yeris Volbann on my own, the moment was close. If I could slip away from the ever-watchful Nemair and their equally attentive retinue. So far I'd not had even a moment's privacy among these people, let alone a full hour when nobody was paying attention to me.

Seeing me dressed, Meri dutifully held out her arms to receive her own traveling costume, mimicking the arrangement of my skirts. She had started off full of excitement, delighted by the grand adventure, but the farther we moved from the familiar safety of Favom, the more anxious she seemed. I couldn't blame her: She was leaving the Decath, the only family she'd known for the last five years, and I knew she wasn't sure exactly what to make of the ones who'd come to take their place.

*I'd be grateful if you'd be a friend to her.* Pox. I slipped beside her and put a tentative hand on her shoulder, steeling myself to keep it there as a swirl of magic flared up around my fingers. I had discovered that even wearing Meri's silver bracelet, I could still see the magic on her whenever we touched. The silver didn't seem to inhibit how magic reacted to me, or my ability to detect it. She turned her gaze from the window and tried to smile, but a quivering lip betrayed her.

"All right!" I backed off. "Let's fetch some breakfast."

"I'm not very hungry," she said.

Meri could afford to skip a meal or two, but some of us woke up starving as a routine and knew that you ate when you had the chance. "I'm getting food for us. Don't eat if you don't want, but who knows what they have planned for lunch."

The inn's common room was surprisingly crowded. This place was remote, and the season for travel was waning, but apparently the colorful wagons and the knot of retainers camped outside with our cargo had drawn out the neighborhood curious. Mostly forest folk, in for a nip before heading to do whatever it was forest folk did. Not the richest pickings, unfortunately. A couple of the liveried Nemair guards sat together at a table near the door. I recognized the big young one from yesterday. Phandre had spent almost the whole day trying to get him to help her forget Raffin.

The mood in the room was strange; most people kept to themselves or smiled at their neighbors, but a current of tension swirled through the diners. I climbed up onto a tall stool at the bar as I waited for our food.

"I'm just telling you what I heard," a wiry man in a much-patched jerkin was saying. "They've increased patrols on the roads, and they're checking everyone's passage licenses. Seems they're on the hunt for somebody special."

I tensed. If they were checking passports, that meant I was stuck with the Nemair. The patrols we'd passed on the road so far had been happy to wave a noble party along with a nod and a bow. But a girl all alone would draw suspicion.

Think *ahead,* Digger. I had to draft myself some documents, just as soon as I could lay my hands on some paper. And a magistrate's seal. Pox and hells.

"I've heard it's Prince Wierolf, trying to sneak back into the country."

"Why sneak?" put in a heavyset laborer coming to join the conversation, a mug of ale in each hand. "Don't he own the whole damn place?"

"Not yet — not till Bardolph says he does."

"Which he *won't.* Old mule. Goddess save him, and all that, of course."

"I heard he off and married some Talancan girl." Somebody gave a chuckle. "I'd be sneaking too."

His neighbor popped him in the head and scoffed. "That's twaddle, and you know it. Milord's met the man and says if it don't involve books or horses, Wierolf's not interested."

Did that include politics, religion, and ruling Llyvraneth? I wondered.

"It's not the prince the patrols are after," said a small, bald man dressed a little better than his friends. The local bailiff, maybe. He withdrew a notice from his coat and smoothed it on the table. "They're looking for assassins. Rumor has it somebody's finally offed Prince Wierolf."

I swung my gaze his way — and I was not alone. The Nemair guards were watching. One of them said something to his partner, who rose and headed straight outside.

Two Ales said, "That's been all over the road to Yeris. They say the city's papered with these notices. Whoever done it's calling themselves the Huntsmen."

"Is that one huntsman, or a pack of 'em?" asked the bailiff.

He shrugged. "It takes a pair, don't it? Kill a royal and claim Zet's favor for it?" Zet wasn't just the goddess of hunting and war, she was the patroness of royalty. Murdering a prince in her name? That even sounded bad to *me*.

"Well, I'll believe it when I see a corpse," said a dark-featured man across the room. "We've heard this rumor before. Just people trying to stir up trouble."

"Or stir up dissenters," the bailiff said quietly. "Toss down a meaty story like that and see who comes out to bite."

"See if they can't stir up a nest of Sarists, you mean." The dark fellow's voice was low, but it carried.

"Well, he's their favorite, isn't he? And they *were* active around here."

"Come now," said the barman. "Surely His Majesty has better things to do with his time than pick at old wounds and bother the fine, upstanding folk of the Carskadon Mountains. And *surely* those fine, upstanding folk have better things to do than speculate about their betters. I know for a fact that you, Merc Kessl, have a fence that needs mending. If your wife comes looking for you here, I *will* tell her all I know."

The wiry fellow stood up from the table. "Aye, you would too. I'll see you, lads." He raised his drink. "Goddess keep Prince Wierolf!"

Nobody matched the toast.

Two Ales spoke quietly. "Careful, Merc — that's treason. If it ain't heresy."

Merc shrugged. "And do you see any Greenmen here, then? When the prince comes through here — and he will — we'll be free to worship as we always have in these mountains. We don't need a king from the city to teach us how to pray."

"Still, what if it is true?" a small man in a brown coat was saying. "The prince could be dead for months before anybody even noticed he was missing. We should do something."

I didn't hear the rest, since the serving girl appeared with my tray. I followed her to Meri's room, helping myself to a coin or two on my way.

I wasn't sure if this lady-in-waiting job paid anything beyond room and board.

Upstairs, Meri was standing in her open doorway, looking down over the rail into the common room. She was quiet and thoughtful as I arranged our plates, not even noticing I took the nob's share of the eggs.

"Do you think it's true?" she finally asked. "About Prince Wierolf? Do you really think they've — assassinated him?"

Startled, I looked up from my food. "There are always rumors like that. I wouldn't worry about it."

"But it might be true?" Her voice was soft and urgent, eyes begging me for answers.

Sure, it might be true. But for some reason I didn't want to say that to Meri. "It's just a rumor, some bored nobs — *people* trying to make a name for themselves, playing on everyone's fears."

"Why would they do that?"

"To scare people, stir them up, sow unrest —" I broke off with a shrug. "You shouldn't think about that."

She turned to me. "But it's our duty to think about it, as the nobility. It's our sacred responsibility to protect our people and our land. I have to understand these things, Celyn." Gods help me, she really believed it. "My parents are heroes, you know. They fought in the last war. I must aspire to be like them, mustn't I?"

She was watching me anxiously, waiting for my answer. But I just bowed my head, saying, "Yes, milady," and thinking that we were all in a lot more trouble than we'd bargained for, if we were counting on Merista Nemair to protect us.

Breakfast was interrupted a few moments later by a knock on Meri's door. "Milady!" a sharp voice barked through the wood. "Your father bids you make haste to depart."

Meri swung the door open. "Now?"

The big guard — Berdal, I thought his name was — nodded. "Aye, lady. He's in a fair rush."

Meri frowned. "Because — because of what they said down there?"

The guard's cool expression never faltered. "Ach, no, lady. They've spotted snow in the mountains above us, and there's a risk of avalanche if we don't get through the pass tonight. Tell your girl to pack your things, and get right down to the horses."

Back on the road, taller and taller trees sailed by the coach windows, black-green things with fierce, triangular bodies that marched like a massive army across the foothills. The closest I'd ever come to trees like this was the great ash that grew at the heart of the Celystra. The Hanging Ash, we called it. It was supposed to be sacred to Celys, but I couldn't imagine what she'd think of it now, its roots watered with the blood of heretics. With Meri chattering away in my ear, I watched the road to Yeris Volbann roll past about noon, and with it my last hope of escape.

The party bound for Bryn Shaer was small. In addition to the five of us who made up Meri's strange family assembly, a handful of servants and some dozen guards rode alongside, all clad in the silver-and-black Nemair livery. Supply wagons brought up the rear. I used the endless hours to try to learn as much as I could about my new company, which was difficult from my position trapped inside the coach, the only member of our party who couldn't ride. Occasionally I could coax Phandre into riding with me and sharing some tidbit of information, but it was never long before she remembered I was beneath her notice, leaving me with little to do but watch the unwelcoming landscape close around me, and wonder what in Tiboran's name I had gotten myself into. She had been included out of sympathy as well; I'd discovered that she was what we called a "loose" nob — orphaned and unattached to any other family. She was as lucky as I the Nemair had taken her in for the winter, though she spared no opportunity to remind me of her superiority.

I thought back over my first meeting with Lord Antoch and Lady Lyllace. Anyone in Gerse would have tied me up and beaten me bloody, demanding I produce proof of my claimed associations before they strangled me and threw my body into the Oss. But with these people, if I said I was a jeweler's daughter, I was a jeweler's daughter. It baffled.

The wagon jostled to an uneven stop, and I heard Merista's voice. "Celyn, come have a look!"

Hopping on one foot to shake a cramp out of my leg, I stumbled out of the coach and joined the party on the road. They clustered at the mouth of a precipice, gazing into the distance below. Meri saw me and pulled me closer.

Impossibly far below us, in a dizzying swoop of trees spotted with crisp gray juts of rock, nestled a miniature model of a castle. Ringed with a double row of heavy stone walls studded with three squat towers, it sat hunched against the black stone of the mountain. At the base of the wall, the cliff dropped straight away to nothing.

"Celyn, get back — you'll fall."

"I never fall," I said, shaking off Meri's arm.

Antoch leaned in beside me. "That's home now. Bryn Shaer, gem of the Carskadons. Another two days' ride, if the weather holds."

In the distance, a few hills and dips past the castle, I spotted a gap in the mountains, a glimpse of open sky. "What's that there?"

"The Breijarda Velde," Antoch said. "The Wide Pass through the mountains between Briddja Nul and Kellespau. Bryn Shaer was built to defend it."

"It looks like it's out in the middle of nowhere. How can it defend anything?"

Antoch gave his rumbling chuckle. "It *doesn't* defend anything now, girl. But back in its day — you can't see it from here, but there's a road leading to and from the castle, and the pass is a straight shot from the guard towers. Anything coming east or west through the mountains, Bryn Shaer has a clear view of it. Critically important in the winter, when the Gerse road is closed by snow."

"The pass is the only way in or out, all winter?" I said.

"And the tunnels," Meri put in. "There's a network of tunnels under the castle, leading all the way to Breijardarl."

"There *used to be* a network of tunnels." Lady Nemair had stepped forward. "They've been closed off as long as we've held the property, and we haven't restored them. So don't any of you girls get the idea to go exploring. Those tunnels are dangerous."

Dangerous tunnels? Bryn Shaer was looking brighter by the moment.

*Carskadon* means "black mountain," and already I was feeling the pressure from that gloomy dark stone. Gerse isn't a pretty city, but there's something about its dull gray buildings that feels . . . normal. Safe. This wild landscape of jutting escarpments and sheer drops into endless nothingness looked like the gods had ripped open the earth in some fit of hunger for what lay below, and left the rent pieces scattered and twisted behind them.

Berdal, the young guard assigned to watch over Meri and her attendants, was apparently native to these mountains and enjoyed pointing out their fascinating hazards to the foreigners of the party. Between bandits lurking among the trees, starving bears ravaging campsites, and avalanches — crushing falls of snow and rock that struck without warning to bury the unsuspecting under a frozen white death — I was starting to wonder why I'd been so worried about Greenmen.

As we climbed, it grew colder; we woke to the landscape frosted silver and a bite to the air, and Antoch pointed out clouds he said were dropping snow on distant peaks. Through breaks in the rock, I glimpsed a night sky with moons that were cold and watching, the stars flickering so close you could almost touch them.

"The scholars at Breijardarl used to study the stars, did you know?" Lady Nemair said as we sat up one night after dinner. We knelt at the fire, the shadows leaping just outside the ring of light. "They named the brightest of them, charted their course in the night. They even speculated that our own sun is a star not unlike its neighbors."

How could that be? "They all look so tiny," I said.

"The moons look small too," Lady Nemair said, "but it would take many thousands of them to equal even the brightness of one sun."

I stared at her until she laughed. Laughed! "I know, you're going to tell me that's heresy. It's not heresy, Celyn, it's astronomy. A science."

"A science they bleed people for."

She grew sober. "That's true enough. But it won't always be that way. Have faith." She said that last bit cheerfully, then told me more stories of the wonders of the college that had once stood at Breijardarl, before King Bardolph declared that knowledge heretical and illegal, and scattered Llyvraneth's scholars to every corner of the known world.

"They taught magic there too, didn't they?" I asked. A dangerous question, but one that seemed tantalizing and mysterious in this remote starlit night.

She nodded. "Not for hundreds of years, of course — there's nothing to teach anymore. But back when this land had magic, certainly they did."

Nothing to teach anymore. I glanced across the fire, where I could barely see Meri sitting with her father and the guardsmen. I spun the silver bracelet on my wrist, and said something guaranteed to earn a Celystra girl the cane. "I heard — people say that magic is coming back." I raised my eyes to see her reaction, but her face was still and calm as the face of a moon.

"I think they've always said that. If it were true, I think it would be a very good thing for a lot of people, and not just in this country."

"Just not Bardolph."

Lady Nemair barked out a short, sharp laugh, then covered her mouth with her white hand. Smiling, she rose and smoothed down her skirts. "That bracelet suits you, Celyn. Good night."

I watched her leave, wishing she'd stayed for me to ask more questions. Every child in Llyvraneth knew we lived in a world of dying magic, no matter what the king and the priests tried to tell us. The Celystra's official position was that magic did not — could not — exist, that Sar had never knelt upon the earth and breathed her power into our world, that those who claimed otherwise were lying or delusional. Dangerous heretics spreading their blasphemy like a plague. Centuries ago Llyvraneth had overflowed with Sar's power, until her temples and priestesses rivaled Celys's own. But now only faint traces remained in the odd charmed antique, the odd nobbish girl, the odd thief — rare, but enough to send the church and the king into fits, until Sar's few remaining faithful had been driven from the island, forced into hiding, or bled on the gallows.

A generation ago, a few powerful families decided Bardolph had gone too far, and had staged a rebellion under Sar's banner. It was hard to say whether any of those rebel Sarists had much to do with magic themselves — and it hadn't mattered anyway, since their strike against the Crown had failed, and they were all soundly crushed by the king's Green Army.

After that, whatever magic there was in Llyvraneth retreated even farther underground, until it was impossible to learn anything about it; that knowledge had crumbled to dust in the abandoned mages' college at Breijardarl, burned in bonfires in city circles, and been locked tight away in convent libraries. I'd never understood this odd skill of mine — there was never anyone I could ask about it, of course. Or show it to. Or trust with it.

Kind as Lady Lyllace Nemair seemed, she was not that person.

Finally one evening, under the faint light of Mend-kaal and a waxing Sar, we crossed one last hump of crumbling rock and rumbled into Nemair lands. I was on the wrong side of the coach and could see nothing, but I felt the caravan stop suddenly, as if we'd all sucked in our breath at once. I leaned my head out the wagon and tried to see something, but there was only gray-dark sky above and gray-dark stone all around.

"Are we here?" I pulled my head back in and looked at Phandre.

"Looks like it." Phandre climbed out of her seat and pushed past me to the door.

Close to, that tiny miniature castle we'd seen across the valleys was *huge*. Not as big as Gerse's royal palace, of course, but nearly the size of the Celystra. Mismatched buildings of stone and brick piled in on one another, watchtowers crowding into walls, all crisscrossed by narrow stone walkways and bridges, until the castle seemed even more a part of the ruined landscape than the mountains themselves. A tight, rocky path twined up the steep slope, the only approach from the treacherously narrow ridge below.

We'd come to a stop on a level plain that spread out around the castle, surrounding it with a great ring of lands and grounds. Still, everyone dismounted and milled about in a tight cluster, as if afraid to stray too far from the safety of the crowd. The night and the cliffs and the utter impossible *size* of the place made it seem risky to take even one step in any direction but toward the castle.

But I saw that tall white tower, with its sharp narrow fretwork, and suddenly wanted to see what Bryn Shaer looked like from *up there*, wondered what was behind all those tiny starlit windows and iron-barred doors. I pushed through the crowd, leaving Phandre and Meri behind. Lord Nemair fell in step beside me, his dark mare whickering uncertainly.

"Celyn." He nodded to me. "Long journey. How are you bearing up, then?"

"Very well, milord. Thank you."

Even in the darkness I could see his broad cheeks part in a smile. "Celyn, my dear, you are a very good liar." He gave me a clap on the shoulder that sent me stumbling, and led the way to the castle gates.

The high wall, maybe three times the height of a man and *begging* to be climbed, parted in a wide double wooden-and-iron gate, large enough to drive the wagons through, three abreast. Liveried guards in Nemair black and silver ushered us through to an open courtyard where torches flickered over a mix of cobbles and lawn. I saw a paddock marked out at one end of the courtyard, while in the shadow of the white tower stood a great half-timbered lodge, still hugged by scaffolding, built around a curved center court.

"Planning an attack?"

Meri's mother's voice in my ear made me jump. "What?"

Lady Nemair laughed. "You looked like you were scrutinizing the Lodge pretty severely, there, Celyn."

I bit back my reply — because that was exactly what I'd been doing: measuring up the walls of the new building for handholds and toeholds and counting windows, just as if cracking this building were one of Tegen's jobs.

"How far is the pass — the Breijarda Velde?"

"Three miles," Lady Nemair said cheerfully. "You can see it from the wall, just there."

She pointed, and under the last wisps of sunset, I could see the gap in the mountains. Three miles, but I could blot it all out with my thumb.

"And that's the nearest habitation?"

"Yes, why? Were you wanting to visit somebody, then?" There was merriment in her voice. "I suppose we could all make a trip of it once we're settled, if the weather holds. There's not much to see, of course — just some farms and a lot of very temperamental goats. I'm not sure how the locals would feel about the neighboring lords descending upon them like an army, though."

Just three miles — yet impossibly far away. Having spent four days twisting through the endless bleak press of stone and trees, I was beginning to have an idea of what a "wide pass" through these mountains might mean.

# CHAPTER EIGHT

We settled in to Bryn Shaer with as much efficiency as the rest of our journey. The brand-new Lodge had been readied for our arrival by a party of servants who'd been sent on ahead, led by Yselle, the Nemair's handpicked Corles housekeeper. The family rooms were on the second floor, above the central public gathering spaces of the Round Court, Lesser Court, Armory, and a half dozen other large and nearly identical rooms an ordinary person would need a map to keep straight. Phandre and I followed Meri upstairs, through a long corridor of dark paneling, flickering torchlight, and impossibly soft rugs beneath our feet. Shadowy and silent — a thief's dream.

Meri led the way a little uncertainly, pausing in stairwells and looking down hallways with a little frown. Twisting her silver necklace in her fingers, she pushed open a door midway down the second floor, and halted in the threshold. Phandre shoved her way past, and let out a long, low whistle. Curious, I followed, leaving Meri lingering in the doorway.

Inside, I wanted to laugh. I had been in nobs' bedrooms before — but city rooms, and never with the lamps lit. And never to *stay*. Even the rooms at Favom couldn't compare to this. The top floor of my entire Gerse rooming house would have nestled comfortably in Meri's Bryn Shaer bedroom, with its high plaster ceilings, wall of leaded windows, and ornate carved fireplace, already burning with a merry glow. And the bed — that *bed*. It was all I could do not to fling myself atop it and roll on the velvet coverlet like a happy dog in a pile of muck.

"Meri," Phandre announced, "I do believe I love you."

Meri still hesitated, but Phandre grabbed her hands and yanked her inside.

"At Charicaux, my window overlooked a garden," Meri said faintly. "There was a pear tree right below, and a dove that would sit in its branches and sing to me."

"Charicaux?" I said, adding, "Milady?"

"Durrel's house."

She looked so lost and forlorn I couldn't help myself. I swung an arm around her shoulders. "Well, *my* last rooms in Gerse looked out on a sewage canal, and my room at the convent didn't have a window, so I think this is magnificent."

Meri gave me a weak smile, but leaned her dark head against my shoulder, her skin sparking faintly as her hair brushed my cheek.

As part of the gathering-in before Meri's *kernja-velde*, Bryn Shaer was preparing to host any number of visiting nobs (among them several prospective husbands for Meri), and apparently there weren't enough servants for all that work. Which is how I found myself, obscenely early the next morning, in the chilly courtyard with Phandre, beating clouds of dust from feather mattresses we'd dragged out of the guest apartments and draped over the paddock fence. The morning was misty and gray; the air smelled of smoke and damp and age, as if with every violent strike of the staves, we were beating some forgotten Bryn Shaerin generation from the linen and down.

"I could be in" — *thwup* — "Tratua right now" — *thwup* — "eating grapes from the fingers of Maharal serving boys." *Thwup.* Phandre brushed an armful of hair from her smudged face and leaned on her staff. "But no! I'm stuck here, at the arse end of nowhere, with mousy Meri and General Lyllace, playing scullery maid with *you!*" She gave another savage thrust to the bed. It was a miracle she didn't poke a hole in it. Hastily I rescued the mattress and moved it to the stack of clean beds waiting to be returned to the castle. I stayed well out of her range and kept the bed between us — Phandre didn't know how to wield a staff as a weapon, but she had annoyance on her side and I wasn't entirely sure she wouldn't crack me upside the skull.

And then I'd have to rough her up a little, and nobody wanted that.

We were both beginning to suspect the truth of it all, though. The grown-up Lady Merista would be expected to know all there was to managing a fine household, and if Phandre and I had any hope of landing husbands in our lady's wake, so would we. There was no sense objecting to this plan; if it came down to it, I didn't think the Nemair could *make* me marry somebody. And Phandre didn't dare protest: She was almost nineteen and an orphan; it was past time she cultivated a few assets that would please a farsighted suitor, and everybody knew it.

And so we all three were to have instruction in housekeeping, tending the stillroom, cheese making, needlework, and the torture of innocent mattresses with technique that would do a Greenman proud. As I hefted the next bed onto the hurdle of twisted vines and twigs, Lady Lyllace sailed by, Meri hard at her heels. Lyllace was rattling off instructions even Yselle would have strained to take in, but Meri was practically beaming — like a puppy thrilled to be included in the games of its older fellows. She was settling in nicely; as her mother's shadow, she'd shed her nervousness. Or maybe she just preferred housework to luxury.

Lyllace paused a moment to inspect our work, nodding briskly. "Good. Stacking the beds like this will keep the moist air out. Be sure you get them back inside before too long, though. We don't want them to mildew."

I thought I saw Phandre's knuckles whiten. Meri gave us a little wave as she scurried after her mother.

"That woman! You'd think she owned the whole mountain, the way she gives orders."

"I like her," I said — not entirely to annoy Phandre.

Phandre glared at me. "You would."

Late that night, we tucked ourselves beside the roaring fire in Meri's bedroom. With the addition of a few more luxuries we'd nicked from adjoining bedchambers — a huge Kurkyat tuffet, a Tratuan glass serving set, a weird painting of a girl wearing a snail amulet on her forehead — we had put the final polish on a set of apartments definitely worthy of a noblewoman on the rise and her two loyal retainers. I stretched my feet out onto the tuffet and bent my head back to watch the shadows leap against the sculpted plaster ceiling. In the distance, the barking of dogs carried on the night wind.

Meri was curled on a cushioned bench, reading aloud from a book of history. "Oh, hear this," she'd say, quoting us some long dry passage about strategy at Valdoth Bridge or the heroic deaths of Sarist soldiers at Aarn. Her silver off, I watched the sparkling dust motes swim about her face and hands. There was something fascinating about it, like the sparkle of a ring on a nob's finger, moving through a crowded market — dangerous and forbidden and right here where I could touch it, if I just reached out. What did that feel like, to Meri? Was the silver restrictive, like a corset or too many hairpins? Did she feel a rush of power when she took those necklaces off?

Phandre pinched one of the Tratuan glasses in her fingers, admiring the way the lamplight played on its gold-dusted rim. "You know, it's a shame to waste these," she said. "We really ought to properly inaugurate our new home."

"How?" Meri asked eagerly.

"I'll bet this place has an impressive wine cellar."

Meri nodded. "It does. They grow fine grapes in Breijardarl."

"And that steward looked like he hadn't missed many nightly libations." That was me.

Phandre grinned. "Excellent. Why don't we see what we can dig up, then?" Her eyes turned pointedly to me. I almost laughed. I was the obvious choice for such a mission, of course. To Phandre I was expendable, and she would be only too happy to get me in trouble, and Meri seemed to think I was bold and daring. I rose and bowed grandly — like a man, not the dainty curtsy of a lady's maid — then ducked out the door.

As I trotted down the corridors, I built a map of Bryn Shaer in my head. Meri's rooms were about two minutes from the main kitchens — down two flights of stairs and past the Round Court (a vast room ringed with carved banquet tables, its tapestry-draped walls soaring up to a buttressed wooden dome). I skipped past the vaulted entryway and its huge arched doors with the heavy iron bindings locking out the wilderness.

I found my way into the darkened service passages, head bowed lest someone see me, but my eyes skirting the shadows, pulling out details. The main kitchens were right behind the central court, and I guessed the wine cellar could be reached fairly easily from somewhere nearby.

Kitchens were never empty, but at this hour they should be quiet; I went a few yards past the doorway first, to check for cellar entrances, but found none. I quickly concocted an excuse, if some overeager scullery wench discovered me here, and pushed my way in.

The great fire had died to embers, and a boy in a tunic that was almost too small lay curled up on the hearth, one sleeping hand on the rake. A single heavy candle burned in a lamp, a plump gray cat eyed me casually from the sideboard, but I saw no one else.

At last — there beyond the butcher block and the great carving table, a pretty painted door with a new, beautiful lock. I seemed to have found my prize; wine was expensive and servants untrustworthy. I slipped a lock pick from my corset and had the door open before the cat could finish yawning. The cellar stairs disappeared into inky blackness, so I borrowed the lamp and let myself down.

Bryn Shaer's wine stores were not quite so impressive as Phandre might have hoped; a few well-stocked racks and behind them, several casks of ale and barrels of wine and mead, but beyond those, the cellars sank deeper into darkness. I cast my lamp into the shadows but caught up nothing but a startled mouse, staring at me with wide dark eyes that for a brief amusing moment made me think of Meri. I turned my attentions to the racks, turning over the dusty bottles to find something suitable — nothing *too* expensive, or someone would notice it was missing; but nothing too cheap either, or what was the point?

Tegen would have chosen a bottle of rare sparkling Grisel from Corlesanne, and nicked the special fluted glasses to go with it. We would have shared the bottle right here, getting recklessly drunk and leaving the bottle and glasses behind, "So they'd know we were here."

Suddenly I didn't want the wine anymore.

With a sigh, I tucked a bottle under my arm and went back upstairs. The door locked as easily as it had opened, and the fire boy slept on. The cat gave me a reproachful look, and I saluted him with the bottle.

That was when I heard the voices, and saw the crack of light beneath a door on the far side of the kitchen — the door to Lady Lyll's stillroom.

If I'd been a smart little lady's maid, I'd have scurried back upstairs to the roaring fire and cracked open the wine warming under my arm. But the smooth wood, and the hushed voices behind it, were just too tempting. I crept closer, and was rewarded by Lady Lyllace's voice, but her normally low, soft tones had turned fierce and definite.

"You tell milord that we are very grateful to Reynart, but that he and his men must leave."

If her companion made a response, I couldn't hear it.

"I don't care — pay them off if you have to. No, you have *my* permission. Now good night."

Metal scraped on stone, and a heavy door creaked shut — the stillroom must have a door that led out to the kitchen gardens. A moment later, the splinter of light opened up, and Lady Lyllace stepped out. I sprang away from the door before it could crack me in the head, but that was the last of my advantage.

"Celyn! You startled me!" Lady Lyllace clapped a hand to her chest. I had never seen her so informally dressed: in just a dark kirtle, her smock sleeves rolled up to her elbows. She dumped a bundle of laundry by the fire, briskly crossed the darkened kitchen to the sink, where fresh water was pumped in from underground springs, and set about scrubbing her hands with the cake of soap. "What in the world are you doing, wandering about at this time of night?"

"Meri — Lady Merista wanted some wine," I said. Not one of my better cover stories, but how else would I explain the bottle in my hand?

Why should I, a mere maid-in-waiting, presume to think my lady was *not* entitled to a bottle of wine in her own home?

Lady Lyllace glanced toward the cellar door as she dried her hands on her apron. "The wine cellar is supposed to be locked," she said, a note of mild reproach in her voice. But she sounded distracted.

"It was on the counter," I said hastily.

She gave me a look that said she didn't believe me, but girls with lock picks clearly didn't figure into her household accounting. "Hmm." She held out her hand, and I found myself handing the bottle over. She glanced at the label and pursed her lips briefly. "I'll have to have a word with Yselle about leaving valuable supplies lying about. Water it well, Celyn. Merista is younger than you, and it's late." To my surprise, she handed the bottle back to me.

I quickly bowed my head. "Yes, milady."

Together we turned back toward the wing where the family was staying. As we walked, Lyllace gave me a bemused smile. "Celyn, why do I think you were probably one of those girls who gave the Holy Daughters fits trying to keep up with your mischief?"

Surprised, I had to laugh.

# CHAPTER NINE

Late morning sun streamed through Meri's windows, making golden puddles on the polished wood floor. I stretched and gazed up at the embroidered canopy with its frolicking deer and fat rabbits. On the table beside the bed — close enough for me to put out my hand and touch it — was a pitcher of fresh cream, a plate of pears and honey, and half a loaf of steaming oat bread. Draped across my feet was a mantle of soft white fur, edged in gold; at the foot of the carved wood bedstead, an inlaid trunk, stuffed with linen smocks so fine I could see my hand through them.

And tucked into a hollow between the herb-scented mattress and the wall, three gold crowns, a dozen silver marks, and a jet ring somebody wasn't using anymore. I was going to have to find a better hiding place for those. Another time. I turned over in the bed, breathing deeply the scent of crisp white linen sheets nobody had ever slept in before.

I heard the sound of the curtain rings being shoved apart, and more sunlight flooded the rooms. Meri stood before me, fully dressed, her hands on her hips and cheeks pink from her early morning ride with her parents.

"Get up!" she cried gaily. "I am to inform you that my lady mother says it's deplorable how lazy you and Phandre have gotten. We have guests arriving today, and you are both to report immediately to the courtyard to greet them." She flung my kirtle at my head.

"Lazy!" Phandre stepped out of the little maid's room adjacent to Meri's bedroom. "You have no idea how much work it is, trying to make a good impression on the household staff." She yawned elaborately. "I was up all hours last night explaining the problem with my door latch to Ludo."

"We heard you," I said, although it was untrue, and Meri shrieked with laughter and turned scarlet.

Phandre just looked haughtily at me, then marched over and carried away the entire tray of food.

"Beast," I said.

"Guttersnipe," she called back as she kicked her door shut. Meri's chambers had a bedroom with an adjacent dressing room, a sitting room, and a small, spare bedroom for her ladies-in-waiting, which Phandre had appropriated on sight. I couldn't mind that much; there were only two beds, and if I had to share with somebody, at least Meri gave off some body heat.

The thing was, I *had* gotten lazy, and it *was* deplorable. Lady Nemair's workload notwithstanding, after two weeks at Bryn Shaer, all my instincts were dulling. Having everything provided for me was making me soft, and I loved it. I added to my little squirrel hoard out of habit, without the thrill it should have brought me. I refused to think about what I was going to do when winter was over. That was an entire lifetime from now, and I was determined to enjoy this one as long as I could.

I unrolled the blue dress Meri had thrown at me and climbed out of bed. Even the floors at Bryn Shaer were warm; you could pad around barefoot, but why? The leather slippers they'd given me had *pearls* sewn around the collar. Tucked alongside my shoes in *my very own* clothes chest was the Decath dagger Durrel had given me. I'd been wearing it strapped to my leg, a curiosity Meri had noticed but never commented upon, but this morning I just held it up to the sunlight and looked at the bowing dog on the pommel.

"I miss him," Meri said quietly. She'd sat on the edge of the bed; her feet almost reached the floor.

"I know," I said, but I was thinking not of her cousin, but of another man with a knife.

"You must miss your — young man too." When I looked sharply at her, she smiled. "I hear you dreaming, sometimes."

Marau's balls. I didn't remember those dreams, I just woke sweating and disoriented and sick with fear.

"It must have been very romantic," Meri pressed. "I gather your brother didn't approve."

For a moment I was confused, then had to choke back my laugh, imagining what my brother — Celyn's *invented* brother — would have made of Tegen. I put the dagger back in the trunk and dropped the lid. "That was a different lifetime," I said.

Out in the courtyard, we clustered together among the bustle of wagons and bodies pouring in. It was probably one of the last warm afternoons we would see for a while. Golden trees I had seen in the distance just days earlier had given up their leaves, and the black hills seemed to loom even closer. Lord Antoch had warned us that weather in the Carskadons can change suddenly, and although he still took hunting parties out daily to catch the last of the hillside game, we girls were cautioned never to go beyond the outer bailey alone, lest we run afoul of bandits or fall off the mountain. For now, the pleasures inside Bryn Shaer were enough for that warning not to chafe. With nothing but thin air above and endless black rolling forest below, Gerse felt as far away as the moons.

Meri stood flanked by Phandre and me, in a bronze damask coat, her black hair caught up in a gold caul. Her curtsies had become less rigid, the hand she offered to her arriving suitors trembled less. Mountain air was good for her, I thought.

And then wondered why, by the Nameless One, I even cared.

The arrivals of the hour included a merchant and his wares, and the press and swirl of people and goods made it like a nob's market day. I half expected somebody to break out pipes or start hawking roasted meat on skewers. I stood behind Meri and curtsied and nodded and freed a few coins and rings here and there.

The merchant, a small, bald man in an expensive doublet, seemed well-acquainted with Lady Lyll, walking her through the heaped-up wagons he had dragged up the mountain from Breijardarl. Their laughter carried across the courtyard as Meri hung back shyly.

"That's Eptin Cwalo," she said. "He's only a merchant, but he's very rich, and he has *six* sons."

"Six?" Phandre broke away, swishing her green silk skirts like the tail of a peacock. I shrugged and followed, curious to see what was in all the crates. Probably cheese and beer and wool — but they might have some of the candied Breijard fruit I was coming to love, which I would be more than happy to help unpack. Nobody would see me in this crowd. I was certain of that. I was peeking beneath the canvas cover on one of the wagons when I heard Meri squeal with delight.

"Uncle Remy!" Meri craned her neck to see over the crowd. "That's my uncle, Remy Daul — my father's foster brother. I didn't know he was coming!"

The man in question strode into the courtyard rather on the heels of everyone else, leading a tense silver horse. He was tall and lean, dressed to accentuate that fact, in a close-cut gray doublet and tight breeches. His hair was impeccably cut, fashionably short, and he wore a thin beard that did not quite conceal the scar twisting the side of his lip. He reminded me of a wolfhound.

"His foster brother?"

"Father lived with him as a boy, and they fought together in the war."

I could believe it. There was a kind of coiled strength in him that reminded me of Tegen, always wound up and ready. He strode across the courtyard as if he owned it, straight to Lady Lyll, who dropped what she was doing to throw her arms around him.

"Remy! Such a surprise! Wherever have you been? We can't keep track of you."

As a groom scurried in to remove the horse, Lord Daul cracked a slight smile. "Here and there. Olin, recently. Very good hunting there."

Meri was still chattering on. ". . . in a grand house on the Briddjan coast, but he isn't there much. He's very much in demand at court as a lunarist, and —"

"Well, go see him." I gave her a little shove, but she froze, rooted to the spot. "What's the matter?"

"I've never met him."

"How do you know it's him, then?"

"Father has a miniature."

Well, if she was shy, I wasn't. I grabbed her arm and tugged her in Lord Daul's direction, over her protests. And then I saw someone *I* knew, and stopped so suddenly I nearly yanked Meri's arm right out of its socket.

A delicate beauty had stepped down from one of the wagons, and was lowering the hood on her sable coat to expose a crown of pale hair dressed a little *too* elegantly, fair cheeks tinged mountain-air pink, light eyes glittering like opals. Even among all the colorful band, I saw her. *Everyone* saw her. That was her whole point.

Marlytt Villatiere, notorious Gersin courtesan. It wasn't as if we mixed in the same circles, if we could help it, but we'd bumped into each other now and again. She was no better bred than I was, but her beauty had propelled her to the top of Gerse society as a concubine to anyone who would keep her, and her list of patrons was reputed to be as long as King Bardolph's list of enemies. I knew her, rather crudely, as Marlytt Doskin — "Everybody's Marlytt."

Marlytt hung on the arm of a rotund young nob in a studded black doublet straining at its laces. The obvious delight and surprise on his face eliminated him as Marlytt's "companion" here; I wondered if she'd recently become unattached, and some natural instinct had drawn her to a house bursting full of noblemen, like a bee to a flowerpot. Behind them, an older woman, narrow and pinched-faced and elegant, gave no effort to hide her disdain.

Marlytt stopped directly in front of us, and her gloved fingers flew to her mouth as she looked at me. "By the gods, I don't believe it!" We stared each other down for the briefest of moments. "Oh, it's been so long," she fumbled, stalling. She clearly didn't know what to call me, since she only knew me by my street name. Fortunately Phandre came to our rescue.

"Oh, don't tell me you know our Celyn," she said, a note of irritation in her voice. "You'll be forgiven for not recognizing her; the local climate has done *wonders* for her."

Marlytt smiled thinly, but I read curiosity and puzzlement in her eyes. "Oh, no, our girl is unmistakable."

"How — how do you know Celyn?" Meri asked, and I was impressed. Most people are hard pressed to manage two words together when meeting Marlytt, let alone a whole sentence.

"I do believe that's a story for her to tell," she said. "But we have much to catch up on . . . Celyn and I." She curled her fingers over mine; they were cold even through the leather of her gloves. "Come see me later, won't you? I'm staying *upstairs*." With a wink, she moved on.

"Well, aren't you full of surprises," Phandre snapped at me.

She had no idea.

"How do you know *her*?"

I shrugged. "From the city. I used to see her . . . sometimes." And she had a history with Tegen, which I was not about to mention.

There was no immediate opportunity to work out what Marlytt's presence at Bryn Shaer might mean for me, for at just that moment, Lady Lyll swept over with the lean Lord Daul.

"Lyllace, beloved, don't tell me this perfect jewel is Antoch's own!" Lord Daul gave Meri an appraising look. "Lady Merista," he said gravely as if speaking to a child, "you won't know me, but I am your uncle, of sorts. Your father and I were boyhood friends."

Meri blushed and mumbled something into her bodice. Daul quirked an eyebrow at Lady Lyll. "Retiring? Where does she come by that trait, I wonder?"

I wasn't sure what he was implying, but I decided I didn't like it. I stepped forward. "Lord Daul, Lady Merista tells us you're a lunarist."

Daul looked at me with as much surprise as if the very floor had started speaking to him. Lady Lyll hooked her arm into his. "Oh, yes — Remy, we're counting on you to entertain us all with your soothsaying."

"Indeed," he said. "I believe I'll be able to tell all your fortunes tonight." He slipped his arm through Meri's. "Lady Merista, I do look forward to getting to know my brother's family once again. Will you do me the honor of showing me around this splendid home?" Lord Daul and Lady Lyll swept Meri away. I looked around; Phandre was still latched on to the unsuspecting wine merchant.

Fair enough; I wanted some candied plums anyway.

Meri's maids were not required in attendance at dinner that night, since the family was having a private meal with Lord Daul, so I ducked away to find Marlytt. *Upstairs*. It was a euphemism, meant for anybody within hearing to know Marlytt wasn't ashamed of her position. Her presence at Bryn Shaer could complicate things for me, but the least little side of me was *glad* to see her — we hadn't been friends, precisely, but at least we could understand each other.

I took the servant's stair, but Marlytt had apparently had the same idea, for I met her on the stairs.

"Digger! You startled me!" She clapped a slender hand to her chest. She was dressed in a loose robe of berry-red velvet, touched at the neckline with Vareni lace that must have cost a fortune. A gift, no doubt, from some besotted client. "What are you doing here? Is Tegen here?"

A dark feeling pierced my breast, but I didn't linger to see whether it was grief, or jealousy, or something of both. "He's dead. Greenmen." It was the first time I'd said those words, and they tasted bitter on my tongue. I sketched out the job at Chavel's, briefly, sparing the details only to spare myself the need to relive them. It certainly wasn't for Marlytt's benefit.

A shadow crossed her pale face. "I'm sorry, I know you cared for him. Still, I hadn't figured you for a runner. I thought you'd be the type to stay and fight."

And I had nothing at all to say to that.

"So what are you planning? Are you here on a job?"

I shook my head and explained how Durrel Decath had whisked me to safety. The story seemed to delight her. "You should have stayed with him," she said. "He sounds like quite the prize."

"Too young for you, I think."

She ignored that. "And now what? Be Merista Nemair's lady-in-waiting for the rest of your life?"

"Until spring, at least. Until it's safe to go back to Gerse." If that ever happened. Marlytt leaned back against the curving stairwell wall, and I thought of something. "Listen — you speak Corles, don't you?"

"Of course. Why?"

"I need you to read something for me." I pulled a crumpled packet of papers from my bodice and handed them to her. Chavel's letters had been rubbing a sore spot in my side for long enough. It was time to finally suss them out.

"I'm sure your Lady Merista reads Corles," she said, flipping through them. "Why didn't you — oh. *Oh*. Digger! Where did these come from? Is that *blood*?"

I pulled in closer. "What do they say?"

Her brows knitted together. "Well, this one is a letter from Secretary Chavel to someone called Vichet, asking if their interests in Corlesanne are being well tended. Do you know what that means?" When I shook my head, she continued. "He wants to know if Vichet has heard from their friends in Varenzia. I don't know. It's just a letter." She slipped the next page forward. "I have no idea what this is." She showed it to me, two meaningless columns of numbers and letters. "A betting book? Some kind of inventory? I can't tell.

"But this one —" Marlytt held out the last letter, and her hand was shaking. "Digger, this looks like a translation of some kind of warrant."

"Warrant? For what?"

She looked at me, and her pale eyes were as wide as the moons. "A price on Prince Wierolf's head. Five thousand sovereigns. And it's signed by the king."

# CHAPTER TEN

Late the next afternoon, I was changing Meri out of her plain kirtle into her evening dress. It had been gray and dull all day, thunder rumbling in the distance. Phandre had heard from her servant friend Ludo that it was snowing down the Gerse road, the storm on its way toward Bryn Shaer. Meri opened her clothes chest and drew out an armful of frothy, ale-gold silk. "Here," she said, smiling broadly, and thrust it into my arms.

"What is it?" I said crossly. "Do you want to wear something different?" We had spent the afternoon doing needlework in the solar, and I had stuck my fingers so many times with my needle I was going to lose all credibility as a nimble-fingered thief.

"Better," Meri said. "You're coming to the feast tonight, and you should look pretty."

"Fat chance there."

Meri's face fell. "I wish you wouldn't," she said, tugging at her hair. In a few weeks' time, that waist-length fall of black would be bound up as she was paraded past the marriage market, and nobody would see it again until after her wedding. Poor Meri; she couldn't stand to see anybody unhappy. I sighed and shook out the fabric.

Which revealed itself as a court gown — not one of Meri's little-girl dresses, made over for my size, but a heavy, stately confection of silk brocade that changed from silver to gold in the light, the sleeves and bodice trimmed in strands of pearls, amber, and tiny glittering silver beads. This was a delicious thing, far nicer than anything I'd ever worn, even when Tegen and I would raid his theater friends' wardrobes for clothes to sneak into Nob Circle houses. This was a real *gown,* meant for wear on public display, laced so tight I would never be able to breathe or sit properly, let alone spend the evening scampering over rooftops or sparring in the street.

"It's beautiful," I said quietly. "Where did you find it?"

"We made it," Meri said. "Mother and I."

"You made this? When?"

"Mostly at night, after you'd gone to sleep. You sleep so soundly, you never notice. Mother did the beadwork. It wasn't that hard," she added modestly.

"I'm sure," I said — at a loss for what I really wanted to say.

She smiled. "I'll teach you. It's something you should know, anyway, if you're going to become 'an accomplished chatelaine.'" Her voice deepened into a fair imitation of her mother, and in a moment we were both smiling.

I traced my finger along one beaded vine. My nails were starting to grow out, but the chill air of the castle was making my skin dry. Thieves keep their hands in good condition, so they can slip in and out of silk purses without snagging. I'd been passing for merchant-class pretty well in Meri's castoffs. Maybe in this thing I'd look like I really belonged in this castle.

And did I want that?

The banquet that evening was the first formal event that gathered all of Bryn Shaer's guests together, a chance to welcome Lord Daul as an honored member of the family and to formally present Meri to the assemblage. We gathered in the Round Court, the tables arranged in a ring along the curving golden walls, the domed ceiling lit by dozens of flickering candles.

Meri sat at the high table, stiff in red velvet and gold, between Daul and her father. Her silver necklaces caught the candlelight from the high iron chandeliers and flashed winking lights against her pale face.

It was the perfect night to drive us all inside; the heavy sky had finally resigned itself to rain — an ugly, sleety mess that made the roaring fire very welcome. I fingered the beaded trim of my bodice. Tart me up like a lady-in-waiting, but I was still just a street thief from Gerse at heart, counting the rings on my neighbors' fingers, the exits in the room. Who had the most valuable jewelry, whose purse seemed the plumpest? What was the quickest way to the courtyard, the roof, the wall? The old lady I was seated with had an elaborate coronet of jet and ruby. I wanted it, and I spent half the soup course working out just how I might twist it from her snow-white hair without her noticing.

"Sparkling Grisel? It's a very fine vintage, coaxed from Count Grisel's own private collection at great personal cost. I'd be wounded if you didn't try it."

On my other side was the merchant, Eptin Cwalo. Having no particular desire to wound the man, I lifted my glass, and spent the rest of the meal learning all about his sons: five worthy lads, plus Garod, son number two, over whose dubious future Mistress Cwalo apparently despaired. I quite liked the sound of Garod, actually, and amused myself by imagining Lady Lyllace's reaction to my announcement of such a match. Cwalo appeared to take a liking to me. It must have been a combination of our common merchant heritage (his was presumably authentic), and our common size: He seemed pleased that I was actually shorter than he was. I let him fill my glass a little more often than was wise.

After the meal, Lord Antoch rose and clapped for attention. "My good gentles, friends and countrymen all, be you welcome to Bryn Shaer, the Bear's Keep! Our home is new, built on this ancient ground, and we are honored to receive your company at this blessed time for our family, when our beloved daughter is preparing to make her *kernja-velde*, and enter society as a young woman."

Light applause and cries of "huzzah!" greeted this toast. Antoch continued: "We are doubly blessed at Bryn Shaer this day, for tonight we welcome back to our family one who has been absent far too long: the brother of my heart, Remy Daul. Lord Remy is known to you all, I believe, so we shall not belabor the introductions, but to say that he has brought a host gift to share with us all: an offer to display his skills at lunarism for our amusement and edification here tonight. Brother?"

Lord Daul rose, looking slender as a blade beside Antoch's bulk, and bowed low to the crowd. "Milord, you do me too great an honor. I am the one blessed, to be reunited with such august company after all my trials. I feel quite the lost sheep returned to the fold, after time amongst the wolves."

"What's he mean?" I whispered to Cwalo, but my companion didn't seem to hear. Lord Daul kissed the hands of Meri and Lady Lyll and climbed down from the high table. During the speeches, servants had brought out a small table covered in a gray velvet cloth and set with the charts and paraphernalia of the moon-casting. Daul took his seat and bowed his head briefly in meditation.

I had seen this done before, of course, though not at such high scales. The back table at every tavern in the Seventh Circle had a resident lunarist — some of them mere scam artists, some with a genuine . . . well, I'd seen a few things I couldn't explain. But the one thing *all* of them were after — fair or foul — was coin. It was officially frowned upon, since foreknowledge of the future was a trait ascribed to Sar alone, but popular lunarists generally escaped persecution. Even Bardolph was said to have one resident at court.

Suddenly a massive crack of thunder shook the Round Court, making everyone jump. When it had faded, Lord Daul let out a quick laugh. "They do quite set the mood for us, don't they?" The chandeliers swung a little, making wolfish shadows on his lean face. "Friends," he said in a low voice that slipped through the hall like a serpent, "who will be first to learn what the moons have in store for us? Lady Cardom?"

"Indeed, no," the woman beside me said, but there was a touch of gay color in her cheeks. "I'm too old for such fancies. I know what my future will bring, young man."

The room erupted in laughter, and Daul inclined his head. "Perhaps her flourishing son?"

"Not me." The fat nob who had arrived with Marlytt gave a good-hearted laugh. "I like surprises."

"Come, come — someone must be brave enough to glimpse what the gods are planning?" Lord Daul swung his gaze slowly through the crowd until he came to rest on Meri. "My lord brother, will you permit me the honor to read the charts for your lady daughter? Since I missed the opportunity to do so at her birth?"

Meri, her color high, turned to Antoch. Her father gave his smiling approval, and she bounded down from the high table. She curtsied very prettily to her foster uncle, then tucked herself at the small table, bending studiously over the charts.

"What do I do?" she said, sounding a little breathless.

"When is your birthday, my dear?"

"The twelfth of next month," Meri said.

"Ah," Daul said. "Very auspicious. The Dead of Winter falls on your birthday this year." The Dead of Winter was a solemn holy day, the full moon of Marau that fell closest to midwinter. Meri's eyes widened as Daul continued, "And, of course, this is a very significant year for you." He cast the stones onto the chart on the table. "Be aware, I tell only what I see, and I cannot be responsible for any shadows the gods have cast upon you."

My thoughts drifted; I was interested less in the future Lord Antoch's bosom friend was predicting for his daughter, and more in the gold strap he wore around his leg. He sat at an angle to me that gave me a clear view of it. It had a clasp that could easily be undone with one finger, but it was a snug fit, to keep from slipping off. There was a design stamped into the metal, and I wanted a better look at it.

I'd give it back, of course. I just wanted to see it. And somehow I didn't think asking for a close examination of Lord Daul's thigh would go over well in this company. Maybe Phandre could get it for me; she knew her way around a few lords' thighs, or so I'd heard. I felt a giggle bubble up inside me, and I took another sip of Cwalo's *very fine* sparkling Grisel.

A peal of applause rippled through the room, and I heard Meri's chair scrape back. "I thank you, milord," she said in her soft voice. "Who shall I send next?"

I glanced up just in time to see Lord Daul beckoning me closer with a narrow finger. "Lady Celyn, do us the honor?"

Ask me twice. I bounced up from my seat beside Lady Cardom, reminding myself to be dignified as I crossed the floor. At the tiny table, I gave a gracious curtsy and settled onto the little stool.

Lord Daul poured the colored stones into my cupped hands. There were seven of them, all different sizes, and the chart on the table was a map of the heavens, with all the moons plotted in their courses through the sky. The stones weren't valuable — just bits of polished agate and marble — and besides, he'd probably notice right quickly if they disappeared from his set.

"Lay the stone of Celys on the date of your birth," he instructed me.

Whereupon we had a problem, since I could no more account for my birth date than I could for my nonexistent mother and father. I hesitated too long.

"Milady does not know when she was born?" he asked. His voice was playful, and everyone laughed. I stole a desperate glance at Marlytt, but she was deep in conversation with Lord Cardom. I was about to put the stone somewhere entirely at random when Daul said, "Methinks you were born under the watch of Tiboran."

My hand stilled in the air and I met his eyes, but there was nothing there but amusement. All right, I could play that game too.

"No, milord is mistaken," I said gaily, or tried, anyway. "I was born in the summer." And plopped the green marble right down in the middle of the month of Celys. It was close enough.

"Milady perhaps exaggerates her age? I would not have guessed you to be quite . . . forty-three, Lady Celyn."

Pox. "Lady Lyllace makes a most excellent salve for wrinkles," I said, to another round of laughter. Tiboran was in high humor tonight; I wasn't usually so good with a crowd. I found the date for sixteen years ago and shoved the stone into place, leaning low across the table, exposing everything I had to Daul's view — and giving me easy reach of him: his belt, his purse, the gold band he wore on his leg.

Daul spread his hands across the parchment, and the stones seemed to bobble and float away from his touch. A sharp's trick — I saw no magic spark for him, and he wore no silver — just simple sleight of hand that any well-trained Gerse thief could mimic.

"Ah," Daul intoned significantly. I leaned in closer still, as if fascinated by the mysteries he was about to reveal. My gaze stayed on his face, though the hand that was supposed to be folded demurely in my lap edged closer to Daul's leg band. Gray fringe from the tablecloth brushed my sleeve. "The shape of your past is cloudy," he said. "There are shadows crossing lines, and I cannot see past them."

"Nonsense!" I said. "I'm as cloudy as a summer day. Tell me what else you see." My fingers came to rest, ever so lightly, against the spring of gold.

"I see your brother is a very powerful man."

My hand jerked, and I felt Daul flinch. Damn.

"Not so powerful," I said tartly — and *loudly*. "He couldn't even get nuns to hold on to me!"

The audience laughed again, and I pulled my hand back, easy, easily. . . .

He slapped me. Under the table, fingertips to the back of my wrist. The look on his face shifted to sharp awareness as he met my eyes, and then back again as smoothly as a moon disappearing behind fog. "Well, I think it's as well that *someone* should look after you, Lady Celyn," he said. "There is a darkness looming in your future, I'm afraid. As well as a new association."

"Not one of the Cwalo boys, I hope!" I tried to laugh with the others, but my wrist stung like I'd been burned, and my heart was a hot frantic flame in my chest. I couldn't believe it. I *never* got caught.

"I think not." He was looking straight at me, his voice low enough for only me to hear. "Take care, Lady Celyn. Beware!" That last was for the crowd, and he dismissed me, but it was all I could do to curtsy like I was supposed to and stumble back toward my seat.

The dinner was breaking up. Antoch had risen, and the others had followed, spilling down into the room and covering me with a merry, laughing crowd. I glanced across the hall, for Meri, for Marlytt —

for the alcove behind the curtains where the servants slipped in and out —

"Very entertaining performance."

I spun. Daul had me by the arm, and was steering me — with perfect decorum — to that selfsame alcove. My heart resumed its panicked flutter as I stared at him.

"Keep walking or I yell, 'Stop, thief!' Don't make a scene."

"What do you want?"

He spoke in my ear, in a low voice. "Satisfaction. You've piqued my curiosity, Lady Celyn. One does not expect a display of *quite* those skills among Lord Antoch's retainers."

"I don't know what you mean." Marlytt could have pulled that off, but I sounded strained and false.

"I'm sure. Sit down." He shoved me down onto a bench half hidden behind a tapestry and leaned over me. He reminded me even more of a wolfhound now, slavering jowls dripping. "Pull yourself together. People will be staring."

I fought for breath. Above us, musicians in the minstrels' gallery had struck up a merry tune, and a knot of people were sorting themselves into a dance. Daul thrust a goblet of wine into my hand as a servant drifted past with a tray. "That was a neat trick," he said conversationally. "You almost got away with it. Another man wouldn't have noticed — you're *very* good, as I'm sure you know."

I didn't say anything, just stared at him.

He shrugged. "Fair enough. Just know, I'm a kindred soul." He popped open the buttons holding his tight sleeve closed. Smoothly he rolled his shirt up to the elbow, revealing a long, iron-black tattoo crudely inked deep into the dark, scarred flesh. I forced myself not to shiver. The scars told me more than the tattoo — the shiny white blots were burns from the scald, the rough skin at the wrist the "manacle's kiss." Silver, superheated until it burned off the hair and flesh, cauterized the blood. The star was a brand. He'd spent time in prison as a Sarist.

The tattoo was a footnote compared to all that — a black blade half-way up the forearm, some dungeon brotherhood, the prisoners banded together for mutual protection against other inmates, against rats, against hunger, against loneliness. Oddly enough, I found it calming.

"Is that supposed to mean something to me?"

"Oh, I think it will. I want information."

"About me?"

"Don't be stupid. Of course not. You're going to do a little job for me."

I stared at him. "Here?"

Before I could ask anything else, the end strains of the music slowed. Daul pulled his sleeve back down, smoothly doing up the buttons with one hand. "Come to my rooms tomorrow before the noon meal."

"I'm not coming to your rooms!" In the space left by the music, I said that too loudly — surprised faces turned our way. "What do you take me for?"

"Stop, thief!" His voice was musical, light — not quite loud enough to be overheard. "And before you say they won't believe me, I saw you slip Lady Cardom's headpiece into your sleeve. So unless you mean to spend the rest of the winter in the Bryn Shaer dungeons, you *will* be in my chambers tomorrow, before the noon bell strikes. Do we understand each other?"

I understood, all right. Understood the way the boar understands the circle of hunters surrounding it with spears. When the music stopped for good and Daul let go my arm, I fled.

Minutes later, there was a pounding on the door to Meri's room. I had stripped out of my frothy gown and was casting through the heap of clothing she had lent me for something I could run in. It was four days back down the mountain toward Gerse — I could never make that on my own. With no woodcraft and no supplies, I wouldn't even make it to the first settlement. But I might have a chance heading east through the pass to Breijardarl, which was only a day's walk. It was still raining, but the moons were out and the path was clear, my own shoes were sturdy, and — damn it! There was nothing here but velvet and brocade. Was I going to have to raid the stable boy's wardrobe?

"Digger!"

I glanced behind me. That wasn't Meri. The door — which I had locked, fat lot of good it did me — burst open, and Marlytt tumbled in, in all her iridescent silken glory.

"What are you doing?"

I ignored her. Meri had wool drawers — I could maybe wear those, for a while —

Marlytt grabbed me. "What are you *doing*? You ran out of there so fast. What happened?"

"I'm getting out of here, that's what I'm doing. I was stupid to think this would work —" I pulled free of Marlytt's grip but stood, panting, at a loss.

She sank onto the bed with some considerable composure. Her eyebrows lifted; she was ready to hear the gory details.

"Do you know that — that Remy Daul?"

A slight frown, no more than a shadow on her smooth forehead. "I've heard of him. He's dangerous. I wouldn't cross him —"

"Well, he's crossed *me*. Says I have to work for him, or he'll expose me to the Nemair. You're the only person here who knows who I really am." I realized it was true as the words left my mouth.

She looked shocked. "Digger, I wouldn't! You know that. I am the very soul of discretion."

She might be telling the truth. She wouldn't stay in her line of work long by being indiscreet. I didn't trust her — didn't trust anyone — but I believed her. Maybe.

"You came here with him."

She shook her head. "I *arrived* here with him. I *came* here with Cwalo, from Tratua. Ask him."

"I will." I wouldn't — I was never going to see the man after tonight.

I threw open another trunk and cast all its contents onto the floor, digging through the mess of small clothes and stockings. "He —" I paused, remembering something. "He said something strange about my brother."

"Celyn's brother?"

I turned to her. "I thought so, but —" Marlytt was one of only a handful of people who knew that Digger of Gerse was not simply some nameless orphan with a blank past. She knew about the convent, and . . . other things. "I don't know."

"Well, what does it mean?"

I sighed. "That Celys really does see everything we do?"

"What?" Marlytt said.

No. It wasn't possible. It was just pure chance Daul had caught me; I'd been drinking and I was careless and I'd slipped up. "It doesn't mean anything." I found my blue wool kirtle and wrestled into it.

"What does he want with you?"

I balled up the rest of the clothes and shoved them back in their trunks. Meri must have a bag here *somewhere*. I ducked under the bed and found my hidey-hole. A nice little stash to get me started on my way to a whole new life. Again. I shoved the coins in my sleeve and the ring down my bodice. I opened the trunk that held the clothes and things the Nemair had given me, and found Durrel's dagger. I weighed it in my hands, then hoisted my skirt and strapped it to my leg.

"Aren't you even curious?" she pressed.

The only way I was going to find out what Daul knew and what he wanted was if I met with him. "Not a bit. I left my curiosity behind in Gerse. With Tegen. I'm getting out of here," I repeated. "Tonight. I don't care how —"

I broke off. A jangle of voices and footsteps carried down the corridor, stopping outside Meri's room. The door banged open, and a breathless, flushing Meri burst inside.

"Celyn — Marlytt?" A cloud of confusion briefly darkened her features, but she ignored the mess in her chambers, waving us toward the corridor. "Come see, it's too exciting!"

I stared at her and the assembled company in the hallway behind her, all dressed, improbably, in their cloaks and coats.

Marlytt rose. "What's going on?"

"We're all off to the east tower to see the Breijarda Velde. That thunder we heard at dinner? It *wasn't*. There's been an avalanche, and the pass is completely blocked!"

## PART II
# DON'T GET CAUGHT

# CHAPTER ELEVEN

Bryn Shaer could make a celebration out of anything, I decided, huddled in my stolen coat beside the tower wall, as the nobs clustered excitedly at the crenellated edge, pointing through the trees at the vast white swell that had been the Breijarda Velde. And, until an hour ago, my only avenue of escape. The sleet had settled to a soft snow, pinkish in the moonlight and just now sticking to the cold wet stones.

"Well, we're stuck with each other now, it seems," said Lord Cardom, accepting a goblet of wine from Eptin Cwalo. "It'll take weeks to dig that out."

"Weeks?" I echoed, my voice a strained squeak. I turned to Lord Antoch. "But won't it melt, or something?"

"The folk of Breijardarl are no strangers to avalanche," Antoch said. "They'll have it clear as soon as they can, but they'll have to wait until the danger of further collapse has passed. I suppose we should send somebody to help, maybe with dogs, dig a little bit from our end as well — and make sure no one was caught in it." He looked up into the snow-filled sky. "This looks like it's shaping up to be a hell of a snowfall, though. Cardom, I think you're right. Could be weeks."

I just stared at them and pulled my coat closer, painfully aware just how inadequate it was. If the lot of them weren't distracted by the excitement, they'd have noticed how strange I was acting. The snow drifted steadily downward, like a soft, white nightmare, as the nobs around me laughed and chattered like a flock of nattering crows.

I spent the night arguing my options with myself, but come morning finally admitted there were none. It wasn't just the avalanche — this freak impediment flung into my path by gods who clearly hated me — but the steady fall of snow on top of it as well. It had drifted up against the castle walls during the night, smothering the courtyard, swallowing the lower stories, pinning the larder and buttery doors shut. Out in the world, a vast white blanket stretched from the bailey wall into the forest beyond. Even the tracks of the messengers and their dogs disappeared again within the hour.

"Don't do anything stupid," Marlytt had said the previous night, as we stood atop the tower. "I know what you're thinking. You'd freeze to death by morning, and your body wouldn't be found until spring. Is that what you want?"

And I'd just looked down into the white depths, weighing death by snow against whatever Daul had planned for me.

Most mornings I would have been entrenched in Lady Lyll's plans for my day — grinding medicines in the stillroom, or marking hemlines for Meri's *kernja-velde* gowns — as her ladyship marshaled the troops to organize the coming birthday feast. The Dead of Winter was fast approaching, a mere six weeks away now, and preparations were mounting, from the planned menu and its stockpiled exotic foodstuffs (Talancan spices and cones of sugar), to the continuing construction work on the castle (a new tile floor to the Lesser Court), to the invitations being dispatched to ever-more esteemed guests — including, I had just learned, His Majesty.

"We don't expect him to come, of course," Lady Lyll had explained. "He hasn't left Hanivard Palace in years. But an invitation is expected, and who knows? He might send a representative. Maybe even Queen Lieste!"

I hadn't been able to tell if that news excited Meri, or frightened her.

Today, however, with the pass closed and snow piling up along the longer route south toward Gerse, Lady Lyll and the serving staff were distracted, scrambling to check that the supplies would hold out until the pass opened up again, sending snowshoed messengers with shovels, axes, and medicines down through the drifts to the site of the disaster, all on top of stirring up the guests into a festival mood. I should have been helping (with the supply-checking, I mean, not with the mood), but I took a chance that one missing set of hands might go unnoticed.

I'd had a lifetime's practice making sure I wasn't noticed when I *was* there. It must work in reverse too.

It took some effort to find Daul's rooms; he was on the third floor, same as all the guests, but I couldn't very well go about asking people at random which door was his. Or knock at every one and wait for the right face to answer. In the end I grabbed a serving boy scuttering past with somebody's mid-morning posset.

"I have an urgent message for Lord Daul. Could you see that he gets it?" I didn't give him time to answer, but plowed on impatiently. "Oh, just show me which room." And I sailed off down the hall with him hurrying to catch up to me. Phandre would have been proud. When the lad stopped at one of the middle suites at the back of the corridor, I caught him by the arm and twisted it behind his back until he gasped. The posset sloshed out of its cup, dripping sticky pink onto the floor.

"Breathe a word of this to anyone, and I'll break your arm. Got it?"

Blinking back tears, he nodded. I let go, and he sped off down the hall.

Before I could knock, the door swung open, and Lord Daul stood in the threshold, looking me over. The scar on his lip stood out in the harsh morning light, and I could see another through the open collar of his shirt. I wondered which were from battle, and which were from prison.

Some of my fear from last night had faded, since I'd survived the night without guards hauling me out of Meri's bed and tossing me into the ancient dungeons. I cast a glance around Daul's quarters, waiting for him to say something. His room was bigger and brighter than Meri's, but more sparsely furnished. The curtains were pulled closed around a tall bedstead, and a ridiculous fire blazed like a furnace. The heat from it hit me like a blow through the open door.

"It seems a serving girl found Lady Cardom's jewels right under her table in the Round Court this morning." No greeting, no explanation. "How fortunate that they hadn't wandered farther afield. I believe our hosts might have launched a castlewide search."

I said something rude, and he grabbed my arm and yanked me inside, slamming the door shut behind me. "How very refined you are."

I rubbed my arm. I'd have bruises where his fingers had dug into my flesh. "What do you want?"

Daul stepped back into the rooms and strode to a carved oak desk by the windows. His rooms overlooked the sculpture garden, where the nymphs and griffins were reduced to formless lumps under their white shrouds.

"Wine?" He lifted an inlaid decanter toward me, twisting the glass stopper with his other hand. He wore an onyx signet ring on his little finger, but I couldn't make out the symbol etched in the stone.

"No."

"Come now, there's no need to be rude. I'm toasting our association."

"I don't drink with people who threaten me," I said baldly.

"Oh, please. I had to give you some incentive. You don't strike me as a girl who's easily convinced." He poured out two goblets. The wine was white, almost clear.

"Convinced of what?" I said.

Daul glanced up. "The value of what I'm offering, of course. A chance to put your considerable skills to good use, and work for me. It seems we're in a position to help each other."

"I don't need your help."

"Oh, I think you do. You have a valuable secret to protect, and that will be much easier if someone doesn't expose you, don't you think?"

I halted, my breath tight. "I'm listening."

"Good!" His cold smile spread. "If you agree to work for me — and you will — I can arrange it so that my friends ignore your petty transgressions, and that their lordships never learn the truth about your identity."

"Your friends?"

He looked surprised. "Oh! I thought I'd mentioned that. You know, you really do look so much like him —"

I was staring at him, tense and cold. "Like who?"

"Your brother."

My entire chest turned to ice, freezing the words in my throat. "My —
Contrare?" I said faintly.

"I think we both know very well who I'm talking about," Daul said.

"You're lying."

"Am I?" Daul said. "We'll see. Now, down to business."

I'd seen a troupe of players once in Gerse — an old man from Sirpal
played the recorder to a thick black snake that rose up from a basket,
stretching its neck like an unfurled cloak. A little girl from the company
dumped a rabbit right in front of it. The terrified rabbit had frozen,
wide-eyed, staring into the snake's gaze. As the music played on, the
snake hung motionless in the air, but the rabbit inched closer and closer
to its death.

I felt like that rabbit now.

"So what are you — like a Greenman or something?" I was nearly at
the desk now. I could *almost* reach the heavy bronze inkwell on the corner. I'm not a great throw, but he was standing right in front of me. I
could do a little damage.

Daul saw where I was looking. With a quirk to his scarred lip, he slid
the inkwell to the opposite side of the desk. "Feisty, feisty! No wonder
your brother thought you unmanageable. Still, I think I like a girl with a
little spunk to her." He reached out his finger and stroked it along my
cheek. I grabbed his hand and bit down — hard.

He slapped me — so hard I went down and cracked the side of my
head on the corner of the desk. Gasping and blind with pain, I fought to
stand back up again.

"We're not playing games here, you little thief. Now listen, and
listen well."

I pressed my hand to my stinging temple and blinked up at him.

"There's something I want in this castle, and you're going to get it for
me. If you don't, or if you fail, I will expose your little masquerade. How

do you think Lady Nemair will like knowing her daughter's been sleeping with a thief and a murderess all these weeks?"

Murderess? What was he talking about? But I didn't say anything — what was the point? He was right about everything. He was Lord Nemair's best friend, a nobleman. He had all the power here, and I had nothing. I was whatever he said I was. Thief or murderer, traitor or heretic — Remy Daul's word was enough to get me killed.

I bit my lip and looked away from him, out into the snowy landscape. My forehead throbbed. In a thin voice, I said, "Fine. What is it?"

"There! Was that so difficult? This should be a simple matter for a girl of your talents. I seem to have been the victim of an oversight. My foster brother invited all our dearest friends to winter with him in his lovely new home, but it seems I, for whatever reason, was not included on the guest list. I'm interested to know why."

"How am I supposed to find that out? Ask them yourself!"

"I have a better plan. I want you to track down one of the official invitations for me. And while you're at it, bring me a seal of the House of Nemair."

That didn't make any sense. "You're planning on forging an invitation for yourself?"

"No! I wouldn't think of doing something so unscrupulous. This is just to satisfy my own curiosity. I'm sure you can understand that."

Don't ask questions. That was one of the first things a thief-for-hire learned. Questions got people killed. "Seal, invitation. Got it." It would be the job of five minutes. I turned to leave.

"Not so fast. The seal I'm looking for is very specific. There will be only one of its type, and it will be held closely by Lord Antoch — or possibly Lady Lyllace. I'm never certain about that one. You're familiar with the Nemair crest?"

I shrugged. "The rampant bear on the quarter field. Of course."

"Very good. The seal you want will have the wrong paw raised."

"The — what?"

"Enough. You have everything you need to know. I'm feeling generous this morning, so I'll give you the day. If I don't have that seal by noon tomorrow — or if you bring the wrong items — it's 'stop, thief!' Understand?"

"It's done. I'll be back in an hour."

His hand came down on my arm, gently enough. "Take the full day," he suggested. "You're only valuable to me if you can follow instructions." He pulled away from the desk and headed for the door.

I paused in the threshold. "Why don't you do it?"

He smiled. "Because I have you."

# CHAPTER TWELVE

It wasn't a good job — Daul had been vague about the location of the target, he hadn't given me enough time to prepare, and there wasn't an escape route. The payment was also questionable. But he'd been convincing. It could be a long time before the snow cleared, and I'd rather spend that time in Meri's warm soft bedroom than whatever served Bryn Shaer for dungeons. I still thought he might be lying about his "friends." Anyone could claim to have the Inquisitor's ear — that didn't make it true. Except that it *did*. Greenmen took even the most frivolous accusations seriously. I knew that better than anyone.

To get the letter and the seal, I'd have to concoct some excuse for getting inside Lord Antoch's rooms, a part of the castle I had never been in and had no conceivable reason to visit. Meri usually went riding with him every morning; that would have been my opportunity, but the stables were under a foot of snow, thanks to the storm that had trapped me here with Daul.

I worked out my plan that afternoon in the solar. The Bryn Shaer women gathered most afternoons for a few hours of needlework and gossip. There wasn't much embroidery getting done today; it was stupidly cold and everyone was still too excited about being snowbound to concentrate. Which was just as well for me, since I was going to have to recruit some confederates for this job, and it would be easier if everyone was already distracted.

"Did everyone make it before the snow, Lady Lyllace?" Lady Cardom had joined the group, and sat beside me, unpacking a workbasket.

Lady Lyll gave a sigh and looked out at the snow, her untouched embroidery in her lap. "No, unfortunately. We were just getting ready to send for the Wolt sisters, but it looks like we'll be missing them."

"Wolt?" Lady Cardom's lips pursed. "Perhaps it's for the best. Your Ladyship, I've brought the stitchery you were so interested in last summer." She drew a roll of cloth from the basket and passed it to Meri's mother. "You'll see it includes the band from Talanca you were asking about, as well as the one from my daughter at Gairveyont."

Lady Lyll unrolled the cloth, revealing an intricate sampler of black- and scarlet-work. She indicated a wide row of alternating lilies, the black threads spangled here and there with gold. "This is the band from Gairveyont?"

Gods, would this conversation ever end? I was ready to poke my own eye out with my needle, and I had work to do.

Lady Lyll said, "I had remembered wrong, then. I thought there were five repeats?"

"No, only four," Lady Cardom said. "She sends her regrets that she could not find the exact pattern you requested."

"Very well. Tell Dressana I am grateful for her help."

Lady Cardom smiled. "She knows, your ladyship."

Lady Lyll took the sampler and rose. "I'll just go tuck this away where I can study it later," she said. "I'll return shortly."

When Lady Lyll was finally gone, I leaned over to Phandre. "Meri has a secret," I said in a low, teasing voice.

Meri looked up, startled. "What? No, I —"

Phandre dropped the book she wasn't reading and leaned forward. "Ooh, come on, Meri, out with it."

"But I don't —" Poor Meri stared desperately at me, trying to figure us out.

"She told me that her father has a book of Vareni love poetry in his rooms." That should tempt Phandre to an adventure; the Vareni weren't prudish about their poetry. And they illustrated.

"No, I —" Meri was still confused. "I didn't. I never heard that."

"Who cares?" Phandre said. "Let's go see." She was on her feet in an instant, with Meri hard on her heels. All I had to do was trail after.

"I don't think we should. Father —" She may have been speaking to the castle walls for all the good it did her. "Maybe we should wait until he gets back from surveying the damage —"

And miss my only shot at Antoch's rooms? Fat chance. Phandre and I grabbed Meri and dragged her from the solar.

When we neared Lord Antoch's rooms in the opposite wing of the Lodge, I skipped forward to reach the door first, blocking it with my body as I popped the lock behind my back. The new locks at Bryn Shaer were flimsy, decorative things that took hardly more than a kiss and a wish to crack. I grinned and swung the door open.

"He must not be worried about intruders," I said cheekily, ushering Phandre and Meri inside.

I almost didn't have to search Lord Antoch's rooms at all, with Phandre there. She flounced through the rooms, touching everything, peering behind tapestries, opening drawers and cabinets, and testing out all the furniture. I just followed in her wake, looking behind whatever she'd moved. I heard a door click open, and Phandre barged into his lordship's bedroom. Meri hurried after her.

"Does your father really sleep in this bed?" Phandre asked, and threw herself bodily atop it.

Meri turned pink. "I — I expect so," she managed.

"And your mother?"

"Sometimes," Meri mumbled.

Phandre turned to her, gaze pointed and mischievous. "Anyone else?"

"Phandre!"

But Phandre only laughed, her hair splayed across Lord Antoch's satin pillows. "I want a bed like this," she said. "Too bad I don't have a father to get me one."

"If you stay with me, I'll ask Father to buy you a great oak panel bed, with a canopy of velvet and lace and crewel." Meri's voice was generous, as if giving away the world was nothing at all in the course of her day.

And Phandre turned on Meri a gaze that was full of acid and ice and every bitter thing. I winced. "I'll bet Raffin Taradyce has an awfully fine bedstead," I said.

Phandre cackled and threw a pillow at me.

"Meri, does your father have an office in here?" I asked, tossing it back on the bed.

She crossed the room and threw back the scarlet curtains covering one wall. Behind was a tiny room, with a much-used desk sitting before walls and walls of bookcases. For a moment I was distracted. Books always did that to me, almost more than a locked jewelry chest or a fat purse dangling from a fat nob. I liked the creamy pages, the smell of ink, all the secrets locked inside. I traced my fingers along one gilded binding after another, thinking I might help myself to a little something extra on this job.

Meri saw me looking. "Bryn Shaer has the finest library in the Carskadons. The owners have been collecting for years."

"Then these aren't all your father's?"

"Oh, no. They were here when King Bardolph awarded the estate to the Nemair."

"What's in here? Oh, books." Phandre strode to the first bookcase and started tipping volumes out at random. "What are we looking for again?"

"Poetry," I said firmly.

Phandre made a face. "*Teska's Bestiary, History of the House of Shaer, A Holy Love* — now that sounds promising."

I made a show of bending over the cluttered desk. "His lordship sure is *messy*," I said, moving aside a map of renowned Carskadon hunting grounds and a book in Corles. And under the map — a stack of letters. I shuffled some around; they were mostly acceptances from the guests who'd already arrived.

"Oh, Celyn, don't —" Meri protested, and I obligingly dropped the map back atop the desk, "accidentally" knocking one stray document to the floor: a folded letter, sealed in gray wax . . . and addressed to someone called Wolt. Perfect. As I bent to retrieve it, I slipped it inside my bodice, careful not to disturb the wax seal. I couldn't tell if the paw was wrong or not, but I had the first half of the job complete, without even getting my hands dusty.

The desk drawer took a little more effort to open, but rewarded me with sealing wax and two heavy brass seals, bears rearing up proudly against a shield. Why would anyone keep a wrong seal of their own house? It was the sort of mistake you'd find on a poorly done counterfeit, not something you'd have deliberately. Shielding the open drawer with my skirts, I turned them faceup, trying to decide which one was wrong. Left or right lifted? I moved my own hands, but I just couldn't remember. Pox, I'd only been staring at the Nemair arms every day for three weeks. In the end I gave up and took them both.

"A *Celyst Reader*," Meri was reading piously. "A *Housewife's Companion*." Phandre gave a snicker at that.

Successful, I turned back to the bookcase. Maybe I'd just take a small one — it didn't have to be anything elaborate. I reached for a thin volume bound in gray kidskin —

And had to swallow back a startled yelp as a thick blur of hazy light suddenly leaped up under my touch. I yanked back my hand as if it had burned my fingers. I'd almost *felt* that. Averting my eyes, I plucked the book from the shelf and squeaked it open gingerly to pages of esoteric scrawl, elaborate diagrams, and detailed drawings in full illumination. But the swirling, sparking mist I saw around it made it hard to make out anything clearly. An image was embossed on the cover — a circle, traced with a seven-pointed star.

"What's that one? Cookery?" Meri said with disinterest. She'd finished going over her shelf and was peering up from the floor.

"No," I said slowly. I wanted to stick it back on the shelf before they saw it, but I couldn't seem to put it down. Meri watched me as I flipped to the title page.

*On the Sacrament of Magecraft.*

"That's a magic book!" Phandre shrieked, ripping it from my hands. "Listen to this! '*Set thy mind and heart to the Holy Sister, most beloved of Celys. Light-bringer, dream-speaker. Give thanks for her Gift. Proceed only with a Purified Soul —* '"

"Put it back, Phandre," I said.

"Are you mad? Look — 'The Seeing Dream.' Who wouldn't want to have dreams that tell the future?"

I had enough trouble with dreams of the past. I couldn't imagine wanting to know what was coming. Meri sat very still, her knees tucked under her skirts, and stared at her hands. "I think we should put it back. I don't think my father would want us playing around in here."

"I'm with Meri," I said, and snatched the book from Phandre as she was absorbed in "To Appear Without Form." She protested, but I tucked it back on the shelf behind the prayer book and a real book on cookery.

Daul was in his rooms when I arrived the next morning, dead on the hour as instructed. It was late, but the curtains were still drawn around the bed, and Daul was not yet dressed, clad only in breeches and a shirt, loose to his narrow thighs. I hung back in the doorway. I really didn't want to be in a room with a half-naked Remy Daul.

"Well?" he said. "In." He slithered into place at his desk, behind a platter of eggs and a thick slab of bacon. "I trust you have the items as we arranged."

I dumped the letter and the seals on the desk. "Happy?"

"Delighted." He eyed the two seals a little strangely, but the letter drew his close attention. "Ah, very nice indeed. Let's have a look, shall we?"

That "we" probably didn't include me, but my curiosity was piqued. Daul slid a lit candle across the desk, and held the letter up to the light. But not to read — the flickering firelight warmed the wax, and Daul carefully peeled it away from the paper in one smooth, unbroken piece. I leaned in closer. Underneath there was a second mark, this one in ink, which had been hidden by the wax.

"What is that?"

Daul smiled. "Curious now, my little mouse?" But he held the letter for me to see. The new mark was slightly stained by the color of the wax: a field of four moons, arched inside a circle of bluish ink. As Daul moved it away from the flames, the mark started to fade from the page. He held the paper closer to the fire before it could vanish completely.

"Disappearing ink?"

He forestalled me, one hand lifted. He took one of the seals I had brought — apparently he could tell which one's paw was wrong — and gave the brass stamp at its base a quick twist. The disk popped right off. As I watched, intrigued, Daul turned it toward me. Hidden beneath the waving bear was a second seal, for stamping ink. Four moons.

"I didn't see that," I said. "What is it?"

But Daul was through sharing. Instead of explaining anything else, he carefully pressed the warmed wax back atop the stamped ink moons and fitted the brass seal back onto its handle. "Very nicely done," he said. "You may put these back at your leisure. Now, the next thing I want might be a little more challenging. Antoch has a journal —"

"Wait." I stared at him. "What next thing?"

"Don't look so surprised," he said, and his rough voice was like a purr. "You didn't really think I was going to let you go so easily? You're far too useful to me."

"I gave you what you wanted," I said in a voice much firmer than I felt. "Leave me alone."

"I think not. I had imagined this more an ongoing partnership."

"We're not partners!"

That slow, oily smile made its appearance once more. "No, you're right about that. I own you."

I felt cold all over, though Daul's fire roared. "I don't work for people who threaten me."

"Really? Why don't I ring for Lord Antoch now, and you can explain that to him?"

"You bastard." I felt my hand creeping toward my knife, and I caught my fingers in my skirts.

"Feign as much bravado as you like," Daul said. "But I think we understand each other. You can either do what I tell you — whatever I tell you, or you can start working on what you're going to say at your trial."

"I'm not afraid of you," I lied.

"Well, then, let's consider the matter a little more closely. I am a man of means, power, and ambition. I have personally dined with His Majesty, traveled with the king's Inquisitor, and been appointed to the Order of the Spur. You, on the other hand, are an anonymous speck of dung from the gutter of Gerse. I think we could say you're disposable."

*Disposable!* It gave me a chill. He was right. Nobody in all the world would notice if I just . . . disappeared. I wasn't Meri, coddled and adored. I wasn't even Phandre, fiercely fighting for a place in the world. I was like he'd said: anonymous. It was one reason I could slip in and out of costumes, roles, identities — because I didn't really have one of my own.

"Don't look so glum! This could turn out to be a very profitable association for both of us. I have powerful friends, and I expect to be well rewarded. I can arrange that your . . . rewards are likewise commensurate with the information you supply."

I stepped back, wary. "What sort of information?"

"What sort of information do you *think* I mean, you brainless slattern?" He leaned forward, his loose sleeves swinging. He'd started to sweat slightly. I could just make out the branded Sarist star on his forearm. He saw me looking, and rubbed his arm.

"Yes, well. I have seen the error of my ways. But I am concerned for the souls of my brother and his family. I know firsthand how deep these dangerous, heretical beliefs may run. I only want to be certain that His Majesty's servants are as loyal as they profess themselves to be."

Oh, and *finally* I understood. "You think they're Sarists."

Daul leaned back and let that thought sink in. "Oh, I more than 'think.' But you will secure me the proof of precisely what my dear friends are planning."

"I won't work for Greenmen," I said. I never would. That was the whole problem between my brother and me.

"That will not be an issue. Do your work well, and no one ever need know you were involved."

This was crazy. "I don't know what you think that seal means, but

Lord and Lady Nemair aren't up to anything suspicious. Ask King Bardolph — he just gave them some kind of medal for their service overseas. Besides, I've been living here for weeks, and nobody's eaten a *single* baby."

"Do you find this so amusing, my little gutter rat? I wonder how you'd laugh with the thumbscrews on. Allow me to determine what's suspicious about Lord and Lady Nemair. You will observe the members of this household as I instruct, report to me, share whatever secrets you uncover in your close association with their daughter — in short, tell me anything interesting you see or hear."

"I see a weasel in one of his lordship's bedrooms. Is that interesting?"

He moved to slap me, but stayed his hand half an inch from my cheek. That time I didn't give him the satisfaction of seeing me wince. "You're very amusing. And now you will fetch me Antoch's journal. Black calf-skin binding, a seal of the House of Daul on the spine. Do you know what that looks like?"

It probably matched the one I'd just palmed from his desk, but I made a pretense of looking dumb. "An ermine?" I guessed. "That's like a weasel, isn't it?" I was seething inside, that this man had me so neatly trapped. Yesterday I was a lady's maid, and now I was a spy.

Pox.

The job was simple: Watch, listen, learn, report. And keep quiet about it all.

I could do that, of course, had been doing it all my life. But I usually chose the jobs I took, although the payment Daul was offering was hard to pass up. *How would they like knowing their daughter's sleeping with a thief?*

I sat now on Meri's lofty bed, my fingers buried deep in the white fur mantle, and stared at the carved plaster ceiling. What were my options? Work for Daul, or take my chances with the weather. I glanced out the window. The snow was still falling, and I'd heard the dogs had found two bodies trapped under the debris in the pass.

I could stroll into Lady Lyll's solar and tell her the truth. Announce that her husband's beloved friend suspected them of Sarist sympathies, and was extorting me to find the evidence. And have Daul tell them some outrageous lie about me. Or even the truth. I clutched at the white fur. That was a sure path to the dungeons — or worse. Did they kill thieves in the mountains?

The evidence. What was Daul even hoping I'd find? A secret stash of Sarist literature? Garderobes full of violet robes?

A daughter with magic?

*Damn.*

That would end this quickly.

I sat very still and cold, pressing an embroidered pillow to my stomach. What did I know? I had seen the magic playing on her skin — but nothing more than that. Not that that wasn't damning enough, but she was a *child*. Merista Nemair wasn't hurting anybody. I'd watched her say her devotions to Celys, right here in this room.

I had worked with dangerous people before. I'd helped sensitive information change hands, things that could get men killed. And maybe *had*. I didn't know. Tegen had always said we weren't spies. Spies had a political agenda. We worked for anybody. We were in it for the money, the thrill, the pure glory of Tiboran, god of thieves and liars. Messengers. Middlemen. Our hands were clean.

I had one skill, one thing I was *really* good at. It had kept me alive for the last few years; why was I balking now? Was this any different from working for Hron Taradyce or the Fealty Guild? I didn't owe the Nemair anything — they weren't my family. And did I really want to spend the next few months in dancing lessons, learning which cup to drink from first, and watching Lady Lyll embroider?

I curled up on the bed, hugging the pillow to my face. "Oh, Tegen," I whispered. Scruples and squeamishness wouldn't bring him back. I could smell Meri's soft, sweet scent on the bed, and pressed my eyes closed. She was nobody to me. Just a warm body and a place to hide. I flexed my fingers and passed my hand an inch above the coverlet on her side of the bed. Faint misty flecks sprang up and swirled to my fingers like silver filings. I thought about the strange way Durrel and Meri had looked at me in the boat, Meri giving me her bracelet. What had they seen?

Tegen had died to keep my secret. He'd killed a guard to keep me from falling into Greenmen's hands, where they'd take special pleasure in making my fingers light up. If I turned Meri over to Daul, he'd start asking all kinds of questions. *She has magic? How do you know?* I couldn't risk him finding out about me. I closed my fist tight. Dying as a thief was better than dying as a heretic.

But if I did my job right, nobody had to die at all.

# CHAPTER THIRTEEN

I was getting careless. That's all there was to it. Life at Bryn Shaer was making me soft. Three weeks of soft rooms and soft food and soft living, and here I was, pressed against a freezing windowpane, my toes curled under, scarcely breathing lest I disturb the heavy fall of yellow tapestry curtains I was hiding behind.

Lady Cardom had come back earlier than expected, and I had not quite figured out how to extricate myself from her chambers without being seen. She was supposed to be at dinner, and I couldn't fathom why she was taking so long getting ready. Was I going to have to stay here until she retired for bed?

I'd spent the last couple of days perusing Bryn Shaer's domestic spaces, and the entertainment was wearing thin. The Cardoms' suite in particular was utterly clean of *anything* suspicious, unless you counted Lord Cardom's vast and inexplicably pink-embroidered smock. That was one mystifying discovery I would happily share with Daul, unable to accept the oddness of it all by myself.

Lady Cardom and her maid shuffled about the rooms, changing Lady Cardom's day dress for — I listened for the rustle of heavy silk or — pox! Was that a loose gown; was she staying in? I didn't fancy the thought of spending the whole night behind this curtain, although I'd fared worse. I imagined a sigh of exasperation and wiggled into a slightly more comfortable position.

My second search of Lord Antoch's rooms had proved less profitable than my first. Not only was there no journal to be found among his lordship's belongings, but when I had gone back to check the library, the magic book was gone. I'd swiped the map of the hunting grounds, though, just so Daul knew my intentions were pure. Daul had looked at it strangely, his fingers whitening on his tight grip of the paper, and offered to remind me, once again, of what I was supposed to be doing. I touched the bruise on my temple — only half hidden by my bulky head-piece — and shook my head.

Still, there was something about working for Daul that — I don't know. I *understood* it. Ever since he'd sent me to fetch that seal, I'd felt something uncoiling inside me, a knot of tension and fear I'd been carrying around for weeks. My fingers itched; my legs wanted to bounce up and down, climb walls, kick somebody in the face. I'd never been good at sitting still, unless I was hiding behind a curtain or under a table or in a black pool of shadow at the edge of an alley. There was a thrill to tempting the risk of discovery, to hovering unnoticed, while people went about their business, no idea their belongings had been touched and examined by a stranger. Daul's work suited me just fine.

A few minutes later, the chamber's outer door finally swung open, and I heard the unmistakable heavy thump of Lord Cardom's footsteps on the wooden floor. "Aren't you ready yet, Mother? Wear the pearls; they make you look nicer."

The footsteps didn't stop. Was he headed for the windows?

"I *am* nicer," Lady Cardom objected stoutly. "Nicer than I ought to be, that's certain."

Stubby fingertips curled around the hem of the drapes, and I pulled back, breath dead on my lips.

"Now, Mother, I know you wish happiness upon your only son."

"She's too young for you. I want your wife to bear me grandchildren, not *be* my grandchild. Don't open those. It's freezing out there."

I could *kiss* Lady Cardom. I heard Lord Cardom lower his bulk onto a bench. "She'll get older. In four or five years it won't make so much difference. Think of everything you could teach her, until then."

She harrumphed. "You know the Nemair are only offering her because they want our help."

"Help that you're only too happy to provide." I leaned a little closer; this sounded almost promising. What kind of help could the Nemair want? I willed them to say more, but Lady Cardom just grunted noncommittally.

"I don't like her maid," she said, and I stiffened. "I don't want her in my house."

"The little one?"

"No, that Phandre. She's too . . . loose. And she's a Séthe. Never did like them much. The other one is fine. She can bring her."

"I don't know, Mother. I think Eptin Cwalo has his eye on that one, for one of his sons."

"Huh. Those Cwalo think they can buy everything. Aren't you ready yet? We want to be there before they serve the duck."

At long last, the Cardom rose together and exited the room. I waited a good twenty seconds before I collapsed to the Corles rug underneath my cramping toes.

Lady Cardom's inconvenient timing had thrown me off my own schedule, and Meri was already dressed and gone by the time I returned to her rooms. I scurried down to the dining room, slipped in the back way behind the tapestry, and threw myself into place beside Marlytt, hoping no one would notice how late I was.

"Where have you been?" Marlytt hissed. "Meri was looking for you all afternoon."

"Hunting," I said crossly, glancing up to see Daul prowling in across the room.

"Bag anything tasty?" she asked coolly.

"A marriage proposal from Eptin Cwalo, if you believe Lady Cardom." I didn't mention what else I'd found in Lady Cardom's rooms. I wasn't even sure myself what it meant. Probably nothing, but tucked inside her jewel chest I'd discovered a band of embroidered linen that looked a lot like the piece she'd given Lady Lyll. But now, inexplicably, someone had gone through and cut several of the stitches, undoing rows of flowers and curlicues. I'd brought it back to Meri's rooms and studied it, trying to work out its significance. Daul had told me to let him decide what was important, but he'd also been quick to show his displeasure when I returned with trivialities. I was smart enough to figure out on my own which category included ripped-up scraps of embroidery.

Dinner that night was informal; we sat where we wanted and collected what food we pleased as the servants strolled by with platters. It had finally stopped snowing, but the cold was impossible, seeping through the floors and walls of the Lodge despite the modern fireplaces roaring in every room. About the only warmth to be had was from dancing in the Round Court. I snagged a passing meat pie and a cup of ale — good sturdy peasant food for a night like this, although I was getting used to the dainties served up on the Bryn Shaer menu too — and settled in beside Marlytt to watch.

Meri was a surprisingly good dancer, bounding along on the arm of Lord Cardom, who flushed red with delight as he swung Meri through a turn.

"They look happy," Marlytt said. "He'd be good to her. I can tell." There was a strange note in her voice.

"I hope she likes pink," was all I said, popping a hunk of crust into my mouth. As the dance drew on, my eyes drifted across the Round Court. Lady Nemair was sharing a pie with the elderly gentleman beside her — a man called Wellyth, whose rooms had revealed only a fondness for tobacco, a couple of law books, and a handful of letters from a young granddaughter, completely free of hidden ink seals. Daul lounged beside Antoch, rolling his goblet between his hands and watching the assembled company with those dark, predatory eyes.

What was he looking for? These seemed like nice people, but maybe my weeks of luxury were coloring my own instinctive suspicions. But I knew someone who never let her sharp perceptions about society be dulled by rich food and soft beds.

I pulled myself closer to Marlytt. "Tell me about these people," I said. She eyed me sideways and sipped her wine. "I beg your pardon?"

"The guests here — who are they? What do you know about them?"

Marlytt hesitated. "Why do you want to know?"

"I just do." When her eyebrows pulled together suspiciously, I changed tack. "Look, I'm stuck here with them for the gods only know how long. It might be nice if I didn't trip up every time I opened my mouth. Help me out?"

"All right. What do you want to know first?"

"Everything. Anything."

Marlytt turned her gaze across the room, to where Eptin Cwalo was being pulled onto the dance floor by Phandre. "Well, Cwalo you know already. Wealthy merchant from an old Yerin shipping family. And by 'shipping,' I of course mean *smuggling*. He's made a name for himself outfitting every army in the known world, but his current passion is reportedly spices from Talanca. He's the sort of fellow you find circling the waters everywhere nobs get together."

I looked at her evenly. "I can't imagine. Go on. I know Phandre too. What about Daul? What's his story?"

Marlytt shook her head, and a delicate swag of crystals glittered in her hair like snowflakes. "Be careful of Phandre. She's a loose nob — orphaned, unattached. Unpredictable. If the moons align in her favor, she'll end up like me. If not . . ."

"I can handle Phandre. *Daul?*"

She tapped her fingers on the rim of her glass. "I don't know much. Boyhood friend of Lord Antoch. Father was Senim Daul, commander of the Sarist forces in the war. He's been away from the court scene for a while, since his familial lands were seized after the war — and of course he spent something like twelve years in traitors' prison."

Twelve years? I was almost impressed. Nobody lived that long in Bardolph's gaols. "That seems . . . excessive."

"I guess that's what you get for being the son of Bardolph's mortal enemy." She pointed a discreet little finger at the Cardom, now sitting with Meri between them. "I've heard Lord Cardom — *that* Lord Cardom's father — only got a year for his role in the conspiracy. Lord Sposa a few months. And Antoch was out —" Her voice slowed, stopped.

"What? What is it?"

"No, it's nothing — it's just —" She paused again and seemed to be making a tally in her head. The strains of the court musicians in the gallery above floated down, the flutes and recorders sounding distant and eerie.

"Marlytt, if you know something . . ."

She turned to me, her eyes gone very serious. "What do you remember about the Battle of Kalorjn?"

"Less than you, I expect." Courtesans trained in history, music, mathematics — anything to make them more appealing companions to accomplished men. "A great defeat for the Sarist cause. That's about it."

"No, *the* great defeat. The end of the rebellion." She nodded slowly. "I think this is them."

"Who?"

"The defeated Sarists. No, look — Daul. Nemair. Sposa. Cardom. Wellyth. Except for Lougre Séthe, they're all here. All the families that backed that last rebellion."

My eyes swung down across the room, to where the dance was breaking up and Eptin Cwalo was leading a tawny-haired beauty from the floor. "No," I said. "Séthe's here too."

A moment later, Phandre swept over and dropped down beside us. "Ah," she sighed dramatically, a hand to her dewy bosom. "I just can't decide. Do I like Lord Cardom for his estate and his allowance, or do I like Lord Sposa for his youth and his beauty?"

It was hardly likely she'd nab either one of them, but she and Marlytt fell easily into sober speculation of the potential faults and virtues of each man, as if they were examining goods at a market. I drew back, wondering how they'd like the corset Sposa wore to achieve that youthful figure, or the blocks in his shoes that added two inches to his height.

I sighed into my ale. My days kept getting wilder, and I wanted someone I could talk to — really talk to, not just this shallow court gossip Marlytt and Phandre excelled at. I wanted somebody who would laugh about Lord Cardom's ridiculous smock or my close call in his mother's rooms. Or help me figure out just what Daul was up to. Back home, there were people I could tell. Tegen would have laughed with me.

Marlytt was watching me now, her pale eyes glittering in the firelight. Together she and Phandre looked fat and pompous and ridiculous, in their crisp silk and heavy jewels, their bodices laced so tight their breasts heaved when they breathed. Phandre had picked up a collar of pearls and a garnet ring somewhere, and she fanned herself elaborately, showing them off.

"What were you two talking about?" she asked in her bored voice.

"Oddly enough, the very same thing you were," I said.

She perked back up. "Really? What were you saying? Have we made matches for everybody yet?" Then she remembered she wasn't supposed to like me. "Excluding poor Celyn, of course, since there isn't anyone here of her rank."

I didn't even need to respond to that, because the music died and Meri collapsed in a breathless heap next to me. Her hair curled in damp tendrils at her forehead, and she was grinning, her color high, her silver necklaces askew in her bodice. I reached to straighten them, but pulled my hand back at the last moment. Suddenly I didn't want to be there. My dress felt hot and stiff, my headpiece was making me sweaty, and the silver bracelet was starting to chafe. I tapped my fingers against the neckline of my dress, looking over the crowd, and wondered whose bedroom I hadn't had the pleasure of perusing yet.

Daul was in the back of the room with Lord Antoch, who was laughing his big, warmhearted laugh at something Daul had said. Heat crept up into my belly and my limbs as I felt the idea take shape. He wanted a thorough job, didn't he? Professional pride as a thief from Gerse's Seventh Circle demanded that I give this my most diligent effort.

"I'm a little tired," I said. "I think I'll get some air." I rose and stifled a yawn, for their benefit.

"She hasn't been sleeping well," Meri said in an exaggerated whisper. Poor Meri — alone with the grown-ups. She was trying so hard.

"I'll walk with you." Marlytt stood and hooked her arm into mine. Pox.

"Not me," Phandre said. "I'm going to give Lord Sposa another turn."

And thus we abandoned Meri to the circling wolves. I could almost feel the suitors pressing in, waiting for their chance to nick in for a sniff.

My blood was rushing as I pulled Marlytt into the servants' stair, curving up the back of the Round Court.

"Where are you going? I thought we were getting air."

"We can breathe upstairs."

"Ow! Digger, you're hurting me! What are you doing?"

"My job — and you're going to help." Marlytt wasn't Tegen, but she'd do for the moment. I didn't know how much time we'd have; not much if the gods' perverse humor held out this evening. With my luck, Daul would suddenly appear, waiting for me to deliver my "report." We slipped out onto the third floor, and I glanced down the hallway. Empty. Everyone from these rooms was still downstairs at dinner. The leaping light from a single torch at the end of the hall cast crazy shadows on the paneled walls. Marlytt's bright face was taut, confused, but I had a good idea she'd keep her mouth shut.

Until we stopped before the door at the end of the hall.

"Are you crazy? These are Daul's rooms!" She pulled her arm out of my grip and rubbed at her shoulder.

"You're the one who said I should be curious."

"Curious, not stupid. What if he catches you — us?"

"I never get caught." The words tasted thin and hollow. They hadn't been a lie, once. "Stand there and watch. If he comes — do what you do."

"Fine." Her eyes mimicked mine, taking in the hall on either side of us, and then she hiked her skirt up an inch or two above her stockinged ankle and leaned casually against the wall outside Daul's door. I knelt beside her, hidden behind her voluminous skirts. She also blocked most of the light, but this was work I could do by feel.

Of course, Daul hadn't been as trusting as the Cardom, or as Lord Antoch, for that matter. The doors on the third-story suites had latches and bolts, not set-in locks — but you can't bolt a door from the outside.

You can, however, padlock it.

Which normally shouldn't be an impediment, but Daul had something special picked out for me: a delicate, barrel-shaped lock clipped over the hasp, its brass case traced with scrollwork. A work of art, really — I had a mind to keep it, once I had it free. I slipped a pick from my bodice and went to insert it into the keyhole, but at my touch, the entire thing sparked up like a firebrand, and a thread of silvery mist seeped from the keyhole, circling the shackle. "Balls!" I swore through the pick in my teeth, and dropped its mate.

Marlytt looked down, a line creasing her forehead. "What's the matter?"

I still had one secret Marlytt didn't know. I scowled and shook my head, fumbling on the dark floor for my dropped pick. I tried a second time, sliding the pick into the lock, following behind with the second one from my mouth. And met with resistance. It was like poking two wrong ends of magnets together, as if the lock repelled my picks.

"Well, how about that," I said in a low voice. I had only encountered one other lock like this. It had been on the Master Confessor's door at the Celystra — and I'd been curious about what kinds of secrets he'd kept behind his too. Magical items were almost as rare as magical people, mostly old charmed objects that had been forgotten about. There was a black-market trade in spelled goods; things changed hands very quietly and for great sums of money. Most of the spells had worn off over the years, of course, but a perpetual charm like the one on this lock would have cost a fortune.

And why was it on *this* door? It was the sort of thing I'd have thought Daul wanted me to find for him, not the sort of thing he had already. It seemed a little strange that a man intent on uncovering Sarists would flaunt a magical item so openly.

Of course, I was the only person likely to discover it was magic, by sticking my fingers where they didn't belong. And it wasn't like I could *do* anything with that knowledge, except glare at Daul and seethe.

"Magic lock?" Marlytt said. "That's interesting. Can't imagine who Daul wants to keep out." There was a trace of wryness in her voice, which I ignored.

"Or in," I suggested, carefully lifting the lock to peer at its back side.

Marlytt shook her head. "It's only locked on the outside," she said. "You can leave the room, but nobody can get in without the spelled key." When I looked up at her sharply, she shrugged daintily. "Valros had one."

Well, Marlytt's "friends" were the type who could afford such a thing — but it seemed like overkill for a man like Daul, in a place like this, supposedly among friends. Maybe the Nemair weren't the only people at Bryn Shaer with secrets. "What's he hiding in there?" I sat back on my heels and frowned at the door, as if force of will could make the lock fall open on its own.

"Digger, I *know* that look. Whatever you're thinking, it's not worth it."

"Oh, it's worth it." I grabbed the lock and held it tight in my fist, letting the strains of magic seep out around my fingers like smoke. "I'll get in there."

I just had to figure out how.

# CHAPTER FOURTEEN

My conversation with Marlytt echoed in my thoughts the next morning as I ground poppy seeds in the stillroom. I sometimes spent mornings here while Meri and her father were out riding, helping as Lady Lyll set medicines to brewing, put up herbs to dry from the kitchen gardens, or recorded remedies in the great bound book she called an herbal.

The poppy seeds had a distinctive sweet smell, and Lady Lyll explained that the flowers grew wild on the sides of the mountain in the spring. She was working on a salve to fight poison in a wound, while a decoction of willow to reduce fever simmered in a crucible. Before this, we'd torn white linen into strips for bandages. I touched the scar on my arm, now a red weal, and thought Lady Lyll might have been a useful ally that night.

"Didn't we make that wound salve last week too?"

Lady Lyll adjusted the flame on the crucible by sliding a perforated lid across the firepot. "Very good. We did indeed. It's very perishable, though, so it's important to always have fresh on hand."

I looked at the little jar she was spreading the ointment into. "But what happened to the last batch?"

Lady Lyll gave me a strange look. "I gave it to the kennels. Some of the dogs have abrasions on their paws from digging in the snow. You're awfully curious this morning. Is there anything else you want to know?"

That felt like a rebuke, and I could feel my face getting hot. "Lady Cardom's headaches seem better," I said instead.

She nodded. "She's suffered from them ever since I've known her. I think it's the tension of having to hold her head up so high all the time."

A high surprised laugh jerked out of me, but Lady Lyll's wide fair face was as smooth and expressionless as a full moon. I watched her a moment, thinking about what Marlytt had said last night. Why bring together all those once-allied families? Maybe Daul was right, and there was something suspicious going on.

Or maybe they were just all old friends, gathered innocently together to celebrate one family's milestone.

"Have you known all your guests a long time?"

"Oh, Goddess, yes. Some of them, like Petr Wellyth, since I was a girl. And some of them came with Antoch, of course."

"Like Lord Daul?"

The bemused smile faltered just slightly. "Celyn, this is some of the most valuable information I have to teach you: Never get between your man and his friends. Theirs is an old, old relationship, and there's no breaking it."

"You don't like him?"

Lyll sighed and rummaged for a vial and funnel. "We've known him too long; it goes beyond liking or disliking. He is the closest thing Antoch has to a brother, and that is that. He has not been so fortunate in this life as we have, and we do what we can for him."

Pox, that told me *nothing*. "I heard he was in prison a long time."

Nodding, Lyll poured the fever medicine into her narrow-necked vial. "There are some things a king can't forgive, and I suppose one of those is being the son of the man who struck war against him. It took all of Antoch's doing just to get Remy decent food, let alone convince the king to spare his life and let him go. Part of that bargain, of course, was that we go to Corlesanne."

"I — what?" I paused in my grinding.

She was looking at the books stacked above the workbench, but her gaze was far away. "I can only assume His Majesty felt it was too danger-ous to have both Daul and Nemair loose in the same country again."

"And it's not dangerous now?"

Lady Lyll's jaw tightened slightly, and she gave a mirthless laugh. "Oh, Celyn. You're so young. You won't remember what it was like, after the war. The betrayals, the exiles, the suspicion. You think it's bad now? Everyone was your enemy in those days." Suddenly she stopped and gave me an odd, appraising look. "Sixteen, and named Celyn. Maybe you do know something about it. The Anointed Children?"

I just kept grinding away with my pestle. "Bastards for Celys, you mean?" After crushing the Sarist rebels, Bardolph had proclaimed that bearing an army of Celyst children to run over the land was a patriotic way for fertile young women to show their devotion to the Goddess of Life. I was just one of thousands of children born those first few years — dozens in the Celystra alone were taken from our mothers and raised by the church. Meri was lucky; her parents had left her with people who loved her, a cousin to watch over her like a brother — and then they'd come back for her. I'd been told my mother was dead, but it had never made much difference to me. Now, inexplicably, I found myself hoping it was true.

Lyll reached out and lifted my chin with one strong finger. "I've always thought that was too great a burden to put on such young backs."

I pulled away. "I'm alive. That's enough for me."

That afternoon was bright and cold, and we were scheduled to take a turn about the castle walls, all the court together. Standing in the freezing courtyard, I clapped my gloved hands together and stomped my feet. Lord Antoch strode over, under a mound of furs, a steaming mug of something in his great bear's paw of a hand.

"Fine day, eh, Celyn?" he said cheerfully, and I nodded through chattering teeth. He laughed. "Don't get much snow where you're from, do you? You'll get used to it. Come have a look; the view from the walls should be spectacular today. We can watch the progress being made on the pass."

Or not being made, more accurately.

I followed dutifully; Antoch at least made a decent windbreak. Winding up toward the battlements, we squeezed past a pair of black-and-silver guards patrolling with pikes. Below us in the courtyard, Daul had Meri on his arm, her pale face looking up into his. I shoved my hands into my sleeves and pressed close to Lord Antoch, who had paused to point out some feature of the valley. Snow glittered in the sunlight, almost too bright to look at.

Eptin Cwalo sidled up beside me, neat and compact in a black felt doublet. "As always, the prospect from your towers is unparalleled, my lord."

Antoch slipped something from his coat, a tube of brass and wood, which he lifted to his eye, then handed to me.

"What is it?" I asked.

"A spyglass. Look through it."

I obeyed, and the distant valley sprang closer, so suddenly it startled me. I yanked the device away, then looked through it again, this time ready for the surprise. "How does it work?" I said, watching the men and dogs, now disorientingly larger, moving vainly against the wall of white.

"Lenses and mirrors," Cwalo explained. "It was invented by a clever astronomer in Corlesanne, and promptly outlawed in Llyvraneth."

"Outlawed? Why?"

"For tempting men to gaze too closely upon the faces of the moons," Antoch said. "But ships' captains and generals find them too useful to give up. If you turn this way, you can see the Gerse road behind us too."

What would be the point of that? I handed back the spyglass.

"And if you look here, Lady Celyn," Cwalo said, "You can see one of the more unconventional approaches to the castle." He pointed straight down, to where the earth fell away at the base of the wall, a sheer drop to nothingness. I liked heights, and I leaned far over the edge, letting the cold crisp air freeze every thought from my head. The path from the ridge looked impassable, little more than a twisting staircase of crumbling rocks, barely one person wide. I couldn't imagine an entire army clinging to that narrow ledge, storming those sheer walls. Along the edge, the floor of the battlement opened up in oblong holes, slanting down like chutes into the sky.

Lord Antoch saw me looking. "For discharging missiles," he said, miming musket fire.

"I've been telling Lady Lyll for years that you need to modernize," Cwalo said. "Build a new artillery wall, shore up the gates. These defenses were fine in the days of magical attacks and siege engines, but with the new cannon, and especially these long-range arms they're coming out with from Varenzia, we also need new approaches in defense."

"Well, you've finally talked us into it, old friend. We've been discussing plans to replace the western and southern bailey walls in the spring."

My brain was frozen, and it took a moment for their words to penetrate. I pulled my head back from the edge and looked at both men. Had Lord Antoch just said they were rebuilding Bryn Shaer's defenses? That might mean nothing; they were remodeling the entire castle, after all. Along with modern roofing and modern windows and modern fireplaces, modern battlements and artillery walls made perfect sense.

But the Nemair had told me that Bryn Shaer was so remote that its military properties were obsolete. No reason to defend the Breijarda Velde, when there was peace in Llyvraneth.

I looked down over the valley, springing away in a bright dip of white so dazzling the sky had turned it blue. Smoke lifted from the Broad Valley, snug behind its blockade of snow. Did the Nemair expect that soon there *wouldn't* be peace in Llyvraneth?

Oh, I was very good. Playing the innocent maid with a sudden interest in military architecture, I drew out everything Cwalo and Lord Antoch would tell me about the castle's defenses, and what they didn't show me, I checked on myself later that afternoon. It took me into the older part of the castle, where they were storing supplies for the renovations, and when I was supposed to be helping Meri practice her lines for the *kernja-velde*, I was instead climbing over dusty ladders and frame-horses and peeking under draped canvas. I didn't know what I was looking at, of course, but I recalled it all faithfully.

By the time I emerged, gray with dust, the sun had dropped behind the mountain, and Zet's moon winked at me from a twilit sky. I crossed back toward the Lodge, pausing to rub a handful of snow over a stubborn mark on my skirt. Berdal, the guard so eager to share his avalanche knowledge on the way up here, was in the paddock yard, trimming the hooves of a white, spotted horse.

I made to curve around back toward the Lodge, but he saw me and gave a wave. I changed directions. "Lady Merista's horse?"

"Sweet little lass, like her mistress," he said. "She does like to ride, that one. I'm surprised their lordships let her ride out alone, though. It's pretty rough terrain in these parts, particularly with the trails obscured by snow."

I stopped. "What — alone? No, she rides with her father." I put those riding clothes on her every morning and brushed them clean an hour later. I *knew* she'd told me tales of Lord Antoch —

Berdal shook his head. "Not since that Lord Daul's been around and taking up all of his lordship's time. Most mornings Lady Merista goes out alone, though I'd feel better if one of you maids went with her." He gave an easy laugh and dropped the pony's hoof. "I suppose it'll have to be that Phandre, since you haven't learned to ride yet, have you?"

I smiled back absently, turning toward the Lodge. If Meri wasn't riding with her father, then where was she going?

Stepping out of the wind, at first I didn't see Daul lurking just inside the pentice, the covered walkway that connected the older Bryn Shaer with the Lodge.

"Learning anything interesting?" he said, his voice a purr as he fell into step beside me. He was clad today in dark blue, a color that made him look sallow and irritated. Maybe it wasn't just the color.

"Oh, yes. You'll be pleased to learn that Lady Lyll is hiding the whole Sarist army in the buttery, and Lord Antoch is — *ow!*"

He'd caught me by the thumb and was bending it backward to my wrist. I gasped and tears sprang to my eyes. "All right, all right!" He let me go, and I rubbed at my thumb. It hurt like seven hells, but wasn't dislocated, thank the gods. I was sure Lady Lyll could have popped it back into place — but I didn't fancy explaining to her how it had happened.

"Stop wasting time. I am not paying you to play the whore for the winemonger and the stable boy."

"You're not paying me at all," I snapped back. "And I've been doing *exactly* what you told me to do. Do you have something to write with?"

His eyes narrowed with interest, but he recovered soon enough. "I'm sure I'll remember."

I shrugged. "The Nemair are rebuilding Bryn Shaer's defensive walls." I sketched out the details of what I'd learned. "The new construction will withstand an attack from artillery fire — cannons."

"I know what artillery fire is, thank you. Anything else?"

Really, there was no pleasing the man.

"It looks like they'll be ready by summer."

He almost smiled. I could see the corners of his scarred lips straining to resist.

"What are you going to do with this information?" I said. "It's not like you can report it to anybody, not right now, anyway, with the snow —"

A finger raised in warning. "You let me worry about that. The only thing that need concern you is learning everything you can. And on that note, what luck have you had recovering my journal?"

I shook my head. "There wasn't anything like it in Antoch's rooms. There might be another place I can look, but —"

"I do not require a blow-by-blow accounting of your failures." Daul leaned over me, his face inches from mine. "I am interested only in success. Believe me, Antoch would not have let that book far out of his reckoning. Find it, bring it. Don't make me find additional motivation for you, little mouse." His voice was hot with warning, and I turned my head away.

"I'm not your mouse," I muttered, as he slipped away down the pentice, and I stood there, rubbing my sore hand.

# CHAPTER FIFTEEN

Somehow, Daul had sapped away all my pleasure over the day's discoveries, and now I just felt cold and dull. Though I was frozen through from climbing around in the cold, unheated older castle, I didn't feel like going back inside, returning to the warmth of the Lodge, and Lyll, and Yselle's hot, heavy supper. I needed space and sky and air. I needed *night.*

It was reckless and I knew it, and I didn't care. From the storeroom by the mews gate, I grabbed the gamekeeper's fur-lined coat and a pair of heavy boots that came nearly up to my knees and even fit *over* my nob's shoes. I hefted the iron bar on the door and shoved out into the night.

It was getting dark, as dark as it ever gets with seven moons looking down on us every night. Only Mend-kaal was full, a shady blot of blue-gray high above the mountains, nothing to worry about. The night watch was far away on the other side of the castle, though that was just stupid blind luck. Hoping Berdal was tucked safely away in his rooms above the stable, and wouldn't take it upon himself to have a last check outside the mews, I stomped away from the light and heat and weight of Bryn Shaer pressing against me.

*Mouse.* It was obvious — I had small hands and sharp eyes and a nose that led me straight into trouble. It shouldn't have bothered me, but it did.

One hot night a couple of summers ago, a brash young thief with a beard had hired me for a job at the Royal Exchequer. It was easy enough, but there had been a sticky spot along the way. My planned exit was blocked, and I had to escape by crawling along a water pipe that opened out over a gutter. Tegen had been impressed. *Just like a mouse,* he'd said, watching me emerge headfirst into the street. I'd laughed and produced the spoils — coin dies for the new silver marks, which I'd hidden beneath my snug hat.

I still remembered the way his fingers felt, brushing through my hair the first time. It had been a warm night, but his touch brought shivers to my skin. Bravely, I had touched his fingers with my own, and thrilled to feel them wrap around my hand. When he lowered his head to breathe my name against my neck, I thought it was the end of the world.

"What's the matter?" he asked, his voice ragged. He had me pressed against the brick wall outside the Exchequer, our twined hands lifted above my head. My eyes were closed, but I felt the solid form of his body inches from mine. I could have traced that shape in the darkness from then on.

I tried to laugh. "Eleven years of convent school?"

Tegen ignored me. One arm stole around my hips and pulled me bodily toward him. "You're magnificent, you know that?"

I felt my cheeks go hot, and shook my head. He was a few years older than me — darkly handsome, very intense, serious in a way that's rare among thieves — and I was a little in awe of him. I still hadn't recovered from the shock of being hired on in the first place.

"Nothing scares you," he continued. "You're game for anything. I've never met anyone like you."

And I had believed him, and I'd let him kiss me.

And I'd let myself believe that that meant something special.

I'd gone a quarter mile or so away from the castle now, pushing through the deep snow toward the fringe of woods. Behind me, the lighted bulk of Bryn Shaer loomed against the mountains. I sank down into a snowbank, my head on my knees.

"You bastard," I said aloud, not even knowing what I meant. Who I meant.

Suddenly, something snapped behind me.

I scrabbled up from the snowbank, my tears freezing in the bitter wind. I wobbled in my loose boots. Looking left and right, glancing behind, I tried to pinpoint the sound. I was terribly exposed — anyone hiding behind a tree or a snowdrift could pick me off and carry me away, and nobody would be the wiser. I fumbled through my layers of coat and skirts and found Durrel's knife, but I wouldn't be able to wield it long before my fingers froze in the open air. I clamped it in my teeth, and shoved my hands back inside the fur sleeves. Not, I may add, a recommended posture for sneaking.

Seeing nothing, I cautiously took a few gliding steps closer to the trees. It could have been a bird, I told myself — one of the black rooks that lingered for the winter. Marau's birds. But there were no branches to creak overhead, no prints in the snow that I could see.

When I reached the trees, a little girl in a purple cloak was standing a dozen paces from me.

I just stood and stared at her, half sure she must be some sort of cold-induced hallucination. Apparently she was thinking the same thing, her eyes wide open in surprise.

I spat my knife into my hand. "I'm not going to hurt you," I said, and she shrank back. Pox. I stuck the knife behind me through the shell of the coat, at an angle so I wouldn't idiotically stab myself or slice the pleats right off the back of my dress. "There, look. All right?" I took a step closer to the little girl — gods ask me why — but she spun and ran back into the woods.

And I ran after her.

I must have had some mad, half-formed thought that she was lost, one of the servants' children, somehow come loose from the castle. But her cloak was like a lure — that impossible, illegal color. Black branches flashed and slapped, silver moonlight sparkled the path of white at my feet, while the purple ducked and wove through the woods. I kept up until I stepped too heavily in a deep place and lost one boot to the snow. I fumbled my way out again. Close to the trees, the snow was not so deep. I kicked off the other boot and picked my way through in just my slippers, the girl in purple always just ahead.

Finally we broke out into a clearing, and I scrambled to such a quick stop that I almost fell over. Clustered around a blazing campfire were at least a dozen people, all of whom looked *very* shocked to see me. A blocky brown dog lunged my way, roaring its objection, but a firm hand gripped its collar and held it back. The little girl flew into the waiting arms of a beast of a man, who scooped her up from the forest floor like she was made of moonlight.

Slowly I snaked my hand toward my knife. Fine night for a campout. I remembered the Nemair's warning about outlaws and eased back toward the trees.

"You are lost from castle?" A tall man bundled in gray stood up from the fire and shook his hood back to reveal a thick mane of light brown hair, just starting to silver. He beckoned me closer. One of his companions said something, in a low, guttural language I couldn't understand, and Graymantle barked back, silencing him.

"Who are you?" I said, my voice a little too sharp.

He smiled. "We are . . . Tigas Wanderers. We make winter camp here at Bryn Shaer."

I nodded, edging farther from the fire. The Tigas were an ancient people from Talanca's hot southern coast — swarthy and dark, with black hair and skin like copper. But my young friend in purple had hair like a flame; the man holding her wore a ginger beard. I looked at the gray cloaks and the motley clothes. More flashes of purple, below collars, inside hoods, and suddenly my crack to Daul about baby-eating Sarists didn't seem so amusing. Memory served up every horror the Celystra had ever ascribed to the followers of Sar: Animal mutilation. The desecration of the dead. Brandings. Burnings. Outrageous accusations, meant to scare us.

They worked.

I couldn't have gone far — a straight line through the trees, and I'd be back at Bryn Shaer, hiding the gamekeeper's mangled coat, in ten minutes.

"You are lost?" Graymantle repeated.

"Yes. No. I'm just going to go back the way I came — I saw your — the little girl, and thought she might be, and — so lovely meeting you all, good night." I made a sort of curtsy-bow cross and turned to leave.

Graymantle gave another order in his strange language, and I froze, one hand gripping the hilt of my knife. A boy about my age or a little younger stood up from the fire. He was fair as Marlytt, with white-pale hair and blue eyes.

"I'll take you back to Bryn Shaer." He spoke native Llyvrin, with a nearly imperceptible Carskadon accent. A local boy.

Still eyeing Graymantle, I nodded warily. The boy brushed past me into the trees.

"Stagne —" Graymantle said, and the boy turned back. The older man said a few words in that odd, smooth language with the disappearing consonants, and the boy — Stagne, apparently — inclined his head. Graymantle accompanied us to the edge of the clearing, and put his hand on my shoulder in farewell.

And I nearly collapsed from the weight of the magic *rolling* off him. Stagne grabbed my elbow and hauled me upright, but Graymantle's hand, his arm, his whole person had lit up like he was consumed by white flame. Why hadn't I seen it before? I had to look away, he was so impossibly bright with it — and saw that Stagne's hand on my arm was flickering steadily too.

"Are you quite well?" Graymantle leaned over me with concern, and it took all my effort to look at him and keep from squinting. I caught a glimpse of his left hand, which I realized he'd been carefully hiding in his mantle, and saw that the palm was branded with a deep purple star — a wizard's tattoo. The Mark of Sar.

Long ago, before magic had faded from the earth, wizards pledged to Sar were tattooed on each palm to show their loyalties. But that was hundreds of years ago. Nobody in Llyvraneth would be so foolish as to put the Mark of Sar on someone. Which meant he could only have received that mark in secret. Or in Corlesanne, where as far as I knew, worshipping Sar was still legal. But what were Corles Sarists doing in the woods outside Nemair lands?

And how had this man come by so much magic?

Oh, this was *not* my business.

It took everything I had not to break free of Stagne's hand on my arm and flee straight back into the night. But I might actually need these people to get me home again. I shook my head. "Thank you, I'm just — very cold."

"Come back to the fire and warm up," Stagne offered.

I felt dizzy, my vision hazing over with all this magic. "No, I'll be all right. They'll start to miss me at Bryn Shaer." Which was no more than the honest truth.

"Very well. Good night, little Bryn Shaer girl."

Stagne led me easily through the trees, keeping up a quiet monologue that I gathered was meant to be reassuring: "Here, watch this branch. It's a little deep there. Would you like to take my arm?" But I just shoved my hands farther into my sleeves and trudged along wordlessly after him. I could still feel the magic on my fingertips, like the prickling of a limb fallen asleep, and I didn't like it. It had never happened before. But, then, I'd never encountered anyone like Graymantle before either.

Back in the castle that night, I threw myself into Meri's bed, crawling deep under the covers. Her warm plump body was like a furnace, heat and light rising from her as she breathed. I stared into the starlit darkness about her, my thoughts a whirl. Who were those men in the woods? Did anyone else at Bryn Shaer know about them? Ordinary Sarists — the kind Daul had me hunting down — were one thing. Disgruntled, passionate, a threat to the Goddess-ordained peace and order in Llyvraneth, yes. But these weren't ordinary Sarists. These people had magic, which meant they were all kinds of danger.

I just couldn't decide if they were dangerous — or *in* danger.

I pulled a feather pillow as tight round my head as I could, but I was still shivering when morning came.

# CHAPTER SIXTEEN

I was edgy and addled as I dressed Meri for her ride the next day, but she didn't seem to notice. My hands shook as I brushed her hair straight, watching the swirl of magic just dusting her skin. I imagined her suddenly flaring up as brightly as the Sarist in the woods, and nearly dropped the hairbrush.

"Meri," I said when she swapped me for the brush and started in on my hair, "have you ever seen anything — strange, on your rides?"

"Strange?" she echoed. "Like what?"

Like the six-foot-tall flaming candle and his merry band of outlaw wizards? That was one danger I'd bet even Berdal didn't know about. "I don't know, people? Your parents told us there were bandits in the forest. Maybe you shouldn't ride out alone."

The brush stroked down the back of my head. "But I don't ride out alone," she said, and there was not a trace of anything but pure Meri honesty in her voice. She smiled at me in the mirror. "Your hair's getting longer. Will you wear it up or down for my *kernja-velde*, do you think?"

I stared at her. What did it matter? But I said, "I'm supposed to be practicing *your* hair."

She shrugged. "I like doing it. Maybe Phandre was right, and I should be a lady's maid."

"Your parents would love that, I'm sure."

"Should I try it?" She struck a formal pose and said, "Mother, Father, I've decided *not* to wed Lord Cardom or Lord Sposa, and instead I'll be running off to serve as Lady Celyn's chambermaid. Will that upset your grand plans overmuch?" She gave a giggle and dropped down beside me on the bench. "You were so brave to leave the Celystra. I'd never be able to do that."

"There was nothing there for me. You have a lot to lose."

"What? Lands and a title?" She said it casually, but I heard an edge of bitterness in her voice.

"No." I turned to face her. "Parents who love you. A big family to take care of you. People like Durrel, and — Morva. Phandre."

"Phandre?" She cocked her eyebrows, but her lip twitched.

"Maybe not Phandre," I said, and she grinned.

Still, a little of that cold dread stayed with me all morning. I made Meri promise she would stay close to the castle on her ride. She looked at me strangely, but agreed. I didn't know what else to do. I didn't want Lady Lyll to find out I'd been running around outside the castle walls at night; I wasn't sure what she'd say, but she was likely to curtail my movements around Bryn Shaer, just when I needed freedom.

Worse, I'd lost Durrel's knife. When Stagne led me out of the trees, I'd seen the lighted hulk of Bryn Shaer and launched myself toward it without a backward look, dumping the gamekeeper's coat in a heap inside the mews, the knife not among its folds of fur and wool. I stuck my head back out into the icy night, but the snow was bare but for the deep furrow of my tracks. All that day I kept moving my hand to my thigh, checking for what wasn't there. It wasn't just being weaponless; there had been something about its heavy presence that I'd found comforting, some tie to the world outside the Carskadons.

I craved the peace and calm of Lady Lyll that morning, but down in the stillroom, my thoughts were scattered and wild. I mistook the order of ingredients in an unguent I could make from memory, and it wouldn't set up.

"Celyn? Are you quite all right? You're not yourself today."

I just shook my head, and cleaned up the mess of the ointment I'd been preparing. "I'm sorry, milady. I won't waste any more."

"No worries, Celyn," Lyll said softly. "I was thinking about you."

Instead of starting a new batch of ointment, I leafed through the pages of her herbal, the heavy handwritten book that guided our hands in the stillroom.

"Where did you learn all this?" I asked her.

Lady Lyll's fingers brushed the pages. "Did they not have herbals at the Celystra?"

"Books like this?" I almost laughed at the thought. "No — believe me, we had no books like this when I was there." Lyll's herbal would have been locked up tight in the bowels of the Celystra scriptorium, or consigned to the balefires.

"But surely the priests and hospitallers have the knowledge of healing? What did they do when someone fell ill?"

Something about her voice told me she knew the answer already, but I answered anyway. "Mostly they just *prayed*. They said Celys would choose to save who she would, and send for Marau to carry away those who did not meet her favor."

"Celyn," Lady Lyll said patiently. "Celys is a goddess of life. She has given us herbs and fruits and flowers that can cure, that can heal, that can save lives and ease pain. Does it not make sense that she would want us to use them?"

I just shrugged, because when did the gods ever make *sense*?

Like a lot of thieves, I knew some basic tavern medicine — how to stanch bleeding, stitch a cut, bind a broken bone — but nobody understood how to keep poison from a wound, save a rotten limb, or bring down a dangerous fever. There were always guesses, of course, and people more than willing to make a profit on those guesses. Apothecaries and potioners' shops abounded in Gerse, selling ridiculous decoctions that were as likely to make you worse as better. And when summer fevers ravaged the city, as they did nearly every year, the Celystra's response was to shut tight its doors to protect its own, and ring the temple bells out in prayer.

But here was *real* knowledge, real medicine to treat the sick and the injured. Forbidden knowledge in Llyvraneth. If Bardolph hadn't closed the Sarist college in Breijardarl, Llyvrins might have learned this too, along with astronomy and anatomy and the other sciences Lady Lyll had talked about.

"How do they get away with it?" I said, reading an entry showing disorders of the liver. I held my fingers to the rusty-red pictures, as if there were some power to be absorbed from the page, beyond the simple, clear meaning of the words. But these words *were* just words, plain and simple and true — and yet powerful in their own way for all that.

Lady Lyll touched my wrist with her warm hand. "We let them, Celyn," she said, and her voice was low and fierce. "We *let* them."

I didn't know what to do with her fierceness, and so I just hid my head in another batch of the ointment I had fouled. Lady Lyll stepped out for a moment to fetch more water from the kitchens, and I was left alone in the stillroom for the first time. I looked around me, almost in awe of this room of hidden knowledge. I was hungry for it — to understand the secrets inside every bottle, every packet, in all those books. It was even more intoxicating than Antoch's library. Taking advantage of Lady Lyll's absence, I pulled another volume off the shelf.

I thought at first it was the gamekeeper's ledger, for there was a detailed listing of game birds, along with numbers and shorthand notations I couldn't make out, but it was in Lady Lyll's firm, tidy script. Tucked between notes on the new construction at Bryn Shaer — tile orders and the payment of Breijard workmen — I found something familiar and out of place: a scrap of embroidery, rows of black and scarlet on white linen, with some of the stitches cut out.

I ran my fingers along the cut bits, frowning. One mangled sampler was strange. Two was suspicious. I cast my eye along the pattern, which was mostly obscured now, but counting the repeats and the images that remained. *I thought there were five repeats. No, she could only find four.* I had dozed through that conversation, but it pricked at my mind now. Was there more to this than just silk and linen?

The more I looked at the stitching, the more I felt sure of it. Hidden in those torn stitches was a message. From Lady Cardom to Lady Lyll, about what? I tried to remember. Something about Lady Cardom's daughter, and the place she lived. Gairveyont. A castle on Llyvraneth's southeastern coast. Four repeats, when Lady Lyll had been hoping for five. Five what? *They're only offering their daughter because they want our help.*

Help with what? I turned back to the page in the ledger book about the construction, thinking about those fortified bailey walls. Five ships? Five cannon? Five — rosebushes? I had no clue what I was looking at.

But Tiboran hadn't marked me as a fool. I knew it was *something*. I stuffed the scrap of cloth into my bodice, just as Lady Lyll pushed open the stillroom door.

I brought the embroidery to Daul, interested to see what he'd make of it. We met in the servants' hallway behind the Round Court, both pieces of cut-up stitchery in my hand.

"What is this?" he said, predictably.

"Isn't that your job? 'Let me decide what's suspicious'?" But I recounted the conversation between Lady Lyll and Lady Cardom. "Maybe it has something to do with the new defenses."

Daul sighed and took them. "Very well. I will look into it. Is that all?"

I bristled. "I went to a lot of work to get those. I hid in a freezing window for *an hour*. You could at least pretend to be interested."

"Bring me something interesting, and I will."

"Fine. But I want to be paid." Enough of working for threats and intimidation. I wanted something *real* out of this job.

His gaze sharpened. "You have something, then?"

I gave a faint shrug.

"The journal?"

"Forget the damn journal. This is better." For the first time, I had something I knew he wanted, and the power of that made my blood feel hot.

He rolled his head back in exasperation. "Five marks — *if* it's something useful."

"Ten. It is. And I'm going to need a knife."

"I need a thief, not a mercenary. Who are you planning to use it on?" But I heard amusement in his voice.

"You."

He did laugh then, a thin sound like the barking of foxes. Something stiff cracked in my own face, and I thought perhaps I was almost smiling.

"You're very amusing, little mouse. Give it to me."

I hesitated. I had to tell *somebody* — this knowledge was too big for me alone. I was crawling with it, like fleas, and I'd go mad trying not to scratch. Let Daul get bitten for once.

"There are Sarists camping in the woods behind Bryn Shaer."

Daul's expression shifted from surprise to . . . something else. "I don't pay for fantasies."

I shook my head, described the camp I'd seen. Well, camp*fire*.

"A band of filthy beggars, no doubt."

"No doubt. And they stole their purple cloaks."

He wheeled his gaze around, leaned very close. "Outlaws. Brigands."

"Not these guys. Their leader had a purple tattoo on his hand."

Daul pulled himself away from me and smoothed down his doublet. "That's worth a half-noble at most," he said, fishing for the coin. I caught it smoothly as it sailed toward me. "Get yourself a knife from the kitchens. I trust a girl of your talents can handle that much." He pushed past me into the Round Court. "I'll give you the rest of your fee when you bring me the journal."

Turning the coin over in my hand, I watched him leave. It was a neat solution to my problem; I had found Daul some real Sarists, and in chasing them down, maybe he'd turn his attention away from me for a few days. I tried not to think too much about what would happen if he caught them.

After dinner, everyone gathered in the Lesser Court for games. I played a match of chess with Eptin Cwalo while the others engaged in a lackadaisical round of riddles, a silly game that usually started out innocent and degenerated after the glasses were filled a few times. Meri excelled at it — both in guessing the answers and in posing cryptic questions.

Cwalo had taken the seat closest to the fire, and the flames leaping all about his small shiny face made him look weird and sinister. Luckily the particular brand of chess he'd chosen, a fast-moving game popular in the south, was one I knew well. I played it by raucous, reckless tavern rules, knocking over his pieces and sacrificing my own with abandon. A slow grin of delight spread across his pasty features.

"My word, Lady Celyn — you have a fearless streak about you."

I grinned back and hooked his Courtier from the game board. "I just hate to lose."

"When it's a cold soup!" Meri exclaimed from across the room. "When is a pigeon not a bird?" She was smiling widely, her color high. Antoch looked on, ever the proud father. Daul sat beside them, thin legs stretched out lazily, watching everyone with a sort of bored, scornful gaze.

"When it's a fowling piece," my opponent offered in a low, smooth voice. I scrunched my face in confusion, and Cwalo explained, "There's a large gun for hunting birds they call a 'pigeon.' No one knows why."

"Master Cwalo, do you know everything?" I turned the game piece over in my hands, a silver figurine in the shape of a nob sketching a bow.

"Perhaps not *everything*, milady." He reached toward me to Bargain back the lost man, brushing his hand against my sleeve. "But do you know who is exceptionally well-informed?" he said. "My son Andor."

"Your sons again! Did you ever think I might like some of these other families, their sons? What would you say then?" I made a ridiculously demure move with my Maid — one that put her directly in sight of his newly reclaimed Courtier.

"I'd say your interest was not misplaced." He sat back in his tall chair, eyeing me through the pyramid of his fingers.

"Indeed?" I slid my Maid down the game board. "If I were a maid in the market for a husband, do you think they'd have anything to offer me?"

"Mayhap. Who are you interested in?"

"I find Lord Cardom pleasing," I said lightly. "What sort of assets does he have?"

"The Cardom are from Tratua. They can offer you ships." He put the Galleon on the board, between the Maid and my Lady.

It was fun playing the nob with Cwalo. "What kind of ships?"

"What kind do you need?" Cwalo's voice was still casual, but he spoke quietly, and his eyes had gone cool and serious. I stared at him for a moment, then hazarded a dangerous, wild guess.

"Warships?"

"That could be arranged."

I breathed in sharply, suddenly sure we weren't playing a game anymore.

"Anyone else catch your eye, my lady?"

What was he doing? Still, Cwalo might have even more information about our fellow guests than Marlytt. It was worth a try. "Uh — Wellyth?"

"Timber."

City girl that I am, I faltered here. "What would I do with timber?"

"For firewood, bridges . . . siege engines. And ships."

I glanced at Lord Antoch. Meri sat at his feet, and he had one massive hand resting softly on her head. Lady Lyll leaned close to Lord Sposa, and was speaking to him in what appeared to be serious tones.

"Sposa."

"Lord Sposa is from Gelnir. He has grain." *To feed your army.*

"And the Nemair?" I asked. "What — what do they bring to this union?"

Cwalo picked up my Lady piece and a Flag that was not on the board, laying them side by side. "Allies. They have friends in Corlesanne. And Corlesanne has friends in Varenzia."

I felt a tremor in my blood. First the castle's new defenses, and now this — Cwalo had as good as told me the Nemair were preparing for war. But was it just the sensible precautions of diplomats reading the political climate? Noble families all over Llyvraneth would want to be prepared, whenever princes Wierolf and Astilan finally came to blows over their uncle's throne. Or was Daul right, and there was something more . . . covert going on here?

A burst of laughter lifted from the other side of the room. "When is a sovereign not a noble?" That was Lord Sposa.

The riddle was about coins, but Daul leaned forward languidly, and said, "When it's Bardolph of Hanival, of course."

Everyone laughed, but I tensed and looked at Cwalo. He was watching me steadily.

"And what does Lord Daul bring?"

Cwalo said nothing, just took the Courtier off the game board and set it on the table. With it he put my Flag, my Regent, and my Cleric. Country, king, and church. It matched Daul's own claims, his implications that he was a loyal anti-Sarist with friends near the Crown.

"Are you sure?"

A shrug. Almost imperceptible. What did that mean?

Cwalo continued rearranging the chess pieces. Galleon, Lady, Courtier, and Knife together on one side of the board; Regent, Cleric, Ring, and Flag on the other. I watched the pieces, confused, but he kept stacking more and more men on the Regent's side, until it utterly overwhelmed the others. What was he telling me? Slowly he turned the Knife toward the smaller force, its own men, and drove it through the center of the line.

"There are questions about the war that have never been answered," he said. "What happened at Kalorjn, who's really to blame for the rebels' defeat. But it's a remarkable turn of events that for the first time ever, all the people who might be able to answer them are here together. All those still living, that is. And among them, there are some who might be, shall we say, strongly motivated to find out the truth."

On the game board, the pieces were starting to twist together into a glittering knot. I wasn't completely sure what Cwalo meant, but I was beginning to suspect there was more going on here than anyone was saying. When Lyll rose and beckoned us to join the rest of the group, I gave Master Cwalo one last hard look. "Why did you tell me all of this?"

"I think it may not be a bad thing for the Nemair to have someone fearless on their side." He eased back in his chair and took a sip of his wine. "You know, Lady Celyn, my son Garod enjoys a game of chess every now and then."

# CHAPTER SEVENTEEN

I was full of questions the next morning — about Daul, about the Nemair and their guests, about Meri's secret rides. I had determined to follow her, make sure she didn't accidentally track into the woodsmen at the same time as Daul. But it was snowing again, a horrible howling blizzard that flung snow at Bryn Shaer from all directions, and Meri happily stayed tucked in bed until even Phandre declared it past time for getting up. It also meant Daul wouldn't be able to go looking for them just yet. Or maybe, I thought hopefully, he might go out and be swallowed up by the storm.

My information about the Sarists was good enough to keep him off my back for a few days, though I still hadn't found his phantom journal. But I'd fallen into a rhythm, and I kind of liked it: stillroom or solar in the morning, breaking into the guest rooms in the afternoon, getting to dinner late, and falling into bed with Meri after.

Daul's obsession with that journal fascinated me, particularly in light of the curious lock on his door, and now Cwalo's cryptic conversation. What was in there he was so eager to find? I also didn't like the idea that the journal might be here somewhere and I *couldn't* find it. That just chafed. If there was a journal, then I'd find a journal, and maybe it would straighten out some of the twining knot of secrets I was caught in. Or at least maybe tell me why Remy Daul was so eager to prove his best friends were Sarists.

I'd already searched the most obvious location, Lord Antoch's suites, three times, and found nothing. There was no journal among the books in Lady Lyll's stillroom, or the cookery manuals in the kitchens. Even Meri's small collection of volumes, lovingly carried from Favom Court, had been gone through. I started looking *under* things, but I'd frankly begun to believe one of three things had happened: The book never existed, it was lost to the ravages of time, or Antoch had long ago tossed it into a fire. There was something appealing about that last option, but only because it supported Daul's interest in the thing.

The snowfall lasted two entire days, putting the work on clearing the avalanche even farther behind. My suggestion that the entire Bryn Shaer court hike down there to help was ignored. At last a morning dawned clear and bright, and Meri got up to ride. I got her dressed, and was fast on her heels, bundling into my coat and gloves, but I lost time trying to find appropriate footwear (I had to sneak into the kitchen and steal the spit-boy's sturdy leather shoes — the only other person in this castle with feet as small as mine, apparently). And then I ran into Phandre in the stairwell, locked in a predatory embrace with Ludo, the servant who was so friendly with her door latch. I had to gag, then slip quietly back up the stair so she wouldn't see me, then down the hall to the main stair, which took me to the utter wrong side of the Lodge — and by the time I got to the stables, Meri was long gone.

I slumped against the stable wall with a sigh. I could still follow, maybe — but when I let myself out the paddock door, I saw no tracks in the snow to tell me where she'd gone. Even I should be able to track a girl on horseback in freshly fallen snow, but a treacherous mountain wind swirled along the surface, brushing everything smooth again.

Pox. I turned back for Bryn Shaer, but something made me pause and go back through the stables. And there in the first stall by the door, waiting hopefully for her mistress, was the white and spotted pony Berdal had been grooming days before. I looked at her, eyes narrowing. Hard to go riding *without your horse.*

"Lady Celyn?" I turned; it was Berdal, coming down the center aisle with a rag in one hand. "Come for that riding lesson?"

"I was looking for Lady Merista," I said.

He shook his head. "She's not been here this morning. But if I see her, I'll tell her you were looking for her."

"No, don't — I mean, don't bother. I'll catch up with her soon enough."

Curious, puzzled, I wandered slowly back up to the house, hardly noticing the cold. Where was our girl going? I was sure Lady Lyll didn't know about it — she hardly let Meri go to the privy alone. I felt a spike of pride. Little Meri, off on an adventure of her own.

Which was none of my business, of course, and about which I cared not a whit.

Back up in our rooms, I shucked off my coat and kicked open the chest where I stored my shoes, since I was just going to have to do this again tomorrow anyway, and the spit-boy had a nice cozy post in the kitchen; what did he need shoes for —

And discovered where Merista Nemair was spending her mornings.

Lying in the chest atop my shoes and belts, where I *always* kept it, was Durrel Decath's pearl-handled dagger.

The one I'd lost in the woods with the Sarists.

I dropped to my knees on the floor, staring at the clothes trunk, those cold, clutching fingers grabbing at my chest again. I picked up the knife, but it swirled now with residual magic, like finger smears on the blade, and when I wiped it with my skirts, it only got all over me. I pulled my dress up, exposing my leg — but it didn't feel safe anymore. I dropped my skirts and left the knife where Meri had put it.

The red jewel in its hilt winked up at me from the pile of stockings and slippers. *Be a friend to her, Celyn.* Pox and bloody hells.

I started with the shoe chest, then the desk and cupboard and the prayer stand. Under the cushions of the window seat. Inside my old hiding spot (I'd found another, in the hollow beneath a loose stair tread in the servants' stair). I even popped Phandre's door and took a peek around her sparse belongings. Where would Merista Nemair store her girlish secrets?

I was lost. They were so much *bigger* than I'd ever suspected from her, but as I looked around the room, I forced myself to stop and *think*. Really think about this. About the dreamy smiles on Meri's face after her morning "rides." About the fair-haired local boy who'd walked me back so confidently to Bryn Shaer. In the dark. It was possible.

As I stood there, the window seat kept tugging at me. It was hollow for storage — we kept blankets there — but the compartment wasn't as deep as it should have been. I pulled the cushions off and flipped the lid, tapping and pressing along all the seams in the boards of the bottom. Was I looking for a panel, a door, a spring? I dug my too-long fingernails into every gap, feeling for a latch. But there was nothing. On the outside, then. I worked my hands along the carvings at the base, the sculpted rosettes and swooping leaves, until my fingers found the place where one rose's center sat a little *too* deep. I gave it a gentle push, heard the click, and watched the panel spring back to reveal the hollow.

"Oh, Meri — *very* nice." What obliging parents the Nemair must be, to outfit their daughter's bedroom with a secret compartment. And to outfit their daughter with two heavy silver chains and a thick silver bracelet. And a protector like Cousin Durrel. And a secure mountain stronghold in which to pass into adulthood unthreatened.

I sat back on my heels. Life for a nob with magic would come with peculiar challenges. Up until now she'd been able to lead a relatively sheltered life — her parents were overseas, and she was young enough not to be much in demand in society. But she was just about to come of age, get married, and be thrust into public life, with all the visibility and gossip and *touching* that came with that life. I knew how easily a nob's secrets could be exposed. Was it possible that along with the training in housekeeping and the social graces, the Nemair had brought Meri to Bryn Shaer for her to learn to manage her magic?

Nobs' children with embarrassing secrets — too many fingers, a susceptibility to fits — were normally offered up to the Celystra for a soft life as honored servants of the Goddess. And the Celystra was only too eager to accept them, and the fat dowries they brought with them.

I could imagine all too well what the Celystra would do with a girl like Merista Nemair.

I reached my hand inside the hidden opening. The cavity was not large — you couldn't hide a whole Sarist rebel down there, or even his spare clothing.

But it was plenty big enough for a couple of missing books. I pulled out the first small volume: the gray primer on magic from Antoch's library. It left behind enough of its not-quite-light for me to see the object that had been sharing its quarters. I fetched it into daylight as well: a worn book of black leather, a mark embossed on the spine: a wide, curving cross inside a circle. The seal of the House of Daul.

First Daul, now Meri? What was in this book that made it so irresistible? My fingers practically itched as I cracked it open.

To — nothing. I flipped through a few pages in smooth black script, but it seemed to be nothing more than some kind of treatise on hunting. There were detailed chapters on dressing the horses, the best weather and terrain for various game, and endless advice on training the dogs. Definitely a nob's book, but why was Daul so keen for it? And why did *Meri* have it?

Pox, this didn't make any damn sense. And it wasn't my business. We never read the documents we stole, not any more than necessary to be sure they were the right ones. What was I doing? Getting involved, that's what.

And that was the third rule.

Stay alive.

Don't get caught.

Don't get involved.

But I hadn't signed on for this job. I'd been recruited. I figured I had some right to know what I was being asked to do. And I didn't like being played.

I sat with the book on my lap and scowled at it. Well, why do people usually want documents stolen? Because the documents say something bad about them or contain secrets they don't want revealed. I turned to the end and made my search more carefully. Sections of pages through the book were blank, as if the author's thoughts had been interrupted and he'd started back up again at random, and as I flipped through the empty leaves, I found something. Someone had filled a page or two with childish, exuberant drawings — a sketch of a typical Gersin river house, a bounding deer whose head was too big, a black mountain menaced by a great dark cloud.

But there in a corner, among a squiggle of random shapes and inky finger-smudges, was something else entirely. Someone had taken blue and red inks, and traced them over each other to make purple. And in that makeshift, forbidden violet ink, someone had drawn stars, a whole constellation of them. Purple stars, with seven points, the seventh longer than the rest. The symbol of Sar.

Was *this* what Daul was after? This page of scribbles in some old hunting guide was the compelling evidence he sought against the Nemair? Even as my fingers trembled, I scowled at the improbability of it.

And then I turned the page, and any desire to hand the journal over to Daul shriveled up inside me. I knew that handwriting — I was getting to know the handwriting of everybody at Bryn Shaer — and I felt those cold fingers scrabbling at my heart again as I read the words Meri had been copying out: *The Seeing Dream. To Appear Without Form. The Sacred Circle. The Dreamless Sleep.* It went on for pages — not just the words, but symbols and diagrams, all copied from the Sarist book we'd found in Antoch's rooms.

Meri was teaching herself magic. Word by word, through rote memorization, using the pages of a half-empty book she'd found in her father's study, she was working her way through the principles and lessons of the old mages.

I held the journal tightly in my hands, wondering. Did she do this alone? Was there anyone working with her, to show her how to shape the symbols, make the words more than words? Or must she do this in secret, late at night, under the guise of sewing by moonlight — her bedfellow and companion possibly even under the influence of this Dreamless Sleep? *You sleep so soundly, you never notice.*

I pressed my fingers to the pages Meri was using as a workbook, watching the mist bunch together on the paper. Somewhere she'd crossed from scribbles to spellcraft. Did she know? Was there some special ink required? What put the magic into the paper? All good questions, and I didn't want to know the answers.

The spring I turned eleven, temple guards captured a man with magic inside the cloistered gates. He was a harmless old gaffer who traded his skills as a tinker for fruit and honey grown inside the Celystra. There was no proof he'd been seditious, or even that he'd ever used his magic. By all accounts, he was a devout Celyst, and came to worship every week at the chapel, laying prayer stones for his family. He liked the convent children, and once brought a small girl a sugar mouse.

When he was exposed, they stripped him naked, cut off his hands and burned them, then suspended him upside down from the Hanging Ash, so he'd bleed to death right there in the green courtyard.

He was killed because someone had seen the magic on his skin.

Because I'd told my brother what I'd seen.

I learned to keep quiet after that, that my touch was dangerous, and secrecy was the only way to ensure survival. There was no way of knowing who to trust, so it became safer not to talk about it at all, just pretend I was like everybody else, I didn't see anything. And as soon as I could, I'd done the thing Meri and Durrel had thought so brave. I'd run away from that place and tried not to look back. Tegen was the only one who knew my secret, and he'd found out by accident. We never spoke of it, and he'd never told another living soul, until yelling, *Digger, run!* with a knife to his throat.

Was it like that for Meri? A fight to always stay hidden, stay unnoticed, pretend she was like everybody else? *My parents are heroes, you know.* Sarist heroes, of a rebellion that would have decriminalized magic. What was it like to be their daughter — their *magical* daughter?

I looked up, past the window seat, out into the snowy world below. Had she found someplace where she didn't have to hide, even for an hour a day, weather permitting?

Without thinking, I reached for the magic book, flipped it open, and laid my hand palm down on the pages, until I had one hand on the journal, one on the primer. The air turned watery and thick, shimmering against my skin. I could only *see* it, and how I hated the hiding and the fear. Being able to wield it must be unbearable.

Carefully, I closed the journal and the book and replaced them inside the hidden compartment. I did my job, tidying up the linen chest and the window seat, making sure the room was perfect and undisturbed. I laid out Meri's clothes, and changed into a fresh dress for the day.

And then I strapped Durrel's dagger to my thigh, right where it belonged.

I'd found what Daul wanted, but there was no way in seven hells I would give it up to him, not now.

# CHAPTER EIGHTEEN

I charged out of Meri's rooms with purpose but without direction. The hallways of Bryn Shaer were empty, and I scurried downstairs to where Lady Lyll would be waiting in the stillroom, but the little workroom was locked, and there was no answer when I tugged on the door. No Meri, no Lyll. I had Daul's journal, but couldn't give it to him. Full of energy and nowhere to fling it, I let myself back out into the courtyard, where wind and servants had swept most of the snow into the corners. It was a cold, clear day, and the rooks wheeled around the white tower, voicing their eerie cries into the thin air.

I stopped for a moment, watching them. Their movements were hypnotic, curving through the sky in smooth black arcs, like lines of ink on a blank page. Something tugged at my memory, but my thoughts were too scattered to draw it out.

One of the rooks dived toward the earth, a straight swift plummet — and my heart went with it. Daul.

I had *told* him about the Sarists in the woods.

Meri's Sarists.

I gave my bodice a yank and set across the courtyard at a run. Now that I knew where Meri had gone, I might actually be able to track her, but instead I turned back to the Lodge. Berdal had told me Daul spent mornings with Lord Antoch, so I headed for the Armory, a long, wide room linking the Lodge with the older Bryn Shaer, where the men often assembled while the women gathered in the solar.

Inside, Daul was fencing with Antoch, while Lord Wellyth and Eptin Cwalo rearranged the markers on a map table. I hung just inside the door. Antoch and Daul were oddly matched, and it was like watching a bear dodge a whip. Antoch moved with an unexpected fluid grace, like Meri when she danced, though Daul slashed at him with a frenzied focus, driving him back and back. Daul struck a point, to a round of applause from their audience — Marlytt and Phandre hanging on the arms of Lord Sposa and Lord Cardom — and Antoch gave a bow, handing over his sword.

Daul stepped back, wiping an arm against his forehead. "Let's go again."

"Nay, Remy, you've beaten me enough!" Antoch laughed. "Come sit by the fire and warm up." He turned away, but Daul grabbed his arm.

"Again." He raised his sword and darted back.

But Antoch turned slowly, with a dark look I'd never seen before. He took three swift paces toward Daul and caught him by the shoulder. "Have *done*," he said very softly, but the room almost shook with the warning in his voice.

Daul went rigid, gripping his weapon. I saw Marlytt stiffen, pulling slightly away from Lord Sposa. Then Antoch's face broke into a grin. "Come, brother — enough fighting for one morning. Peace?" He held out his hand.

Daul shook him off, stuck the practice swords carelessly into their rack, and stalked off across the room. I pulled back, deciding this probably wasn't the best moment to talk to him, but he stopped at a long table and poured himself a drink. Across the room, Lord Antoch shook his head and turned back to the fire.

Very well. Daul and Meri both accounted for. Now what? I wandered more slowly down the hallway, until I found myself back in the courtyard once more. I looked up at the white tower, still occupied by its family of rooks, marching along the crenellated battlement, poking their beaks through the narrow slits. Why did that seem so strangely familiar — and significant? I watched them, tapping my fingers against my lips, until I finally tapped something loose.

I slipped back inside, straight for the stillroom, and nicked Lady Lyll's account ledger. I would have to bring it back *immediately*, of course — there was no way someone as efficient as Lady Lyll wouldn't notice it was missing. But tucked in the stairwell, I slowly flipped through the pages until I found the catalogue of the birds at Bryn Shaer:

Pigeons: 125
Falcons: 15
Gyrfalcons: 12 and two very fine
Drakes: 5
Crows: 24 by count

"I found you," I whispered into the neatly inked pages. *When is a pigeon not a bird?* I knew Lyll kept precise records, but I had been to Bryn Shaer's mews, and though everyone here enjoyed poultry and falconry as much as the next nob, they didn't have a hundred and twenty-five pigeons. I had seen one or two falcons, not a dozen or more. Lady Lyll had taken a careful account of something — something that would look innocent to prying eyes.

But it wasn't birds.

*A fowling-piece called a pigeon*, Cwalo had said. A gun.

I cornered Marlytt the next day. I had to drag her away from a tennis match between Daul and Lord Cardom (who was surprisingly good, for all his size). In the hall, she clutched at my arm, looking anxious.

"Digger, please be careful. Someone is bound to notice."

"Did you tell me Eptin Cwalo was an arms merchant?"

She just looked at me. "I suppose — why?"

I paced down the hall. Marlytt didn't need to be involved in this, but she was still my best source of information. "But you said he was from Yeris Volbann, didn't you? That's west of the Carskadons."

"Digger, you're talking nonsense."

"Am I? Cwalo came here with you and Daul — from Breijardarl. That's east. What was he doing over there?"

She gave her dainty shrug. "Exactly what he said he was doing — buying fruit and wine? I think you'd be glad of that too, that he and

Lyll so thoughtfully stocked the larders before we were all snowed in here."

I let her go. The Nemair had been sending shipments over the mountains for months before we arrived, and big things too: furniture, cloth, casks of ale, tapestries, all the fine wood and stone used to build the Lodge. The disassembled crates were stacked in the older part of the castle, but it would hardly be a difficult matter for a man as shrewd as Eptin Cwalo to label something "pears," when what was really inside was — gyrfalcons. It made too much sense; what good were new artillery walls without new artillery? What if Cwalo wasn't just a wine merchant desperate for daughters-in-law? Cardom, ships. Wellyth, timber. Sposa, grain. In his account of what the assembled families had to offer the Nemair, he'd left one out: *Cwalo, guns.*

It was like having an itch under my corset — it was going to niggle away at me until I scratched it. *Daul* was going to niggle at me. With a whistle and a wave to the rooks who'd given me the idea, I set off to find Bryn Shaer's missing birds.

My search took me back to the old part of the castle and its raised battlements. I wanted another look at the walls — not that I'd know what I was looking at. Maybe I could persuade Eptin Cwalo to give me another tour. Marau's balls. A stair inside the white tower wound up to a wide walkway overlooking the whole castle. Arrow loops spiraled up alongside it, making a series of tiny windows in all directions. I remembered Antoch miming a firearm on the battlement. Would these tiny slits be useful for the new artillery, or were we too far away from anything to get good range?

And then I banged my head softly against the wall for even having such a thought.

I pushed my way through a short arched door onto a raised walkway ringing the tower. Wind whipped at my head. I could see all of Bryn Shaer's lands, down to the dip of the Breijarda Velde. Men and dogs were still working at clearing the snow, and from up here, they looked tiny and ineffectual. They probably looked tiny and ineffectual down there too.

Something in the snowy distance closer to the castle caught my eye — a lone figure on a white horse, bundled in a red coat, streaming across the white fields toward the trees. *Oh, Meri,* I thought. *We need to teach you a thing or two about stealth.*

And then I remembered she had eluded me already, and kept her lone morning jaunts a secret to everyone except perhaps the groom. Maybe she wasn't doing too badly on her own after all.

I pulled my coat closer and tried to recall what Cwalo and Antoch had told me about defending Bryn Shaer. The way they had talked about artillery and artillery walls, it had sounded more hypothetical than real, but there were five main towers — each corner of the outer bailey, the white tower I stood upon, and a square gatehouse perched right above the sheer drop Cwalo had so enthusiastically pointed out to me. Five towers, five drakes. Even I knew you'd need a *big* gun to defend a tower. Like a cannon.

So where were they?

Behind me, I heard the door being shoved open. Startled, I spun, and Daul stepped out onto the ledge with me.

"What are you doing here?" I glanced past him; the curve of the tower partially blocked his view of Meri, moving with excruciating delay toward the fringe of trees. I made a mad decision and headed *toward* him.

"Looking for Sarists?" he said, a note of amusement in his voice.

"Of course I am," I snapped. "Don't you know they've added snow and crow droppings to the Inquisition's Catalogue of Transgression?" I made to push past him, but his arm came up and blocked my path.

"Not so fast. Any more entertaining lies to sell me this morning?"

"What?"

"Sarists in the woods," he said, his voice a low, dangerous slip of sound. "Very diverting. You truly are Tiboran's own child. To think I very nearly believed you."

"I wasn't —" I stopped myself just in time. "You didn't find them."

"'You didn't find them,'" he echoed. "You're fortunate I enjoy riding out into the wilderness chasing the fantasies of little girls, but I would advise you to adhere more closely to the truth than you're probably accustomed to, if you don't want me to dissolve our little partnership."

"Good! I wish you would."

Daul leaned in close enough that I could smell his clove-scented breath. "I think you misunderstand me. If you stop working for me, little mouse, you'll never work for anyone again." The icy wind shrieked around the tower. "Just remember how many sheer drops there are in these mountains, and how very much snow."

I pulled back. "I'm tired of your threats," I said, but I sounded unconvincing.

He held my arm and squeezed. "Show me some good work, then, and perhaps I won't feel so compelled to make them."

Below us, Meri had finally reached the woods. Smoothly she dismounted and tethered her horse to a tree. And then *just stood there*, stroking its nose.

"Why are you doing this? Going after the Nemair?"

His gaze went straight over my head, out into some shadowy distance. "Because someone has to. You know that too — I've seen the way you look at them. What is it you called them — nobs? Men like Antoch Nemair think they can get away with anything, and it has to stop. He'll find out soon enough that lands and a title won't protect him from the Goddess's justice."

"I don't understand."

His gaze fell on me, clear and sharp as ever. "You don't need to understand. You need only to obey. Go along now; I believe you have a report due."

I wasn't *budging*, not until Meri disappeared into those dark trees. "Report of what?" I asked wildly. "I haven't found anything else!" Just the hints from Cwalo and Lady Lyll's weird notations, which, without evidence, added up to exactly nothing. Oh, yes, and the little matter of magical Merista Nemair and the wizards in the woods.

A figure in violet, with a fair pale head, stepped out of the trees and opened his arms to Meri. Stagne. I had to keep Daul occupied until they turned back into the forest.

"What's in that journal you want so badly? Don't you have enough evidence yet to send your Greenmen friends?"

Daul's expression darkened. "No. The journal is . . . a personal interest."

"A personal interest?" I repeated. Mainly because Meri and Stagne were still lingering by Meri's horse, stroking and patting it. Sweet Tiboran — was I going to have to kiss the man? "I charge extra for personal interest."

"Enough." He loomed over me, and for a moment really looked like he could send me over the edge, and it would be nothing for him. "What was amusing grows tiresome. Do the work you're capable of, or there will be consequences."

"Wait — what about this?" In desperation, I dipped into my bodice and pulled out the letters I'd been carrying for weeks, crumpled and warm from being up against my body. "They're not from Bryn Shaer, but I think they might be useful to you, in some way."

Daul's gaze sharpened, and he released his grip on my arm. I used my freedom to unfold Chavel's letters. "Look. Here's a letter from Secretary Chavel to somebody in Corlesanne — asking after 'friends' in Varenzia. That could be suspicious," I added hopefully. "I don't know what that second page is, but that last one —"

Daul's eyes lifting over the paper and settling on my face were enough to stop me cold.

"Well, you can see for yourself," I finished.

"Where did you come by these?"

I shrugged. "Are they any use to you?"

Daul was difficult to read, but he gave the third letter — the one that had so shocked Marlytt with its news of a royal bounty on Prince Wierolf — only a cursory glance.

"I thought that was the important one," I said. "That's not news — a price on Prince Wierolf's head?"

Daul gave a mirthless laugh. "No, little mouse, that's not news." He folded the letters carefully and slipped them inside his doublet. "In fact, they're worse than worthless."

"Then why are you keeping them?"

That slow, dangerous smile I was coming to hate. "Because clearly they have some value to *you.*"

"Give them back, then!"

"When you bring me something I can use. Incriminating letters written *by the Nemair.* Evidence of treason. My journal."

I glanced down to the woods. Meri and her purple friend had stepped *away* from the trees. If Daul turned to go now, there was no question he'd see them. I grabbed for one last wild chance. "Stockpiled weapons?"

Daul wheeled around and looked hard at me. "Did you say weapons? Firearms?"

I stepped back, nodding warily.

Daul broke into a wide, wolfish smile. "But that would be a grave offense," he said. "According to the Covenant of Kalorjn — which Antoch himself signed — former Sarists are strictly prohibited from owning any artillery, let alone raising a standing army. If the king were to find out that the Nemair were secretly buying and storing weapons on this property . . ."

"I get my life back?"

"Exactly, little mouse."


Meri had actually given me the best place to start looking, the very day we'd arrived here: *Tunnels under the castle, all the way to Breijardarl.*

Lyll and Antoch had made it very plain that those tunnels were in dangerous disrepair, that they weren't part of the restoration. But if the tunnels were one of Bryn Shaer's most important defenses, then surely they'd want to make sure they were as war-ready as the walls and towers.

And just a tiny thread of a voice whispered that those tunnels went to Breijardarl. Right *under* the snow-blocked pass. Away from Daul and too-shrewd merchants and wizards lurking in the trees and Sarist revolutionaries planning their next rebellion.

And Greenmen waiting for Daul's report. My report.

After leaving Daul, I joined Lady Lyll in the stillroom, where she put me to work sorting through a bowl of seedpods. She stood with her back to me, cataloguing our work, moving easily through the motions of labeling bottles and scribing notes in her ledger. The heavy pleats of her skirt fell in smooth, even folds that never seemed to wrinkle. Watching her now, it seemed impossible that this peaceful woman might be mixing up a war as deftly as she stirred a batch of headache tincture. I *wanted* it to seem impossible. I wanted her to just be Meri's mother, the bighearted, soft woman who had taken me in without a question. I wanted to be a girl who didn't find that suspicious.

"Milady, did you once tell me there were tunnels to Breijardarl underneath the castle?" I blurted it out like that, hoping — I don't know for what. For her to laugh and give me some reason to think I was crazy, that Daul was crazy and a bird was a bird, and for her to put her hand on my head and smooth my hair and say, *Digger, you worry too much.*

Lady Lyll scrubbed with a rag at a stain on her workbench. "There were. Before Llyvraneth was one nation, there was frequent fighting between Kellespau and Briddja Nul — particularly who laid claim to exactly what land in the mountains. Bryn Shaer was constantly in dispute, so one of the landholders — Ragnhald Shortbones, I believe he was called! — supervised the excavation of almost the entire mountain between here and the pass. It was really quite an amazing undertaking. Though of course they had magic to help, in those days. I don't know how you'd accomplish such a thing without it."

I buried my hands deep in the seeds and let them pour through my fingers. "I'd love to see them."

Lady Lyll turned to me with a smile. "Wouldn't it be exciting to explore them? Unfortunately, the cellars here are unstable, and part of the tunnels collapsed about a hundred years ago. There's been no reason to open them up again, of course, now that Briddja Nul and Kellespau are at peace. Not to mention the expense. Even Antoch and I haven't been more than a few hundred yards inside them."

"Oh," I said, and I was almost relieved.

"And so I must urge you, Celyn — I know how much you like to wander off by yourself — not to go looking for them. It's much too dangerous. I can't imagine what we'd tell your brother if anything should happen to you."

I blinked at her. Her broad face looked gentle, genuine, but there was a core of iron in her words, just the slightest edge of something I couldn't make out. She *never* mentioned my brother; was that meant to be a threat of some kind? Or merely the sensible cautions of an overprotective mother? I shook my head, said, "No, milady," and told myself that I was definitely imagining things.

I rose to join her at the workbench, but I set the bowl too close to the edge, and Lyll's next movement knocked it to the floor, scattering seed-pods everywhere. I bit back a curse.

"No matter," Lyll said. "We'll just count them again." She crouched on the floor with me to gather the spilled seeds. The spiky pods snagged in the fringe of the rug as I picked them up, lifting the corner of the rug off the floor, and I couldn't help peeking under it.

Impossible. Tiboran didn't love me this much. I glanced toward Lyll, but her back was to me, so I lifted the rug as high as I dared, and reached my hand under.

My searching fingers found something that was not a lost seed: a cold smooth curve of iron in a recess big enough for my hand. I pulled my hand back and gave it a look to be certain. In Lady Lyll's stillroom, set into the flagstones and hidden under a rug, was the iron pull ring of a nice-sized trapdoor.

I love trapdoors. They mean secrets and hiding places and the thrill of discovering things you were never meant to see. Of course, this one might be nothing more than a cold-box, set into the chilly floor and the cool stone beneath to keep perishable medicines fresh. But then why hide it with a rug?

I could find out right now — flip the rug back, grab the handle, and haul it open with Lady Lyll watching, there to explain away its very mundane purpose. And lose my chance at anything that might *really* be hidden down there.

I folded back the edge of the rug and smoothed the fringe. *Tonight*, I promised it.

# PART III
# DON'T GET INVOLVED

# CHAPTER NINETEEN

The hours until Bryn Shaer fell asleep were an agony of mindless impossible boredom in the stillroom and solar and Round Court. I felt edgier than I had since that first nob banquet at Favom Court — was it only a month ago? Though we'd been ticking off the days until Meri's *kernja-velde*, my sense of the time passing had been buried by the barricade of snow, added to almost every day, that trapped me here in Bryn Shaer.

Finally, finally, the family and guests all went to bed, and by some miracle Meri fell instantly asleep beside me. I slipped out of bed and crept down the servants' stair to the kitchens. I had timed my hour precisely; the kitchen staff was asleep and I passed no servants on my way.

I slipped my lock pick from my seam and tumbled the stillroom lock. With the door shut behind me, the light from the hallway was swallowed up immediately. Inside the stillroom it was dark and freezing; the moonslight filtering through the small, high window didn't help much, but I had some good idea where I was going.

I knelt on the floor by the workbench, flipped back the rug, and, cringing against the possible shriek of stubborn hinges — and the possible disappointment of a cavity full of chilled medicines — heaved hard on the pull ring. It came open easily, revealing a square opening large enough for a person to fit through. I flattened myself to the floor and reached a hand down into the hole. I don't know what I expected — a cache of documents, perhaps, maybe valuables — but my outstretched fingers found nothing, brushed nothing but darkness. I scowled. Nobody took this much care to hide an empty *hole*.

I peeled myself from the floor and rolled a scrap of paper into a taper that I lit from the tinderbox on the workbench. Carefully I lowered the burning taper into the hole and found what I was hoping for: stairs. Moving slowly so the taper didn't blow out, I slid feetfirst over the polished edge of the opening and dropped easily down onto the stone floor below.

Well. I was in it now. The opening above me glowed with square silver light, making it easy to see the distance I'd have to climb to get out again. One good jump, and I'd be able to grab the edges. But that was for later. I gathered my skirts in one hand and edged downward, the flickering taper throwing the passage into uneven light.

The stairs twisted downward in a tight spiral, each tread barely wide enough for even my small feet; this passage had been constructed for secrecy, not for convenience. There was no dust on the stairs, but I didn't know if that was because they were used often, or just that no dust ever found its way this deep.

When I found myself on flat ground once more, I paused for a moment, feeling the darkness press all around me. When I was small, I'd spent a lot of time hiding in dark spaces like this — tucked behind shelves in a root cellar, or curled up tight in a catacomb. I felt safe in the dark and silence; the world went on, however wicked or righteous, far above, never touching the lives of the mice and spiders below.

The little landing was hardly big enough to turn around in, let alone conceal anything as bulky as a stash of firearms. I moved the taper in a slow arc, showing up the space I'd found myself in. Shadows flew out of its range, up into the darkness above me and against stone walls barely an arm's reach away. After turning three quarters of the way around the space, I came face-to with a smooth wooden wall.

Wood was good — it could conceal hinges, a squint with a view to the room beyond, a catch for a secret door. . . . I shone my dubious light over the wall and found a seam, tracing along it with my fingers until I felt the notched-out hollow of a latch. Just an easy toggle with my finger, and the door eased open, inching toward me with a click.

The overwhelming silence of the passage pressed in on me, making my rushing heartbeat feel as loud as stomping feet and slamming doors. Something was behind that door — something somebody didn't want found — and I was on the other side.

I grinned. *Perfect.*

I squeezed through the door, ready at any moment for someone's great hand to grab my shoulder and yank me bodily into — wherever. The taper lifted high, I squinted into the darkness. It seemed to be a relatively ordinary Bryn Shaer chamber, maybe a little smaller and less drafty than most. Bare stone floors, half-paneled walls, hardly any furniture. I stepped a little farther into the room, watching beneath the shadows, but could see nothing suspicious. No hidden cache of documents or weapons, no Sarist priestess tucked away under an eave, no secret alchemical laboratory.

I sighed. I was getting ready to shake out the taper before it burned my fingers, when I heard something.

I froze, listening. Was someone on the stair behind me? Or in the stillroom above, getting ready to close the trap? No — the sound was closer than that, and quieter.

Whoever had gone to the trouble to hide this room had also done me the favor of hanging a lamp beside the doorway. I lifted it down and lit it with the taper, and the chamber sprang into bobbing light.

The shadows in the far corner revealed themselves to be heavy woolen curtains draping an alcove, parted slightly in the center. I crept closer and lifted a hand to move the curtains aside. But my hand stopped midway, and the lamp swung as I stared at what lay behind the drapery.

It was a bed. With a man in it, fast asleep and breathing in fitful, gaspy breaths as his fingers curled and uncurled around the hem of his blankets. He was pale and sweaty, with dark curls sticking to his damp forehead. I sprang backward, nearly tripping on my own hem, and clamped my mouth tight to silence my own breathing. The light made a wild streak of brightness on the walls; I hastened to steady it, but not before it threw its light across the sleeping man's chest and abdomen, tightly wrapped in bandages seeped with blood.

Abruptly, I saw everything — the basin and sponges on the table behind his head, the roll of linen for bandages, the vials and packets of herbs. This wasn't a laboratory — it was a sickroom. And its injured occupant? The light also showed up the massive signet ring on his thumb — a rampant stag crowned with ivy — the mark of the House of Hanival, Llyvraneth's royal family.

My heart flew into a crazy rhythm, and I squeezed my fingers tight on the handle of the lamp to stop their trembling. Only a handful of people would wear such a sign. And only one of them was famously missing.

I should have turned back, rehung the lamp, climbed back up the stairs, pulled myself through the trapdoor, locked Lyll's door, slipped into bed beside Meri, and thought no more about it.

But I didn't.

Because in the next moment, exactly the wrong thing happened.

He woke up.

A muffled snore turned into a moan, and as the lantern light swung across his face, he winced and turned his head away. I lowered the light and shaded it behind my skirts, but I was too late. The flickering eyelids parted, and a frown formed on the sweaty forehead.

"Hullo," he said in a breathless voice, still thick with sleep.

I bobbed a curtsy.

"Are you supposed to be in here?"

One might ask the same question. "Of course," I improvised. "They've sent me to . . . see to your wound . . . s."

He tried to sit up, but grimaced. Impulsively I stepped closer to him, set the lantern on the table, and reached one arm behind him for support. Well, if this was the role I was going to play, I might as well fling myself into it. He had clearly once been a big man, but injury, sickness, or inactivity had wasted him, and he was not difficult for even tiny me to lift. Now propped up, he made a sound that was half sigh, half groan.

"Water?"

There was a pitcher behind him, and I poured out a cup, realizing, as I had to crack the ice on the surface, just how cold it really was in here. Shouldn't he have a fire going, hot bricks in his bed at the very least? Trying very much not to care, I lifted the cup to his lips. His own shaky hand came up to meet mine, steadying the vessel. He managed a sip or two before his head fell back, his eyes closed, breathing heavily.

"Thank you."

My mind raced. What had I stumbled onto this time? And what was I going to do about it? This was worse than finding the love letters Lord Keran had written to his squire. Worse than uncovering the plot to assassinate the Brion ambassador. This man, in this condition, in this castle, was more kinds of danger than I could count.

"Milady?"

I blinked and wrenched my thoughts back to the present moment.

"I —" He waved a hand weakly in a vague direction. I shook my head, not understanding. "I need the chamber pot."

Oh, gods. I won't record the details of the utter absurdity of me, Digger the gutter rat, dressed up like a nob, helping one of the dueling princes of Llyvraneth take a piss. But I'm sure I heard Tiboran laughing at me.

I finally got His Highness lowered back into his bed, with entirely too good a view of his bandages as I was maneuvering him about. Well, my cover was that I was here to see to his wounds, so see to them I would. Fortunately or unfortunately, I had cleaned up after enough bar fights to have a pretty good idea of what I was doing. I bade him sit up so that I could unwind the old wrappings, which I did as gingerly as possible. He was short of breath and too pale. And all the while, he looked at me out of deep brown eyes that harbored their own share of secrets, as if he wished to ask me something.

"What?" I was a little short, I admit it. He was leaning heavily against me as I peeled the linen strips from his bare chest.

"What's your name?" It came out in a gasp as I stripped the last bit of cloth from his skin, and he seized my hand and squeezed until I thought my fingers might break.

"Celyn," I gasped back. "You're hurting me."

"Sorry," he mumbled, freeing my hand. "It's just — stings a little."

The beads of sweat that had sprung up on his brow in this frigid room said it hurt a little worse than that. "Sorry," I echoed. "I'll try to be gentler." Under the bandages, his body was a horror. One giant gash, obviously a sword wound, stretched from his breastbone almost to his pelvis. Sickly green-and-violet bruising spread all across his flank, and one shoulder bore the marks of an arrow — or a musket ball — that had pierced straight through. His body had once been well-muscled, but now his skin hung slack and sallow. The largest wound had been stitched closed with neat, competent stitches that threw a brief, insane image of Lady Lyll and her embroidery into my mind. What in the name of all that was holy had happened to this man?

And how, by Marau, did he get *here*?

"This wound is inflamed," I said, indicating the sword gash. "What have they been treating it with?"

"There — there's a powder, in a packet —" He tried to gesture, and I reached behind him before he could strain himself. Inside the pouch was glittery gray dust.

"Silver. Good." It wasn't a treatment we'd had much access to in the back rooms of the Mask & Barrel, but of course one spared no expense when treating a prince. According to Lyll's herbal, the metal fought poison in a wound. I sprinkled a liberal amount down the length of the wound, wishing I could do more. If he didn't die from the injury, fever would take him. It was beyond a miracle that he was conscious and alert.

"Don't look so optimistic," he gasped out when I had finished rebinding the wounds and had him laid back as gently as I could. He tried to smile. "It's not that bad."

I stared at him. "You're dying. You must know that."

"Impossible. I'd be disappointing too many people." He winced. "Besides, I have this." His hand fumbled for the chain around his neck, with a bronze pendant like a small coin suspended from it. He held it out with shaking fingers, and I was just about to touch it, to see the design stamped in the metal, when he said, "It's magic."

I curled my fingers back. "Right." He had to be feverish to tell a total stranger that.

"I've worn it all my life," he said. "My nurse gave it to me. I guess I should thank her, shouldn't I?"

"Don't be premature," I said. "Those wounds are serious. How long have you been here?" The bruises weren't fresh, and the wound had had time to become infected.

The prince shook his head carefully. "If I had to guess, probably a couple of weeks."

Frowning, I pondered this. Before the avalanche? It had to be, but who had brought him here? There hadn't been any other new arrivals since then, and this man certainly hadn't gotten here on his own.

*This is not your business.* That voice was a very wise warning, and if I was smart, I would heed it. I rose from the side of the bed a little too quickly, and a shadow of pain flashed across the prince's face. "I — I have to go," I said. "They'll be looking for me."

"Don't go." The voice was a hollow thread, a weak plea from a man used to being obeyed.

"I have to. You're right — I'm not supposed to be here." A question crossed his eyes, and I forced a little smile. "I bribed the other girl to let me come in her place" — praying that there *was* another girl — "and she'll get in trouble if they find out. Please, don't tell anyone?"

He eyed me steadily, but I could see he was flagging. "On one condition," he breathed.

Damn. It was never good when your betters put conditions on things. I nodded.

"You'll come back and see me again?"

"Why?" His face had taken a grayish cast I didn't like. I rummaged among the vials until I found one that smelled right. Poppy. It was a dangerous decoction for a man in his condition — like I needed the death of the prince on my hands — but I feared pain would keep him awake. I dipped my little finger in the vial and held it to his lips. He shook his head.

"Not unless you promise to come back," he whispered, so softly I could barely hear him. His face was twisted with pain.

"Oh, all right!"

The prince parted his lips and allowed me to smear the poppy juice inside his mouth. "Tomorrow?"

I yanked my hand back. "Certainly not." But I caught a glimpse of something familiar in his dark eyes — something that all too often went with fatal wounds. Fear. Who was I to try and alleviate this man's pain and fear? Nobody, but he kept *staring* at me, damn it. "All right," I said. "Tomorrow. If I can get away."

His head sank back against the bed. "I'll be waiting."

Oh, gods. I got out of there as fast as I could.

# CHAPTER TWENTY

I didn't sleep that night, and by the time the mountains outside were tinged pink from the rising sun, I was in a rage of panic. I'd thought I'd understood what I was piecing together about the Nemair — the cryptic embroidery, their magical daughter, Bryn Shaer's new defenses, the possible gathering of weaponry — but this shook my neat stack of secrets into a pile of rubble and made everything else seem minor by comparison. They were hiding the missing prince, literally beneath our feet. Who else knew about him? Hardly anyone, surely, or why keep him down there in that freezing cell, instead of up in a guest room, where Lyll could tend to him properly? I'd seen Prince Wierolf's wounds; they weren't the wild random mess of cuts and bruises you'd pick up in a casual fight — even a bad one. They were made with skill and deadly intent. Everyone had heard the rumors, and I had seen the order, signed by the king, that put a price of five thousand sovereigns on his nephew's life. Clearly someone had tried to carry it out.

And I had given that order to Daul. Oh, hells. However the prince had come to be hidden down there, Daul was the last person who should find out about him. It didn't take much to figure out what his Greenmen friends would do with that information. As if Meri and her Sarists weren't bad enough, now I had the biggest secret in all of Llyvraneth to keep from him too.

This was getting exhausting.

I paced from the window to the bed. Meri was fast asleep, her breath a swirl of shimmer in the half-light. On another night, she'd have been the one awake, writing in her secret journal. I glanced back toward the window seat. Maybe I could use one secret to cover another.

Obviously the prince was worth more than the journal — more than any of the Nemair's secrets put together, for that matter — whatever it was that Daul was so interested in. Was there any chance Daul might back off and let me go if he finally got his hands on that book? Or would he keep pushing me until I gave up everything, turned over every loose stone in this castle until the secrets crawled out like beetles? Could I say, *Stop, enough, I won't do this anymore*? I couldn't risk it. I'd have to find a way to steadily dole out smaller secrets to him, or —

I knew what the "or" was. It wasn't just the pressure of revealing my deception to the Nemair anymore. Lady Lyll liked me. She'd be disappointed, but she might not *kill* me. But if Daul really had the connections he claimed —

*Or.*

I held my fingers just above Meri's fanned-out hair and let the thick, watery air waft between them. He was *not* going to find this out. The Inquisition would not have Meri. Maybe there was a way to give Daul exactly what he wanted, without risk to anyone else.

While Meri slept, I pulled out the hidden journal again. I stroked my fingers over the shakily written pages. That might work to my advantage, although where I was going to find a binding to match this —

I was crazy.

But I knew I could do it.

I was going to have to copy the whole damn book.

I awoke to a crick in my neck, the white fur mantle tucked around me, and Meri gone. Gods — what now? Stumbling to my feet, I almost fell over the breakfast tray. Meri — riding. Or not riding. My head was fuzzy from a night spent cramped — apparently — in the window seat. I'd done one thing right, at least: The hidden chamber under the bench was tightly shut, Meri's secrets safely tucked away inside.

I changed my smock and shook out my kirtle, did something more or less respectable with my hair, and headed off toward the stillroom. I told myself it was absolutely *not* to visit the prince again; I had to pretend everything was normal, for one thing — and for another, I still hadn't satisfied my curiosity about the bird-guns. The trapdoor in the stillroom was my only clue about the tunnels; could I help it if it also happened to lead to Wierolf?

I passed Phandre along the way, coming up the corridor in a sunny yellow gown, her hair bouncing as she walked. She gave me a significant look as we met.

"I'd call you lazy," she said, "but you were still dressed, so I think you were actually *up* all night. What were you doing, I wonder?" She twirled a packet of papers in her hand. "Something with Lord Daul?"

"What?"

"Don't snap at me," she said. "People are noticing. I'd say it takes a pair to set your aim on his lordship's best friend. But I don't think you have it in you."

I could have laughed, if I wasn't staring at her in astonishment. "Me and Daul? Sure."

Phandre shrugged. "Well, I don't know. Maybe there's something about gutter rats he finds exotic."

I knew better than to let her bait me. "Have Ludo's parents given their approval yet?" I asked sweetly. "Because I heard Lord Wellyth ask if Lyll knew any well-bred girls with no prospects. His granddaughter needs a governess."

Her face darkened briefly. "She wouldn't," she said, but there was doubt in her voice. I'd struck a nerve. "You're lying."

I wasn't, exactly: I *had* seen a letter from Lord Wellyth to his daughter-in-law, proposing "the Séthe girl" for just such a role. "Apparently she needs to learn how to shake her tail at everything that moves."

But Phandre wasn't listening anymore. She twisted the papers in her hand and stalked off down the hallway, back the way she'd come.

Downstairs, the stillroom was empty, so I went next door to the kitchens, where I managed to work out from Yselle's halting Llyvrin and my nonexistent Corles that Lady Lyll was in the solar this morning. I should go and make sure of that, but if Lyll saw me, I wouldn't get away again, and I had a command to appear from someone who outranked her. I had meant to ignore it, but it was like trying to set a bowl of cream out of reach of a cat. Sooner or later she'd nick in for a taste. I'd just have another nip down, take a proper light and see if Lyll's tunnel led anywhere else, and then *maybe* check in on the prince on my way out.

Accessing the hidden stair was even easier by daylight, even if I did have to crawl under the rug and pull the trapdoor shut above me. As I trotted down the twisting steps, I decided the architects who had designed this castle must have been great friends to Tiboran. This time I'd helped myself to one of the stillroom candles and I shined it now around the stairwell, looking for more doors or passages that had slipped past me last night. The prince's presence here made such a thing even more likely; there had to be a route in and out of his hidden chamber that made a little more sense than crawling underneath Lady Lyll's stillroom. That hardly seemed a practical way of bringing an injured man treatments or clearing away his soiled bandages and chamber pots. Chamber pots — *pox*! I'd been smart enough to carry the changed bandages away, and stuff them into one of the great ovens kept burning all night in the kitchens, but that hadn't even occurred to me. Oh, this was all kinds of foolishness, and I was being stupid about it, to boot.

The little landing at the foot of the stair seemed to lead nowhere else, though I tapped all around the space and inspected every crack in the wood with my candle. If there was another passage, it was through the prince's rooms. Of course.

He was awake this time, propped against the pillows with a tray beside him on the bed. He smiled weakly when I came in. "Hullo," he said hoarsely. "I thought I'd dreamed you."

"That would have been nice," I said, "but no. I'm as real as you. You are real, aren't you?"

Wincing, he maneuvered an arm out from beneath his linens. "This certainly feels all too real."

"I'll bet." The hanging lamp was lit already, and I stuck the candle in a brass holder on the shelf behind the bed. I glanced around the little room but, even with twice the light, there wasn't all that much to see.

Just the bed and the prayer stand and the shelf full of medicines. "When was the last time you had something for the pain?"

He closed his eyes briefly. "Someone was here a while ago; she gave me something. What time is it?"

"Morning, late," I said. "The other woman — does she always come in the way I came?" His dark eyes clouded over with confusion. "Never mind." The milk and bread looked untouched. "Did you eat anything?"

"She tried, but . . ." He trailed off.

I scowled. It didn't seem like Lady Lyll to leave a tray of food in bed with an invalid, but the prince clearly wasn't strong enough to move it himself. "Can you feed yourself?" That was probably not how a nurse was supposed to talk to a prince, so I tore off a piece of bread and dipped it into the milk, then held it up to his mouth. He took it, swallowing slowly. I gave him another couple of pieces, and though he seemed willing to try more, the bowl had been nearly full when it was left here with him, and I didn't want to arouse suspicion.

When I didn't offer any more, his fingers fumbled for the bread. I let him; all the better if he made a mess himself. I was looking around the room, trying to decide how I was going to tap my way around the paneled walls until one of them popped open and became a tunnel . . . without him noticing.

Abruptly, Wierolf's hand fell heavily to the tray, splashing milk. "Damn," he said weakly. "Thirty-one years old, and I have to be spoon-fed like a baby."

"You're tired. I should go —"

"You just got here." The protest was feeble and almost whiny and, damn me, he *was* the prince, even if nobody was going to say so. So I knelt beside the bed, my cold toes tucked under my skirts. "Tell me something, Lady —"

"Celyn," I said. "But I'm not a lady. I'm just a maid."

"Tell me something, Celyn just-a-maid."

I waited, but he didn't finish. "Milord?"

"Tell me something — anything. About yourself, about this place, about the weather. By the gods —" He broke off, a cough racking his whole body. His face twisted with pain, but he shook me off when I tried to help. At last he sank back down against the bed, pale and sweating. "Just — talk to . . . me." The last word was merely a movement of cracked lips.

"All right," I said finally. What I really wanted was for him to talk to *me*, but he obviously wasn't up to it. "It's winter," I began. "It's cold here; there's a lot of snow, and . . ." For the love of Tiboran, I was a better storyteller than *this*. What had happened to me?

I didn't know which way to lie, that was the problem. I didn't know what this man knew, what he was supposed to know, and who might be keeping what from him, and why. And until I knew that, I had no idea what to say or not say.

"I saw a lion once," I said utterly at random. "At a street carnival in Gerse. Its fur was gold, and it had huge golden eyes that looked right at you, like it knew every secret you ever had. They had a baby there too, and for a silver piece they'd let you hold it. It was heavy and soft — the softest thing you've ever touched. Softer than velvet." I was looking at my hands as I told that stupid story that wasn't even a story, just a scrap of pointless memory, and the prince was silent so long I decided he'd fallen asleep. But when I looked up at him, his head was turned toward me, and he was listening to every meaningless word I said, great dark eyes watching me intently. "It — it reminded me of the sun," I finished lamely. I didn't even know what that meant.

"Go on," he whispered.

"I —" I faltered. "There isn't any more to tell."

"Gerse," he murmured. "Is that where you're from?"

I nodded.

"I thought so — your voice . . ." He briefly closed his eyes, as if gathering strength. "Where were you raised?"

"At the Celystra," I said without thinking, and could have bitten back the words. His dark eyes were still on me. *Like they knew every secret you ever had.* I dropped my gaze.

186

"Convent school," the prince said. "I'll wager you don't miss that."

"You have no idea," I said, and thought he smiled.

He turned his head a little, working his eyes. I wondered if the pain — or the poison in his wound — might be making him dizzy. "How did you end up here, Celyn just-a-maid?"

"Milord, I ask myself that question *daily*."

A sound squeaked out of him, raw and painful. It took me a moment to realize it was a laugh. Surprising myself, I grinned back. It made me daring. "What about you, milord? You haven't told me your name."

A sigh. "My name," he said, his voice raspy. "I don't get asked that very often. I think . . . I'll be no one for a while. See what that's like."

"Fair enough," I said. I wasn't going to be the one to press someone about his identity. "You'll like being no one. It's better than commonly reported."

"Is it?"

"Oh, yes. Nobody expects anything of you, nobody makes demands on you, and if nobody knows who you are, you can be anyone you want. I highly recommend it."

"It sounds splendid," the prince said, but my list had spun out further in my mind: *Nobody tries to kill you.* Did he know his own uncle had ordered his death? I shivered in the icy room.

The prince was clutching at the little amulet he wore, his face drawn tight.

"Can I see that?"

He leaned forward so I could lift it from his neck. I held it by the chain and gradually pooled it into my palm, until the bronze pendant touched my hand, and the magic around it shifted and swam, twining across my fingers, my wrist. The prince winced and put his hand to the bandage on his chest.

"It doesn't seem like it's working." As gently as I could, I hung the pendant back around his neck.

"I don't know, it hurts, and she's not sure why it's taking so long to heal. Maybe —"

I thought through what I'd learned from Lady Lyll in the stillroom, but kept staring at the pendant, the way it fell against the bandages, and — *pox*! I was seven kinds of a fool.

"Are they still treating you with silver?" He just blinked at me. Lyll must not have known about the amulet. "Silver inhibits magic. You've got — two kinds of medicine there, magical and mundane, and they're fighting each other."

He eyed me strangely. "You didn't learn that in the Celystra," he said, surprising a laugh right out of me.

"I should go," I finally said. "You need to rest."

"All I do is rest." He sounded petulant again.

"Yes, and why is that, do you think?"

"Point taken," he said. "Very well, Celyn just-a-maid. You may go. But come back again with more stories of Gersin lions." He settled back against the pillows, closing his eyes.

I'd been dismissed, but I lingered as he fell asleep again, then crept around the perimeter of the room, casting my candle over all the seams in the paneled walls until I found one that matched the way I'd let myself in. It wasn't even that well concealed; it was just so dim in here that it looked more like a wall than a door. I cracked it open, shining my light into the hollow behind it, but the shadows were too deep for the candle's glow to penetrate. Wierolf shifted restlessly on the bed, and I slipped through the door, feeling it click shut behind me.

The thrill wore off abruptly. The passage continued straight — east, at a guess, though it was hard to be sure, underground — for a few dozen yards, then ended at a short flight of stairs that opened out behind a storage bench in the kennels outside. The dogs gave me a roaring welcome as I popped up between the cages. Convenient, perhaps, but not exactly good for stealth. And utterly free of firearms. The only birds here were the real kind, rooks perched low, taunting the dogs.

Meri was still out on her "ride" when I dragged myself back up to her rooms. I used the time to gather supplies for my new project: forging a copy of Daul's journal. Ink and pens we had aplenty, but leather for the binding and pages to match were going to take a little more effort. Meri's magical fingertips had left flickering traces of power on some of the journal's pages, but mostly the book behaved itself. The whole thing was about eighty pages, written in a smooth swift hand; with a little practice I would have that script down as naturally as if it were my own. Daul would never know the difference. I'd made a living making sure of that.

I wrote a few quick practice lines to see how hard it would be, feeding the sample pages into the fire when I was done. The careful, familiar work was soothing, but every time I looked up from the page, my thoughts drifted down to the prince below, or out into the snowy morning with Meri. To Daul. Normally I liked secrets, but these were beginning to wear on me. I could have spent the whole winter in cozy luxury, with nothing more difficult to do than labeling medicine bottles — but I'd had to go poking my fingers where they didn't belong. And now I was caught in a tangle of lives, lies, and mysteries that had nothing and everything to do with me.

Meri finally came in, half soaked, her thick hair speckled white with melting flakes. I'd watched out the window for her approach, and had cleared away all the signs of my work.

"Celyn — mulled wine! How clever of you." Meri crossed the room and shed her gloves, dropping them on the tapestry tuffet.

"Did you and your father have a good ride?" My voice sounded sharp.

"Snowy," she said, sinking down beside me. "It got a lot colder than I expected." She looked out the window, into the thickening snowfall, and I wondered where her gaze tracked to.

"Meri, you would tell me, wouldn't you, if you had a secret?"

She blinked at me in surprise. "A secret? What do you mean?"

I shrugged. "You know, anything. Like if you had — a lover, or something?"

"A lover? Celyn, what in the world are you talking about?" She seemed guileless, confused. "If I had a lover, you can be sure I wouldn't keep him a secret!" She laughed. "And anything else? Of course I would tell you.

Unless I was commanded not to by my lord father and lady mother, of course. But those would be official secrets that really weren't my right to dispose of any way I wished to."

And that was the crux of the problem before me. The things I knew, I had no right to know. They weren't my secrets to keep or give away. "I'm no good at secrets," I said, looking at the patterns in the red and gold of the tuffet. "I always have to tell *somebody*, or I'll go mad with the feeling — it's like holding on to a hot ember."

Meri gave me an odd look for a moment, and then smiled. "Well, then," she said, "I guess I shan't be telling you any of my secrets, after all!" She stood and brushed droplets of melted snow from her skirts. "I'm soaked," she said. "Help me change?"

She raised her arms expectantly, so I came to her side and unlaced her wool riding gown. The folds of heavy damp fabric slipped easily to the floor. Beneath the wool gown and her linen kirtle, her smock was very sheer, and as I helped her step out of the kirtle, I thought I saw something strange. Crossing the boundary between curiosity and shocking rudeness, I pulled her smock down off her shoulder, exposing the bare pale flesh — and the tiny tattoo, still slightly pink and swollen, at the base of her shoulder blade.

The purple tattoo.

Of a seven-pointed star.

I stood there like an idiot, the corner of her smock still in my hand, too stunned to say anything.

"Celyn!" Meri pulled away, tugging it back over her shoulder.

"Meri, are you *crazy*?"

"What?" She held the smock closed with one hand balled up at her breast. "It's nothing."

"Nothing? A *tattoo*? And — and of —" Ridiculously, I almost couldn't bring myself to say it. I had to whisper. "*The Mark of Sar*? When did you get this? *Where* did you get it? Who gave this to you?" Who would have the skills — and the nerve — to commit such a work of madness? Branding the Mark of Sar into the heir to Bryn Shaer?

"I don't have to tell you anything!"

"No, you don't, but — what if someone saw it?"

She frowned. "Who's going to see it?"

"Anyone! Your mother — a seamstress! Your husband?"

She made a sound, but I couldn't tell if it was derisive or hopeless . . . or something else. "You have one."

Now how in the world would she know that? It was just my Guildmark, three tiny black dots on my hip. I'd had it since becoming a thief. Officially.

"I saw it once. In the bath." She sounded defensive.

"Meri, I don't think you realize how dangerous this is."

"I do!"

I grabbed for her shoulder again. "No, I don't think you really do! That's not something you do on a lark, for a thrill! What do you think would happen to you if someone found that?" I shoved my own sleeve back from my arm, revealing the gash that had faded into a long pink stripe on my forearm. "Look. Look! I didn't get this falling into some rosebush at the convent. I got it from Greenmen. *Greenmen*, Meri. I'm lucky that's all they did. And I don't have the Mark of Sar branded into my body."

Meri's eyes were wide and sober, but I saw a flash of defiance in them. I wanted to be proud of her. I also wanted to slap her, shake her, club her upside the head and drag her down the mountain by her hair. I wanted not to feel *anything* about this.

"Stagne," she whispered finally.

"The Sarist boy," I said, and she nodded. "Oh, Meri."

"But he's not my *lover*," she insisted. "At least — I don't know, Celyn. It's all so strange."

She didn't have to explain it to me. But apparently she was going to, anyway. They had met, entirely by accident, soon after Daul's arrival when she started riding out alone in the morning. Stagne had been gathering firewood near their camp and had foraged too close to the castle grounds. They had been meeting ever since, and —

When she faltered, I realized Meri was trying to figure out how to tell this story without mentioning magic. And I was just so tired, and I didn't have the energy to lie anymore, or keep one more secret. So I pulled off the silver bracelet and caught up her hand, holding it tightly right before both of our faces, so she could see the tendrils of magic weaving our fingers together.

"I knew it," she whispered.

I shook my head. "No, I just *see* it. It's not the same."

Her eyes were wide and eager. "Durrel said —"

"Durrel! What are you talking about?"

She was nodding, transfixed by the air swirling around our hands. "In the boat, he thought you had magic, and that's why you ran away from the Celystra, and he told my parents —"

"Your parents think I have magic?" I yanked my hand away so fast she stuck her stinging fingers in her mouth. "Pox and hells."

I felt stupid; thoughts died only half formed. "I *did* leave the Celystra because of my magic," I said slowly. "Because that's where they torture people with magic. You *have* to be more —"

Behind us, the door slammed, and we both jumped. In a flash, I draped Meri's gown across her shoulders and spun to face the door, my heart racing.

"Well, don't you two make a pretty picture," Phandre said, crossing the room. "I heard you yelling from halfway down the hall, and here I find you, practically naked in each other's arms! Is there something going on I don't know about?"

Her voice was teasing, but Meri's white skin flushed pink.

"I — got wet. In the snow," she stammered, her defiance evaporated.

"You don't have to explain it to me," Phandre said, raising her hands and walking through to her own room. "Let me know when the wine is hot." Her door shut with a click.

I didn't say anything else to Meri after Phandre was gone. What would have been the point? She had the tattoo — it was hers for life.

Until some Inquisitor's fire burned it off of her.

# CHAPTER TWENTY-ONE

I approached Marlytt after dinner that night. I had to secure some free hours in which to balance my growing list of insane responsibilities, and the prince was already eating into my schedule. "I need you to look after Meri for a while tonight," I said.

"I thought that was your job," she said, shifting in her seat. "What are you doing? It's something for Daul, isn't it?"

I leaned closer. Across the room, Meri was playing chess with her father; but she'd likely follow me if she saw me leave abruptly. "Just stay near her. Keep her entertained."

"And what will I tell her when she asks after you?"

"Anything. I don't care. I'm sure you'll find a way to keep her so busy she won't even wonder."

Marlytt's brow creased. "What's this all about, Digger?"

"Nothing. He's convinced himself the Nemair are up to something, and I need to get him off my back. So try and keep Meri out of trouble for a couple of hours, can't you?"

She softened. "All right. But what sort of trouble do you think she'll get into?"

"Don't ask that."

She fingered the necklace at her throat, her expression calculating. "Wait — is this what you were asking me earlier? About Cwalo — and guns? What are you involved in?"

"*Nothing*," I repeated. "And stop asking me questions you don't want the answers to. Can I count on you?"

She rose and shook out her skirts, giving me her sunniest smile. "Of course. Lady Meri and I will be close as sisters tonight."

I probably should have asked Marlytt to keep an eye on Daul instead; he was still skulking about, and I had a feeling he was expecting something from me. I hadn't come up with anything new since stupidly handing over Chavel's letters, and he'd be getting bored and restless. So I dodged him too.

I slipped upstairs to swipe Meri's journal, then lit off for an unused guest room in the old part of the castle. It was poorly furnished and freezing, with a broken window whose low stone sill I could use as a desk. Nobody was likely to find me up here. I'd need a few days at least for what I was going to do, and privacy and light to do it in. I kept waiting for Lady Lyll to ask me where all her candles were going.

Kneeling by the window, I spread my supplies on the cold floor: a stack of papers of approximately the right size from Cwalo's rooms, black leather and needles from the tack room, a variety of inks and pens I'd gathered here and there. I wrapped my fingertips in strips of cloth, to keep as much ink from my hands as I could. I didn't want Meri or Lyll to ask what I'd been writing, and I absolutely didn't need Daul sniffing around my fingers and getting suspicious.

Most thieves — common street scum, anyway — couldn't even read, let alone write. But I'd been clever with a pen since I'd first nicked one from my brother, wondering why he was carrying a feather around, when he scarcely ever went outside and certainly didn't care for birds. But he'd shown me that feather's amazing secret power, helping my little fingers master it. He'd sit for hours at one of the high Celystra desks with me in his lap, shaping my hand around the pen, tracing the letters on the page, until the day finally came when he judged me good enough to get me work in the manuscript room. My first memories were of those candlelit hours bent over words together. It was hard to believe we took such different lessons from our days writing out scripture.

Tegen had been fascinated by my writing, curving his lean body behind mine as I worked, swiping the pages before they were dry and holding them up to the light. "What's this say?" he'd ask, kissing the back of my neck to try and make my hand slip.

"It's a harbormaster's report, and if you don't give it back, it's going to say Lord Verin has been shipping Talancan *pigs* into Gerse instead of Talancan gold."

Harbormasters' reports, forged passage licenses, copies of sensitive letters — Tegen found me work doing all of it. I was good, and I knew it. Lord Taradyce had never found out the incriminating letter from Minister Engl he'd paid so handsomely for was a forgery. Tegen had gotten a better price from Engl to keep the original out of unfriendly hands. *She's just that good.* I could still remember Tegen telling the doubtful minister those words, how he'd laughed later over the double cross.

Daul's journal was a mix of strangely varied handwriting — in places smooth and precise; in others untidy, like it had been done in the dark, during a rainstorm, possibly by someone with a fever or a broken hand. And I had to match those bits, letter by letter, ink blot by ink blot, constantly recutting the tip of my quills to match the thickness and precision of the original text, testing on scraps to make sure I had the proper pressure on the pen.

It would have been an interesting challenge, if not for the sparkling pages that kept reminding me how important it was that I get this exactly right.

Revealing my magic to Meri didn't seem to change things between us, except she now considered me her confidante, which brought a whole layer of intimacy I could happily have done without. That night in bed, I heard more details of her tryst with Stagne, which sounded more heartbreakingly innocent the more I learned. And she wanted to talk about *magic* — what she was learning from the people in the forest, what it felt like, how it was to use it freely, to have a friend who understood her.

It took me a brief, paralyzing instant to realize that she meant me.

Lady Lyll knowing somehow bothered me more. As I worked beside her in the stillroom the next few days, preparing medicines I now gathered were going to treat the prince, I kept stealing sidelong glances at her, willing her to give up some clue that she suspected — had *always* suspected — me of harboring magic, like her daughter. It made my skin itch unpleasantly, thinking that I'd been working side by side all these weeks with someone who knew my secret.

And the more time I spent with Daul's journal, the more confused I became. I'd hoped copying it out might give me *some* hint at its importance to him, but I was more than halfway through and still couldn't see how it connected to the Nemair's secrets.

I wanted to put all the pieces together, and I had a feeling that the prince was at the heart of them. But I certainly couldn't just *ask* Lady Lyll what I wanted to know, so it seemed my only option was to keep slipping down to the hidden chamber under the stillroom, and prodding at the only person who seemed to know even less about what was going on than I did.

Those first few days the prince was still drifting in and out of fever dreams, and half the time I wasn't sure he even believed I was real. I expected him to slip up any moment and tell Lady Lyll — or whoever was tending to him — that a maid named Celyn had checked his bandages and dosed him up with poppy. But days went by and Lord Antoch's guards never seized me by the hair and had me flung into the dungeons, so I figured I was more or less safe.

"Someone's bound to find out I've been here," I said on my third or fourth visit. He was clear-eyed and lucid, but his face still had that ragged, sickly look. "I'm not helping you, and I don't even want to think about what they'll do if they catch me." I'd had the good sense to stop playing nurse, at least.

"You're helping. Look, I'm getting stronger already." He pushed himself up in bed to prove it, though the movement left him pale and breathless. "Besides, you're the only person who stays long enough to talk to me. The others hardly say anything — and I think that one of them doesn't speak any Llyvrin."

Yselle. So that answered one question. "She's Corles," I said. "I don't understand a word she says either."

"Tell me more about this place, Celyn just-a-maid. Where is it? What is its name, who are its keepers?"

"I —" I hesitated. I still wasn't sure what he knew, or was supposed to know — but then, he was the one in the most danger here, and Marau's balls, if the man was ever going to be king, starting off completely ignorant about his own situation was a stupid way to begin such a career. But maybe we two befuddled wretches could help each other. "Only if you tell me what happened to you."

Finally he nodded. "What I remember, anyway."

"You're at Bryn Shaer," I said. "It's a fortress in the Carskadon Mountains."

"I know it. I was in Olin . . ."

"Bryn Shaer is held by An —"

"Antoch Nemair." The prince gave a cough that sounded weak and strained. "Right. His wife — what's his wife's name?"

"Lady Lyllace." He mouthed the name even as I said it, his face screwed shut as he fought for the words. "Do you know them?"

"No, I just —" He didn't have to finish. He just knew the names of major nobs and landholders. Of course he did. "It's hard to remember," he said. "Thank you."

"Olin?" I prompted gently, the name twitching at my memory.

The prince looked at me a long moment, and I couldn't decide what was in that steady, unnerving gaze. Why didn't people mention *that* about him, when they told tales of what kind of a man he was? Finally he dropped his head back and spoke to the ceiling. "It's a hunting lodge. It belongs to an old friend of my mother. I was there for the stag."

I wondered what kind of figure he must have cut, just weeks ago, riding through the forest on his great royal horse, a bow in his hand. Suspecting this might be a long story, or at least a difficult one, I poured him some water. His hand lifting the cup to his mouth was steadier than it had been even a few days ago. Fighting with the silver in his wounds or not, that medallion he wore must be very powerful. I wondered what such a thing might be worth — a charmed pendant, to keep a prince alive.

"We had chased the quarry into a clearing, but when I got there, it was empty. My — companions were nowhere to be found, and nor was the deer." Wincing, he said, "I heard a shot, and I remember falling, and that's it. I don't know about —" He gestured to the bandages binding the gruesome sword wound. Then he turned to me, and the expression on his face was anguished. "Celyn," he said, "we don't use firearms for deer."

"No," I said gently, and although I had no idea if that were true or not, I understood what he was asking me. "Nor swords, I imagine."

"No." He looked into the distance then, and his eyes were damp. I fought a weird urge to reach out to him, although there wasn't a thing I could do to make what had happened to him any better. Lured by his friends into an assassination attempt? What did you do with that?

"You're very lucky," I said, though the words were hollow. How lucky did I feel when I got away from the Greenmen who'd killed Tegen? I pulled away and stared at my knees.

Finally I heard a sigh. Thinking it was my cue to leave, I rose, but the prince spoke again. "What kind of woman is she?"

I blinked. "Milord?"

"What kind of woman would you say Lady Lyllace is? Is she trust-worthy? Scheming? What is she like?"

"I —" Gods, how to answer that question? "Trustworthy? I hope so, though I haven't had cause to test that. She's — good, I think. Kind. Wise, strong. What?"

The prince was smiling strangely at me. "I hear your answer in your voice, Celyn just-a-maid. You've said enough."

*But I haven't even gotten to the best part yet*, I thought a little wildly: the collection of former Sarists, the possible rebellion she was planning, the guns she probably had stashed behind his room. . . . I pressed my head back against the ledge of wood behind me. "Milord, I think —" I took a hard swallow and launched myself toward madness. "I'm going to tell you some more names."

He eyed me strangely. "Go ahead."

I listed them all: Nemair, Cardom, Sposa, Wellyth, Séthe, and Daul. The fog from his injury had affected his memory, but if he'd managed to dredge up Lord Antoch and Lady Lyll, who'd been quietly living overseas for years now, then he should hear the rest. His face remained impassive when I started my list, but midway through I saw him start to tense up — just barely, just a hint of anxiety he was trying to hide. I had seen that look when I had tended his wounds.

A frown creasing his brow, he shifted himself into a new position. "Are those the other — guests? Wintering at Bryn Shaer?"

Somehow it didn't surprise me that he'd worked that out. "Do you know who they are?"

"Oh, yes." Wierolf said gravely.

"I just — I thought you should know."

"I'm glad. I think I need to have a conversation with the woman who changes my bandages."


Daul's journal remained an irritating distraction all that week. Though I made good progress on my forgery, I still had no idea why anyone would care so much about this dull little book. It didn't mention anyone or anything of note, beyond a few choice hunting grounds or notable huntsmen who'd died a hundred years before the writer put ink to paper. In fact, Meri's scrawlings, scattered throughout the book's once-empty pages, were the only thing of interest.

Once I had the text in hand, I turned my attention to the binding. It wasn't my best skill — lacing the pages into the leather cover involved a *needle*, and I was just sure I'd botch the job by bleeding all over it. The cross-shaped seal I'd nicked from Daul's desk was meant for pressing wax, not leather, but with the help of a little water and a heavy stone wrapped in linen, I was able to pound a convincing approximation of the seal of the House of Daul into the binding.

Finally, a little more than a week after finding the prince, I was done. It was good work: nice, the binding tight; the script convincing; the missing pages of Meri's notes now accounted for by a new set of page numbers. The one peculiar thing I noted was that a leaf at the very front had been sliced out of the original volume, so I carefully drew the point of Durrel's blade along the spine of my copy, nicking the leather with the tip, just like the real one. When I checked my work against the original, I saw that the scratches continued under its pasted-down endpapers.

Taking care not to tear anything, I slid the knife blade under. The glue was old and brittle and the whole sheet popped away in one piece, revealing a strange series of cut marks incised into the wrong side of the leather. It was as if someone very angry with the book had attacked it, but as I examined the scratches, I started to make out a meaning in all those sharp, intersecting diagonal lines. I took one of my pieces of scrap and laid it over the cover, tracing the lines lightly with a dry nib of my pen, until I had scratched the same shape into the paper. Meri would have recognized it: It matched her tattoo.

It was a peculiar thing: a Sarist's book, with a hidden Sarist symbol, but no Sarist content? I wondered yet again what Daul was after. In the end, the binding on the new one was a little less black, and a little less flexible — but I doubted Daul would notice.

I waited until Meri had ridden off to meet Stagne one morning, then slipped off for Daul's rooms.

"I have it. Let me in."

It was almost as if those words were the magical key that sprang the lock on that door. I should have tried them before. The door swung open, and Daul gave me a slow, thin smile.

"Mouse! This is an unexpected pleasure. I'd nearly given up on you, after your last report. Well, don't just stand there; let me see it." He stepped back and ushered me inside.

As usual, his rooms were much too hot. Daul's beard had gone scruffy, and apparently I'd interrupted him in the act of shaving, for he held a sharply curved blade in one hand. Calmly I passed him my work of the last several days. He stopped, stared hard at me for a moment in which I was very good and did not fidget at all, and then took the book from me, almost reverently. He held it in his palms a moment, and the strangest thing happened — he closed his eyes and seemed to slump just a little.

"Thank you," he said, and I stared at him. Thank you? From Daul? He held the book before him, thumbs stroking the leather. "Eighteen years." The words were a sigh.

"All right, so what is it?"

For a second there he almost looked like an ordinary person. "This book was written by my father. During the war. It's the only thing that could lift his mind away from the battles for a few moments."

I bit down on my tongue before I could say something unkind about military commanders staying focused on wars they were losing. Daul leafed through my pages, fingering the letters, and for the briefest of moments I almost felt sorry. His father had never touched this book, never written those words. The memory that Daul was experiencing now was a forgery.

"He left me a message in this book," Daul said quietly — and there, it was back: the edge in his voice.

I shook my head. "I don't think so. And yes, before you hit me, of *course* I read it." Unless he meant the star under the endpapers, but what did that say that the world didn't know already?

Daul actually smiled, a flash of genuine amusement that disappeared as soon as it was born. "It was a message to share," he said. "Half went to Antoch —" He held up the journal. "And half to me. 'In these pages, I have recorded the truth.'" He leafed through the text, reading swiftly, hungrily.

"What truth?"

"About Kalorjn." He shut the journal with a snap.

The truth about Kalorjn? He was the second person in recent days to say those words to me. "What does that mean?"

Daul's hard gaze came back up and met mine. "Before he died, my father was convinced he knew how we were betrayed. This will tell me what he knew."

"How? And why didn't you just ask Antoch for it?"

And like that, the moment of confidence was gone. Daul opened the drawer of his carved desk and withdrew a leather purse. "You have done very fine work today, my little thief," he said. "And since I am a fair man, a man who keeps his side of a bargain . . ." He took out a gold coin, gleaming brightly in the morning light. I almost didn't catch it when he tossed it to me — it was a *sovereign*, the highest coin of the realm, a coin so rich that no common person dealt with them. This was the money affairs of state were conducted in. I gaped at him. I wasn't even sure what I would do with that kind of coin. I could probably *buy* a ship to Talanca.

But that wasn't all he'd promised me. "I want my letters back."

He leaned back, as if considering me. "I think not."

"Why not? You said —"

"My, my. For a lying thief, you're awfully prickly about people keeping their word, aren't you?" He was slowly edging me back toward the door. "By the way, it looks like we can expect a break in the weather soon. Mail will be going through again; I'll be sure to send your regards to your brother."

He shut the door in my face. I stood outside, fuming. I had half a mind to bang on his door, but had the good sense to get out of there before I did something stupid. We were shortchanged on jobs sometimes; it was a hazard of our trade, since there was hardly anybody to complain to. I'd just have to get them back some other way.

I turned down the hall, forcing myself to walk calmly. The truth about Kalorjn? What did that mean? Cwalo had said there were questions that had never been answered — about the battle, about how the Sarists were betrayed. But Daul was at Kalorjn; surely he knew what had happened. And why would someone with his fingers in the Greenmens' purse care about an old battle that the Sarists had *lost*?

# CHAPTER TWENTY-TWO

An excitable Meri caught me by the hand as I got out of bed the next morning. "Come with me today," she pleaded. "They want to see you again."

I frowned, not really liking the sound of that, but reluctantly pulled myself into my heaviest kirtle and the wool damask coat they had given me. I suspected it had belonged to some Bryn Shaer child before me, but it was warm, which was all that mattered.

We walked, thank the gods, though I convinced Meri to take a more circuitous route with better cover: around the side of the old castle, in the shadow of the bailey walls, until we reached the woods pressing in on the northeast side. A few snowflakes drifted down from an overcast sky, and Meri's cheeks turned pink in the cold air. The last several days, much of my freedom had been bought because Meri and her parents were meeting privately with the suitors in the afternoons, which Meri recounted to me now, concluding with, "It's all very strange."

"Well, what do you think of them all? Are they nice?" *Do they appear to be making war against the Crown?*

"I do like Lord Cardom, and Lord Sposa has been very nice. But Celyn! What am I supposed to do about Stagne?"

"Do your parents know about him — about his friends?"

Meri looked shocked. "Of course not! Mother would be mortified, and Father would probably kill him. They wouldn't understand."

We reached the trees and ducked under snowy branches, and there, standing in a clearing just inside, was the fair-haired Stagne in a thick blue coat, and the wizard in gray whose power had so blinded me. He was still bright with it, but it wasn't so overwhelming now. Meri ran to them, but I hung back, the ominous warnings of Celystra masters echoing in my thoughts.

Meri spread her mittened hands wide to include us all. "Master Reynart, this is the girl you've asked me about, Celyn Contrare."

Reynart. That was the man I'd thought of as "Graymantle," and something about that name sounded vaguely familiar, but I couldn't place it. He bowed to me, and I squinted and stepped backward.

"And this is Stagne Crevin," she continued. The fair-haired boy came to her side and took her arm.

"Wait till you see what Master Reynart has devised for us today!" he said into her ear.

"More fire?" she asked, hope in her voice, and he grinned.

I followed Meri to their camp, saying little as Stagne and Reynart spoke with her. Our path brought us toward the mountain, to a ruined cemetery and a shrine to the gods, half reclaimed by the woods. A tendril of steam rose from an iron cooking pot set up in the doorway of a squat round crypt, tended by a plump woman with a crow perched on her shoulder.. The stone globes that marked the graves were dusted with snow, and the shrine's domed roof had fallen in, the icons inside missing or broken. A squirrel scampered about the snow-strewn rafters, kicking flakes onto the broken benches.

"We practice here," Stagne explained. "The power's stronger near Sar." He pointed to a white statue in the corner, the figure of a robed woman kneeling to kiss the earth, a blazing star like a halo behind her. Her face was a bashed-in scar of shattered rock, a vicious crack spreading down her neck and shoulder. The same blow had knocked some of the pointed tips from the star — but she was still very obviously Sar, goddess of magic.

I stepped across the branch blocking the threshold and approached the statue. I put a hand on the cracked marble, stroked fingers over the folds of the robe, poked the gilded star. "There's no magic here," I said without thinking, and then flinched from my own words.

Reynart looked at me quizzically. "No power here? What do you mean? Show me." His voice was curious and gentle, still with that low, rock-on-rock timbre to it. He gave me an encouraging nod.

"I — I'm not sure what to do."

Reynart passed his hand over the statue's head and body, and though I could see the air around his fingers waver and glow, none of it came up from the statue itself. I put my hand on her, and nothing happened. I shrugged.

"How do you know this?" Reynart said. "Forgive me —" He reached out his hand to take mine, and at my touch, the magic radiating from him flared up. He gave a little jump, and then laughed — an odd sound, full of surprise and pleasure. "I have never seen your power before," he said.

"It's not —" I stopped, because he *clearly* knew more about it than I did.

Reynart took my shoulder, still smiling at the way the magic arced between us when we touched. "Come, Celyn. Let us show you how we shape this gift the Goddess has given us."

And I spent that morning watching Reynart teach Meri and Stagne how to make magic. I was stunned and in awe of all of it — the ease and confidence with which Reynart moved and spoke, sparks occasionally flying from his hands as he demonstrated some point; the calm and accepting way Meri and her friend listened and worked; the impossible thing they were doing, here in broad daylight where anybody might see.

Meri knelt in rapt concentration before the statue of Sar, looking almost like she was praying, while Stagne crouched behind her, one hand pressed flat against her shoulder. Meri glowed steadily, looking hazy and indistinct, and I watched a wide band of power wrap itself up Stagne's arm, lifting strands of Meri's hair like static. He murmured words, low and unintelligible, and the magic seemed to roll across his body and up to his outstretched fingertips. A ball of magic hovered above his hand, then slowly turned from a thick haze to something invisible, licked by tongues of flame. He saw it, gave a yelp, and yanked his hand from Meri. The ball of fire vanished, sucked back to nothing in the cold. They both started laughing.

"We've never gotten that far before," Stagne said, sounding

triumphant. "Let's go again." He touched Meri's shoulder and turned back to the shrine.

Reynart explained that fire made a good place to start learning the manipulation of magic, because it was easy to turn the energy of magic into the energy of fire.

"Meri's magic is different," I said, watching them. I could not say how, exactly, except that it seemed . . . more solid, somehow. "Is it because she's a girl?"

Reynart looked pleased again. "No, it is because she is *Reijk-sarta*, a Channeler. The boy and I are *Kel-sarta*, you would say, I think, Casters? The Goddess requires two to work together to use her power: one to draw the magic up from the earth, and the other to shape it to its new form. Your Merista, she has much power, but she cannot make it leap and play and become flame or wind or weapon. The boy can bend the magic into a new form, but without the Channeler's power to draw from, he can do nothing. We do not know why, but the *Reijk-sarta* are very rare. We have not seen one for many years, so you may imagine how special she is to us.

"Stagne is a good boy," Reynart added, looking at them both. "He was abandoned by his parents in Breijardarl, and friends brought him to us."

"Friends?"

He drew me closer. "All across this island are those who take great risk to protect those with magic, and arrange safe passage for them across this land."

"Is that who you are? Is that why you're here — for Meri?"

"No. Ours is another purpose here. Finding Lady Merista was a happy accident."

I wanted to ask him more — what his plans for her were, what they were training her to do. *Fire or wind or weapon.* What did that mean? But Meri was on me, grabbing my arm and chattering excitedly.

"I wish you could stay and meet the others," she was saying. "You'll have to come back again, can she? They're wonderful — there's Kespa, she's their healer — I'm learning that — she has the dearest little baby. And Hosh, that's Stagne's dog —" and on and on. She waved to the woman with the cooking pot, who poured out a measure of soup for a little boy. Fireballs aside, these people hardly seemed the horrific threat the Inquisition would have everyone believe. Not if they'd been consigned to spending the winter camped out in the most remote part of Llyvraneth. What harm was that small boy with his soup? What harm was *Meri*? I flexed my fingers, but did not look down to see whether they were sparking.

"That's — that's a lot of you." I broke into Meri's chatter. Far more than I had seen the night I stumbled on their campfire. "Where is everyone?"

"They've been camping in the tunnels." Meri pointed across the cemetery to the little crypt.

"Tunnels?" I turned to look. "The Breijardarl tunnels? Can we see? I thought they were blocked off."

Reynart shook his head. "They're clear, all the way through the mountain. Perhaps unstable in places, but we've developed . . . methods of shoring them up."

I blinked at him, wondering how Lady Lyll would like knowing she had excavation contractors specializing in magic holding up the foundations of her castle. I turned to Meri. "Did you help with that?"

She nodded happily. I shook my head in amazement. Then something occurred to me. "You have somebody watching the other end, right? In Breijardarl?"

Reynart nodded. "Of course. There are many more of us than you realize."

"How many?"

"These are interesting questions for a lady-in-waiting," he said.

I flushed, remembering that I had told Daul about them. "If the Greenmen — the Inquisitor's men come through here, all of you will be the first to be targeted. Don't you care?"

Meri squeezed my arm. "You mean all of *us*, Celyn."

No, *no*, I most certainly did not mean that — but Reynart put a hand on me and said, "We have ways of protecting ourselves, of remaining hidden."

I watched the power swirling around his hand, bright as a flare where my skin touched his, and wondered. "Let's go back through the tunnels," I said to Meri. "You have a dress fitting, and your mother will be expecting us." And I had artillery to look for. Now more than ever.

I waited at the crypt door while Meri bade Stagne farewell, rising up on tiptoe to kiss him briefly on the lips. She led me confidently around the tombs, to a stairwell hidden beneath a plinth in the floor. She was changing, our timid little Meri. And for no accountable reason, that made me feel strange.

Meri lit the way with the glow from her own hands, and I wondered if this was part of the way she purged herself of excess power picked up while she was "Channeling." Pox, live until my tenth age and I would *never* get used to this.

"The tunnels do pass beneath the fields and into the woods, but mostly they go underneath the castle itself," Meri was saying. "And I guess some parts aren't really tunnels at all, more like extra storage rooms, wine cellars and such."

*And weird little hidden bedrooms*, I thought.

These tunnels were built to the same Bryn Shaer standards everywhere on the property, with arched brick ceilings and a hammered-earth floor that had turned nearly to rock over the years. I wanted to scurry like a rat down every dark turning of the entire network. Here and there we passed a bit of broken brick, or a spot of ceiling that seemed to sag — and I could see the patchwork the Sarists and Meri had done, bands of magic wound like straps around the weak parts.

"How long will it stay like that?" I asked, and Meri shrugged.

"Forever, I think. We used a permanent charm."

"You're learning so much," I said.

She shook her head, ducking as we crossed beneath a wide stone beam. "Oh, no. I can't imagine ever knowing as much as Reynart or even some of the others. They've been studying it all their lives, and I —" She trailed off, the glow of her hands fading just slightly. "Here, we're at the garden wall — that's the buttress we just passed under. The kitchens are just ahead."

Meri passed by another room, the bulky shapes within briefly illuminated by the swoop of light from her hands.

"Wait, Meri." I had another mission in these tunnels. "Can you shine your light here?"

Meri turned back and joined me, and we stepped into the little alcove. Inside the room were two long, canvas-covered humps. They were low to the ground and the wrong shape to be cannons, but there might be muskets wrapped up in there.

"Oh," Meri said. She added in a low, respectful whisper, "Those are the bodies of the avalanche victims."

"What?" I stepped closer, drawn by morbid curiosity. "I want to see."

Meri frowned, but stayed by the door and looked out into the hallway as I crept closer and pulled away the canvas covers. The bodies were pale and cold — it was freezing in here; apparently an appropriate place to store someone until you could bury him when the earth thawed out again. I knelt there with them, looking at their still forms, imagining what it must have been like to die like that, under a ton of snow.

"Who were they?" I was shivering, even wrapped in my heavy mountain coat. They did not seem to be related; one was heavy and muscular and fair, the other older, slighter, grizzled.

Meri shook her head. "No one knows. They don't belong to Bryn Shaer, so they must have been coming up from Breijardarl. Someone there will probably claim them in the spring."

Over their bodies I made the signs for Marau, meant to bring the crows to find them and carry their souls to the gods, although someone had done so already — their arms were laid out properly, one crossed over the chest, one pointing toward the feet. Their hands were bare, and the big one wore an onyx signet ring on the little finger of his left hand.

Inscribed into the stone was an arrow. Frowning, I looked at the other man. He wore the same ring.

"Meri, come and look at this." She approached and reluctantly shone her light on the bodies, where I pointed at the hands crossed over each man's chest. "Lord Daul has a ring just like that," I said, and she leaned in closer.

"What do you think it means?" she whispered.

"I wish I knew."

I took the rings, when Meri wasn't watching, wrestled them from the stiff cold fingers and stuck them inside my gloves. It was just one more thing that didn't fit — that two dead men were connected somehow with Daul? Who were they?

The arrow was the symbol of Zet, goddess of royalty and the hunt. Black was the color of Marau, god of death. What did Zet plus Marau make?

More math than my poor brain could figure out.

"Maybe it has something to do with hunting," Meri suggested as we covered the bodies and left. "A guild, or something?"

"Have you ever seen Daul go hunting?" I asked, knowing full well Daul never left the Lodge if he could help it. Probably because he hadn't had the benefit of his father's treatise on the subject. I choked back a half-hysterical laugh.

"Something to do with the war, maybe?" I said, but we dismissed that as well. The bigger man had been far too young to have fought with Daul and Antoch.

Well, there was only one answer: I was going to have to ask Daul himself.

Pox.


There were workmen in the Lesser Court, so that evening's entertainments were held in the Armory. Nobody had thought to modernize this room; it was Old Bryn Shaer, every inch: rusting shields and polearms on the stained walls; a massive iron cage of a chandelier; a great model landscape of Llyvraneth, left over from the last days when people had planned wars here. A fire blazed, flanked by life-sized marble Spear-Bearers of Zet, their stone hair flowing over their bare shoulders, naked bodies cleverly concealed behind their oblong shields.

Eptin Cwalo offered to walk me through the weapons displayed on the walls, but I declined, watching Daul instead. His moon charts were spread before him, but he seemed edgy and cold tonight, reading the fates of his fellow courtiers with less than his usual humor. When he predicted that Marlytt would have a fat husband and fat ugly children, her pale face reddened and her smile grew tight.

"I'm tired of this game. Let's have another," she said softly, pulling her hand away.

Something in Daul's face went very hard. He bowed to Lady Lyll and Lord Antoch, who clapped politely, then, to my dismay, he headed in my direction. I looked around desperately — but Cwalo was all the way on the other side of the room, pointing out the features of one of the fencing swords to Phandre and Lord Cardom. I turned to cross back to where the Nemair now chatted with Lord Wellyth, but Daul sidestepped me, cornering me near the map table. From across the room, I saw Phandre's gaze sharpen.

"What do you want?" I hissed. "People are staring."

He bent over the model landscape, tapping his fingers on its rim. On the map, Gerse was a mass of gray bricks in the south; the river Oss a painted silver ribbon stretching from the city; the Carskadon Mountains, built up with lumps of plaster, rising like the spine of some beast. Purple and green markers made of painted lead sat in the corners of the board, along with tiny matching flags.

I leaned against the wall, waiting for him to say something. But he ignored me, playing with the figures, placing flags and men across the board — purple on Tratua, western Gelnir, near Breijardarl, matching the markers to the families here at Bryn Shaer. There was something calculating and concentrated about his focus on the map, and I watched his eye draw repeatedly to the southeastern quadrant.

When Daul still didn't say anything, I picked up one of the green figures and tossed it into the air, catching it neatly. "What's that ring you always wear?"

He looked up sharply. "A sudden interest in me? Perhaps our little game has gone to your head."

"Some game," I snapped, my voice low. "But fair's fair. I bring you information all the time. Now I want some."

"You bring me worthless information!"

I jumped, and looked to see if anyone had noticed. But everyone else was occupied on the other side of the room, listening to Lord Antoch tell some amusing story. Almost everyone; Meri had turned toward me, brow furrowed with concern, but Marlytt's hand on her arm turned her back to the party. Daul's eyes were with mine, watching Antoch across the Armory. But he said, "My ring? Say it's a token of my commitment."

I scowled. "Commitment to what? What's the arrow mean?"

He turned back to the table, shifting some pieces on the map board. I watched him, perplexed. Across the room, Marlytt had evidently engaged Lord Sposa in conversation with Meri, pouring wine for both of them. *She'd* know precisely how to get a man to talk. Maybe I could use my own talent to annoy Daul to crack something open. "What's the matter? Bad news in the journal?"

For one cold, deadly moment, I thought he might actually hit me — there in front of everyone else. He gripped the edge of the map table. "Have a care for your tongue, little mouse," he said in a tight voice. "I fear it will get you in trouble someday."

"What did it say?" I pressed — but softly.

"Nothing. It said nothing. As I believe you mentioned, when you were so forthcoming about admitting you had read it." Daul took up one of the violet armies and flung it into the center of the map. It skidded on the rough surface and came to a stop at the foot of the bony spine of the Carskadons. "No matter. I know the truth of things, and Antoch does as well. I will just have to find some other way to prove it. He's the one. I know it."

"Celyn, come back to the fire," Meri called. My head shot around.

"In a minute," I called back in a strained voice, then whispered to Daul. "What are you talking about?"

Daul slowly drew one of the pawns down the southern tip of Gelnir, to a low sea-bordered plain between Gelnir and Kellespau. "Antoch Nemair is the Traitor of Kalorjn."

I stared at the armies scattered across Llyvraneth, and tried to make sense of the words Daul had just said. I heard Lord Antoch's huge, jolly laugh, the clink of glasses raising a toast. "He can't be," I said.

Daul turned on me. "Do not speak of things you cannot possibly understand."

"*That's* what this is about? You were never after Sarists?"

Daul looked darkly into the model landscape and its multicolored armies. "Oh, trust me, I am happy with whatever evidence of disloyalty you can find, but as I mentioned, this was a personal interest."

It was insane to be having this conversation, out in the open in front of everybody, but maybe Daul was half crazy. And me? Well, that was established.

"I thought you were after Lord Antoch because he *was* a Sarist," I said. "But now you say he betrayed them? I don't understand."

"Everything points to it!" Daul's normally measured voice verged on shrill. He leaned closer, speaking low and harsh. "How else is a man — an avowed Sarist, the left hand of the commander — appointed ambassador to Corlesanne, awarded a lavish mountain estate, allowed to escape the prosecution of his fellows — while the rest of us spend years in exile or prison?"

"I don't believe it," I said, just to fill up the dead, crushing quiet left after Daul's words. The trouble was, maybe I did. Prizes like Bryn Shaer and a post at a foreign court weren't things the king normally lavished on his mortal enemies. If Antoch was the traitor, if he had engineered the fall of the Sarists' last hope of rebellion . . . that might have been a valuable favor indeed for a grateful king.

"But Lyll told me they were sent overseas for helping you get out of prison."

Somehow Daul's cold gaze grew even icier. "That's the official story, is it? Don't believe everything they tell you, little mouse. I remember that gaol — twelve stinking years of it. Ask Antoch how long he spent there."

Laughter drifted closer, and Lord Antoch rose from his spot near the fireplace. "Remy, Remy — leave the poor girl alone. You'll put her off her dinner." He crossed the room in a few easy strides and threw a huge arm around Daul, who stiffened. "Celyn, my girl, this snake of a brother of mine isn't bothering you, is he?"

For a moment I felt dizzy. Daul couldn't be right.

Could he?

# CHAPTER TWENTY-THREE

All evening long I stole glances at Lord Antoch. Was he really a man who would send his own people to their deaths in return for a post at a foreign court and a run-down castle in the mountains? Daul was convinced, but I just didn't know — Antoch doted on Meri, and there was nothing but love in his gaze for his wife. But that was no good measure of what a person might do when pressed hard, or when tempted. And I knew better than anyone not to judge somebody by his relatives.

Lord Antoch's best friend was trying to destroy him. The prince insisted he was nobody. The wine merchant was an arms dealer. Lady Lyll was hiding *everything*, and Meri was a wizard. There had to be *somebody* in this castle who was exactly what he seemed, with no treacherous secrets or betrayals to conceal. There *had* to be.

And what about me, sneaking around spying, working for Daul? Why could I accept such treachery from Daul — or myself — but it seemed unforgivable in a person like Lord Antoch?

I was still stewing over it all the next morning when I ducked down to check on the prince.

"Celyn just-a-maid! You're just in time for my debut." Wierolf was sitting on the edge of his bed — in a shirt finally, thank the gods — and he held up his hand. "Wait — stand there." Very carefully, he pushed himself to standing, wavering only slightly. He took a few tentative steps, then lurched for me, grabbing my wrists.

"Very impressive," I said, leading him back to the bed. His color was better, and dressed now, he didn't look quite so frail. "You'll be storming the castle in no time."

This drew one of Wierolf's rare frowns. "I don't think so," he said quietly.

"What did Lady Lyllace say when you talked to her?" I asked.

"Surprisingly little," he said. "And I scared the other one when I tried to speak to her in Corles." With a sigh, Wierolf leaned back against his cushions. "What is going on here, Celyn? This place, with its mysterious silent keepers and spare accommodations and its strange little maids who show up in the middle of the night?"

I sank down as well. "I don't know." I thought for a moment. Maybe the missing piece to the puzzle upstairs could help untangle this whole mystery. "Do you know anything about the Battle of Kalorjn?"

"I've studied it, of course. The Sarist and Royalist forces were evenly matched, and the Sarists had the advantage of terrain. By rights they should have carried the day."

"I was thinking more about the end of the battle."

Wierolf turned, propping himself on his elbow. "The unknown traitor? Well, that's the great mystery, isn't it? There are rumors, theories — but only the dead know for certain."

"What theories?"

He shrugged. "Names, suspects — Daul, for one."

"Daul — Remy Daul?" I blinked.

"No, Senim. The commander. There's no evidence, of course."

"Did anyone ever say it might have been Antoch Nemair?"

He eased back and regarded me carefully, letting out a long, low whistle. "Are you serious?"

I stared at my hands and gave a shrug.

"All right," Wierolf said. "Let's think about this. The Sarists were defeated because they were given false intelligence about the size and movements of the Royalist troops. Nemair had command over the Sarists' right flank, which was supposed to protect against a charge coming at them on their seaward side. That charge never came, Nemair's men never mobilized, so Daul's forces faced the full brunt of the Royalist attack. By the time Nemair's men got word, it was too late. More than twenty-five hundred rebels were killed in the battle alone. Vorstig — the Royalist general — had the surviving common foot soldiers rounded up and executed. Their commanders were arrested."

I'd heard the rest of that story. "So . . . it *was* Nemair's fault? If he'd attacked when he should have —"

Wierolf turned up his hands. "Who can say? Most people give the blame to the reports he and Commander Daul relied on to plan their strategy. Unfortunately no one has ever been able to determine the source of that information."

"But how can they be sure it wasn't just a mistake?"

"No. The Royalist attack was too specific — they knew exactly where to strike, and how hard, knowing that a third of their opponents' forces would be distracted elsewhere. That could only have come from spies within Daul's camp."

I sighed. Maybe it *was* true.

The prince was watching me. "Look, I've never met the man, and apparently I'm not quite the judge of character I thought I was" — he gestured vaguely toward his wounds — "but everything I've heard of Antoch Nemair would suggest he's not your man."

I was silent, turning that over and over in my mind.

"Eighteen years is a long time. Maybe it doesn't matter anymore."

"It *does*." I was surprised at the vehemence in my voice.

Wierolf touched my arm with a cold hand. "Why?"

"Because it does." But Wierolf was right. Why did I even care? The Battle of Kalorjn had nothing to do with me. I sighed and tried to explain it, even to myself. "They took me in when — when I left the Celystra. They gave me a home and a post and a —" I faltered. "I just need to know."

"Would it change anything? He'd still be the man that took you in."

"The truth *always* changes things."

"He might not be the same man he was, eighteen years ago."

I made a skeptical sound. "People don't change that much."

Wierolf lay back against the pillows. "What happened to becoming anyone you want if nobody knows the truth?"

"That isn't what I meant."

"Oh," he said. "Because that's what it sounded like to me."

*   *   *

Meri was getting anxious and fussy. For the last several days, she'd been told to stay away from the Sarists' camp. The weather had been clear, and with no new snow to obscure her tracks leading to and from their little settlement, apparently Reynart felt it too risky for everyone for them to continue to meet, until he sent word that it was safe.

"Why can't you take the tunnels?"

She was actually *pacing* in front of her tall frosty windows. "Reynart said not to. They've gone deeper into the forest for some reason, and they're not camping in there anymore."

That was strange, but Meri didn't have an explanation for it. Was there something in those tunnels that Reynart and his men didn't want Meri to see? The bodies, perhaps? That didn't make sense.

"I have an idea," I said — before any such idea was even half formed. "Let's find out."

Meri looked at me blankly. "Find what out?"

I grinned up at her. "That's what I want to know."

She was a little harder to coax into an adventure than I'd expected, and we ran into an obstacle on the way: Berdal, outside in the snowy courtyard, mounting up on a tall brown horse. He was bundled heavily into his coat and mantle, a hat pulled low to protect his face. He lifted a hand in greeting.

"Morning, Lady Merista, Celyn. Haven't seen you much about these days."

I pulled my coat closer. "It's too cold out here. I have a soft post, inside."

Berdal grinned. I'd known boys like him all my life — common, plain-speaking lads who didn't cloak themselves in courtly flattery. Or conspiracy. I missed them.

"You can keep that," he said. "I'll take the fresh air out here any day." The horse made its own commentary just then and I gave Berdal a look. With a laugh, he said, "It still smells better in the barns, if you ask me."

Meri giggled. "I think so too."

I glanced at the horse and the heavy saddle packs. "Are you leaving?"

"It looks like we're finally getting a string of enough good weather to go on a mail-and-supply run down to the inn. I'll be back in about a week. Want me to carry a letter for you? I can wait." He smiled at me, wide and friendly, but at the word *mail*, my stomach clenched.

"Who's sending letters?" I tried to sound curious and casual.

He flipped the saddlebag open and pulled out a packet of papers. I edged nearer, trying to see. "Lady Nemair, that Lord Wellyth, and Sorja from the kitchens. Lady Merista, are you sure you don't have one to add? Maybe to that Decath cousin of yours?"

Not Daul. I restrained my relief. "I thought I heard Lord Daul mention a letter to — friends, in the city," I said. "Did he get that to you?"

"Nay, I've not seen Lord Daul," Berdal said. "Maybe I should wait —"

"Oh, I'm sure he wouldn't like to delay you," I said hastily. But I was confused. "Is — is this the first time mail's gone out, since the avalanche?"

"Aye."

"And there's no other way a message could have gotten out, before now?"

Meri was looking at me strangely. "Celyn, what are you talking about?"

I glanced at her. "Nothing," I said firmly, but my thoughts were astir. Why hadn't Daul sent his report? Did he have another way to get messages in and out of Bryn Shaer? "Let us know when you get back," I said to Berdal. "We can hand the letters around, so you won't have to breathe the foul air in the Lodge."

Berdal grinned again. "Deal." He swung up onto the horse and, clicking at it, turned and rode out through the snow.

We took the outside entrance Meri had shown me before, the one that led from the covered pentice down beneath the Lodge. Today we'd brought a conventional lamp and descended the narrow steps carefully.

"What are we looking for?" Meri asked. She was clutching my arm, which made it harder to maneuver in the dark, even with the light bouncing all over the low, arched walls.

"Show me the route you take to meet them."

She led me back through the freezing tunnels, and I shone the light into every corner and alcove. After an hour or so, we still hadn't seen anything suspicious — but I had to admit dragging Meri through dark tunnels wasn't a terrible way to spend a morning.

"How did you get that wine?" Meri asked abruptly. "That first night?"

"What?" We'd paused by a narrow gap in the stone, and I could see straight down the tunnel . . . into the back of the Lodge wine cellar. Well, why not? Cheaper to use the tunnels that had been here for centuries than dig your own. "I stole Yselle's keys." I was about to move on when the bobbing light flashed on something just beyond the gap — an empty wooden crate, stamped with Eptin Cwalo's insigne. I stepped toward it.

"Oh, I know what's back there," Meri said. "I saw the crates when Mother and Master Cwalo unloaded them. Loads of wine, and I think the other crate was pears."

Wine and pears. I'd seen the falconry inventory in Lady Lyll's account book, and something had to account for the entries recorded there. Cwalo's cargo was the missing piece that made it all make sense — the ledger, the mangled embroidery, the armies marching across the model landscape that Daul rearranged again and again. Those green toy soldiers weren't massing in the sculpted foothills because of wine and pears.

"Meri, wait here." Forgetting I was walking off with our only light, I squeezed through the gap until I stood behind the storage racks, the lamp casting a wan glow into the empty space beyond the last shelves. My little mouse friend was nowhere to be seen — but there in the deepest shadows was something I'd missed, my first time around.

Another door.

I was starting to think that Bryn Shaer might actually have *too many* secret passages.

One of the shelves had been dragged over from another part of the room to hide the door; black smudges on the stone wall opposite showed me where it had formerly stood, and lines in the dust on the floor gave up its path across the room.

"Celyn?" Meri's wavering voice floated out of the darkness.

"Hold on," I said. I drew closer and felt my way around the shelf. It had been cleverly positioned to look like it was flush against the wall, but there was plenty of room for me to wriggle behind and reach the latch.

It was locked, of course. And not one of the flimsy Bryn Shaer locks that fell open if you shook them hard enough. This was a serious, heavy iron padlock. I had to rest the lamp on the shelf to work it with my picks, but three tries in, I had it. The tumblers fell into place, and the latch clicked open. I gave the door a gentle push, and it swung inward easily.

I lifted the lamp and stepped inside — and shone the light on something I was never meant to see. "Sweet Tiboran's breath," I swore, and clutched the light so hard its brass handle bit into my fingers. I didn't want to drop it — not in here.

Barrels — no bigger than small ale casks — stood stacked all around the room; sixty, a hundred, maybe more. They were end-up, not sideways, as you'd store wine or beer, with a crest in Vareni stamped on each one. I crept in, lifting my light as high as I could. Behind the barrels, tucked deep into the retreating darkness, I saw the blacker black of iron, the bulky shape of a small wagon. I sucked in my breath. A cannon. I turned, casting the glow around the room. Two more cannons. Four. A row of matchlock muskets, mustered up against the raw stones — polished and ready to be hefted and fired. There were dozens, scores . . . I lost count. This wasn't some forgotten artillery, tucked away for storage and abandoned years before. These guns were modern, new, and *ready*. Waiting.

And they were hidden. With barrels and barrels and *barrels* of gunpowder.

"Celyn!"

Meri surprised me and nearly knocked the lamp out of my hand. I gave a little shriek and fumbled to hold my grip. She pushed past me into the storeroom.

"Celyn, what is this?" Meri turned slowly, taking in the scene. "What does it mean?"

"You *saw* your mother unpack those crates? Are you sure?"

"Well, not *unpack* them. What's going on?"

And that was the point at which even Tiboran apparently ran out of lies. I just couldn't think of a single thing to say to Merista Nemair that explained away the armaments hidden beneath her parents' castle. Well-fortified castles were proud of their armies and fortifications and their weapons stores. They didn't tuck them underground, behind locked doors concealed by heavy furniture.

"We're not supposed to have weapons," she said slowly.

Meri wasn't stupid. No matter what I'd tried to tell myself. This was the girl who'd talked us past the Greenmen in Gerse, who'd been teaching herself magic in secret for weeks, who'd ingratiated herself with a band of outlaw wizards, who'd gotten a Sarist tattoo and possibly even a Sarist lover. Who'd figured out that I had some kind of magic.

Who'd saved my life.

The girl who'd told me it was her duty to be ready when war came. Like her parents, the war heroes. I turned to her.

"I think your mother is planning another rebellion."

"With *Eptin Cwalo*?"

"With everyone here." Briefly I sketched out the hints from Cwalo, the Kalorjn connection all the guests shared, the coded embroidery. I left out Daul, the prince, the Traitor of Kalorjn . . . and my part in all of this. Meri listened thoughtfully, nodding, and interrupted me while I described Lady Cardom's stitchery.

"Four, not five? Gairveyont has five dependent houses," she said. "They were all loyal in the war, but the smallest, Bryn Gairve, borders on Kalorjn. Maybe Lady Cardom's daughter couldn't convince all the houses to support them, if Gairveyont went to war with —" She faltered. "With us."

That was a better theory than any I'd come up with. Would Daul work that out from the scraps of stitchery?

And then Meri said something surprising. "Do you think Master Reynart is working with her?"

"Now that," I said, turning to look at her, "is an excellent question."

Meri was somber all the rest of that day, uncharacteristically silent when I tried to talk to her about it. She just shook her head and kept saying, "I need to talk to Reynart." Not her mother — I supposed that was something.

I'd found the guns, but that only made my questions niggle at me more. I thought maybe Wierolf could help me make sense of things, so at the next opportunity, I slipped down to see him. He was getting stronger, fast, and it was starting to worry me a little. Once he was well enough to move around, what was to keep him confined to this little space? The last few afternoons, I'd found him standing or pacing his rooms — first a tentative shuffle from the bed to the prayer stand and back, then the weary walk of a man whose very boredom was exhausting him, now the wound-up stride of a lion determined to slip his cage and run free again. We'd not discussed the Traitor of Kalorjn again, which was fine by me. I had enough on my mind, now that I'd found Lyll's "birds."

Today he stood in the middle of the room, shirtless, shifting his stiff body through a series of measured poses. The shiny pink skin near his wounds twisted as he moved, and I feared they would break open again. He reached for his shirt and fumbled into it awkwardly. His left arm was still not much good to him.

"Thank the gods, are you going to feed me?"

I had nicked a loaf of spice bread from the cooling tables in the pantry, and I laid it on the shelf behind the bed. "Your arm was high, just now," I said. "You need to keep your elbow down or you'll expose your . . . flank." I winced.

The prince gingerly fingered his side. "You think?" He eased himself down on the edge of the bed. "You know the *Kaal-haia*? You are full of surprises, Celyn just-a-maid."

"The what?"

"The *Kaal-haia*, a technique for self defense and hand-to-hand combat. It was developed by monks — and you don't care."

I'd never heard its nob name before, but I'd learned my share of street fighting over the years. "Brothers," I said simply.

"Ah." Wierolf cupped the heel of the hot bread in his hand. "How many?"

I started. "What?"

"Brothers. How many? Older or younger?"

I clamped my mouth shut for a heartbeat. "One. Older. But there were always other . . . guys around." I was mixing my stories now. Tiboran help me untangle them later.

Wierolf nodded. "It was like that back home too. There were always cousins or wards or hostages to spar with." He seemed to trip over the word *hostage*. "In fact . . . you remind me of my cousin Deira. She was always kicking me in the shins when we were kids."

"Hey! I can leave you to starve, you know." But I knew who Deira was. She was the sister of Astilan, the nephew Bardolph *hadn't* issued a death warrant for. I watched him eat, talk of brothers and cousins making me feel inexplicably sad. Why were the families of the world so unfairly parceled out? I'd have loved a big brother like Wierolf, maybe even a little sister like Meri, but instead I'd had . . . oh, hells. What was the point of that line of thinking?

"Here." Abruptly — or as abruptly as his injuries would allow — the prince rose and held out his hand. "Do you know the Fifth Forms — the ones that start with the crow postures?"

Stupidly I nodded yes, and before I realized what I was agreeing to, he had pulled me to standing with his good right arm. "What are you doing?"

"I need a sparring partner. Can you see Lady Lyllace running through the Wolf-and-Boar with me?" The prince moved me into place in the center of the room. "Good. So, just stand there. You don't have to do anything." He gave a slow twist to his neck, a roll of his shoulders. "Hey, relax. Think of it like we're dancing."

I barked out an involuntary laugh. "Even better," I said, but backed up a pace and stood as still as I could.

As Wierolf slowly worked his way through the poses, clumsily trying to make his reluctant limbs obey him, it was all I could do to keep my mouth shut and not offer commentary. *Shoulders down. Turn your hips out for that kick — you'll get better reach.* But he knew all that; he just couldn't make his injured body bend to his will.

Yet. I saw determination in his face — in the set of his jaw, the evenness of his gaze, the steady rhythm of his breathing as he moved through the forms, drilling the moves over and over. There was no doubt that this prince of the realm would *make* himself heal, pushing through the pain and weakness until he had control again. And once he had conquered his own body, he could turn his will to other goals.

He tracked closer to me, swinging an arm toward my ear, darting a punch at my eyes. I blinked, and Wierolf grinned. His weak left arm was slow to respond, and flew awkwardly, but I could see him learning, adjusting to its limits. As I watched, something flashed to *my* left, just at the edge of my vision.

"Was your brother at the Celystra with you?"

I struck out, whapping his fist away from my jaw and seizing his other wrist, twisting it upward so he stumbled to his knees.

We hung there a moment, the prince gazing up at me, bemused and breathless, me frozen in place, unable to move from the shock of striking His Royal Highness.

A grin spread across Wierolf's sweaty face. He pulled gently on his arm, and after a moment, I let him go. "*Nice.* I think, Celyn just-a-maid, there's a little more to you than you're letting on. What other secrets are you hiding? Maybe a knife in that basket of yours?"

"That's not funny!" I was tired of pretense, of *nobody* being what they said or appeared, and of trying to keep everyone's lies straight. "And what about your secrets, Your Highness?"

To his credit, he barely reacted — just watched my face for a heartbeat, gave the shadow of a nod, and backed off a few paces. "How long have you known?" he asked, reaching for a towel.

"Since that first night."

"*How* did you know? We haven't met before, have we?"

I managed not to laugh at that. Instead I opened my fist to reveal the ring with the royal crest I'd palmed when he struck at me.

He did react to that — his dark eyes grew wide and he glanced hastily at his naked hand. "How did you —"

"It slipped off when I blocked your blow." Well, there was *technical* truth in that. I handed it back. He gave it a strange look, as if expecting it to speak to him, before sliding it back onto his thumb.

"Just who or what are you, Celyn of Bryn Shaer? One of Bardolph's spies? Is he training little girls as assassins to kill me in my sleep now?"

"It's a little late for that, I think."

His gaze shot to my face. "Is that what you were doing, then, hovering over my bed that first night? Plotting a new and stealthy way to murder a prince? Bardolph making sure they finished the job?"

The thing was, I *could* have been — and both of us knew it. But I shook my head. "I was trying to figure out how not to get involved."

It was Wierolf's turn to laugh. "Too late for that," he echoed, but his voice was bitter. He finished mopping his face with the towel, and dropped it in a heap next to the washbowl. "Do they know you've been coming here?"

I shook my head.

"Then you haven't been spying on me?"

I flushed guiltily. Brilliant. If there was one time for Tiboran to desert me . . .

"I see."

"Your Highness —"

He didn't look up, just gripped the edge of the bed with white knuckles, his breath ragged. "I'm tired, Celyn. Leave me." And, at last, I heard the royalty in his voice. There was no disobeying that.

As I slipped toward the hidden door, he spoke again. "And tell your friends I said hello."

I paused, my hand on the edge of the door and took a deep breath. "Are you a prisoner here, or a guest?"

He finally did look up, then. "Sometimes I'm not sure."

# CHAPTER TWENTY-FOUR

A few nights later Meri, Phandre, and I sat together around the fire, our feet on the Kurkyat tuffet, just like that first night a month ago. Phandre was ranting on about some injustice Lyll had done her — forcing her to pot honey or seating her in the wrong place at dinner, or some other atrocity — but Meri and I were lost in our own thoughts. I hadn't gone to see the prince again, telling myself it was just too dangerous now. It was too easy to be unguarded in his presence. It had been a stupid thing, visiting him, and it was past time for me to start *thinking*, before somebody really got hurt. I told myself I didn't care what he was doing, down there in the dark and cold, all alone.

As my thoughts circled the bottom of my cup, Meri's door burst open, and Yselle flew in, yammering a storm of frantic Corles. She crossed the room, curtsied to Meri, and hauled me to my feet.

"Yselle!" Meri broke in and separated us, then tried to listen to what the housekeeper was saying. She said a few words in Corles, then turned to me with a look of confusion. "I don't know, but she says she wants you. My mother wants you."

I stared at them both. "For what?" I said, my voice a lot shakier than I liked.

Meri shook her head. "I'm not sure. Maybe I should come along." She reached for her robe, but Yselle forestalled her in a fierce snap of Corles.

"No, it's all right," I said. "I'm sure it's nothing."

But I wasn't sure. This was how it happened — someone bursting into your bedroom in the middle of the night and dragging you off with no explanation, so your family never saw you again. Had Wierolf given me up to Lady Lyll? Would Yselle throw me into some secret chamber here at Bryn Shaer, to rot in the dark and cold until the world forgot about me? How long would that take? Not that long.

The worried expression on Meri's face did little to reassure me. I gave her a faltering wave and followed Yselle into the corridor. She continued to speak to me in swift, rattling Corles that washed over me like a chill, and I trailed along in her wake, my dread building with every step.

Lady Lyll was rummaging about in the stillroom. I paused in the doorway. "Your Ladyship, I —"

She turned, and a look of — what? Relief? — passed across her face. "Oh, good, Celyn, you're here. Come with me, please." She dismissed Yselle with a nod and steered me into the stillroom. Once inside, she thrust a basket into my arms, crammed full of bandages and bottles. The trapdoor was standing open, and I couldn't help staring at it.

"There's an easier way, but this is quicker," Lady Lyll said. "How are you with ladders?"

"Ladders, milady?" I said stupidly, as Lyll reached behind the workbench and drew out a short, simple frame ladder — the obvious bit that the trapdoor passage had been missing all along. "Uh, passable, I suppose."

"Good. Follow me."

I just stood there, completely undone by surprise. Lyllace was halfway down the ladder, but she looked back up at me. "There's a — situation," she said. "I don't have time to explain properly, but I need someone with a cool head and a steady hand."

Immediately I was overwhelmed with worry for the prince, but I stopped myself from questioning Lady Lyll; I would find out what happened soon enough. Down in the passage, she lit a lamp and led the way down the stairs and through the narrow corridor. I saw the box of light from the prince's open door well before we actually crossed his threshold.

He was back on the bed, stretched out awkwardly, weakly pressing a ball of rags to his abdomen. It was soaked red, a red pool spread below him on the sheets. I balked at the door and could move no farther.

"Celyn!" Lady Lyll barked, and I sprang forward. The prince's eyes fluttered, but I didn't think he saw me. As Lyll knelt beside Wierolf and gingerly lifted his hand and the rags away, it was all too obvious what had happened.

The barely healed wound — the one that had nearly killed him scant weeks ago, the one he'd been straining overmuch by practicing his fighting moves — had broken open, and was bleeding freely. All over. Everywhere. It looked fresh, like someone had stuck a knife straight into him again.

If I hadn't stood there like an idiot and *let him* kick at my head . . . "Is — is he going to die?"

"Die?" Lady Lyll looked up sharply. "Of course not! What do you think we're doing here? Quickly, now — give me a hand."

Her words were like a good sturdy slap across the face. I dropped down beside her and wordlessly began to empty out the supplies she'd need.

"Have you stitched a wound before?"

"No." I had, but nothing like this. My needlework was no comparison to Lady Lyll's. Certainly not good enough for royalty.

"Then watch me."

For the next half hour, we mopped up blood, pressed torn flesh back together, and looked for healthy skin to set the stitches in. Lyll's hand was steady and swift — her stitches here were every bit as exact as the ones she set with gold on linen. Wierolf's eyes blinked open once or twice, and once I even thought he recognized me, but mostly he lay still, panting and pale.

"What happened to him?"

"I — I don't know," Lady Lyll said, tying off the last stitch. I pointed the tips of the scissors and snipped close to Wierolf's skin. Apparently she hadn't worked out any sort of explanation yet.

"Who is he?" I pressed. If Lady Lyll trusted me this much, would she come all the way?

"He's — Yselle's nephew," she said, only the ghost of hesitation in her voice.

"Yselle's nephew," I repeated.

"He's a fugitive. He — got in trouble with the bailiff at his village, and she hid him down here without telling anyone. Celyn, I know I can count on your discretion."

I could teach Lyll a thing or two about lying, but I let it go. I handed her the next thing she asked for, a bottle of vinegar from the basket.

She carefully cleaned the freshly sewn wound, wiping away every trace of blood from the prince's body. I held him as she bandaged him, his body heavy and hot against mine. My face was pressed in close to his clammy neck, and — something was wrong here. "Milady —"

"Yes, what?"

I said it without thinking, and I had to wait until we had gently shifted Wierolf onto the ice-cold floor so we could change out his bedding. Where was it? "He needs —" And there I was, crawling around on the prince's bloody, unmade bed, digging beneath the soiled mattress for —

"What are you doing? What are you looking for?"

"This." I found it, the chain snapped, caught in a crevice between the bed and the wall. If a spark of magic hadn't leaped at my fingers as they brushed the edge of the pendant, I wouldn't have seen it at all. I held it out to Lyll. The symbol I'd never been able to make out looked clear and crisp tonight: a seven-pointed star. Of course.

Lady Lyll looked at me for a long moment before she took the charm, threaded it onto a length of silk, and put it back around Wierolf's neck. "I normally don't like things like this," she said. "But I suspect this man is an idiot who will never let a wound heal properly without a little . . . help." And she tucked the pendant itself neatly inside a wrap of linen, close against his ravaged flesh.

Finally when all three of us were beyond exhausted, and Wierolf was sleeping peacefully in a clean bed, Lyll sank against the bare stone wall with a sigh. "Thank you, Celyn. I can't tell you how much I appreciate your help."

I glanced at the prince again. His breath came in shallow, ragged bursts, but his color was better. I wanted Lyll to tell me something true about him, and wondered how much she knew I had guessed.

"Shouldn't someone stay with him?"

Lady Lyll frowned, and I could see the worries warring behind her eyes. What might the prince say when he woke up? Would he have the good sense to keep silent, or would his drugged mind spill secrets she'd worked for weeks to protect? It was odd, seeing this stalwart woman nervous and faltering.

"You'll be missed," I said firmly. "Tell me what to look for, and I'll stay."

Finally she agreed. "Very well. He should be fine now, but watch for more bleeding, of course. If he turns paler, or if he doesn't seem more alert after a few hours, send for me. You can find your way back to the stillroom?"

"In the dark, milady."

Lady Lyll still hesitated.

A dark thought crept its way into my mind and would not stop squirming. *Was* it just a breaking-open of the old wound? That had been an awful lot of blood for someone supposedly healing. Maybe someone else at Bryn Shaer had found out about the prince's presence here, and decided to finish what the would-be assassins had started. But who?

"Forgive me, milady, but —"

"What is it, Celyn?"

I gestured vaguely toward the patient's new bandages. "That — it looked like an old wound?"

An odd look crossed her face, but she nodded briefly.

"How can you be sure? That it's not a new injury, I mean."

She watched me a moment. "Well, for one thing," she said, "there is no way he could have survived a new injury. Are you sure you'll be all right down here by yourself? I could stay —"

"Milady, I'll be fine. He'll be fine." Besides, I really wanted to be the first one to see him when he woke up — so I could give him the smack upside the head he deserved.

Lyll finally agreed and headed for the chamber door, looking heavy and weighed down by the supplies she carried.

"Milady?"

She turned back.

"Why did you send for me? You could have stitched that up yourself. I wasn't really that much help."

She looked at me evenly, and I could not read the expression in her brown eyes. "Because," she said simply, "he asked for you."

Wierolf slept fitfully through the night; Lady Lyll had dosed him with enough poppy to keep a horse immobile, and I was nearly that tired. I managed to fall asleep propped up against the stone wall, my head pressed forward into my chest.

When I woke, confused about the time, I was freezing and achy and disoriented, and at first I didn't remember where I was. It was dark and cold, and for a strangled moment I thought myself back in the wine cellar in Gerse. I jumped to my feet —

"Easy, easy." A soft voice came out of the darkness. "You're with me."

"Wierolf?" I found his name somewhere, but it sounded scratchy and strange in my voice. I had never said it aloud before.

"The candle's gone out. There's another one on the shelf behind the bed. You know where, right?" His voice was surprisingly strong. "Were you here last night?" the prince asked, as I rose and got the candle lit. "I don't remember."

"What do you remember?" His bandage looked fine — just the slightest bit of pink dampening the linen. His forehead was cooler than he had any right to be.

"Um, I was doing a little stretching —"

"A little stretching? It was that damned Raven, wasn't it?" I said. "You know you're not ready to —"

"And there was lot of blood," he finished. "I couldn't stop it, and it seemed like hours before anyone came. I was afraid to call out, and I thought you'd come back, but —" He sighed heavily. "I guess I shouldn't have expected you to."

"Well, you nearly bled *to death* this time," I said. "You have no idea how lucky you are that Lady Lyll found you when she did."

He looked solemn. "I do. Can you — can you tell me where you thought you were, a moment ago, when you awoke? You sounded scared."

I shrugged faintly. "Home. Gerse."

"At the Celystra?"

"Why would you say that?"

His voice was gentle. "You were — mumbling a little in your sleep. I couldn't really make out any words."

*Liar.* But I was grateful. "Just so you know, apparently you're Yselle's nephew."

He blinked. "Yselle?"

"Your Corles nurse. You got in a fight with your bailiff."

"I see. Did I win?"

"Not from what I can tell."

"I'll have to learn to — control my temper," he said, wincing as he tried to shift position. "I hate this."

I edged him over slightly on his pillows. "I know."

"I'm accustomed to being useless," he said. "Not *helpless.*"

"Nobody likes a whiny prince."

"You'd be surprised," he said. "That tone of voice is usually quite effective on women."

"Ew." I waved him off, but at least he was almost smiling again.

"So, Celyn *not*-just-a-maid, are you ever going to explain to me who taught the Celystra girl to fight? Was it this mysterious brother of yours?"

I sank down beside him. "He's not mysterious," I said. "And no."

"So it wasn't your brother?"

"No, it wasn't my brother," I snapped. "What?"

"You know my story," he said softly. "Tell me yours."

I shrugged. "Nothing to tell. I left the Celystra, he didn't. End of story."

"And the Nemair took you in, and you left Gerse with them."

"There, see? Now you know everything."

He gave a little sigh. "Do you ever think about what's happening — out there? Back at home? What would you be doing right now?"

Leaning my head back against the wood railing, I tracked my thoughts back to the city. It seemed unreal, no more than the dream I'd just had and couldn't remember. "It's almost midwinter," I said, my voice thin and thready in the flickering candlelight. "I guess we'd be getting ready for the last of the street fairs and river festivals before everything closes for the Holy Nights of Marau."

"Tell me about them," he said. "I was officially banished from Gerse when I was nine. I haven't been back since."

Something about that made my throat feel tight. Not to *ever* go back to Gerse? I'd thought I was used to that idea. I closed my eyes and recalled aloud how the twisted cobblestone streets filled up with crowds in ornate, fanciful masks, and the boats on the three rivers lit up with paper lanterns like huge fireflies.

"That sounds pretty," he said softly. "Tell me more about the rivers."

I told him what I remembered, about how the Big Silver rose and fell with the tides; and Wierolf asked about the locks on the Oss that moved great ships in and out of the city. When I described our rainy winters, he wanted to know if the main streets were ever impassible because of mud. And when I talked about walking along the great wall that surrounded the city, he inquired about the gates and the watchtowers.

I hesitated; something in the questions he asked me was shifting away from casual conversation. The city wouldn't have changed much in twenty-two years — but Bardolph hadn't barred Wierolf from Gerse because he didn't want the prince to see the festivals. I rose and crossed the room, where he could see me without straining, and drew a great ring on the wall with my finger, pointing to places as I spoke.

"Gerse's wall has seven gates," I said. "They lead into different areas of the city. The Oss Gate, here, on the northwest side, for boats. It's always heavily guarded, but they never close it. The Harvest Gate, what locals call the Green Gate, is open sunrise to sunset. The Green Gate road goes almost straight through Gerse, right to Hanivard Palace, if you can clear the market traffic. . . ."

I glanced at him through a strand of my hair that had come loose. He was watching my hand, though a fine sweat had broken out on his forehead. "Go on," he said.

And I continued, explaining to Prince Wierolf exactly how he might breach my city, should he ever decide to bring an army marching on Hanivard.

# CHAPTER TWENTY-FIVE

The prince finally fell into a light but peaceful sleep, and Yselle came to fetch me, ordering me to Lady Lyll's quarters, where a scalding-hot bath had been drawn up in the dressing room. As the steam drifted into the wan morning light, I scowled into the water and imagined blurting everything out, just to see what Lyll would do. What's with the guns in the wine cellar? Ever plan to let the prince out of that little cell? Do you know that Daul hates you? Was your husband the Traitor of Kalorjn?

I gave the water a frustrated splash. She might not even know the answer to that last one; I remembered that she hadn't even married Antoch until after the war. Back at Favom Court, Morva had told me their marriage was "His Majesty's doing." The idea that Lyll could have married the traitor without realizing it made the hot steamy air hard to breathe.

When Lyll returned, she had a fresh white shift and a clean kirtle draped over her arm. Mine had gotten covered with Wierolf's blood. As she sat beside the bath, I saw in her face a reflection of all my own thoughts. I braced my legs against the copper wall of the tub to stop from sinking below the water.

Lyll fussed a little, testing the bathwater, refolding the shift, adding a few drops of oil to the tub. Finally she looked at me gravely. "Thank you for your assistance last night, Celyn."

"Last night, milady?" I said, and for a wild moment even I wasn't sure what I was doing. "I'm afraid I don't know what you mean. I was with Lady Merista all evening, as you know. We were abed early, but milady woke in the night with a cough. Yselle brought us some mead to soothe her throat."

The edge of Lady Lyll's lip twitched as she watched me, her expression shifting slightly.

"And I am certain you will find no one to dispute that account. I remember the hours quite clearly, in fact."

Lyll eased back into her chair. "And how fares my daughter this morning, Lady Celyn?"

"Very much improved," I said smoothly. "I'm certain she'll be able to make her morning ride with her lord father."

"I see," said Lyll. After a long pause, she added, "Has my daughter suffered many such episodes?"

I nodded carefully. "And it would not surprise me should she suffer them again in future."

"Celyn —" She braced the heel of her hand against her forehead. "He has demanded that you be allowed to continue to visit him. But by all the gods, *please* use discretion. I cannot overstate the delicacy of our situation here. You know we are expecting a representative of the king for Meri's *kernja-velde*, and I hope I don't have to tell you how critical it is that our — guest remain anonymous and invisible. Everything depends on him, Celyn."

Her words gave me a chill despite the steamy water. "I understand, your ladyship."

Lyll watched me one long, hard moment, then gave me one of her crisp nods as she rose from the stool. "Thank you, Celyn," she said — and, inexplicably, I wanted to hear that warm low voice speak my real name.

I climbed out of the tub, and Lyll left me to towel off and get dressed in private. Her dressing room was a snug, warm space with paneled walls and no windows, filled with cabinets and chests and lovely little ladies' things. I pulled open a drawer in the dressing table, looking for a hairbrush, and saw a tiny face looking back at me. I dipped my fingers inside and retrieved two miniature portraits, carefully set in delicate bejeweled frames. One was of a boy who could be Meri's twin — round-faced and pale, solemn. The other was of a much younger child, scarcely more than a baby, done up in a brocaded frock and posed stiffly, a golden rod clutched in chubby fists.

Lady Lyll returned just then, and I started, questions poking at me from all directions. Lyll, a shadow crossing her face, smiled faintly. "Those are Meri's brothers." She gingerly took the miniatures from me. "My sons from my first marriage, Ralth and Sandur."

"Where are they now?"

"With their father," she said, and I was surprised. "It's all right. When I was very young, my parents married me to a nobleman who had more ambition than virtue. Our families were not rich, and he was the younger son; at the time neither of us expected to make any better match. He and I got along; by all accounts it should have been a successful marriage. I bore him two healthy, beautiful boys, a feat I have not been able to replicate for Antoch. And then his brother died, and suddenly he stood in line to inherit not only his own family's estate, but that of his brother's betrothed — and she *was* wealthy. He cast me aside, and that was that."

"But you were married to him."

She smiled bitterly. "Not anymore. Not under Bardolph's new decree that only marriages performed in a Celyst temple were valid. My family had let him persuade us to be married by a priest of Mend-kaal. At the time I thought it was quaint, perhaps even a little romantic. But one swipe of Bardolph's green pen, and suddenly I had never been a wife, and my sons were bastards."

"Why aren't they with you now?"

Her lip twisted in a way that was not quite pleasant. "His new wife proved . . . disappointing in that regard, and after a time, my former husband agreed to legitimize his sons — if I surrendered any claim to them." She sighed, stroking the face of her older son. "I had lived two hard years in my father's house with two small boys who hated me for leaving their father. At the time it seemed like the right thing to do. I haven't seen them since. Meri has never met them."

I watched her soft pale hand draw circles on the face of her boy, and I wanted to squeeze her hand or hug her or something. "I'm sorry," I said — because I couldn't think of anything else, and because it was true.

"It was a long time ago," she said, her voice suddenly brisk. She placed the portraits back inside the drawer and snapped it shut. "Let's get you dressed."

But I watched her out of the corner of my eye, and I wondered. I remembered something else Morva had said, back at Favom Court, about Lady Lyll's children being taken away from her, for being married to a rebel. Well, she had some of the details wrong, but the gist right. It seemed to explain a great many things about Lady Lyllace Nemair.

I was a little surprised that Lyll didn't keep me close the next few days, but she had an injured prince to tend and must have decided against a repeat performance of our late-night drama. It was just as well; I didn't know what I would do with both of them there and conscious together. So I wandered a little aimlessly through the halls of the Lodge, trying to remember what it was like when I'd first arrived here last month — when carpeted corridors and rich mountain breakfasts were enough excitement for one lost Gersin thief.

Before Daul came and spoiled all of it.

Late one morning I found myself peering between the half-open Armory doors, where Daul and Antoch usually fenced. Curiously, Antoch sat alone there now, leaning back in the bench before a blazing fire. Before I thought about what I was doing, I slipped inside.

Crossing from shadow to shadow across the long cold floor, I took the space in, liking it less and less the longer I was here, with the suspended weapons and the Spear-Bearers guarding the fire. Bryn Shaer had been built for defense, and this was a room for war. Had the last Sarist conspirators planned their rebellion in this room? Or maybe Bryn Shaer was still a property of the Crown then, and in this very room, from that same scarred bench where Antoch slumped before the fire, the king's generals had studied their maps and pointed their fingers and wiped an entire religion from the face of Llyvraneth.

*No,* I thought, *someone had* helped *them do that.*

"Celyn, my girl!" Antoch rose at the sight of me, and pulled me into a huge embrace. "Have a seat. Will you take wine?"

I shook my head.

"Miserable morning," he said cheerfully. "What have my girls found to do with themselves today in all this snow? I see one's here to keep an old soldier company, but what about the others?" He waved me to the chair across from him.

"I believe Lady Merista and Phandre are trying on their gowns for the *kernja-velde* this morning."

"And not Celyn?"

"No, milord. Her ladyship had need of me this morning." The lie came easily.

"Good, good. And how are you getting along, then? The other girls treating you well?"

"Meri is, of course, milord."

He gave a little chuckle. "No answer about Phandre, I see. Well, we try to be fond of her. Old family friends and all. I know Lyll worries what will become of her — always scheming, my lady wife. But I've told her the Séthe always land right-side up." He shuffled the papers before him on the table, and I leaned in slightly for a look. There was a map of Llyvraneth — old and well-worn, a crack at one edge where it had been folded instead of rolled. The ink had nearly rubbed away in parts, but I could still make out the name scribed over a green plain on the coast of Kellespau. *Kalorjn*.

Was that why Antoch sat here so often? The Spear-Bearers were the handmaidens of Zet, her loyal guard. They were said to hunt down traitors, harrying them with their dogs and spears until the end of days. Was Antoch waiting for those guardians of loyalty to step away from that hearth and strike him down? I stared at the leaping flames on their bare marble shoulders, their carved quivers. Maybe the arrow ring that Daul and the avalanche victims wore *did* have something to do with the war, after all. Perhaps all the survivors of Kalorjn had them. Maybe Antoch had one himself. *A token of commitment,* Daul had said. To the Sarist cause? But that didn't make any sense; why wear Zet's symbol, then? And why would Daul be wearing his now, when he had so clearly thrown off his Sarist leanings? Pox. *None* of this made any sense.

"Did your people fight in the war, Celyn?"

I looked up at this unexpected question. What was likely to be useful here? "My father. But —" I ducked my head as if embarrassed. "Milord, he named me Celyn and sent me to the Celystra."

"Ah. There were decent men on both sides in that war. Just remember that. A lot of losses on both sides too." He sighed heavily. "Damnable world that makes a thing like war the only answer to a problem."

The Spear Maidens staring down on me, I found myself in complete agreement. "He never spoke about it, though."

"It was a dark time. We all did things we're not proud of — necessary things, but ones we don't like to remember nonetheless."

I held my breath. "What sort of things?"

Antoch gave me a soft look. "I'm sure your father served honorably, Celyn. But war casts a long shadow, and sometimes you're trapped under it for years after." His voice changed as he touched the map with his blocky fingers. "I made a mistake eighteen years ago. At the time it seemed like the right decision, the only way to save some good people's lives, but —" He shook his head. "I've been trying to undo it ever since, but it never seems like enough."

I felt my pulse quicken. "A mistake, your lordship?"

Antoch rolled the wine around the bottom of his goblet. "It's a sorry matter, to be defined by the worst thing you've ever done." He was looking into the fiery distance, the spears glowing in the strange uneven light. "I let down a lot of good friends."

Was he about to confess? I leaned forward. "At — at Kalorjn?" I said softly.

He looked up sharply, but his broad, bearded face softened. "Listen to me ramble on," he said. "A lot of nonsense for young ears, when you should be enjoying yourself. Don't let my lady wife work you to death, my girl. You make sure your own gown is just as splendid as the others'. And if it's not, you'd better report to me."

Antoch's words echoed and rumbled as I sped down the hall, no clear destination in mind. *I made a mistake eighteen years ago. I let down a lot of good friends.* Daul was right. Antoch was everything he said. A traitor.

And why did that bother me? I wasn't even born eighteen years ago. How could it possibly matter to me whether Antoch Nemair or Eptin Cwalo or — or Marlytt — was the Traitor of Kalorjn?

But I knew why. And the knowing sent me running down the long soft halls of the Lodge, where every paneled wall and hanging tapestry hid another secret. Where people smiled while they twisted knives, and nobody — not even me — was what they said.

When I'd run myself out, I was only half surprised to find myself standing outside the prince's chamber door. There was nothing he could do for me — but something about him felt simple, uncomplicated. Which made no sense at all, because he was the most dangerous person here.

Wierolf was sitting up in bed, looking a little healthier. Instinctively I laid a hand on his forehead, checked his bandage, helped him into a clean shirt, happy to have something besides my own gnawing thoughts to focus on.

"Are you going to read my water too?" he asked with a grimace as I eased him back against his pillows.

"Keep it up," I warned, and he forced out a laugh.

"You look worried," he said.

"And you look . . . annoyed. Your Highness."

"I'm going mad in here," he said. "Do you know how I spent the morning? Counting the ceiling tiles. *Seventy-four times.* At this point I think I'd even take you cleaning my wound again, just for the novelty."

That coaxed a grin from me. I knew how he felt — to be accustomed to a life of running and climbing and *danger,* and then be shut up tight in some castle, with nothing to do but sit, while the world closed in all around you. I settled down beside him on the floor — wearing a groove in the stone by now — and leaned my head back against the frame of the bed, looking at the well-accounted-for ceiling tiles.

I might be the only Gersin thief ever to make friends with one of the royal family of Llyvraneth. It was a heady thought, one that made me alternately want to throw back my head and laugh . . . or shiver with fear.

"Celyn, honestly — you look like you'll unravel if somebody gives a tug on the wrong thread. What's wrong?" He watched me carefully, and I could see him measuring his words, calculating and wary. "Does it have something to do with me?"

"No." Not really. *I'm not sure.* But then, before I could think better of it, I blurted out, "Did you know your uncle put a price on your head?"

His eyes widened, and he was silent a long moment. Finally he said, "I guess I shouldn't be surprised, but it's still a bit of a shock to actually hear it out loud."

We sat in silence for a bit while Wierolf took this in. "I can't really remember anything about the men who attacked me." His voice sounded weary. "I would hope I'd recognize them — but I don't know. Were they my friends? Strangers?" He gave his head a frustrated shake.

"I think we can safely say they weren't your friends." My hands tucked inside my heavy sleeves, I fingered the rings I'd taken from the avalanche victims, which I'd been carrying around with me like a sort of strange talisman. "Do you think someone at Bryn Shaer might try to claim the bounty, if they knew you were here?"

"Well, how much was it?"

Ridiculously I found this funny, and though I clamped a hand over my mouth, a laugh escaped through my nose as a very un-noblike snort. Wierolf watched me patiently, his mouth twitching. "That's nice. Should I be watching my back for you?"

"I'll be good," I promised, glad he'd stopped me when he had.

I could see the prince run through the roster of Bryn Shaer's guests in his mind, but he finally shook his head. "I don't think the people you've mentioned would sell me out — but I'm not sure of anything anymore. Those families were loyal during the last war," he said. "But that might not mean anything now."

I looked at him. "They weren't all loyal."

He held my gaze. "You think Lady Lyllace might be hiding me from Lord Antoch."

Not even sure myself, I just looked back, fingernails in my mouth. The prince lay back heavily in the bed, panting slightly from the effort.

"I've got to stop coming in here and scaring you to death with bad news," I said, checking his forehead for fever. "You'll have to find another hobby. Do you have any pastimes that don't involve you nearly getting killed?"

He didn't laugh, but he looked almost wistful. "I actually used to be a passable carver," he said. "I made a set of chessmen for my father once. I was proud of those."

"We've got rocks in abundance," I said. "Why don't you see if they'll bring you the supplies to do that, then?"

Wierolf looked straight at me. His eyes were clear and bright and very serious. "And do you think Lady Nemair will give me a knife?"

I looked at him a long, long moment, weighty silence filling up the space between us.

"I think you should find out," I finally said.


Before I could learn whether or not His Highness was successful in coaxing a weapon from his host (captor?), I had another encounter with Daul. I had not seen him — alone — since the night he'd accused Lord Antoch of treachery, and I wasn't happy that it was looking likely that he was right. He cornered me after a busy dinner, when everyone had assembled in the Round Court for games and music. Marlytt was teaching a new dance to Meri and Phandre, while Lords Cardom and Sposa looked on. I was trying to sneak across the room before I could get pulled into the demonstration, when Daul slipped up beside me and pushed me into the hall. I didn't have the energy to struggle.

"Enjoying your holiday?" The words were friendly, but the tone was icy and hard.

"Terribly. It's always such a delight to be snowbound with a madman. I can't think why I haven't made this trip before."

"Easy there. My friends are very impressed with your work," he said.

"Are they?" I said. "That's fascinating, because we've had mail go out exactly once, and your report wasn't with it."

Daul's face darkened. "What —"

"What the hells is going on here?" I said. "If you're not reporting suspicious Sarist activity to the Greenmen, then what are we doing?"

Daul pressed close to me. "Have you brought me any suspicious Sarist activity, little mouse? I'm having trouble remembering. Let's see. Are there Sarists hiding in the woods? No. And what about these guns you promised to find? You talk big, but I've yet to see any real evidence."

I pulled away, but I could hardly protest. He was right, and I was running out of little things to string him along with.

"Enough games. I know you've been holding out on me. From now on, I want *everything* you find, the moment you find it. Do you understand me?"

"That's what I've been doing!"

"Really? Then tell me what you and my brother were discussing the other morning. You looked so cozy there together in the Armory."

"How did —" I gave up. Daul already knew; telling him couldn't make things any worse. "You were right. He as much as admitted it to me."

His hand on my arm gripped tighter. "As much as? What does that mean?"

I explained what Lord Antoch had said to me, about making up for a mistake he made eighteen years ago. Daul's breath quickened, and he stared into my eyes.

"And you're not making this up?"

"Why would I make that up? It's horrible."

"It's not enough," he said, almost to himself. "We need proof."

"Why? You're the only one who cares."

He brought his face very close to mine. "And I'm the only one who matters, to you. Remember that, little mouse."

# CHAPTER TWENTY-SIX

I couldn't sleep that night, and Meri was just as restless. She kept turning over in the bed, an arc of sparks flowing over her. I stared up at the embroidered canopy, listening to Phandre snoring noisily in the other room. I knew I should be worried about Lord Antoch, but the shadows on the canopy kept shaping themselves into long black arrows instead.

"Did you ever talk to Reynart?" I whispered.

Meri flipped over and looked at me. "I couldn't. I was going to, but I got there and couldn't think what to say to him! Celyn, I don't know why those guns are down there. I trust Master Reynart, but —"

"We need more information," I said, and Meri nodded. She was so solemn and earnest, and she was ultimately at the heart of all the secrets that Bryn Shaer twined together. If her mother was planning a war, if her father was the Traitor of Kalorjn, if Daul was passing information to the Inquisition, Meri deserved to be more than to be a helpless pawn carried along by their machinations. And I thought she'd demonstrated she could handle more, as well.

Daul had claimed his father's journal could prove that Antoch was the traitor, but whatever he'd found inside it hadn't been what he'd expected. Yet he still insisted it was true. And those *rings*. That damn niggle wouldn't let up. Something was wrong there; I could taste it.

There was one place in this castle that I had never searched, one person whose secrets dictated every move I made. And there was only one person in this castle who could help me get inside those mysterious rooms. I turned to Meri. "There's somewhere we should look," I said.

"Where?" she whispered.

"Lord Daul's rooms."

She propped herself up on one elbow. "What?"

Well, I was committed now. "I'm not sure I trust him, Meri. He's definitely hiding something about his connection to the avalanche victims. We need to find out what it is." She gave a tentative nod. "He has a magical lock on his door. Do you think you can open it?"

At the word *magic*, she brightened. A real chance to use her powers for something that might be important. "Can we go now?"

"Now?" I said. "But it's late; he's probably in bed —"

She shook her head. "He's reading a moon chart for Yselle. I heard her tell my mother. For her sister's birthday. It has to be done at midnight or something."

I just blinked. It was completely preposterous, and try as I might I just couldn't imagine Daul tucked into the kitchens, reading fortunes for the housekeeper. "Good," I said. "Yes. Now."

Getting up to Daul's rooms was not a problem; it was getting *into* them that would require Meri's specialized skills. We sneaked up the stairs, keeping to the shadows along the edge of the hall, and stopped before Daul's door.

"Go on," I urged, but Meri hesitated.

"Why are we doing this?" she asked.

I stood beside the door. "He's dangerous," I said quietly. "He knows my brother, and he's threatened to — report me to the Celystra." That was all true enough, but somehow I still felt like I was lying to her.

Her eyes widened in indignation."Your brother! But —"

"I just want to make sure he's not telling the Celystra anything *else*, as well."

Meri set her mouth decisively and gave her attention to the lock. "This would be easier if we had any kind of a key," she said. "But if it's really just magic keeping it shut, that shouldn't matter." She looked at it, whispered to it, stroked and tapped the case and shackle. The lock's magic seemed to shudder under her fingers, but it wouldn't dissipate. Finally she stepped back. "I think it's a permanent charm. You need the original spellcaster to break it."

Pox. "You tried," I said generously, but my voice sounded thin.

"What now?" Her fingers were hooked together at her waist, and she looked eager to do something else.

"Nothing now," I said. "We go back to bed." I pushed her toward the main stair. We had to be cautious going back past Lady Lyll's rooms; Lyll was getting used to finding me in strange places at all hours, but Meri was new to this.

I miscalculated. Meri trailed behind me down the stairs, and I stepped out into the hallway just as Lady Lyll rounded the corner, carrying a heavy journal and moving with determination toward the public section of the Lodge. I ducked back, swearing silently, waving Meri deeper into the shadows.

"Celyn!" Lyll gave me a curious look. "What are you doing up?"

"I needed to use the privy," I said. Never mind that I was fully dressed and heading in the opposite direction. I said a silent prayer that Meri would have the good sense to stay tucked tight into the darkness.

Lyll didn't believe me, I could tell that immediately. But she nodded anyway. "He's been restless all day. Maybe you can calm him down, convince him to sleep."

Relief surged through me, though I found a little space to reflect that that was probably the wrong reaction. "I'll try, milady," I said. "Would you like me to use force or persuasion?"

Lady Lyll cracked a smile. "At your discretion."

Since I was now supposed to be on my way toward the stillroom and the prince, I had to turn around and walk with Lady Lyll, leaving Meri behind on the stairs and hoping she hadn't overheard that little exchange. "Where are you off to at this hour, milady? If I may ask."

Lyll consulted the timepiece she wore on her girdle, and sighed. "There's some castle business I must attend to," she said. "We've not heard back from the messenger we sent down the mountain several days ago, and he is overdue."

I felt a stab of worry. "Berdal? What do you think happened to him?"

Her expression softened. "Probably just got caught by some bad weather. But we were hoping he'd bring news we've been expecting for several weeks now."

"What sort of news?"

"Word from the Crown, regarding the representative we hope they're sending for Meri's *kernja-velde*. Nothing serious, but we thought we'd send someone after him, just to make sure. Lord Antoch and Lord Daul are going to ride out in the morning."

"Together?" The word squeaked out of me.

She frowned. "Of course. Celyn, what's the matter?"

I shook my head — what was I supposed to say? Don't let Antoch ride off alone with Daul? They'd been alone together every day for weeks. If Daul was planning on throwing Antoch off a mountain, he'd had ample opportunities before.

But Antoch hadn't ever confessed to treachery before.

"Isn't it dangerous on the roads? With the — bandits?"

"They'll have guards. And I expect they'll bring back some good game, as well. They've spotted some wild sheep on the hills below us. We'll have mutton stew next week!"

*Now. Now is the moment to tell her.* "But Daul never goes hunting," is what made it past my lips. Lady Lyll just gave a little chuckle and kept walking, while I hoped desperately that whatever guards Antoch brought with him wouldn't turn on him if Daul suddenly shouted, "He's the Traitor of Kalorjn!" into the windswept air.

We'd reached the Lesser Court doors, and Lady Lyll took her leave and went inside, followed soon after by Lord Wellyth, who gave me a brief, stately bow. I lingered, suddenly suspicious. Why would Lord Wellyth care who was coming for Meri's *kernja-velde*?

"What's going on?" Meri slipped up beside me, and I jumped. Blast — I *was* getting soft. She never would have gotten the jump on me in Gerse.

I edged to the side to let Meri peek through the crack in the doors with me. "Some kind of meeting," I said.

"They've been having a lot of those. Usually after we meet with the suitors in the afternoons — Mother makes me leave, and the others come in, and they talk there for hours."

"The others?"

"Everyone — Lord Wellyth, and the Cardom, Lord Sposa . . ."

"I want to hear what they're saying." Through the gap in the doors, I tried to see a place to sneak in and conceal myself. Was there a back entrance to the Lesser Court? I couldn't remember.

"We could try the gallery," Meri suggested. "The minstrels' gallery for the Round Court backs onto the Lesser Court, and there's a grille, so the people in the Lesser Court can hear the music."

I turned and stared at her. She was grinning. "Mother made Phandre and me polish it one day. I don't remember where you were."

I tossed up my hands. "Lead the way."

Tucked behind the musicians' seats was a fretwork panel that screened us from view but let us hear everything from the Lesser Court with perfect clarity. Listening to the shift of bodies and voices inside, I guessed there were five or six people there besides Lyll. Meri crouched beside me, trying to peer through the gaps in the grille.

"I can't see anything," she said. "Just a lot of chair backs."

"Just listen," I whispered.

"Lord Wellyth," said a warm voice I had no trouble identifying as Lady Lyll's. "If you'll remind us all where we left off last time?"

"Certainly, my lady." I heard a rustle of papers, a cough, and then Lord Wellyth's thin, reedy voice. "We had settled on the restoration of properties and council seats to exiled families, and on the relief of the Heresy Tax levied against those families — but we were still disagreed on the matters of liberation of lands claimed by the church —"

"The *Celyst* church," somebody put in.

Meri turned to me, her brows pulled together. I shook my head and turned back to the grille.

Another reedy cough. "Yes, well, as I was saying: liberation of lands claimed by the church in the last twelve years."

A chair squeaked angrily. "Since the Edict of Crenns? That's nothing! We must demand back *all* the lands the Celysts have taken since Bardolph took the throne!"

"And you know he'll never agree to that." That might have been Lord Cardom.

"Let him refuse. We're ready. The timing couldn't be more perfect, not with Bardolph sending Astilan to bully Corlesanne —"

Lady Lyll broke in. "We're not ready," she said, speaking low. "This is the path we agreed on. It will take at least another seven months to pull together enough resources for a military operation."

"Then the first thing we must address is that intolerable concession barring us from rearming." That was a woman's voice, and it sounded familiar — Lady Cardom, perhaps?

"And that will be the first thing they look for. What do you think Bardolph will do the moment you ask to put a couple cannons on those warships you build?" I definitely knew that voice: Eptin Cwalo.

"We might as well roll over and capitulate, to take your position!" cried another man. Lord Sposa, I thought.

"Gentlemen! Play nicely or go home." Lyll's voice was light but firm. Amid some squeaks and mutterings, there were reluctant grumbles of assent. "Good," said Lyll. "Lord Petr, please continue."

The debate went on, Meri and I listening as they hashed out the finer points of King Bardolph's offenses against the people of Llyvraneth, and the actions by which His Majesty might avoid an armed uprising of his subjects.

"It sounds like some kind of charter of grievances," I said. "They probably mean to present it to whoever the king sends to Bryn Shaer."

"Mother said they're not ready to go to war. But we saw all that artillery, which means —"

I nodded. "They don't think the king will agree to any of their demands."

Snow fell thickly as Daul, Antoch, and a handful of guards rode off the next morning, burying their tracks and obscuring their path down the mountain. I stood on the tower walk and watched them go, and within moments they were lost in a swirl of white.

Lyll swept us into a flurry of preparations for the *kernja-velde,* a mere two weeks away now: final fittings for Meri's gown, elaborate rehearsals of the ritual, and endless yardage of embroidery for the ceremony. Meri had formed quite an attachment to Marlytt, who instructed her on everything from dance steps and hairstyles to — I suspected — how best to comport her affair with Stagne. Not that I thought Meri would actually be so foolish as to *tell* Marlytt she was secretly seeing a Sarist magician behind her parents' backs, but if I were a young girl in need of romantic advice, I knew the one person at Bryn Shaer I would turn to.

When I wasn't pinning up hems or sampling delicacies for Yselle in the kitchens, I was keeping the prince company. Lady Lyll had consented to a small carving knife, and Wierolf whittled halfheartedly at a lump of wood that might have been on its way to becoming a cow. I could tell he was restless, though, so to keep him from overexerting himself before his wounds were ready for sparring, I dragged a plank of wood in from the kennels, and we took turns using the knife for throwing practice. Wierolf etched a circle in the center of the board for a target. My aim was almost pathologically bad, but with the prince's coaching, I was improving. I could actually hit the wood, blade first, almost every time.

It all kept me busy enough to — mostly — take my mind off of Daul and Antoch and the missing Berdal. I did make one last, fruitless search of Lord Antoch's rooms, hoping for evidence that would prove he was or was not the Traitor. But aside from a curious door hidden behind his bed, which appeared to lead nowhere interesting, there was still nothing incriminating among his belongings.

More than anything, my fingers were itching to get inside Daul's rooms and rifle through them. I was determined to find out what he was hiding behind that charmed lock. The more I thought about it, the more I wanted to do it, and the more I resigned myself to the fact that there was only one way to get in there that I hadn't tried yet. I was going to have to go in from the *outside* — up or down the side of the building.

And directly below Daul's rooms, by some stroke of Tiboran's genius, were the rooms occupied by Lady Lyll. Rooms I was already well familiar with.

Opportunity came when Lyll and Meri were in the kitchens one morning, working with Yselle on Meri's birthday menu. Last night's snow should keep everyone safely tucked into the warmer rooms at the center of the castle, and no one would be wandering the statue garden at this hour.

Letting myself into Lyll's rooms took no effort at all, and I crossed to the leaded windows. Everything was white and brilliant outside, making it hard to judge the distance to the ground. I put a hand to the latch and cracked the casement open. A whip of icy air snapped through the gap and a dusting of snow scattered off the sill and into nothingness below.

I poked my head out the window, squinting against the sting of cold air. Daul's windows were exactly above the ones I stood at; I'd just climb up, trip the latch with my knife, and slip inside.

If the icy wind didn't knock me off the side of the building.

I pulled my head back in and made a check of myself. My kirtle was a sturdy, serviceable wool, and I had tucked the skirts high into my belt; they shouldn't pose much of a problem. The elaborate stonework had lots of hand- and toeholds. And there was no need to climb back down again; I'd just let myself out into the hallway on the third floor, shake out my skirts, and breeze down the corridor. I slipped Durrel's knife into my belt, held in place by a ball of skirt beneath it.

I hopped up to sit on the windowsill, nothing but cold behind me, and pulled my stockinged legs up onto the ledge, one after the other. Holding tightly to the window frame, I eased myself to standing.

Gods — that wind! It knocked the breath out of me and the sight from my eyes. I pressed my cheek against the rough stones until the blast of ice slackened, then cracked an eye open to judge my next move. Grasping a jutting brick tightly with out-of-practice fingers, I hauled myself up.

Gloves. Why hadn't I thought of *gloves*? The stones were rough and freezing; it was a good thing I only had to go one floor up — my fingers would be numb (and useless) before too long. I stretched my right leg up and found the top of the window frame. Pushing off, I grabbed a stone above, and straightened.

*Close the window.* I reached down with one cautious toe and gave the window a tap. It swung wide and almost caught; a little breeze might sneak in, but whoever found it would think only that it had come loose in the wind. Muscles stiff with cold and disuse, I made my way up the side of the Lodge, my hair whipping in icy strands against my eyes. Next time I'd wear a better hat.

Finally I felt my fingers close on the window ledge above, and pulled myself up until my chin was level with the sill. The wavery glass was inconveniently draped with heavy dark curtains, and I could see nothing inside. I held fast to the sill and twisted an arm behind my back to liberate my knife, then slid the blade between the two glass panes. It caught the catch easily, flipping it open. With the blade clamped between my teeth, I eased my fingers beneath one pane and tugged it toward me. Ducking as it swung overhead, I waited a moment, then spit my knife out into the room. I didn't hear it land — either the howling wind or a cushion of Corles rug muffled the sound.

*Almost there.* I searched the wall with one foot until I found a good-sized stone with a ledge just big enough to hold all my weight. I pushed off hard, high enough to hit waist to windowsill, then tumbled into the heavy drapes, scraping my back against the sill as I skidded down to the floor inside.

Corles rug. Not quite so soft on the tailbone as one might wish. I sat, frozen and breathless, just in case somebody had heard me, until the cold caught up with me and I started shivering. I eased to my feet and pushed into Daul's rooms. The chambers were stuffy and thick with heat from the fireplace, which blazed ridiculously, even considering the snow.

I tried to remember what I knew about Daul — not just the very little he'd hinted to me, but anything I'd heard him tell others, any clues I'd picked up from Cwalo and Lyll. He'd arrived here the same day as Marlytt and Cwalo — I thought back, picturing that scene. He'd been traveling lightly, no baggage. Where had he told Lyll he'd been? At the moment I couldn't remember.

I flipped through the papers on his desk, but there was nothing suspicious. Daul was smart and devious — he'd probably taken anything valuable with him — but he was also arrogant, and wouldn't have counted on me going to such lengths to get in here. What was I looking for? Keys, notes — anything with that single arrow on a black ground, like the rings. My letters. I popped the lock on the desk drawer, sliding the whole unit out from the desk and laying it gingerly on top. There was nothing fastened to the underside of the desk, or the underside of the drawer, or inside any kind of false bottom.

Inside the drawer itself I found the Carskadon hunting map I'd swiped from Lord Antoch's rooms. I should return it to Antoch; the thought of Daul knowing I was in here while he was gone, magic lock still perfectly undisturbed, gave me a malicious thrill. Tucked beside the map was the forged journal, and though I leafed through it I still couldn't tell what Daul had wanted it to say. The rolled-up map stuffed in my bodice, I shut the desk drawer and fiddled the lock until it snapped to, gazing around the rest of the room.

The problem with castles is that they have all sorts of hiding places: nooks in the fireplace façade, loose flags in the floor, decorative urns or boxes, spice cabinets, hollowed-out stones in the walls . . . there could be anything hidden anywhere. I tapped my knife blade flat against my palm, looking around. Exactly like Antoch's apartments, Daul's bedchamber was set off from the rest of the room, up two polished steps and curtained off. I pushed aside the copper damask hangings and stepped inside. The massive bed filled up most of the chamber, and for a moment I considered the possibility that I might have to climb up there to look above the canopy. I found nothing in the rosewood chest beside the bed, or beneath the seat cushion of the ebony dressing chair, or under the rug. I grasped the crewelwork bed hangings and flung them open.

And found something — but not the secret I sought.

The slender form wrapped untidily in the linen sheets winced against the sudden influx of light and raised a bare arm in defense. I stared down, one hand still clutching the bed curtain. Silver-pale hair scattered over the pillow, and ice-blue eyes squinted open to meet mine.

"Digger?" Marlytt's voice was thick with sleep, as if she couldn't quite fathom what I was doing there. She fumbled with the sheets. "Digger — wait!"

I didn't wait. I dropped the bed hangings and skittered back down the wide steps and was halfway to the door — the door with the lock that only opened *from the inside.* And how had Marlytt known that? *Idiot.*

"Digger, *wait.*" That cool voice stopped me. Marlytt, still wrapped in the bedclothes, grabbed me by the arm. "This isn't what —" She paused in the lie and pushed a handful of tangled wispy hair from her face. "This is exactly what you think it is. Every thought you're having is absolutely correct."

I looked around the rooms once again. The evidence of her presence was subtle — no silk dressing gown thrown over a chair, no hairpins scattered on the night table — yet Marlytt was obviously at home in these rooms. The roaring fire — I was seven times an idiot. Rooms whose occupants are away for a few days don't need to be *heated.*

"Daul's mistress?" I finally managed to get out. "You're *Daul's* mistress?"

She eyed me steadily. "Daul's whore, you mean? You can say it."

"But —" I grappled for words, as the events of the past weeks tumbled through my mind, each with a new significance. The things Daul claimed to know about me, the way Marlytt had urged me to avoid getting involved, the information she'd helped me piece together. Her cozy companionship with Meri. "How long?"

"Long enough. He brought me here."

"Everything I've told you, every *word* I've said — or Meri! — has gone straight to Daul's ear?"

"Don't try to play the wounded innocent here," she said coldly. "It doesn't suit you."

"But you know what he's been making me do!"

Marlytt's face was hard. "Yes," she said, "and now you know what he's been making *me* do."

I had to get out of there. I shoved past her toward the door, and snapped the bolt without even bothering to check if anyone was in the corridor outside. I ran down the hallway, not caring who saw me. How could I have been so stupid? I *knew* better than to trust Marlytt. And I'd put Bryn Shaer's most precious secrets practically right in her hands.

# CHAPTER TWENTY-SEVEN

I avoided Marlytt over the next few days, which was easy enough, as she kept herself scarce. Off scaring up other dupes to spy on for Daul, I supposed. What secrets had she managed to coax from Sposa or Cardom, with her soft voice and cool eyes? I tried to remember everything I might have told her, and how damning it was, but there was nothing to be done about the situation now except take even more care — and keep Meri away from her.

I tried to be angry with Marlytt . . . but I *knew* what Daul was — and I knew what Marlytt was, as well. She had her own priorities for survival; had she done anything worse than I had? Would I have done *any* of this, if it hadn't been for Daul prodding me? The hidden weapons, the secret Sarists, this stupid mess with Antoch and the Traitor of Kalorjn? Daul's whore? Well, that was me too. Even worse, after all that, I still hadn't managed to find anything useful in Daul's rooms.

The rest of that long week was interminable, following Lyll through an endless list of irrelevant tasks until I was ready to stab someone to death with my tiny embroidery needle. The snow never let up, building in slow, inexorable drifts on the windows and in front of doors. One freezing afternoon we gathered in the solar, where Lady Lyll supervised Meri working out the seating arrangements for her birthday breakfast. She shuffled people back and forth, while Lyll looked on and made suggestions.

"I wish Marlytt was here," Lyll said. "This is the sort of thing she excels at."

My eyes jerked up from the knot I was trying to untangle in my thread. "I think she's taken to bed —" I winced. "With a headache."

Phandre laid her stitching aside and gave a languorous stretch. She went to peek over Meri's shoulder, but as she read the chart, her face grew red.

"Cwalo?" she said. "You've seated me by the *wine* merchant?"

Meri looked up, confused. "I — I thought you'd want to," she said. "His sons —"

"You thought I'd want to sit with a common shopkeeper while *she*" — she glared at me — "gets the place of honor beside you? Who is she? I am a noblewoman, from a family older than yours!"

"You can have my seat; I don't care."

Phandre spun on me. "Of course you don't! You're *nobody*!"

"Lady Phandre," Lyll began ominously, using her title, but I was annoyed.

"Honestly, don't you ever think about anything important?" I snapped.

Phandre's face went white with fury, but Lady Lyll stepped between us. "Celyn, dear, why don't you run down to the stillroom, and check on that — preparation we've been working on. Lady Phandre and I will finish this conversation."

"Oh, what's the point?" Phandre said, heading for the door. "You always take her side." And she slammed out of the solar, the rest of us staring after her.

"What did I do?" Meri said.

"Don't worry about it," Lady Lyll said with a sigh. "Sooner or later she'll have to accept the realities of her situation. We'll find her a strand of pearls to wear, or something, and she'll get over it."

I took Lyll up on her suggestion anyway. Wierolf was kneeling on his bed, rummaging one-handed through the medical supplies on the shelf, his other hand stuck in his mouth. I could see the outline of the fresh bandages beneath his linen shirt, and wondered briefly if Lady Lyll was ever going to get him more clothes.

"Celyn, thank the gods," he mumbled through his fingers. "Can you help me — I can't seem to find anything to stop this bleeding —"

"You're bleeding? Again?" I crossed the room. "By Marau, Your Highness, you are *truly* the clumsiest man I've ever met. What have you done now?"

What he'd done was cut himself — badly, in the webbing between his finger and his thumb — on the dumb, dull knife Lady Lyll had given him to carve with. I dabbed the cut with a rag dipped in poppy. "Here, press down hard. What were you making?"

"Ha — here; you'll like this." He patted the rumpled bedclothes and found a disk of wood the size of my palm. "I'm making a new device for myself. What do you think?"

He handed it over: a skillful rendering of a lion, silhouetted against the rising sun. The sun's rays spread like flames to the edge of the disk, mingling with the flowing mane of the lion, its sinuous tail, its outstretched paw. I fingered the spokes of the rays, stretching out into forever. It felt like gold in my hand, warm and smooth from his touch.

"What do you think?"

The sun. Neither Celyst moon nor Sarist star, but something separate and above them. It was a daring statement — something I wasn't sure the world was expecting from Wierolf, Lazy Prince of Llyvraneth. I held the device of the lion and the sun up until the carved flames shone back the flickering lamplight.

"I like it," I said, absently watching the light hit the wood.

"Something's troubling you."

I glanced up. "No."

"Liar. You only come down here when you're upset."

"Not true! I also come down here when you're bleeding."

He smiled faintly. "What's the matter?"

With a sound that was half sigh, half growl, I sank beside him on the floor. "Nothing. Everything. I just saw a grown woman throw a fit over a feast seating chart. Nothing makes any sense anymore."

I couldn't sit still. I jumped up and grabbed Wierolf's knife, pacing before the wooden target. For the first time I realized the circle in the middle might actually have been more than just a ring to aim at. A round full moon, to strike at with a blade.

"I used to love secrets," I said. "Exploring rooms I wasn't supposed to be in, looking through locked keyholes, reading forbidden books. There was a *thrill* in knowing something nobody else knew. It made me feel — I don't know. Less small and powerless."

Wierolf leaned forward on the bed, listening. I paced a few more steps, and he finally said, "So what happened?"

I took a toss at the target, but the knife bounced off. "I met you."

He strode over and retrieved the knife. "Oh, come now," he said, handing it back. "I must be just about the best secret you ever had."

I wasn't in the mood to smile. "Almost."

"Really? Now what could possibly compare to me?" He sounded teasing, and I ignored him.

"This isn't funny. I don't know what to do. I know things, and I wish I didn't. I've never collected secrets about — about people I *know*, before. . . ." I shook my head. "It's different."

"Don't do anything," Wierolf suggested.

"I can't. They're too big. Somebody's going to get hurt." I flung the knife again. "Damn it! I wish I didn't care whether or not Antoch was the Traitor of Kalorjn! Or that Lady Lyll was stockpiling weapons — and princes — under her castle. Or that Meri —" I broke off. "This is impossible." I sank down on the bed.

He sat beside me. After a moment he said, "There's more, isn't there?"

"More? What are you talking about?"

"This isn't just about Lord Antoch or Lady Lyllace, or whoever your Meri is. Something else is weighing on you." He was looking at me with those steady deep brown eyes.

"Don't do that," I said.

"Do what?"

"Look into my — soul, like that. I don't like it."

"That's it, then," he said, and there was a hint of discovery in his voice, like a man finally figuring out a puzzle he's been working on. "This is about what *you're* hiding. About your secrets."

"I told you. I'm not hiding anything."

He looked at me softly. "Simple Celyn, just a maid."

"That's right."

Wierolf eased back. "All right. Well, if you're interested, I've never been that fond of secrets, myself. I think they're at the heart of a lot of what's wrong right now — the fear and suspicion, the secrecy. Neighbors turning on each other, parents hiding their children, people hiding their faith. That can't be what any of the gods intended. Bardolph and Werne have it wrong."

"Werne?" The name slipped out, a faint little whisper.

"What happened to you at the Celystra?" Wierolf's voice was gentle.

I pulled back. "Nothing."

"Did it involve your brother?"

I turned to him. "What? No, I told you —"

"Do you know you flinch anytime someone mentions him?"

"I do not!" But I did. I knew I did. "Why am I talking to you?" I got up again and found the knife where it had fallen, across the room at the base of the target.

"You want to," Wierolf said easily. "Celyn, you're not small and power-less anymore. Whatever it is, it can't hurt you now."

"Oh, yes it can." But somehow, it suddenly seemed intolerable that *Daul* was the only person who knew this, when I was surrounded by people who wouldn't use that knowledge to hurt me — Meri and Lyll and Wierolf. The prince was wrong; this was very dangerous, but hiding from the truth couldn't keep it at bay forever. Wierolf had shown no interest in the throne — yet he'd been attacked by his uncle's men any-way. And I couldn't keep pretending that renouncing my brother meant the connection between us did not exist.

I took the knife and sat back down beside Wierolf. He looked at me expectantly. "Let me see that pendant you wear," I said. He quirked an eyebrow at me, but handed it over. "What does this look like to you?" I asked.

"Uh — bronze? A circle, with a star on it? Why, what does it look like to you?"

I gripped it in my hand, until the magic frothed through my fingers. "Like sunlight on water. Like — heat haze. Or a fog."

"You have magic." Somehow, there was no surprise at all in his voice.

"I *see* magic. You don't want to see magic at the Celystra. My brother was the devout one; he told me I was unclean. He called me an *abomination*, a corrupt thing unworthy of the gods."

Wierolf touched my hand. "That's unforgivable."

"No — what's unforgivable is that I believed him. For years, I thought somehow, maybe he was right. Surely he *knew*, right? Hadn't Celys chosen him to speak for her? If the Lord High Inquisitor calls something unholy, it must be so."

The prince's dark eyes grew wide. "Wait. Your brother is —"

I was halfway there already. I took a breath and undid the lie I'd been hiding behind for five years. "Werne the Bloodletter."

He just *looked* at me a moment, utter disbelief on his face. Then he made a strange, strangled sound, and covered his face with his big hand.

"Laughing. You're laughing? I tell you my brother is the king's Inquisitor, and your response is to laugh."

"I'm sorry," he said. "Truly, Celyn — that's just so much *bigger* than I expected! I knew you had a secret, but by Tiboran —"

"Did you ever think that maybe this is one of the reasons people want you dead?" I snapped. "No wonder they favor Astilan."

The smile dipped. "I deserved that," he said. "I know what it cost you to tell me this. But you speak truly? You really are the Inquisitor's sister?"

I closed my eyes and kissed the knuckles of my left hand. "I swear by Tiboran and the Nameless One, I would not lie about that."

"No, I believe you — it's just . . . I've never heard that he had any siblings." He uncurled my fingers from his medallion. "But I suppose the reason for that is obvious." There was a long, silent pause, as Wierolf seemed to try to place this new information in his understanding of the universe. "So it's Celyn Nebraut, then? Who's Celyn Contrare?"

"An invention. And it's not Celyn at all. It's Digger."

He looked amused again. "The Inquisitor has a sister called Digger. What's your real name?"

"Children born inside the convent aren't given names until they take their vows. I wasn't there that long." The prince was still watching me in astonishment. "It's a long story."

"Then tell me." His voice was gentle, inviting. *Go ahead, Celyn, give us your tale.* And somehow, there I was, telling him everything. About the Celystra, about the man who'd died when I'd informed on him, however unwittingly, about leaving the convent and making a life on the streets as a pickpocket. How I'd buried myself so deep in the slums, as Werne rose so high in the church, that I was sure we'd never find each other ever again.

"Who were your parents?"

My voice was rusty and stiff on this unpracticed story. "My mother came to the Celystra when she was pregnant with me, though Werne always liked to claim I was one of the priests' children. She'd been married to *his* father, a potter who died when Werne was small." A monk had told me that once, meaning to be kind. "She died when I was born, so I don't even know her name. Werne would never tell me. She died in grace, he'd say, and her life before meant nothing."

I sighed and looked into my skirts. "I've always wondered what kind of life she had hoped for, coming there. What she'd wanted for us. She got it with Werne, at least." My voice sounded bitter.

"How old were you when you left?"

"Eleven. I really did just climb up over the wall and drop down on the other side — smack in the heart of Gerse. That first night — I was sure I would die. Everything was so *loud*, and disorderly. A horse from a passing coach nearly ran me down, and I thought it was Celys, come to drag me back inside. I ran. I'm still running." I took a breath, remembering. "But another girl found me when I nicked a roll from a cart, and she took me to a tavern and told me all about Tiboran. And everyone there was messy, and devious, and they laughed at *everything*, and they gave me a knife and told me to go cut a man's purse strings — and I did it, and I was good at it. And I liked it. I loved it."

"And somehow you ended up at Bryn Shaer."

I explained how that had happened as well. Wierolf mulled this over for a bit, then surprised me by standing, and by pulling me to my feet too. "Well met, Digger of Gerse," he said. "I am Prince Wierolf, and I've a few questionable relations of my own."

Now that the words were said, I felt horribly exposed, as if someone had stripped away my clothes and pushed me out into the snow. "What now?" I said. "What happens next?"

He regarded me solemnly. "Now you can figure out the next secret on that list."

# CHAPTER TWENTY-EIGHT

I felt raw and hollow after my confession to the prince, like after a bad sickness. I had said the words, and they hadn't killed me, but it would take a while before I felt like myself again. I took the kennel route from Wierolf's chamber, to delay the moment I'd have to face people. Afternoon had faded to evening, and Tiboran's moon was high and bright in a deepening sky. I looked up at it gravely, then sketched a formal, actor's bow. "Thank you," I said aloud. He had guided my performance all these years, after all. I had to have faith that the timing he'd chosen for the end of my masquerade was the right one.

The next few days were peaceful ones at Bryn Shaer, even amid the birthday preparations. Lady Lyll's late-night meetings with the conspirators continued; Meri and I "attended" another one together, and they seemed to be piecing together their final arguments for the king's representative. I knew Lyll nursed some concern for Lord Antoch's party, now a day or so overdue, but for me, with Daul gone, it almost really was like a holiday.

One morning I came back from the stillroom to find Phandre pawing through Meri's clothes chest.

"What are you doing?" I crossed the room and slammed the lid shut, unfortunately missing her fingers.

"Looking for Meri's pink sleeves," she said haughtily. The garments in question were balled up in her hand. "Not that it's any of your business. I wanted them for luncheon this afternoon."

"Wear your own sleeves," I snapped, snatching them away from her. As I smoothed the silk, I saw a little tear in the lining. "Phandre . . ."

Phandre ignored me, just strode across the room, looking around like she didn't live here too. "Where is she this morning?" she asked sweetly. "She disappears a lot, doesn't she? Like you. I came in late last night, and what a suprise to find your bed empty."

"I'm sure you find that strange," I said. "If Meri wanted you to know what she was doing, she'd tell you."

"Oh, yes, I forgot. *You're* her great confidante now." Phandre gave me a little sniff and headed off to her own room — but not before plucking the pink sleeves from my hands again.

I shook my head. *Nobs.*

Meri returned a few minutes later, bubbling over with excitement. "Stagne and I materialized a ball of flame for a full minute before it dissipated!" As I helped her out of her riding clothes, she added, "I saw Marlytt in the courtyard. She'd like to speak to you."

When I didn't respond, she squeezed my arm. "Say you'll go. I don't like to see you two quarreling. She says she has something to give you."

Outside, a figure in blue descended the east tower steps and came to meet me, long hem trailing behind her in the snow.

"I know you don't want to talk to me," Marlytt said. She held the neck of her coat closed with one shivering hand. "So just listen."

Warily I nodded, and she set off walking toward the moonlit sculpture garden. I followed close behind.

"When Daul found me, I was in Tratua with a man called Mils Rhonin. He was a low-level city official, a widower. I had been with him almost a year." She paused and looked up into the sky. Ice crystals had formed on her long, pale lashes. "He wanted to marry me."

She kept a measured pace, and her voice in the whipping wind was soft but distinct. "I think he mostly wanted a mother for his children — a girl and two little boys. They had a house with a view of the sea, and a courtyard where the children could play." She looked straight at me. "It was the kind of life that girls like us never dream of having.

"And then one night I met Daul at a banquet — some city function that Mils had to attend. I danced two dances with him, and by the end of the night he'd told me to leave Mils and come with him. I refused, of course. The next day I saw him again, when Mils's daughter and I were drawing water at the city fountain. He claimed to have contacts in the

Inquisition. He again told me to leave Mils, this time in much less . . . subtle terms. Mils's daughter had to stand there and listen while Daul called me a whore.

"A week later, five Acolyte Guardsmen arrested Mils at our house, in front of his children. Daul was there an hour later. And that time, I went with him."

She arranged a strand of fair hair that had slipped loose. "He brought me here to spy on Antoch, to seduce him. But when it came time, he wouldn't let me. I guess Daul turned out to be a jealous lover after all. Not that Antoch would ever have been tempted; I saw that immediately. He's too good a man. And then you showed up, a new toy Daul just couldn't resist." She shook her head. "I'm sorry, Digger. I didn't mean to get you into this."

Her eyes were as icy as I'd ever seen them. "Daul is cold and he is ambitious. When he wants something, he gets it. When he hurts you, he leaves no marks — but you bleed to death on the inside, from a thousand invisible cuts." She turned her gaze into the distance, toward the wall and the mountains and, maybe, the canals of Tratua. "I saw Mils one more time. Daul took me to see them release him from prison. It had only been a few days, but he'd changed so much. The worst thing, though," she said, so softly I almost didn't hear her, "the worst was the look in his eyes when he saw me standing in the boat beside Daul."

She turned to face me. "So you can stop giving me that look like I've plunged a knife into you, and don't you dare judge me. Because I know what it feels like to betray someone I care about, and believe me — this is nothing."

Before I could say anything, Marlytt pulled something from her sleeve and held it out to me. A packet of letters, a little road-worn and rumpled still from being crushed against someone's rib cage for a month. Her hand was blue with cold, but steady somehow. "I think you were looking for these," she said. "Don't lose them again."

She lifted the sable hood up over her face, turned, and walked back to the castle with measured dignity.

I didn't follow. But in the fading light, I unfolded Chavel's letters. And there, along with the letter to Vichet and Wierolf's death warrant and the incomprehensible list of odd markings, was something new: a worn and much-folded slip of paper that read *In these pages, I have recorded the truth.* I knew that dark, spidery hand all too well: Senim Daul, my expert huntsman. Beneath that pronouncement, the page was covered in numbers that spread onto the back side. Folded with it was another sheet, in a hand I didn't recognize, but could guess: Senim's son. This one was filled with little notes and scratch marks, as if he'd been trying to puzzle something out. And, standing there in the late morning chill, I thought I knew what.

"Thank you, Marlytt," I whispered into the dusting snow.

I had to wait until everyone else went to dinner, but as soon as I could, I hastened back to Meri's rooms and popped open the little compartment beneath the window seat. Her books were still there, and I pulled out Senim Daul's hunting journal. Beside it, I spread out the two pages Marlytt had given me: the sheet of numbers, and Daul's efforts to decipher his father's message about Kalorjn. *A message to share,* he'd said: half to Antoch, half to Daul. Antoch had received the journal, and Daul the list of numbers. How did they fit together?

I turned a few pages in the journal, glancing not at the words but at the book itself, the margins, even the page numbers, carefully rendered in tiny, neat script. I'd had to renumber them in Daul's version, to account for the sections his was missing — Meri's sections. Daul had said the journal was worthless.

It wasn't worthless. Not the real one. Not the one I held in my hands, carefully arranged by a system of page numbers to say precisely the right thing at the right spot on the right page, so another reader could find that reference easily.

I had seen a coded book once before in the Celystra manuscript room, a volume of heretical scripture disguised beneath a lackluster history of foreign rulers. The Scriptor had explained to me how it worked: One conspirator wrote out a message using words in the book, and then sent a coded version of the message referencing only page and word numbers. The recipient could then look up the numbers, and reconstruct the message by finding the right word on the right page. It was a neat little system, and in theory it worked beautifully.

Unless you had a forged version of the book that was off count by some fifteen pages. Then your reconstructed message, instead of saying *I can identify the man who betrayed us,* would read *Boar the and bloody fowl tossed there water.*

Precisely what had happened to Daul.

I got up from the floor and made very certain Meri's door was locked. Then I knelt in the dark by the fire, trying to decide if I really wanted to do this. *In these pages I have recorded the truth.* Senim had meant this information to be known, at least by a very few people that he trusted. But eighteen years had passed; the damage was done long ago. Wierolf was right: Did it even matter anymore?

It mattered to Daul. The truth he thought was hidden in this book had twisted friendship and love into something awful and vindictive. Maybe it was best if I just threw the note and the journal both into the fire, let this secret die with Senim Daul, like it should have.

*Antoch is too good a man.* Even Marlytt sensed that, and her instincts about people were infallible. If it was true, if Antoch was the Traitor, it would destroy a lot of that good. And what would it do to the alliance growing right now at Bryn Shaer, if Lady Lyll's allies discovered Nemair had betrayed them?

I held the book close to the flames, but something stayed my hand. Wierolf had spoken of how damaging secrets like this could be, as if they ate at the heart of the country like a poison. And it seemed Tiboran had ordained this hour for the unraveling of secrets. First mine, then Marlytt's — and now the truth about Kalorjn.

With a weird weight pressing on me, I fetched fresh paper and ink, and set about uncovering one more secret.

The contents of the message unfolded before me. What Senim Daul had carefully hidden among the falconry lessons and mating habits of the wild boar was the account of what the Sarist commander had discovered about the Battle of Kalorjn. How under only mild duress, and with weak promises of paltry rewards, someone had agreed to leak false intelligence to the Sarist troops.

But who was it? Daul's book contained no proper names, but when I searched through its pages again, I discovered a handful of strange spelling errors — letters repeated in certain words. I had taken them for fatigue or carelessness when I'd made my copy, but now I wasn't so sure. When I rearranged the extra letters, they sorted themselves out into a name. I was hoping it would be harder, that the shape of the words would be unfamiliar, that it would reveal a name I didn't know from the halls of Bryn Shaer.

But it didn't.

According to Senim Daul's convincing account, the Traitor of Kalorjn was not Lord Antoch Nemair.

Commander Daul had named Lougre Séthe.

Phandre's father.

I sat in the roar of the flames, feeling hot and sick. The strange things Antoch had said about her in the Armory finally made sense. No wonder the Nemair felt sorry for her. They were just that generous.

What would Daul do? What should I do? I folded the account up with Daul's papers and the journal, and tucked everything under the window seat. I had to tell Daul when he got back; he needed to know Antoch was innocent. But that might turn his wrath on Phandre, which, however I felt about her, she didn't deserve. And there was no way to convince Daul without also showing him the real journal — and nothing had changed there: I still couldn't do that, not without endangering Meri. To say nothing of the trouble Marlytt would be in, for stealing Daul's papers.

Meri came in before I had made up my mind. She swished over to me in her red velvet gown. "We missed you tonight," she said. "Are you all right?"

Was I? I had no idea. But I nodded.

"Master Cwalo asked after you. He wanted to partner with you at riddles. He told me all about his son Viorst, who manages a winery in Yeris Volbann. It sounded very romantic."

"Meri, I'm not going to marry one of Master Cwalo's sons."

She smiled. "I know. But it's fun to think about."

I watched her, something tight in my chest I didn't understand. She wasn't the daughter of a traitor; if she'd had any clue there was ever a risk of it, she'd be delighted that it wasn't true. Was there any chance that Phandre knew what her father had done? "I'm sorry about Phandre," I said without meaning to, and Meri frowned.

"What about her?"

"She took your sleeves," I improvised. "I think she's still mad about the seating arrangements for your breakfast."

"Oh, she's always like that." Meri looked at her hands, smiling faintly. "My parents always insisted we be kind to her, and we have so much in common, anyway."

"Like *what*?"

"Both of our parents were exiled, while we had to stay in Llyvraneth as wards of the Crown. She didn't have a family to take her in, like I did, just a lot of tolerant houses that would keep her for a season or two. Lord Ragn was always kind to her, and the Decath usually let her stay longer than most. But she'd always move on, and then when she came back . . ." Meri trailed off.

A daughter cast to the fickle sympathies of random nobs seemed like pitiful reward for Séthe selling out his brethren. Why had he done it? Meri curled up beside me on the bench and leaned her sparkling head against my shoulder. "I'm glad you came to Bryn Shaer with me, Celyn."

That weight on my chest pressed harder. "Me too, Meri."

The door to Meri's rooms swung open, and Phandre walked in. She took one look at Meri and me sitting together, and her face clouded with disgust. With an angry shake to her head, she walked straight past us and slammed the door to her little room.

*  *  *

As soon as Meri set off to meet Stagne the next morning, I nipped down to see the prince. He was carving again, this time with a better grip on the wood and a lot less blood. He looked up when I came in.

"It's not Antoch," I burst out. "He's not the Traitor."

The prince's face lightened with relief. "Good. That's wonderful. Did you find out who it was?"

"It's no one at Bryn Shaer. It's someone — dead. I think it doesn't matter anymore."

Wierolf studied me a long moment, eyes dark and soft. I looked away before he convinced me to make any more spontaneous confessions, but I sat down on the floor, feeling strangely light and free. Daul was gone for the moment, I'd survived revealing my identity, and Antoch wasn't the traitor. Maybe Wierolf was right, and this secrecy business was overrated. "What are you working on now?" I asked.

Wierolf handed me the scrap of wood he'd been whittling. It wasn't much of anything, really, just a series of scrolls and edge-fluting and faint, tentative markings, like he'd been trying out ideas before committing to them. "I'm carving you a miniature of the Celystra, for a souvenir," he said with a grin.

I punched him in the shoulder. "Oh! You're very amusing. When winter's over, maybe Lyll can find you a post with a troupe of traveling —" I stopped, staring at the carving. Among the random sketches on the back, one thing stood out. Scratched in the wood was a long, thin arrow, etched inside an oval.

Suddenly I was *freezing*. I turned the piece around and showed it to the prince, my finger on the symbol.

"What is this?" My voice was faint.

Wierolf scowled. "I don't know. I keep seeing it, whenever I get flashes of — that day at Olin. Why?"

"Because I've seen this symbol before," I said. I reached into my dress and fished out the onyx rings. "On two dead men, and one living man with a serious grudge against Sarists."

Wierolf turned the rings over in his fingers, his brows drawn taut together. "Where did you find these?"

"They were on the avalanche victims. Does it have something to do with the men who attacked you?"

"I — maybe. I can't remember. The avalanche victims?" Wierolf's frown intensified. He looked like his head hurt. "I don't understand."

But I did. For the first time, I understood *everything*, and it was so sickeningly, perfectly obvious. "I have to go," I said, getting to my feet.

"What? Go where? Digger!" Wierolf said. But I was already gone.

I flew up the little passage and hauled myself into the empty still-room and out into the hallway. In the servants' stair, I dug through my hidden stash for the hunting map I'd taken first from Antoch's and then Daul's rooms. I unrolled it on the stairs. Where — where was it? There — about a day's ride northeast of Bryn Shaer was a marking for what looked like a good-sized country house, in the midst of a forest labeled *Miniver, Stag, & Grouse. Olin.*

Two people had told me that the hunting was good at Olin this time of year.

The prince, who had been hunting stag.

And Remy Daul. Who never hunted. And yet wore a huntsman's ring.

*Somebody claiming the name Huntsmen says they've offed him.*

# CHAPTER TWENTY-NINE

For a moment I couldn't move, couldn't breathe, couldn't stop staring at the name on the map. Good hunting at Olin. The rings. The *sovereign* he'd paid me with. His utter lack of surprise over Wierolf's death warrant. *No, little mouse, that's not news.* An order to kill the prince *wouldn't* seem like news to the man who'd already carried it out.

Somehow I was on my feet again. I had to find Lyll. Daul surely didn't know he'd failed. The "avalanche victims" must have been his accomplices; had he dispatched them too, while crossing the Breijarda Velde to Bryn Shaer? Grabbing the rings and the map, I banged up the stairs to Lady Lyll's rooms.

She swung the door open to my frantic knock. I pushed inside.

"Celyn, what on earth's the matter? You're white as milk."

"Daul tried to kill the prince." There wasn't any other way but blurting it out. My shaking hands dumped the map and rings on the rug, and Lyll bent to retrieve them. "It's not safe — we have to move him."

"What's this?" Lyll asked, an edge of concern in her calm voice.

I tried to nick a little of that calm for myself. Taking a deep breath, I started again. "I think that Lord Daul is responsible for the attempt to assassinate Prince Wierolf."

A little of the color leached from Lyll's face, and she rose and clicked her door shut, pointing to a low bench. "Sit. Explain."

I obeyed, while Lyll examined the map and rings, her expression growing sharper when I got to the avalanche victims in the tunnels.

"He must be one of these Huntsmen that the rumors are about," I said. "He called the ring a token of his commitment to something — and if he's already killed his accomplices . . . Milady, Wierolf isn't safe here."

"This is very disturbing," Lyll said slowly. "What made you . . . look into this?"

I wanted her to be brisk and decisive, sweep through the halls of Bryn Shaer and somehow whisk Wierolf to safety, but instead she was cautious. I could tell she was tracking back over my movements of the last few weeks — my perpetual lateness, my pointed questions, my late-night wanderings, my discovery of the prince. She'd convinced herself that I was just impetuous and curious, but now she'd be reconsidering her assessment of me. And she'd get to the truth.

I searched for the words to explain. "Your ladyship, I — I find things."

"You *find* things," she echoed. "I had noticed. Is it too much to hope that finding is all you've done?" When I couldn't answer, she pursed her lips. "I see. So besides spying on Lord Daul, what other things have you 'found'?"

I made a strangled sound. How many masks did Tiboran expect me to shed all at once? "Not *on* him, milady," I said. "For him."

She drew back. "Ah."

"Lady Lyllace, please. I didn't know he was going to turn out to be —" I faltered and gave up. Daul had shown me what he was the day I met him. The only surprise had been how I had come to feel about the Nemair. "I'm sorry. He's been collecting information to send to the Inquisition."

Lyll nodded slowly and crossed the room. "We know," she said finally.

"You *know*?"

She opened a locked compartment behind a drawer in her spice chest. "We've intercepted one of his messages. It was in code, so we have no idea what it says, but the Gerse address is a false one known to be used by His Majesty's spies. We made a copy, but had no choice but to let it go through. We slipped it back among the other messages before Berdal rode out. At least we're aware of him now." She took a folded paper from the chest.

There were a dozen questions I wanted to ask. "How long have you known about him?" I finally managed.

"I've *wondered* for some time, but it's only been since Berdal left with the mail that there's been anything concrete to confirm my concerns. We read all the messages before they left Bryn Shaer, and we recognized the address. That's one of the reasons Antoch took Daul with him this week — to keep an eye on him, somewhere he couldn't do any more harm."

"Milady, I — I don't know what to say," I said honestly. "This is all my fault, and —"

"I can't pretend to be pleased by this news, Celyn," Lyll said crisply. "But I have to suspect there was some fairly significant pressure brought to bear to . . . encourage your cooperation."

I nodded unhappily. "But what about the prince?" I said. "We have to do something, before Daul discovers that he's failed."

Lyll was grim, pacing between the chest and the bench. "Normally I would agree with you, of course. But, Celyn, he's not well enough to ride, and I'm afraid there's nowhere nearby to send him safely, and no one I trust, for that matter. I don't know what we can do."

"Then at least give him some guards or something!" I sounded desperate.

She considered this. "Good, yes. We have a little time, I hope. I will try to come up with alternate arrangements for His Highness before Daul returns and becomes an — urgent threat. But in the meantime, Celyn, I must ask you not to see the prince again."

I recognized the iron — the *disappointment* in her voice. "I understand, milady." There was so much I wanted to explain, to *make* her understand, but all my explanations would sound false. Lyll would never trust me again.

She was still holding the paper from the spice chest, folding it and refolding it in her hands, and I caught a glimpse of the contents — a collection of symbols and numbers that seemed oddly familiar. "Milady, may I see that?"

She hesitated, but apparently decided I couldn't do any more harm either. I studied the strange notations in Daul's coded message, and for a moment everything went absolutely still and quiet. "I know this," I whispered, dipping into my bodice. I pulled out Chavel's papers — the letter, the death warrant, and the third page that we hadn't been able to identify. Wordlessly, I passed the lot to Lady Lyll. She took them, her breath growing quicker as she read.

"Where did you come by these?"

I looked at her. "Milady," I said, "I'm not really a jeweler's daughter."

She glanced up. "I was beginning to wonder."

Slowly I explained about the job at Chavel's, about the Greenmen waiting for us. About Tegen. Everything I had worked for Daul to keep hidden. As I spoke, Lyll took the packet of letters to her desk and lit a candle. Exactly as I had seen Daul do, weeks ago, she held the papers up, one by one, to the flame. Chavel had not had time to seal his letters with wax — but on the lip of each page appeared a faint circle of ink, showing an arrangement of four moons.

Lyll put a hand on my arm. "Your friend died recovering a Celyst code key," she said. "You have no idea how important this is. This will change everything for us."

I watched the hidden ink seals darken over the flame. "Secretary Chavel?"

"A Sarist sympathizer," she said. "He was taking enormous risks, sending sensitive information out of Hanivard Palace. I'm sorry to say we heard that he had been arrested, but perhaps the fact that you removed this evidence will spare his life."

"What is that symbol?"

Lyll reached inside her desk and found another letter. As she held it over the flame, I saw the same symbol appear — no, not quite the same. A circle with three moons. She layered one paper over the other, so the seals overlapped, and held them before the light. Together, they made a circle with seven moons showing the seven points of a star.

A knock struck her door, making us both jump. Lyll extinguished the flame and tucked the papers into the heavy folds of her sleeves. "Get that, will you?" she said, and I swung the door open to admit Eptin Cwalo.

"Excellent," Lyll said. "Cwalo, come. I have news."

"I have as well, your ladyship," he said. "Your lord husband has returned."

I shot a panicked look at Lyll, but her practiced calm never wavered. "Good," she said. "Did our friends come?"

Cwalo stepped inside, shutting the door behind him. "Unknown, milady. But apparently his lordship brings further news: Workmen have succeeded in clearing the snow from the Breijarda Velde. The pass is open."

"More good news," Lyll said brightly. "Lady Celyn —" She paused, and a cloud of something passed over her face, but I couldn't tell what it was. She slipped the packet of letters from her sleeves and turned them over in her hands. "My dear," she said, "may I hold on to these for a bit?"

I reached out to touch the softened edges, the dried spots of Tegen's blood. *Love letters*, Phandre had called them, and I'd been wearing them pressed against my heart as if that were true. "Keep them," I said. "I've been trying to deliver them for two months."

Lyll squeezed my arm. "Go and see what tidings my husband brings," she said.

I stiffened. *Daul* was out there. "But what about —"

"Do nothing," she said firmly. "We must give no cause for alarm, do you understand me?"

I nodded, not at all confident I was that good a liar. But Lyll held me steady in her gaze. "All *will* be well, Celyn. Have faith." She gave me a nudge toward the door, and I left, wanting desperately to believe her.

Men and horses bustled in the paddock, unloading supplies and milling about Lord Antoch. I counted well over a dozen strange faces; where had they come from? Berdal had ridden out alone, and Antoch and Daul had taken only a handful of guards. Lord Antoch spotted me and gave me a crushing hug. "Ah, Celyn, good to be home," he said.

"I think her ladyship wants to see you," I said. Daul was glowering at me over the back of his horse, and I couldn't help noticing that his hands were bare. His ring was gone. I was dismayed — without that ring, there was nothing to tie him to the prince. Lord Antoch set off for the Lodge with Daul, most of the men trailing behind them.

"Welcome back," I said to Berdal, even daring to reach my gloved hand up to touch his horse's face, as I'd seen Meri do. It bumped back at me in a snuffling, hungry way I didn't altogether care for.

"She likes you," Berdal said. "You come out when the weather's better, and I'll teach you to ride."

"Right," I said, curling back my fingers. I'd make time for that. "How was the trip? We were worried about you."

He looked embarrassed. "Sorry about that. We had a little drama at home. One of my cousins has joined the army." He shook his head, hauling off his horse's saddle.

"Bardolph's army?" I said, and he actually spat into the snow.

"Worse. Astilan's! I thought my aunt Thilde would die of the shame."

I looked at him in surprise; people normally didn't speak so freely. "You don't support Astilan's claim?" I said tentatively, but guessing what the answer would be. He worked for the Nemair, didn't he? I remembered that woodsman in the inn saying the mountain people had supported the Sarists in the last rebellion.

"Not me," Berdal was saying, heading with his saddle toward the stables. "I'm strictly Wierolf's man, when the time comes."

*He'll be glad to hear it,* I thought. Berdal reappeared, still talking as he worked. "My father died at Kalorjn," he said. "A lot of boys up here are just waiting for a chance to fight that battle again."

I turned to where the liveried Nemair guards were leading a knot of commonly dressed fellows into the older part of the castle, and recalled Lady Lyll asking *Did our friends come?* The Nemair had no army; who did they plan would wield the guns waiting in the wine cellar? "Uh, how many boys?" I asked, and Berdal grinned.

"I guess it wouldn't do any harm to say her ladyship had better instruct that housekeeper of hers to start cooking meals for about five dozen. We brought about twenty home with us, but more are on their way. And more will *be* on the way soon, now that the pass is open."

"You weren't just delivering the mail," I said stupidly.

Berdal looked toward the castle. "It's not much, unfortunately, but it's a start. Men will come, now that word's out that Bryn Shaer is recruiting."

I hoped there would be time for Lady Lyll and Lord Antoch and their allies to gather all the troops they'd need. Bardolph had had eighteen years to build up his army, while the Sarists had been barred from retaining more than a handful of guards. Oddly, a little thrill went through me, knowing everything Lyll and the others were doing to prepare themselves.

Which would all be for nothing, if we couldn't safeguard the prince.

Upstairs in the Lesser Court, Lady Lyll and Meri were reading a letter together, their matching heads bent over a sheet of green-dyed parchment, a cracked seal of gold wax making two half-moons on the paper. Antoch stood behind them, looking grim. Meri was pale, but Lyll's face was set. She glanced up and waved me over.

"Milady?" I said. "What is it? Is it from the king?" Would the conspirators finally get their opportunity to present their demands to Bardolph's representative?

Wordlessly, Lyll passed me the green letter, and I felt the chill in the room descend as I read it. This document didn't offer anybody at Bryn Shaer a chance to do anything except turn on each other in a bloody scramble to dodge the scald and gallows.

The letter was from Bardolph — and, as anticipated, he was declining the Nemair's invitation. And he *was* sending someone in his place. But this representative would not be interested in the complaints of a handful of disgruntled nobs.

Because the king was sending Werne Nebraut, the Lord High Inquisitor.

# CHAPTER THIRTY

I held that letter tight, my head buzzing. The name Werne, in thick black script, marched across the page like a roach, but I couldn't make myself drop the paper. Werne, coming *here*.

"When?" My voice was a mere thread of sound.

"The letter is more than a week old," Lord Antoch said. "They'll have word that the pass is open by now. With clear weather, Gerse is no more than five days' ride. If there's another storm, maybe a day or two more. But soon."

"By my birthday?" Meri said faintly. Somehow I had forgotten, but the Dead of Winter was only a few days away.

Meri's mother nodded grimly.

"Milady, what about —" *About Wierolf, and Daul?* I stared urgently at her, but she shook her head.

"There's no time," she said simply. "It's too late."

Five days, a week at the most, and the Inquisition would be at Bryn Shaer. I didn't want to believe it, but they were riding even now. Werne and his six Confessors on their dun-brown palfreys, with their snooping noses and their air of authority and righteousness, coming to comb their fingers through Meri's things. Through Lady Cardom's perfectly composed embroidery. Through Lord Wellyth's sweet letters from his granddaughter. Through every inch of Bryn Shaer, prying up loose floorboards and wall panels, digging into every crevice and crack until they found all the evidence I'd helped Daul alert them to.

Coming here to find *me*, stinking of Sarists, and lighting up like a candle in the presence of magic. I knew they had tools — their blue jasper lodestones, charmed by specially trained priest-confessors to light up when held by someone with magic, their treated silver chains that burned the skin. It didn't always work, but it would be enough to condemn me.

My very face alone was enough to condemn me.

And what about Meri, with her silver and her tattoo?

And Reynart, Stagne, Kespa, and all the others?

And Wierolf — would he be safe?

After the Inquisition came through Bryn Shaer, the only person left standing would be Remy Daul. They'd burn the hangings, smash the new glass windows, leave the Lodge a tower of smoke to be seen for hundreds of miles, rising above the Carskadons and telling all of Llyvraneth that we were powerless against them.

What had I thought would happen, when I agreed to help Daul?

The next days were dark ones at Bryn Shaer, everyone in a pall of defeat and dread. Lyll directed a tense masquerade, leading us through a steady progression of feasts and games and *kernja-velde* rehearsals as if nothing was out of the ordinary, but all of the Sarist conspirators had been alerted to the Inquisition's arrival. Meri reported raised voices from the Lesser Court gallery more than once, but I'd lost the heart to eavesdrop with her. The promise I gave Lady Lyll, to stay away from Wierolf's cell, only made things worse. I *knew* nobody else would tell the prince that the Inquisition was coming, but I was desperate to show Lyll that I was not some wanton gutter brat bent on pulling apart everything she'd worked for. Besides, I was too busy stalking Daul.

Lyll had said to give Daul no sign that he'd been exposed, but it wouldn't have mattered if we did. He strode the halls of the Lodge like he owned them, walking into the kitchens and helping himself to wine and food, ordering the servants about and rearranging the furnishings in the Round Court and Armory, which Lady Lyll always quietly put back into place again.

I found him late one afternoon in Lady Lyll's apartments, lounging before the fire and eating an apple, his wet boots propped up on a silk damask robe thrown across a bench. I suddenly realized what Daul thought he would get out of all of this. "Ah, mouse," he said lazily, "now we shall reap the rewards of our labors."

I stalked over and yanked the robe out from under his feet. "Get out of here!"

The oily smile spread. "Our friends are on their way. The world will finally know what kind of man Antoch Nemair really is. And I know they'll be particularly interested in hearing from you, all your fascinating discoveries about our hosts."

I felt something hot under my breastbone — and I liked it. I looked him in the eyes. "I don't have anything to say."

Daul looked surprised. "Don't tell me you've grown scruples, mouse. That won't save them."

"Maybe not, but I might feel compelled to volunteer some other information I've gathered here and there."

He rose so fast he knocked the bench over. "You're bluffing. You don't know anything."

"I *know* what you are, and I know what Antoch is," I said fiercely. "And you're wrong about everything. Now take your hand off my arm before I break it." I didn't wait, but shook him off and pushed past him out into the hall.

Daul was right, as usual; I wasn't bluffing, but his crimes weren't anything the Inquisition would care about. Still, I couldn't just stand and *wait* for all of Daul's plans to destroy us. That fire in my breast propelled me all the way out onto the east tower, where the icy air woke me out of my fog. Master Cwalo was walking the battlement, holding his hands up to the walls as if estimating measurements. He was bundled in a long Kurkyat coat in shades of fiery orange and gold, a fluffy fur hat covering his bald head.

"Fine afternoon," he said as his words were whipped away by a brutal wind and snowflakes swirled before his face.

"Where are you from?" I snapped, and he laughed. In the distance, the Breijarda Velde was a wide white gash in the hills. For weeks the avalanche had trapped us here; now, without it, we were suddenly vulnerable. "We have to do something."

Cwalo turned and leaned against the wall, eyeing me strangely. "Not much to be done at this point," he said. "Everyone here knew the risks, and we knew what would happen if we were caught. Now, Lyllace will try to bluff, but it's difficult to make a cannon look innocent. And if they were to find anything worse . . . well."

"And nothing happens to Daul." I was sure Lyll had confided in Master Cwalo.

"He hasn't done anything wrong," he said.

"He tried to kill Prince Wierolf!"

". . . Not in the eyes of the law, anyway," Cwalo continued calmly. "Exposing traitors to the crown, carrying out an order to kill the prince. Everything *Daul's* done has been absolutely legal. No, Celyn, the hard truth of it is, the people we care about are the criminals here."

His words hung in the windswept air. "What did you say?"

He watched me evenly. "I said we're the criminals here."

It was like he'd slapped me, and suddenly I felt the tightness in my chest disappear, like I'd shucked off my silver or stepped out of a fog. "You're right," I said. *The people I cared about were criminals.*

Well, so they were. That wasn't anything new. And as I turned this odd idea over in my mind, something else started to stir, as well. Just a faint little niggle — but I'd learned to trust those niggles. I couldn't get rid of *all* the evidence against the Nemair, but there was one thing I could do. One thing I had to do, before the whole thing came crashing down around us. *Everything depends on him.*

Impulsively I gave Master Cwalo a kiss that brought flames to his cheeks. "Thank you," I said, and started to run off.

"Wait — Celyn!"

I turned back.

"What are you going to do?"

Snow flew up all around me, and the moons were just winking to life in the pale afternoon sky, and the Breijarda Velde glowed with a faint dusty light. I turned my face to Tiboran and Zet and Sar and the rest and grinned. "I'm going to steal something!"

Meri was in her rooms when I got back, my plan half-formed. When I saw her, curled into the window seat with a lamp and a bit of needlework, I was seized with inspiration.

"I need your help."

She looked up expectantly. "Of course. What is it?"

"Something brave. But, Meri — it's going to be hard."

"I'm ready."

"I'm serious. You know that the Inquisitor is riding here now, and you know what that will mean to Reynart's men, to Stagne."

Her face was solemn, and I knew that this was something that had not gone undiscussed during their rendezvous. "Yes." She was looking at her embroidery, a cipher of a star of violet silk, intertwined with a heart, stitched into the corner of a handkerchief. I touched the hem.

"For Stagne?"

She looked tearful, but she nodded. "It's not finished," she said sadly.

"You can finish it when you see him again," I said firmly. "Here's what I have in mind."

It was nearing midnight when I found my way back to Wierolf's vault. Meri had gone off on her part of the mission, though she had soundly rejected one facet of the plan, no matter how I tried to convince her. The prince was barely asleep, but I struck a flint and woke the chamber into light.

"Celyn — Digger — what is it?" Wierolf fumbled for his bedclothes. I stooped and threw him the braies he'd dropped in the middle of the floor, then turned my back.

"Get dressed, Highness. It's time for you to go."

"I don't understand. What's going on? I haven't seen you since you ran off that day."

"Questions later. Will you hurry?" I put the candle on the prayer stand and shook out the bundle I'd brought with me: a coat and boots for Wierolf, in a nice, invisible dun-brown wool, fur-lined mittens, and both a linen coif and wool cap, all of it nicked from Berdal's rooms above the stables. Nothing could hide his height, of course.

"What are we doing?"

I turned back. "You're leaving."

He stood to tie his hosen. "You make that sound so ominous. I'm hoping you haven't had a change of heart and decided to kill me after all."

"You're not funny," I said impatiently. "Now *move*."

Infuriatingly Wierolf sank back down to the bed. The half-healed scar stood out pink and furious on his wan skin, his magic pendant a blurry blot of light on his chest. "I think I want you to explain yourself first."

"I have a plan."

"A plan? Does Lady Lyllace know?"

"No."

"And why not?"

My face was hard. "Because what she doesn't know, she can't give up under torture."

"What are you talking about?"

"Werne is coming."

The prince hesitated a moment, letting the words sink like stones in water. "Start over," he said.

I sketched out the situation: Meri's *kernja-velde*, the arrival of the Inquisitor and his men, the *incredible danger* we were all in if Werne found Wierolf here. He frowned and heard me out, but when I finished, nearly breathless, he shook his head.

"I'm the prince — I have nothing to fear from the king's Inquisitor."

"You've been in hiding for a reason," I reminded him.

"Yes," he said slowly, "and I'm still not entirely sure why, exactly."

"Because people are trying to kill you, remember?"

He shook his head, but fingered the scar. He said nothing — he didn't have to. I recognized the look of someone lying to himself. "But the Inquisitor —"

"Won't care that you're the prince. Trust me, Highness — I have known him all my life, and he is without mercy, without inhibition. And if the Lord High Inquisitor discovers His Royal Highness, Wierolf of Hanival, in a nest of Sarist traitors —"

He hauled himself to his feet. "All the more reason I should stay, help protect them!"

"Protect? Are you crazy? You're barely fit to *stand*. What kind of protecting do you think you'll be able to do here?"

"Digger, you worry too — *Aaagggh!*"

My hand shot out and jabbed him under the breastbone, where the scar was still healing. The prince stumbled backward with a gasp, all the color drained from his face. "Point taken," he panted. "He really scares you, doesn't he?"

"He should scare everybody."

Wierolf struggled into his shirt, looking like he wanted to say something more.

"Can we talk about this when you're not in mortal danger?" I said.

"We're in mortal danger every second of our lives," he said gravely.

"Now you sound like me."

He grinned at that, and against my will, I had to smile back. He was good at that — at looking deeply into people and knowing exactly what to say to them. It would be a good skill in a king.

If he survived that long. "Can you move a little faster, Highness? I don't know how much time we have, and they're waiting."

He looked up sharply from his coat laces. "Who's waiting?"

"That's a little hard to explain. You kind of need to see them."

A worried crease lined his forehead. "Just how *planned* is this plan of yours?"

Finally I got the man dressed and his few belongings packed. As Wierolf crossed the threshold before me, he gave one last glance around the room. Strange, indelible things had happened in this room the last several weeks, things that had changed both of us. I knew I wouldn't soon forget them — and it seemed Wierolf of Hanival, prince of the realm, would not either.

We took the kennels route, though Wierolf stopped to say hello to the sleepy dogs, crouching down to put his fingers through the cages.

"Aren't you a pretty beast?" he murmured as a slavering hound turned to pudding at his touch. "Those are very impressive spots —"

"*Wierolf!*"

He swung his head around. "Sorry." As we resumed our flight, he said, "I could hear them barking, sometimes. Before you appeared out of the shadows, sometimes it was the only way I knew there was still a real world out there."

"Yes, and if anyone hears them barking now, we're done for. Down here." Using the path Meri had shown me, I led the prince down through the hidden entrance near the pentice, taking odd turnings through the roughest and most abandoned path I could plot out for us, avoiding the bits that ran past wine cellar and mews. On my own I could make up a lie if I were caught, but I'd be hard-pressed to explain why I was making off with the prince. As we went, I explained how the tunnels below the old castle continued through the mountain.

"Unless they've collapsed in the last few weeks, they go straight to the Broad Valley."

Wierolf halted. "Collapsed?" he said, a note of alarm in his voice.

I shrugged. "Don't worry — they've been using them all winter. I'm sure it's safe."

"They?"

"Your new allies."

At last we came to the cold rough stones that marked the foundations of the oldest part of Bryn Shaer, where the tunnels left the castle and became caves beneath the mountain. I fairly pushed Wierolf into the passage. He had to duck — I'd forgotten how bloody tall he was. I scurried ahead and found a lamp and the flint that hung beside it. A second later, leaping yellow light danced with shadows on the cave walls.

"Tiboran's breath — you weren't kidding," Wierolf said, coming forward to take the light. I hefted his pack over my shoulder and let him wander down the path ahead of me.

A few hundred yards in, beneath the makeshift camp in the old tomb, we found them. Wierolf stopped short and gave me a questioning glance, lifting the lamp to shine on a cluster of expectant, anxious faces. Faces I didn't need the light to see.

The whole band was there, men, women, and children crouching against the tunnel walls, waiting. I made out a handful of violet cloaks, more than one tattoo — on hands, necks, foreheads. A great many packs and bundles lay about them; Hosh sat patiently swishing her tail against the cave floor. These people didn't look like a mighty army that would boldly march our prince to safety; they looked like what they *were* — a band of half-starved refugees. Well, so was Wierolf. He'd fit right in.

Closed, expressionless faces turned our way, and for one freezing moment I decided that this had been a dreadful error. I was going to get the prince killed — if not *by* these people, then along with them.

"Digger?" Wierolf's voice was soft, questioning.

As the light filled up the space, I saw Meri speaking with Stagne. She turned, saw Wierolf, and then froze, eyes wide with astonishment. A second later, she dropped smoothly to one knee, her head bowed. Every single person with her did the same. It gave me a strange, hollow feeling, all those men in violet bowing to the prince.

"Your Highness," Meri breathed, and the prince strode up to her and took her hands, lifting her from the rocky floor.

"Prince Wierolf, Lady Merista Nemair, heir to Bryn Shaer," I said. That almost sounded like it was supposed to.

"Well met, Lady Merista," Wierolf said smoothly, and Meri dipped another perfect curtsy — and it was all just so ridiculous! We were in a freezing *cave*, for gods' sake, at the dead of night, with a band of outlaw magicians and their *dog*, all running away from the Inquisition, and they were playing nob.

Meri clutched my arm. "I knew it!" she whispered fiercely. "I knew you and my mother were hiding something, since that night Yselle came for you." But instead of hurt or disappointed, she seemed excited. "My prince," she said gravely, "please allow me to introduce a good friend of this house, Tnor Sarin Reynart."

From out of the cluster of bodies, a wiry man in gray rose and doffed his hood, freeing the mane of wild hair. "My prince," Reynart echoed Meri. Wierolf was staring at Reynart, a puzzled, pained expression on his face. The wizard took a step closer. "We are relieved your royal person has recovered from such grievous injuries."

"You —" the prince said. "It was *you*. At Olin — you saved my life."

Reynart was smiling. "And my companions, Highness. The lord of Olin has been a friend to us; long have our people camped in those lands. We knew the lady of Bryn Shaer has a reputation as a skilled physician — among other things — and that she could care for you in better comfort than could we." He drew one of his companions forward, the plump woman with the pet crow. "Kespa, our healer."

She bowed briefly, then set upon the prince, a hand on his forehead, lifting his shirt hem, nodding with satisfaction. I saw the tattoos on her palms, winking violet in the lamplight. "The touch of the Goddess can heal," she said, standing on tiptoe to peer inside Wierolf's collar, where the musket ball had struck, "and we can ease hurt, cool a fever, sometimes even stave off Marau, for a time — but I don't have your Lady Lyllace's knowledge of anatomy and surgery. You required a real physician."

Wierolf took her hands. "Perhaps this is knowledge that may be shared one day."

Reynart's serenity never wavered. "Highness, we are blessed to serve you. Only command us, and we obey."

Wierolf gave a strange half grin and looked at me. "Actually I believe Celyn is giving the orders here tonight."

I explained again how the tunnels led to Breijardarl, how Reynart's men would slip beneath the mountains just as the Inquisitor rode above them. Soon, easily, Reynart and Wierolf took over on their own, Reynart gesturing into the tunnels, Wierolf listening keenly and asking questions, both oddly at ease. The prince was among his people; as Reynart introduced his companions, Wierolf reached out to touch hands, heads, dogs, knelt beside a small girl with wide eyes who held her purple-clad dolly tight to her chest.

I hung back, feeling useless but satisfied. This would work after all. With a strange, closed-off feeling in my chest, I backed off a few steps and turned to leave. Tucked together under a magically reinforced seam in the cave ceiling, Meri and Stagne held each other closely, her dark head against his fair one, both of them flickering with their strange, watery light. He clutched the scrap of her unfinished embroidery.

I heard my name. I turned to see Reynart standing near me, holding something toward me in his tattooed hands. "Celyn of Bryn Shaer," he said solemnly. "Friend to Merista, the *Reijk-sarta*."

"The Channeler," I said, and he nodded, pleased.

"I have spoken with the others," he said. "We believe that we may have an answer to your magic." He cupped a tiny book, no bigger than his palm, bound in dark velvet that was worn and thin at the corners. I reached toward him, and a flume of light poured over and frothed the air around our hands. "I told you of two magics — *reijk-sarta*, the gathering, and *kel-sarta*, the shaping. But this ancient book, passed down among hidden mages for many centuries, speaks of a third magic, the rarest of all: *erynd-sarta*. The finding."

I repeated the word softly to myself, and something felt warm and alive — and new — inside me. Placing the book in my hands, Reynart opened it to a page of faded script, hand-inked an impossibly long time ago: *And unto the world Sar gave a third blessing, the Eryndeth, or Finder, given the power to see the Breath of the Goddess, or track Her footsteps.*

"When magic was abundant, there was no need for someone with a special skill to locate it," Reynart said. "All knew where it could be found. But not now." He was smiling, but there was something sad in it. "Your path lies elsewhere," he said. "You are called by a different god. But when you hear the voice of Sar speak your name, you will find us again." He closed my fingers around the book, turning back into the darkness toward his men. I held the little volume tightly, awash with wonder. Eryndeth — the Finder. Well, I may not have a real name, but I was certainly collecting a share of nicknames that fit.

"Digger." Wierolf strode toward me, across the cave. "A plan," he said, a playful note in his voice. "A good one, I think."

I had to smile. "You're not afraid of small spaces, I hope."

Wierolf barked out a powerful laugh. "Come with us?"

I paused, a hand lifted to my mouth as I realized it had never occurred to me. I could stroll down the tunnels along with the prince and the Sarists, and never have to face Werne and the Inquisition. "It's tempting," I said.

"But you're not coming." It wasn't a question, and I found myself shaking my head.

"I guess not."

He reached a hand toward me, held mine tightly. "Thank you, Digger. And good luck." As he pulled his hand away from mine, I realized he'd left something small and smooth in my palm. In the flickering light, I held it up: a small disk of wood, no bigger than a coin, in the shape of the prince's new device. The lion passant, against the rising sun.

"My favor," the prince said. "Should you ever need it." And then, quick as that, he stepped away from me and raised both arms in a salute. "You are braver than you know," he said firmly. He looked my way one last time. "May Tiboran guide you home."

Meri and I went back to his room after that and stripped away the evidence. It took hours and a heavy stone I'd pried from a crumbling tunnel wall to break apart the bed — all the gods damn me, I thought those things were supposed to be *portable*! — but before we'd lost all the night, Wierolf's chamber looked like what it was supposed to be: an adjunct to the stillroom. We left the prayer stand but dragged in a little shelf, stashed bottles everywhere, spilled a little oil on the floor, lit and put out a tiny fire to scorch a circle on the shelf and fill the room with heady, acrid smoke. It was good work: I was a practiced forger, after all, with experience making things appear to be what they were not.

Still, I had to quell a little pang as we rolled a dirty rug over the floor. I'd never see him again, but that was hardly new; I'd parted from most of the people I'd known in my life. Funny how one winter at Bryn Shaer could make me grow attached to people I shouldn't even know. I leaned up against the door frame and sniffed. It was a tiny, stuffy, poorly heated room; I should be glad to be rid of it.

By the time we climbed back out to the main corridors, darkness was starting to fade from the sky. Tired as I was, I wasn't quite ready to just slip into bed. I took Meri out onto the battlement, where I'd once watched her meet with Stagne.

I leaned over the wall, looking over the spread of mountains. This early they were barely more than hulking shadows, tipped with moonslight. Six moons in various phases dotted the sky — all but Zet, protector of royalty, who must have ducked into hiding with her prince. I hoped she'd watch over him, wherever Reynart and his band took him. Tiboran was a fat pink blob to the northeast, disappearing behind the crest of a hill, or into a cloud, or into a broad valley somewhere — it was hard to tell, in the darkness. I grinned at it. Fair enough; I could do this on my own.

# CHAPTER THIRTY-ONE

At dusk on the eve of midwinter, the Inquisition came riding to Bryn Shaer. And they brought the king's army with them.

Everyone gathered on the east tower, where we had watched the avalanche pin us to the mountain, to see the soldiers flood through the pass and spread up the sides of the mountain like poison in a wound. Beside me, Meri made a stricken sound and clutched tight to my arm. I felt sure we'd done right, sending the prince off with the Sarists, but as the Green Army crawled inexorably toward us, I wondered. If Werne and the Confessors had found Wierolf here, would that be a big enough prize to leave us alone?

I knew the answer to that.

I had seen no more of Berdal's "friends" from the mountains, but I knew Lord Antoch rode out every morning with Meri, and I hoped our little Bryn Shaer family was growing. The missing member of our strange assemblage had not gone unnoticed however. The morning after Meri and I had our last late-night adventure, Lady Lyll confronted me. We were in the solar, putting the finishing stitches in Meri's ceremonial embroidery.

"Celyn, dear, I seem to have . . . mislaid an item of some value. You would not have seen it anywhere, by chance?"

"Item, milady?" I looked up. Lady Cardom was watching us over the edge of her embroidery hoop.

Lyll bent closer. "This is no time for games. Do you know where he is?"

I studied my own needlework. "No, milady, not precisely. And more to the point, nor do you or Lord Antoch or Meri. Or Daul. But he's safe. I'm certain of it."

She looked vexed — she *was* vexed, but there was nothing she could do about it. Finally she sighed. "I hope you know what you're doing."

Now, back at the battlement, Lord Antoch lifted his spyglass — that new, heretical invention from Corlesanne, with which we could look up and examine the faces of the moons — and trained it on the Breijarda Velde. "I'm counting about two hundred fifty men," he said.

Lyll reached for the glass. "Why so few? That's not an invasion force."

"No," Cwalo put in. "It's a statement."

I understood him. It meant Bardolph could reach us here, at the most remote place in Llyvraneth, and that only a handful of soldiers would be required to subdue any brewing rebellion.

"Our supplies are low; we can't hold out a siege."

"No siege," said Lyll. "No siege engines. But perhaps they mean to occupy us."

A tremor of revulsion went through me. Greenmen billeted in every Bryn Shaer bedroom, touching the Nemair's belongings — and the Nemair's guests? I turned to Lyll. Her face was set, impassive, even though all her plans were surely at an end. Even with the men Berdal had brought, we were no match for the king's soldiers.

"What's going to happen?" I asked.

She was grim. "The Inquisitor and his men will ride to the gates, and we'll let them in. There will be some formalities — an exchange of greetings and such — and then Werne will request we give lodging to his men."

"And if you do?"

Lyll shook her head. "We'll be prisoners in our own home. They will hold us here until Bardolph decides we're no longer a threat."

"How long will that be?"

She just looked at me. "Forever."

I felt sick. I had done this — Daul and I had worked together to bring Werne here.

We stayed there in the fading light as the Green Army filled in the dip below Bryn Shaer, that impossibly narrow ridge of plain that was the only place to launch an attack on the castle. They were all in green, the same bright-grass color, and it was hard to tell them apart: soldier from Greenman, ordinary priest from Confessor. But one figure stood apart.

Small and slight against the fighting men, astride a mule at the head of the cavalry, the Inquisitor rode with his six Confessors, and something about him, so still and singular and composed among the tumult of the army, made the hundreds of soldiers at his back seem irrelevant. The Goddess's pale light shone only on her most beloved servant, and Werne the Bloodletter looked like he could sack Bryn Shaer all on his own.

Meri watched him, her gaze fixed. I put a hand on her arm to pull her back, but she wouldn't move. In the dusky light, my hand on hers pulsed brightly.

"I told you you should have gone with the others," I said, but she pulled away from me.

"My place is here," she said — and she didn't sound so young, suddenly. She held fast to the tower wall until the stones started to glow under her grip.

"Meri, they'll see you!"

She set her jaw. "Good. Let them."

On the ledge below, Werne dismounted awkwardly from the mule, shaking out the skirts of his robes. The Confessors followed, surrounding him in a circle of green that moved as one toward the path leading up to Bryn Shaer's gates. As Werne disappeared beneath the jut of rock, Lady Lyll stood back from the wall.

"Time to greet our guests," she said.

We had always met visitors out in the courtyard, but tonight Lyll and Antoch arranged themselves in the wide flagstone entry hall before the massive arched doors, now flung open to the snow and wind. Firelight flickered from torches set around the space. Flanked by a dozen of their black-and-silver guard, the Nemair looked like an extension of the stone walls of Bryn Shaer, ancient, austere, immovable.

I did what I had done since I could remember: I hid. I tucked myself onto a narrow balcony overlooking the entry court, drawn back behind a tapestry so no one below could see me. Meri joined me after a while, though by rights she should have been beside her parents. I was glad she'd grown a measure of caution and knew better than to present her magical self before Werne the Bloodletter — though she'd have to, eventually. There was no hope that the Inquisitor could come to Bryn Shaer ostensibly for Merista Nemair's *kernja-velde* and not ever meet her.

The seven figures in green strode as one into the Lodge, moving from the snowy courtyard to the dark stone floor in perfect unison, even the damp hems of their robes and cloaks swinging together across the threshold. They fanned out into a half-moon, Werne at their center. A dozen Greenmen stood at attention behind them. The Nemair were all grace, sinking just as smoothly to their knees, heads bowed.

"Be you welcome to Bryn Shaer, Your Worship," Lady Lyll said, her voice as warm and strong as ever, lifting her face to meet Werne's. "We have been expecting you for some time."

The Inquisitor placed a hand on her dark head and gave a murmuring reply that I couldn't make out. Meri frowned a little. "He doesn't look like I'd thought," she said softly. "He's just . . . ordinary."

It was true, I thought, looking down on that face I hadn't seen in so many years. My slight build, my dark curly hair. At twenty-six, he had filled out some, but he wasn't very tall. The hands that touched Lady Nemair's head and accepted a kiss from Lord Antoch were smooth and tan and delicate. A great round of blue-and-brown chalcedony — earthstone — hung from his belt, but instead of the moon-shaped beads worn round the wrist by most servants of Celys, he carried a blade at his hip. It was probably only ceremonial — the image of Werne in a knife fight was almost amusing — but it was his badge of office as an inquisitor, not just a mere priest.

The Confessors carried swords. And I had no doubt that theirs were sharp and practiced.

Lyll and Antoch rose, and Werne stepped aside to introduce his party. "My confessorial staff and my personal guard," he said.

Lyll gave a serene smile. "Confessors, your Worship? We are honored, of course, but are surprised your Grace would require them to preside over our daughter's *kernja-velde*."

"Not to mention the armed escort that brought you here," Lord Antoch added quietly.

Werne's dark gaze shifted to Antoch. "A show of friendship. His Majesty wishes to remind his subjects that we are all one family in Celys."

"Good," Lyll said. "We thought perhaps he was feeling . . . over-protective."

The Inquisitor glanced backward at the waiting Greenmen. "Quite. I told his Majesty I did not require them, but as you can see, they are here nonetheless. I do not expect them to interfere with my . . . work, here."

"Ah, then we shall consider the troops merely decorative," Lady Lyll said brightly. "You may thank His Majesty for us, but do mention that we should have been more than happy to provide our own 'ornamental' guard for the occasion." And with that, she hooked her arm into her husband's and led everyone to the Round Court.

"What will happen now?" Meri asked, squeezed tight to me.

A voice behind me startled me, and I glanced up and found Eptin Cwalo sharing our vantage point. "Tonight Bryn Shaer will feast the Inquisition and its men," he said as if this was all part of some pre-arranged plan. "And tomorrow we'll all be asked to report on one another's habits, secrets, heresies, and petty blasphemies."

Meri turned wide eyes to him. "What does that mean?"

He bowed his pale head. "Even in houses that are blameless, there are always people frightened enough of the Confessors to inform on some-one else. If we're lucky, they'll find only minor transgressions, and consent to merely confine your parents to the castle."

Even Meri didn't bother to ask what would happen if we weren't lucky. Because Bryn Shaer was far from blameless, and we all knew it.

No one ate much that night — at least no one from Bryn Shaer. Yselle and the cooks had prepared a sumptuous feast from Meri's stockpiled *kernja-velde* food, because everyone knew that you did Celys honor by feeding her servants well. Closer to, Werne certainly didn't look like he'd missed many meals. I happily sat as far as possible from him, since ladies-in-waiting were hardly worthy of His Worship's exalted company, down across the room with Phandre and Eptin Cwalo. Poor Meri was pressed between her parents, looking terrified. Beside Lyll, Werne ate steadily, scarcely looking up the whole meal.

"I do hope you'll try the roast pork, Your Worship," Lady Lyll said smoothly. "It's rather a Bryn Shaer specialty. Our cook is Corles, and I'm afraid we picked up some foreign customs while abroad."

"His Worship prefers to dine in silence," one of the Confessors said sternly.

Lady Lyll smiled and ignored her. "Will you take wine, my lord?" she asked cheerily.

The Confessor glared at her. "His Worship never indulges in spirits."

"Pity," Lord Antoch said, pouring himself a great draught from the flagon. "Splendid local vintage. Tiboran truly smiled on the vineyards that year. The Masked God's blessing to you, Your Worship."

I nearly choked on my own splendid vintage. Were they *deliberately* baiting him?

But Werne looked up only briefly. "Your hospitality does the Goddess honor," he said. "I look forward to acquainting myself with all the . . . comforts of this place. I'm sure I'll find it edifying."

"What are they *doing*?" Phandre fussed, as the female Confessor's placid expression grew strained. "They make us all look like mannerless rustics!"

But Cwalo, beside me, was smiling faintly. I caught his eye, and his grin spread. "Is that how it looks to you, Lady Celyn?"

"No," I said, and my voice was unexpectedly bright. "We look unafraid."

"I'll drink to that," said Cwalo, clinking my goblet.

The other Bryn Shaer guests were not so easy, though I could see them straining to follow the Nemair's lead. The only one who seemed to be succeeding was Marlytt, as icy and charming as ever, her delicate fingers on a Confessor's green sleeve. Even Daul seemed twitchy; he kept darting glances toward the Inquisitor, as if he wanted to scurry over and whisper something in his ear. It bothered me, but I didn't see what I could do about it. No matter how brave the Nemair seemed, Daul had won.

After dinner, I pulled Lady Lyll from the crowd streaming out of the Round Court. "You were magnificent!" I said. She gave a faint smile and squeezed my shoulder. "I almost forgot to be afraid of him."

"We'll pay for it, I'm afraid," she said. "Still . . . it *was* hard to resist. Go be with my daughter now, Celyn." She touched the silver bracelet on my arm, and her voice was sad.

Meri and I had been spared the task of billeting the Inquisitor's men in the spare Bryn Shaer guest rooms, and we trailed back to her apartments, both of us quiet. All along the hallways between the Round Court and the family suites, people stood and whispered, guests, guards, and servants turning worried faces to Meri. Finally she stopped and looked at everyone.

"Be easy," she said calmly. "Lord Werne is one of many guests my parents hope to host at Bryn Shaer, and it is our job to make him and his men feel welcome. And now I suggest we all retire for the evening, as I'm sure we'll all have much to do tomorrow. Good night."

The startled residents didn't react for a moment, then came murmurs of "yes, milady," and "good night, milady" as people drifted off to their rooms. Meri nodded, satisfied.

Back in her rooms, she sank onto her bed with a deflated sigh and looked up at me with frightened eyes. "What will we do, Celyn?"

I sat beside her and took her hand. The magic flared up between us, and I only squeezed harder. "Whatever we have to."

# CHAPTER THIRTY-TWO

Morning came, Meri and I waking together to stare at one another.

"It's my birthday," she whispered. I had almost forgotten. Though her gowns were laid out in her dressing room, and we had all memorized our roles, the coming celebration had been eclipsed by everything else. The ceremony itself would be delayed for a couple of days, to fall on a more auspicious calendar day than Meri's actual, Dead of Winter birthday. That had always been the plan, but it seemed impossible now to think about a feast of celebration, with the Inquisitor and his men walking the halls of Bryn Shaer and casting their dark green shadow over everything.

I tried to smile. "All grown up," I said softly.

Though Meri was to have breakfast this morning with her parents, there would be no riding out of Bryn Shaer today, or any other day, probably. It was only beginning to dawn on me that my fate was sealed with the Nemair's. I would likely be spending the rest of my life here in the Carskadons. At least until Bardolph died and Astilan took the throne, and decided that the Nemair were even more of a threat than his uncle had thought, and had everyone brought to Gerse to be executed.

*That's it, Digger. Start the day on a positive note.*

I dressed Meri in her kirtle of soft pink wool, and I brushed her long fall of black hair straight down her back, tying it back from her face with a gold ribbon. During her *kernja-velde*, if it even happened now, Marlytt and Phandre and I would plait and pin it up into an elaborate confection of braids and jewels, as a symbol of her reaching adulthood. But until then, even though she was technically an adult today, she would wear it loose.

Phandre came out of her chamber, looking sullen and thoughtful. I almost said something snide just to lighten up the heavy air — but she didn't seem worth it anymore. Meri crossed to the window to kneel by her prayer stand as I pulled on my own blue dress. I saw her from the corner of my eye, hands resting on the stand's edge, head bent.

"I hate them!" she cried out suddenly, and gave the prayer stand a shove that sent the candles and prayer stones scattering.

"Meri!" I said, shocked more by her behavior than anything. She stood staring at the mess, her hands balled up at her sides. I went to her, to help gather the spilled stones, then stopped myself. What did it matter anymore? I took Meri's hands in mine, and a thread of light twined our fists together.

Phandre just stood in the corner, dressed wisely in green, and watched.

Meri spent the morning with her parents, and Phandre wandered off wherever she normally wandered off to, but I was too restless to stay anywhere for long. Though Werne had only brought a dozen Greenmen inside the gates with him, we felt their presence everywhere: drinking Yselle's mead in the kitchens, standing guard by the Armory, patrolling the battlements. It was like Gerse all over again, only worse.

At last I went up to the white tower. I'd nicked a packet of seed for the rooks, an offering to Marau's messengers on this holy day, and as I scattered it against the snow, I cast my thoughts to the year's dead. I said a prayer for Tegen, that pain still a hot knife in my breast; for the dead men in the tunnels, Daul's conspirators; and for my tinker at the convent.

As the black birds circled down, wide wings lifted, I watched the soldiers outside the walls circle the castle like a green moat. Why hadn't I run with Wierolf and Reynart? Why didn't I grab my stash and head straight down those tunnels now? Why was I still here?

I went back to Meri's rooms, which still suffered from this morning's mess. As I bent to right the toppled prayer stand, I found a scrap of paper, torn no bigger than my thumb, with writing on it. My writing. It was a piece of the page I'd been using to decode Daul's journal — the page on which I'd recorded the identity of the Traitor of Kalorjn.

I was staring at that scrap of paper in my fingers when Marlytt burst into the room, her hands gripped together at her waist. "I can't find Meri," she said simply. A furrow creased her forehead. But Marlytt *never* let worry show.

"She's with her parents."

"Lady Nemair is downstairs, supervising decorations in the Round Court, and Lord Antoch was in the Armory with Cwalo and two of the Confessors."

I stood up, moving toward the door with her. "Why were you looking for her?"

"I don't know where Daul is either."

The cold room suddenly felt hot. We stared at each other, a vise of worry pulling us together. Maybe the two had nothing to do with each other, but it was awfully strange that Daul and Meri would *both* disappear on the very morning of the Inquisition's arrival.

On the very morning of her birthday.

"Sweet Tiboran, I know where she is," I breathed. "She's fourteen now — the Age of Authority. She's answerable for her own crimes."

Marlytt shook her head, confused, and I remembered that of course she didn't know that Meri had magic, let alone that she'd been consorting with wizards and getting the Mark of Sar branded into her skin. Well, this was still no time to go spreading it around the hills. "Get her parents," I said. "I'll find Meri." And I took off down the hallway, Marlytt staring silently after me.

I ran down the soft rugs, trying to keep my breath measured and even. I was probably overreacting, but a thread of fear twined around my heart, pulling tighter as I ran. Marlytt didn't know about Meri's magic — but might someone else? Had Meri guarded her secret well enough, or had she grown careless after meeting Stagne? Even in the absence of magic, her tattoo was enough evidence to send her to the gallows. How long would it take the Confessors to find it?

I tried to remember where they'd put the Inquisitor's men. Would Werne have taken over some public space? Not the Armory — Marlytt had said Antoch was there. I started toward the Lesser Court, but saw, down at the end of the far hallway, a pair of Greenmen flanking Lord Antoch's door. I skidded to a stop and ducked back into an alcove. Pox. I couldn't just run up and barge through the doorway — that wouldn't help Meri, if she was even there.

*Easy, Digger.* Interviews, Cwalo had said. Everyone at Bryn Shaer would have to appear before the Confessors and say whatever would save our own skins. Meri might just be having her interview. Questioning by the Inquisition was never a good thing, but it was better than an arrest.

And then I saw Daul step out of Antoch's rooms, and knew better. Hot bitter bile rose in my throat and I had to fight down a murderous urge to run for him. The first thing I had to do was find Meri, assess her situation. Satisfying as attacking Daul would be, it was unlikely to help.

I paced the little nook, considering my next move. The easiest way to get inside those rooms was to march up to the guards and announce that I could identify traitors and heretics, and I was ready to do my holy duty by Celys and the king.

The next easiest option was to stroll up and announce that I was the Inquisitor's long-lost sister, and demand to see him.

Neither option was good. Both would get me in, but I wanted to get *out* again too. Thinking a moment, I came up with a third alternative. I ran back to Meri's rooms and grabbed the untouched breakfast tray. The posset had gone cold, but who cared? I didn't actually intend to feed anybody. I hesitated, wondering if I could do anything useful here, add something to the tray to gain some kind of advantage. A knife wouldn't help Meri. Could I drop some potion or poison from Lyll's stillroom into the wine or honey? I had a bottle of something I'd nicked, weeks ago. But chances were too slim that the Inquisitor would actually consume it — and what if Meri got hold of it instead?

In the end I gave up and just took the food. Observe, learn, report. I could do that, without getting anybody killed.

I carried the tray back across the Lodge to Antoch's chamber, the plates and pots rattling as I hurried. I was sweaty and agitated from all this running, but the Inquisition was probably used to sending people into such a state.

At Antoch's door, the Greenmen looked me over suspiciously. There were two of them, one looking bored, the other small and surly and glaring up and down the empty corridor. Like all Greenmen, he was armed with a nightstick, which was technically the only weapon they were authorized to carry, but I saw a sheath in his boot, and a matching one in his partner's. Did guarding the Inquisitor merit additional weaponry — or did these guys just like knives? In a fight, I might have a chance with the smaller one, but the bigger guard had at least a foot and a half on me, and probably double my weight. This was going to take charm. Thank the gods I'd spent the last two months with Phandre and Marlytt. I looked up sunnily and said, "I have His Grace's tray!"

The smaller guard scowled at me. "Go away."

But the other, older and softer, smiled back at me. "We didn't order anything."

"*Everyone* at Bryn Shaer gets breakfast," I said. "Here — there's honeyed Breijard pears. Go ahead, His Grace won't notice if one's missing."

"He's eaten already. Go away."

That little one was starting to get on my nerves. I wondered if I might take him out — the tray was heavy; one quick club to the back of his scowling head —

"Ease up a little, Arrod. The girl's trying to be hospitable. That's rare enough."

I turned to Older-and-Softer. "One quick peek inside the rooms, and I'll disappear. You'll hardly even know I was in there." For good measure, I stole a glance at Arrod. "And I can make sure the next tray has an extra bottle of sweet Brennin red on it."

Finally, finally they relented, stepping aside and swinging open Antoch's unlocked door. Inside, Meri sat in a chair by the cold fireplace, weeping and obviously terrified. Werne stood before the tall windows, a green shadow, flanked by guards. His head was bowed over the earthstone in his clasped hands. One of the Confessors looked up briefly when

I entered, but nothing more. The red drapes sectioning off Lord Antoch's office were thrown open, and two Confessors were working their way quietly and methodically through Antoch's desk and bookshelves. Suddenly I was sick with relief that I had never brought back the seal or the letter I'd stolen.

Not that it mattered. Werne already had Antoch and Lyll's most valuable possession.

"Celyn!" Meri's voice was a sob. She stared at me with wide red eyes, straining her hands, and I saw that she was bound to the chair — with silver chains. I took a calm breath and set the food down quietly on the desk beside her.

"They have Stagne!" Meri whispered urgently.

I shook my head. "Impossible. He's safe, Meri, I promise."

Desperate, awful hope burned in her eyes. "But she said —"

"Who said?" My voice was a hiss, and I made a pretense of noisily arranging the food to cover our conversation.

She looked at me miserably. "Phandre."

"What!" A hot sickness spread through every inch of me, and on a table a few feet away I now saw what I had missed at first: two small, leather-bound books, one black, one gray . . . and both of them held down by a thick silver weight. Beside them was a flat, grayish-blue stone — one of the lodestones carried by the Confessors to detect the presence of magic — and a host of wicked-looking instruments with orbits and dials and compass faces. The kinder tools of the Confessors' trade. Everything in me crumbled. If they had her magic books . . . But I saw that Meri was fighting for bravery now that I was here, and so I knelt beside her and squeezed her hand. "It's all right, Meri. They won't hurt you. We'll get you out."

She nodded tearfully, but I could tell she didn't believe me. I held her hand tightly, fiercely, my fingers digging into hers, but no spark, no thread of light twined our hands together. Meri pulled her fingers out of my grip, curling them back under her bound hands, giving her head the faintest shake. Desperately I wished someone else were here to help me —

anyone. Wierolf. Lyll. Tegen, who would have devised an escape for Meri bordering on genius. Tegen — who had not been able to free himself from three Greenmen. But who had saved me.

A strong hand grabbed my arm and yanked me away from Meri. "What's this, then?" said a dangerous voice, and I looked up into the pockmarked face of a leering Greenman. "Another little magic-lover, no doubt. Let's strap her down as well, see what she'll give up."

"Guardsman Jost! This is a nobleman's home, not some dockyard ale-house." One of the Confessors gave him a chilling look. "Try to comport yourself with some dignity, if that's even possible."

"Yes, Your Grace." The Greenman dropped my arm and stepped away from me.

Well, they knew I was here now. "Don't you people know who this is?" I said. "That's their lordships' daughter — and you have her chained up in here like a common criminal. I demand to know why!"

"Silence, wretch!" the Confessor snapped in a voice like a whip cracking. "You presume to question the work of the Holy Mother's servants? Begone before we're moved to take another prisoner."

I remembered those voices. The man was older, graying at the temples, and he looked mean. Not fighting mean, but dark and cruel, the sort of person who could sit for hours, pulling out a girl's fingernails. I took an involuntary step backward — but a voice like a tether grabbed me and held me steady.

"Be easy, Brother Hessop." The Lord High Inquisitor turned away from his contemplation at the window. "We must be always ready to explain why our Holy Mother makes the demands on us she does."

I remembered that voice too. Soft, soothing, always so utterly reasonable — Werne had always been able to convince anyone of anything. He moved toward us in a practiced, gliding step that made him seem to float above the floor.

"Tell me, child, who are you?"

Hysterically I almost laughed. But before I could make up my mind how to answer, Meri spoke up: "My maid, Celyn. Don't you touch her!"

Alarmed, I grabbed for Meri's shoulders. Werne spun his gaze on her, and like that it switched from benevolence to venom. He leaned over her and almost spat in her face.

"If you speak again in this room, sinner, I will have your blaspheming tongue cut out."

"Don't talk to her that way," I cried. "This is *her father's* room!"

"Celyn!" Meri sobbed, her voice raw and full of terror.

Werne slapped her. Hard, backhanded, across the face with a gloved hand. I flew at him, forgetting every calm and disciplined fighting move that had ever been drilled into me, screeching, kicking, flailing madly with my hands, until strong arms grabbed me from behind and lifted me bodily from the ground.

Vaguely I understood that this was all going horribly wrong; I was making everything unutterably worse for Meri and myself. I stopped screaming, at least. I had to — a hand was clamped hard across my mouth. Blessed Tiboran, for once I had the good sense *not* to bite.

The Greenman gave me a violent shake. "How dare you touch His Worship with your filthy Sarist hands!" He drew his nightstick and pressed it up beneath my jaw. "We'll cut off those hands and feed them to you, little girl."

"Enough!" Werne was unharmed, stumbling backward briefly before regaining his footing and his composure. He brushed his robes down, but he looked shaken. He put his fingers together and stared at them a moment, with dark brooding eyes — did *mine* look like that? — taking slow, smooth breaths. My chest tightened, watching him, his movements too familiar, and I looked away. We *weren't* alike. We weren't.

No, I was an impetuous fool who was going to get Meri killed, and he was the pillar of icy calm who was going to wield the blade, right in front of me where I could watch. *Oh, Meri, I'm so sorry.* I couldn't say the words aloud, with the guard's hand over my mouth. Meri slumped mutely in her chair.

"Forgive me," Werne said, and it was a shrieking, insane parody of an apology. "While the work of Blessed Inquiry often inspires —

passionate — reactions, we do not normally witness such displays. My daughter, it is worthy that you have inspired such devotion in your maid. Perhaps our Holy Mother will look upon you both with mercy." He glanced briefly at me. "Get . . . that out of here."

The guard holding me carried me to the door — but Werne was still looking at us strangely. "Wait."

The Greenman halted, mid-turn, his hand dropping away from my mouth.

"Your face is familiar, child. Do I know you?"

I could have gotten out of there. One word would have dumped me safely in the corridor, so I could flee back to Lyll and Antoch with the news of what I'd seen. One word.

I didn't say it.

"Of course you know me," I said recklessly. "I used to be your sister."

# CHAPTER THIRTY-THREE

The look that came across Werne the Bloodletter's face at that instant was priceless. I would have cherished it, if it hadn't been so deadly dangerous. He stared at me, eyes ink-dark and penetrating, but I refused to look away. I heard Meri gasp.

"Speak that lie again, blasphemer." But there was confusion, doubt in his voice.

"No lie," I said, struggling a little in the Greenman's arms. He set me back down on the floor but didn't quite release me. I still felt a little wild, and I had the strange sense that Werne had *always* made me feel that way, as if all his goodness and restraint brought out the recklessness and insolence in me. Like the moons of Celys and Marau, always pulling each other in opposition through the heavens. All these years, I'd been so afraid of him finding me again — but it was like he'd forgotten he ever even had a sister.

Werne crept closer, as if concerned I might strike out at him again, or that something noxious on me might rub off on him if he got too close. "I had a sister once," he said softly, almost to himself. "But she died, long ago. A heretic, unclean. It was the greatest sorrow of my life."

"Unclean!" I spat back. "You said those words to a child! A child, Werne!"

An arm gripped me tight. "Do not speak so familiarly to the Lord High Inquisitor," said a voice of iron in my ear. "Do you wish me to remove her, Your Worship?"

The Inquisitor — *my brother* — was looking at me, and through me, his fingers pressed together again. I could not tell what might be going on behind those intense, brooding eyes.

"You are somewhat like her," he said finally. "But it's impossible. Yes, Jost, return this . . . person to her people. I — I must have solitude to pray for guidance in how to deal with these outlandish claims." He lifted the hood of his robe and turned toward the door.

"Your Grace?" One of the Confessors, a tall woman with steel gray hair, spoke up. "What shall we do with the prisoner?"

Werne turned to her like the wall had spoken, and it baffled him. "What do we always do with them?" he said, and stepped out of the room.

By the time the Greenman dumped me in the hallway and I'd scrambled to my feet again, out of reach of the guards at the door, Werne had disappeared. What would he do now, my strange confession nagging at him? I was sure he was telling himself he didn't believe me, that I was just another lying heretic who'd say anything to save herself or a loved one, albeit one with a bizarre claim. There was no chance of a loving reconciliation here, even if either of us wanted it. Most likely, I'd be arrested before I could spread my lies any farther afield. Before anyone might suspect I was telling the truth. Before anyone realized that Werne Nebraut's sister might be magical.

Would that ruin him? Magic in the family had ruined plenty of others, highborn and low; by rights it should do no less damage to the High Inquisitor himself. But I hadn't known the gods to play fair yet. It would probably only manage to increase his esteem.

I pulled myself together a little, beating the wrinkles from my skirts and tucking loose strands of my hair back in place, and went to tell Meri's parents.

Marlytt had gathered everyone together in the Lesser Court — Antoch and Lyll, Cwalo, Lords Sposa and Wellyth, and the Cardom. Evidently she had not been successful in locating Daul. I had thought I was calm, but then I saw Phandre.

"You *cow*! How could you!" I got one good blow in, a beautiful jab to her beautiful jaw, and she dropped, shocked, a hand pressed to her cheek. Somebody little caught me from behind — Cwalo, probably — and Lyll and Antoch rose, looking horrified. Phandre saw them, and something shifted across her face, from fear to fury.

"Did you see that?" she cried. "That gutter rat struck me! I'll see you flogged for that!"

"Hard to see anything with your traitorous eyes cut out!" I yelled back. Cwalo pulled me back against him.

"Easy, girl," he said in his low smooth voice.

"She —"

"Girls!" That thunderclap could only have come from Antoch, and it shocked the entire room to silence. Lyll swept over and stood between me and Phandre, who had started to whimper just a little. She was lucky I didn't kick her.

"Celyn, Phandre! What on earth is the meaning of this?"

Before the lying snake could say a word, I pulled away from Cwalo. "Milady, your lordship — Meri's been arrested."

All the iron seemed to go out of Lyll just then, and I was suddenly sorry I hadn't thought of a gentler way to say it. She wavered and sank against Antoch, who caught her.

"But this is outrageous!" Lord Wellyth cried. "In your own home, your own daughter?"

I went to put my arms around Lady Lyll, and she gathered me to her. "What happened?"

I was so angry I could hardly speak, but I restrained myself for Lyll's sake alone. "She was betrayed by Lady Phandre," I said. "She stole her books and lured Meri to their room by *pretending* they had arrested someone else."

"You're lying," Phandre said simply, but there was no real effort to convince anyone. "Prove that it was me."

"I don't have to prove it!" I said. "Meri told me."

Lyll turned slowly to Phandre, who wilted a little.

"She's making it up," she said, but couldn't quite meet Lyll's eyes.

"They have her bound with *silver*, milady," I said.

Lyll's smooth face went white, and she squeezed my arms tight. "How —"

Everyone else pressed close, trying to hear. I hesitated, but nothing could be served by sparing the rest. "She has a Sarist tattoo. They're bound to find it. Phandre must have known about it." That was a guess, but it seemed logical. And Phandre, for her part, just stared back boldly, hatred in her green eyes.

"Lady Phandre?" Lady Lyll's voice was hard and cool.

Phandre dragged herself to her feet. "I just did what everyone else was too afraid to do. She was a risk, to all of us."

"What did they promise you?" That was me.

She tilted her chin up. "They didn't have to promise me anything. Anyone can see where the real power is."

Slowly, Antoch turned his back on her. "You saw my daughter?" he said softly to me.

"She isn't hurt. Please, your lordships — I have information, but I can't report it here." I glanced toward Phandre.

Swiftly, Lady Lyll pulled herself upright and issued a series of crisp, quick orders. Cwalo and Lord Sposa dragged Phandre off to her room, with orders to post a guard on her door, and Lord Wellyth was dispatched with Lord Antoch to verify my report.

"I think I may have made everything worse," I added, before they left. Everyone looked at me expectantly. "I may have — said something to the Inquisitor about being his sister."

I winced, but was met with absolute empty silence. It really didn't get easier to say. I pushed a loose bit of hair back behind my ear. Lyll took me gently by the shoulders.

"Celyn?" Her eyes searched my face. "It's true, isn't it?"

I think I nodded. Vaguely I was aware of voices in the background, but I didn't really hear what they said. Lyll touched the silver bracelet on my arm. "And *this* is why you ran from the Celystra."

Uncertainly, I glanced around the room, but everyone there — Sarists all — was somber. They could guess that Werne the Bloodletter's sister wouldn't wear a silver bracelet just because it was pretty. I nodded — more firmly this time.

"All right," Lyll said with another little squeeze. "Thank you, Celyn. Petr, my lord husband, go now. We shall hear the rest of Celyn's tale another time."

They weren't gone long — just long enough for Lord Sposa and the Cardom to press against me, full of questions I couldn't answer. Marlytt finally broke them up by handing warmed wine around to everyone. I gripped my hot cup hard until my hands stopped shaking. When Lord Antoch and Lord Wellyth returned, their faces were grim. Lyll rose half out of her seat.

"We couldn't see her," Antoch began, but seemed unable to go on.

Wellyth stepped forward, unfurling a document and slipping on a pair of spectacles. "We spoke to one of the Confessors, but we did not see the Inquisitor himself. Lady Merista has indeed been arrested. The charge is heresy."

Lady Lyll's hands on her wine were white. "Go on."

Wellyth continued. "They are gathering evidence in advance of pressing formal charges against your lordships, for harboring a heretic —"

"Harboring? She's our daughter!"

"And fomenting rebellion," Wellyth finished heavily. "Apparently they are in possession of some evidence regarding illicit Sarist communications, and they're looking for proof that Bryn Shaer has been building a standing army." Lord Wellyth looked everyone over, his gaze falling a little too long on me. "Still, we are authorized to report that they are willing to forestall charges against anyone in the house, provided —" He hesitated.

"Provided what?" Lord Sposa demanded. "Out with it, man!"

Suddenly I knew *exactly* was Lord Wellyth was going to say. I looked up at him calmly as he read the rest of the order.

"Provided you deliver Lady Merista's maid, one Celyn Contrare, by sunset today."

I jumped up. "Fine. I'll go now." If I got back in there, maybe I could —

Lady Lyll grabbed my hand. "Celyn, sit down." She turned to Wellyth. "No, of course not. It's out of the question."

"Why not?" I stared at her desperately, though part of me was crumbling with gratitude.

"Because we wouldn't turn anyone over to them, least of all a friend who has served our family with honor and devotion."

I made a strangled sound at that and looked at Wellyth. "Go back and ask if they would take me in Meri's place."

"You don't give orders here," he said, but added gently, "It wouldn't do Lady Merista any good."

"The Inquisitor wants *me*," I insisted.

"But he'll take you both." Lyll leaned over and took my arm. "Celyn. We'll find another way. Petr, please convey our regrets to His Grace's men concerning their generous offer. Find out what their demands are regarding Lady Merista's ransom, and when we can have her returned to us pending trial."

Wellyth looked even grimmer. "I'm sorry, Your Ladyship. There's to be no ransom."

Lyll finally sighed and pressed her eyes closed, a hand covering her face. "Then there's nothing we can do," she said.

"No!" I cried. "How can you say that? Milady — they only have twelve Greenmen. I know the Confessors are armed, but I'm sure the Bryn Shaer guard is strong enough, and —"

They were staring at me, brows drawn, faces hard. I blinked back. "What?"

Lady Cardom spoke up. "Are you suggesting we mount some kind of — rescue mission, girl?"

"Why not?"

"With the king's army camped outside?" Sposa said. "Impossible."

"But it's *Meri* —"

"Enough!" Lord Antoch's voice boomed out. "Have done. Everyone —

just go back to your rooms and wait for word. I'm sure we'll learn their next move soon enough."

I was about to make another protest when Lyll shook her head. "It's over, Celyn. They've won. It's time to cut our losses and retreat."

"What does that mean?"

She glanced briefly at her husband. "We'll begin negotiations to turn ourselves in for conspiracy. Maybe then they'll be persuaded to spare Meri."

"No, you *can't*," I said, my voice desperate. I felt dazed; how had it come to this?

Lady Lyll gave my fingers a faint, fluttering squeeze, but didn't meet my eyes as she rose to leave, Lord Antoch close behind her. The others drifted away as well, until I was alone with the Cardom, Marlytt, and Eptin Cwalo.

Cwalo sat beside me. "I said you were fearless," he said softly. "Good girl."

"And I told you I hate to lose."

Lady Cardom regarded me evenly across the court. "I always did find Lyllace Nemair and Petr Wellyth a little overcautious for my tastes," she said.

I looked up sharply. "You don't agree with them?"

"No," she replied. "Any pretense of negotiation is delaying the inevitable, and the longer Lady Merista is in their custody, the worse it will go for her."

A chill went through me. She was very direct — but it gave me some hope. "Will you help me do something?"

Lady Cardom almost smiled. "Antoch saved my husband's life at Kalorjn," she said. "What do you propose?"

# CHAPTER THIRTY-FOUR

An hour later, bent over the desk in Lady Cardom's chambers, we had the framework of a plan. Eptin Cwalo and the Cardom were eminently practical, devising the all-important leg of the journey that came *after* the comparatively minor matter of freeing Meri from the immediate clutches of the Inquisition. We recruited Berdal, who was more than happy to sign on for any adventure on behalf of the Nemair, though he sobered when Cwalo explained his role in the mission.

"Your job will be to get Lady Merista as far from Bryn Shaer as quickly as possible. Pick up horses where you can, and use the network of informants and sympathizers to send word to the Nemair when you reach safety."

I'd nicked a map of the castle and its grounds from the white tower workroom, and Berdal studied it now. "But where should I take her?"

"Don't tell us!" I put in. "Just pick a direction and *go*. Deep into the mountains, if you have to. And trust Meri; she knows the land around Bryn Shaer." But I quietly added, "If you're looking for allies, a party of Sarists known to Lady Nemair left via the Breijardarl tunnels two nights ago. They may still be reachable."

He pointed to the map. "I've been watching the soldiers' movements since they arrived; there's a period of about ten minutes when the patrols don't overlap — here, near the mews — during every shift. We should be able to get out unseen then."

The only hitch in this plan was that there was no time to consult Meri regarding her feelings about any of this. "She didn't want to run," I said, recalling her adamancy when I'd pressed her to go with Wierolf and Reynart. "She wanted to stay and defend Bryn Shaer."

"I'm sure she'll find it preferable to the Bloodletter's gallows," Lady Cardom said drily.

I took Marlytt to find Lyll and Antoch. Her role was to attach herself publicly to the Nemair, making sure they remained visibly blameless in their daughter's escape.

Moving around Bryn Shaer was not as easy as it had once been. The dozen Greenmen seemed to be everywhere, and they were not particularly inclined to let a couple of waiting women pass freely. We had to stop and account for our movements more than once — as well as fend off the wandering hands of one lecherous guard on duty near the Armory, who thought I looked like easy prey. Marlytt talked him down before I broke his fingers.

The Nemair were in Lady Lyll's quarters, a Greenman stationed at the open door. Lord Wellyth sat with them, shuffling through a sheaf of papers. Lord Antoch rose to meet us, and I saw with some shock that he'd been crying. Impulsively I opened my arms to him, and let him squeeze me until I felt a rib crack.

"Milord," I whispered, holding tight to his arms. "Where is the opening to the passage behind your bed?"

His massive, blocky body stiffened, but he murmured into my hair. "The roof. It — it's for stargazing."

I let out all my breath and squeezed him back. "Thank you."

"Celyn —" He caught me as I pulled away, and looked hard into my eyes. "Don't do anything foolish."

What was one more lie? "Of course not."

The Cardom had agreed to divert the attentions of the people guarding Meri long enough for the rest of us to affect the rescue. Lady Cardom had smiled thinly and predicted that this should pose no problems.

And my job? Nick a priceless treasure from Lord Antoch's rooms without getting caught, of course.

It was a solid plan, once Berdal and I had worked out the logistics of the job. Roof access was inconvenient, but not impossible. There was one tense and ridiculous moment, when Berdal and I were slipping up the servants' stair and heard footsteps descending toward us. I flung myself at him, pulling him into a passionate embrace — which probably had the opposite of the effect I'd intended, making us actually *more* noticeable, particularly since I had to stand two steps up from Berdal to even make the maneuver possible. When the guards finally spiraled down out of view, Berdal broke away from me, his face purple from the effort of not laughing.

"Sorry," I sputtered. "I panicked."

"Just glad I was here," he said smoothly.

"Hopefully that was the last of the Greenmen," I said, tallying them up in my head, and continued on up. The Lodge attics were little more than cramped, narrow passageways extending the length of each wing, but doors beneath the eaves opened onto tiny stone walkways running along the roofline. I'd been up there only once before, my first week spying for Daul, and I'd loved the exhilarating height and the blasting wind.

There were no locks on these little doors; there was no point. Particularly in the dead of winter, when ice coating the frame and the hinges and the latches had frozen everything shut.

"Hells," I said, giving the door a fruitless tug. This was as bad as the lock on Daul's door. I hated to use such a pretty blade for such an inelegant purpose, but I pulled out my dagger and started to dig away at the crack between door and frame.

"Stop," Berdal said. "Here." He threw his shoulder hard into the door, then braced his foot against the wall and heaved. The door popped open with an ungodly sound, shards of shattered ice raining down on the attic floor. "Gods — do you think they heard that?"

I shook my head, slipping my knife back into its sheath; weird attic noises were beyond the scope of Greenmen's duties. As we stepped out onto the ledge, a swirl of snow rose up in the icy wind, and I had to lift my hand before my face. "This is horrible," I said, trying to keep my voice low, even in the screaming wind. "Are you going to manage?"

"Lead the way," Berdal cried back, crouching as he moved along. "And remind me to ask how you got so adept at climbing about on castle rooftops when you can't even ride a horse."

"You're a fair hand at this too."

"I'm a mountain boy, remember?"

We followed the footway to a terraced landing behind the Round Court's domed roof, which shielded us from the worst of the wind. A flight of narrow steps linked the landing to the battlements curving past the Lodge. The door to Lord Antoch's passage was hidden behind a decorative corbel shaped like a bear and buried under a foot of snow. Inside we could see a narrow iron ladder fixed to the wall of the snug passageway.

"Are you sure about this?" Berdal said, staring into the darkness.

"It's nothing," I said, lowering myself over the edge. I gave him a grin I didn't quite feel. "I'll have her back in a minute. Try not to fall off the roof."

The ladder led to a narrow crawl space almost directly above Antoch's rooms, then a tight staircase dropped into the space between his chamber and the servants' stair. I knew I was near when I heard angry voices, muffled through the walls of wood and stone. I couldn't make them out, but I prayed it was the Cardom, starting their performance. I felt through the dark for the end of the stairs, the back of Antoch's paneling, a latch in the wall. My fingers had just worked out the mechanism when a shrill voice in the distance declared, "Absolutely disgraceful!"

Lady Cardom, right on schedule. I took a deep breath.

I flipped the latch, *easy, easy,* just tapped it open . . . The door slid silently sideways, tucking back neatly inside the wall. Listening first, I could hear nothing between Lady Cardom railing in the hallway, and the almost soundless rustle of the heavy tapestry hanging in front of me. Now behind Antoch's bed, I sank down, feeling for the bottom of the bed frame.

As Lady Cardom carried on outside, I slid onto my belly and pulled myself under the bed, pushing forward with my toes. My shoes were wet and my feet were cold, and I left a trail of damp behind me that we'd have to crawl through again. Fortunately there was plenty of daylight seeping through the heavy bed-hangings, and nearly enough room underneath for me to sit up without hitting my head on the straps holding the mattresses in place.

"Is this how all His Grace's interrogations are carried out? I tell you, the things I've seen in this house —"

I inched forward and found a gap in the curtain panels, lifting them aside so I could see into the room. Meri's chair was still by the fireplace — which was *still* unlit, the savages — and I only spotted one pair of green boots beneath a long green hemline. I eased myself to the far side of the bed and slipped out into a snug alcove between the bed and the wall, still mostly hidden from view, unless somebody decided to look straight at the bed itself.

I peered round the corner. Meri was facing the wrong direction; she'd have to turn halfway around to see me, and I was going to have to cross half the open room to reach her. As I waited, debating my next move, a Confessor appeared, carrying a book, and seated himself right across from Meri. Pox — he was going to read scripture to her. This could take all afternoon.

Blessedly, at that moment Lady Cardom's protests hit a new level. "I will not be manhandled by you, young man!" she cried, quickly followed by the outraged voice of Lord Cardom: "Take your hands off my mother! Can't you see she's frail? Guard! Help! Guard!"

Meri turned her head toward the door, startled, and as she glanced across the room, her eyes caught mine. They went wide suddenly, but darted away again just as quickly. She was pale, and there was no way to tell what she was thinking, but my heart was hammering wildly.

"Take your hands off me!" Lady Cardom's voice was loud and incensed. "In my day, servants of the Holy Mother would never have disgraced themselves this way!"

Suddenly Meri spoke to her Confessor. "Oh, don't you think you should see what's happening?" she said, her sweet voice wavering with concern. "I think he might hurt her!"

For a brief, deadly moment, I worried the Confessor would ignore her. But he was young, and kept casting nervous glances toward something in the corner I could not see. Finally he set the book down in his seat and got up to investigate.

*Now!* I scurried out into the room, but Meri was shaking her head wildly. I edged backward, frowning, and she nodded toward the obscured corner, carefully mouthing one word to me.

*Werne.*

Damn.

I had to get Meri out of here before the Cardom got themselves arrested too. A moment later, Meri looked straight at me and yelled, "Help! Help! I think he's going to kill her! Your Grace, come quickly!"

I froze, my heart in my throat, but Meri showed no fear.

"What is it now?" said a cross, low voice, and Werne stepped into my field of vision. He stared at Meri with contempt and loathing, but she met his gaze, her eyes wide and innocent.

"Your Grace," she pleaded. "Might you go see what that fuss is? I truly do think someone might be hurt."

"I told you *silence*, blasphemer!" He turned back, and Meri looked at me despairingly. I had just decided to dash forward anyway and fight it out as I could, when from the hallway, Lady Cardom gave one piercing, heart-stopping scream.

"What in Celys's name?" Werne spun on his heel and headed toward the door. I dived for Meri, skidding across the floor and then searching through the silver chains for the tiny locks. I fumbled through my bodice for my thinnest lock pick. Could I *snap* the chains? They were so thin — I bent my head to take a link in my teeth and gave a yank sideways with my head. The delicate chain popped apart, but something burned on my lips and tongue, and for a moment my vision blurred.

Out in the hallway, I heard Eptin Cwalo's smooth voice trying to calm everybody down. I frantically unwound the chains, but my fingers felt strangely fat and I couldn't work them fast enough. I finally got one of Meri's hands free, and she fought through the bonds with me, until they were loose enough for her to pull her other hand out.

"They're coming back," she whispered, and I grabbed her bodily and shoved her, none too gently, down underneath the bed.

"Go, go!" I hissed, right behind her.

"Where?" she said wildly, her face pressed to the floor.

"Straight back — there's a hidden door, you'll go right through!"

Meri found it, thank the gods, just as Cwalo's voice grew closer and more distinct. He was *in* the room now, and he had to keep them occupied long enough for Meri and me to reach the roof. Otherwise they'd tear the room apart until they found our escape route.

"Quickly now, or they'll find us," I said, coming up behind Meri in the passage. I slid the little door closed, wishing I had some way to jam it shut.

"Here," Meri said, and she passed something thin into my hand in the darkness. It felt like a hairpin, long and flexible. I bent it open and thrust it between the back of the door and its narrow track. It wouldn't stop anyone determined — but it might keep the hidden door from being discovered immediately. "I took it from one of the Confessors when she bent over me to check the chains," she explained. "I thought it might be useful, somehow."

I was too astonished to say anything, just nudged Meri forward, up the narrow stair. "Can you make a light?"

In the darkness I felt her shake her head. "There was something — wrong about the chains," she whispered. "It wasn't ordinary silver; it *burned.*"

That would account for the strange taste in my mouth. "That's all right," I said. "Just go quickly and try not to bump your head. Two flights up, and we'll be on the roof."

She barely faltered in her climb, and in a moment we could see the square of light from the open trapdoor above. Weak with relief, I pushed Meri upward. "Berdal's standing guard," I said. "Do you see him?"

She climbed out onto the snowy terrace, and I could see her looking down the roofline. "Yes, he's —" but whatever else she said was lost to the wind. I saw her stumble forward, out of my view, and I climbed up after her — as a dark, scarred face bent low to meet mine.

"Hello, little mouse," Daul said, and something hard and cold smashed into my face.

# CHAPTER THIRTY-FIVE

Something was dragging on my arm, and I heard whimpering. I felt myself stumble, then get jerked to my feet again. Gradually the red fog of my vision cleared, and I saw that I was being pulled along the roofline by Daul, who was prodding Meri along before him, a silver-handled pistol at her back.

"Daul!" I tried to shout, but my voice was slurred and dull, and my mouth was full of blood. I must have bitten my tongue when he hit me, probably with that pistol-butt. He glanced back, saw I was alert, and grinned cruelly.

"Welcome back, little mouse. We missed you."

"What are you doing? Let us go!" He was jerking me along so erratically I couldn't get to my knife; it took all my effort just to stay upright and keep up. I yanked hard on my arm, but didn't even throw him off stride.

"Not yet, I don't think," he said. "You'll enjoy this next part." He pulled me toward him, trying to line me up with Meri. "I'm going to return His Grace's prizes to him."

"Don't do this!"

Daul ignored me. He was leading us from the roof toward the broad ramparts of the bailey wall. Meri was shivering — from cold or fear I couldn't tell. I'd only meant to have her up here a moment, before Berdal bundled her in fur and whisked her to safety inside the attic.

Berdal — what had happened to him? Had Daul — I tried to glance backward, up to the Lodge roof, but the snow was blinding, and I could barely see Daul and Meri. If I could get Daul's gun —

He pulled me tighter, and I fell forward, bumping into him. "His Grace expects you both in good condition, but I think he might find you a little . . . disappointing." Daul was panting, his words coming in choppy bursts.

"Why are you doing this? Antoch's not the Traitor!"

He ignored me. "Imagine my delight when I discovered that the Inquisitor seemed to have a particular interest in *you*."

"You knew that already!" But no. He'd never said anything about Werne specifically, and he'd hardly needed specifics to intimidate me. *You flinch anytime someone mentions your brother.* Marlytt's limited knowledge would have been enough. A brother in the church, one chancy remark, and my own imagination filled in the rest. Oh, stupid sneak thief! I *deserved* to get caught.

But Meri didn't. I had to get her away from him. He took us down a few more snowy steps, and now I could see the Green Army in the distance, a faint mossy blot below us through the snow. We were at the east tower now, with its stair that led straight down to the gates. *Gods, he means to go through with this!*

At that moment, the tower door exploded open. Daul and Meri stumbled back a few steps, and in that second of confusion, he let go of my arm. I lunged for Meri, but Daul had a better grip. He had her back in his arms, the gun poised, in a heartbeat.

"Daul! What's the meaning of this?" Antoch's roar carried even over the wailing wind.

I could see Meri straining to break free and run for her father's arms. "Let the girls go!" Antoch cried.

Daul yanked Meri back, the barrel of the pistol pressed into her bodice. "I don't take orders from you anymore, Antoch!"

Antoch looked baffled. "What do you want, Remy?"

Daul gave a shrug. "This."

"Daul, *he's not the Traitor*!" I cried.

"Lies!" Daul yelled back. "You said he confessed!"

Antoch fell back, like Daul had struck him. "What?"

"No, Daul, it was never Nemair! I found the proof!"

Daul twisted Meri in his grip and peered out at me over her shoulder. "What proof?"

I inched a little closer. When I could grab the gun — "It was in the journal."

"There was nothing in the journal! You know that. It was worthless nonsense."

"No, there was nothing in the journal I gave you. The real one has everything."

"Real one?" His knuckles on the pistol whitened.

"The one I gave you was a copy. I forged it. The real one — I held on to it." Even now I found I couldn't say what Meri had been using it for.

Meri was trembling so violently, I was afraid she'd set the gun off.

Antoch was struggling to catch up. "Daul, I don't understand how she knows, but what Celyn is saying is true. I swear by Sar herself that I did not betray our people. Please, just let my daughter go, and we can talk about this like rational men."

"You're lying!"

"No!" I cried. "Listen to us."

"If it's not you — who was it, then?"

I waited for Lord Antoch to say, but he hesitated. "It was Lougre Séthe."

"Impossible." But Daul's voice wavered, tinged with doubt. "Séthe couldn't find the privy by himself — how could he give over troop movements to Bardolph's forces?"

"It wasn't what Séthe told them," Antoch said. "It was what he leaked to us. False intelligence; we relied on it, and —" His shoulders sagged with the old memory.

Daul was shaking his head. "Séthe ended up with nothing. He died in exile — a beggar!"

"Remy —" Antoch's huge voice was gentle, pleading. "It will all make sense if you just let Merista go and allow me to explain it to you."

Daul's arm was tight around Meri's body, and her lips were turning faintly blue with cold. A shadow moved behind Daul, a ghost in the snow. I froze, scarcely willing to breathe — but Daul saw that my attention had been diverted, and he turned.

Just in time to have the tower door bang open once more, hard against the side of his head. Daul stumbled again, and this time I was quicker — I grabbed Meri by the arm and yanked her free, pushing her across the snowy walkway to her father.

Daul whirled toward the turret, and the shadow in the snow slammed into him, nearly knocking him off his feet. The figure was tall and dark-haired, and for a moment I took him for Berdal — until I saw that brown wool jerkin. I bit down on my sore tongue to stop from crying out.

They grappled together against the bailey wall: Daul, lean and wiry, and Wierolf, tall and sturdy. I had not seen Daul fight before, and though the prince was skilled, Daul wasn't recovering from near-fatal wounds. He got in one good blow to the prince's body, and Wierolf dropped back, stunned.

And then Daul saw his attacker, and all the color bleached from his face. "You!" he breathed. "Impossible. You're dead!" But his words were almost lost in the wind. Wierolf was bent double on the pathway.

"I guess your friends didn't finish the job," he said, struggling to his feet. I ran to grab him — prop him up like I'd done so many times before — but before I could reach him, Daul gave a strangled cry and jumped off the bailey wall, into the blinding snow.

For a moment there was shocked silence on that walkway. Even the wind seemed to have lost its voice. Then Meri screamed, a half second too late to be useful, and it knocked me to my senses. I flew to the edge where Daul had jumped — the pentice roof was just below, an easy distance — and Daul was on his feet, disappearing into the white.

I had swung one leg over the wall when Wierolf grabbed me. "Digger, are you crazy? That's a fifteen-foot drop!"

"Let me go — I can catch him!"

"There's nowhere for him to go. Let him run."

I met his pleading gaze with a hard one of my own. "There's been enough running." I slipped over the edge.

And fell hard, with a loud thump, on the slippery pentice roof below. Damn snow. I slid off onto the ground. My hip was sore, but that was about it. Hiking my skirts in my hand, I sprinted across the courtyard. Daul was halfway to the siege gates, and he had a lot of leg on me.

He also had a pistol, and I only had a dagger, but for the moment I didn't care. All I could think about was catching him, hitting him as hard as I could, hurting him. Making him pay for the threats, the intimidation, the knocks on the head, the scene with Werne that morning. For Meri. For Marlytt.

For the prince.

We ran through the empty courtyard, straight for the gatehouse overlooking the sheer cliff and the army on the ledge below. Opening the siege gates cost Daul some time. I threw myself into his back, slamming his body against the half-open gate. The pistol went skittering toward the ledge.

I was fast, but Daul was stronger. I was mad, but Daul was bigger. We struggled for a moment, but I couldn't match his reach or his power. In no time his hand was crushing mine, twisting Durrel's knife from my grip. He writhed out from under me, edging back out through the gate, toward the rocky precipice and the steep path down to the waiting army. I scrabbled after him, fighting to find my feet in the snow and my skirts. If I could get the knife back —

"What are you doing?" he yelled, but my shoulder hit him squarely in the back, and he stumbled. I knocked his arm aside and grabbed his wrist. He tried to shake me off, and my half-frozen fingers protested — but I'd been building up to this for two months, since the night I'd run from Greenmen instead of standing and fighting with Tegen. I turned under Daul's arm and pulled his hand with me, bracing it against my hip as I leaned into him, trying to get him to drop the dagger. A hand shoved hard against my head, and my feet slipped, dumping me in the snow. But I had the knife.

It was a stupid, scrabbly, awkward, unlovely sort of struggle, each of us unbalanced by the slippery rocks and the wind. We were also getting precariously close to the edge of the mountain — in the whiteness it was impossible to tell where land turned to air. My foot caught in my skirt as I lunged for Daul, knocking him off balance. I slashed at his flailing legs; the knife stuck in his boot leather and threw me sideways with a kick. My head swung through empty air, inches from the dizzying drop.

I hopped back from the ledge a few paces, regrouping, and the knife flew from Daul's boot and whizzed past my left ear. I flinched in time to see him looming up beside me again. I grabbed for his doublet, as his arm snaked upward from his belt, something glinting bright and silver in his hand.

"Digger, *watch out!*" The prince was pounding through the snow behind us, kicking up plumes of white as he ran. I saw his arm lift just a fraction before Daul did, and I let go of Daul's doublet and dropped back onto the ground.

The prince's knife — that tiny dull carving knife begrudgingly loaned by Lady Lyll — came tumbling through the air and hit Daul, hilt-first, in the shoulder. It fell uselessly to the ground. Daul paused for a moment, glanced down at the knife, and then laughed. He fixed his gaze on the prince.

For a heartbeat, I was frozen with indecision. Somehow my body decided for itself, and my arm stretched out far above my head, searching in the snow, until I found something solid under my numb fingertips. I grabbed it, flung my arm forward as hard as I could, and watched my dagger sail awkwardly through the air and bury itself in Daul's side, just above his belt. Daul stumbled, shook his head as if to clear it, and lost his footing on the narrow ledge.

"Daul — look out!" I'm not sure I really said it, but his eyes widened briefly as the earth fell away behind him. Wierolf dived for me and pulled me to him — but over his shoulder I saw the surprise on Daul's face turn to a thin, wicked smile. He sailed backward over the edge, swallowed up by snow and sky.

"NO!"

I did scream that, into the roaring wind, into Wierolf's shoulder as he held me down. I stared and stared, but all I saw was endless, swirling, deadly white. Wierolf eased off slightly, and I cried out. "I didn't mean to kill him —"

"Of course you didn't. Easy, now."

But hadn't I? "I chased him — you said stop, but I chased him, and if I hadn't, he'd —" My voice was strangled, raw — something I couldn't recognize.

"Listen to me." Wierolf turned my face to his and spoke firmly. "He had a gun. He was going to kill someone. Maybe you, maybe me. You're lucky to be alive. *Merista's* alive, because of you." He stopped. "Gods — Digger! You're bleeding."

I shook my head. "No, it's Daul's —" and I looked down, to see the prince holding my hand up by the wrist, streaming red against the snow. I'd grabbed Durrel's dagger by the blade, and hadn't felt the edge slicing into my frozen fingers. The prince found his own dull knife a few feet away and tore it through the hem of his shirt. His pale, scarred skin was nearly as white as the world around us.

"Here." He bound my wounded hand, then eased me to my feet, and we both wavered.

"Digger," he said gravely, putting one arm around my shoulders — for comfort or support or both.

"What?"

"I've seen you fight better."

Leaning against him, I laughed until the sobs came.

# CHAPTER THIRTY-SIX

Wierolf guided me back to the courtyard, leaving the siege gates open to the snow that would, within minutes, bury Daul, my blood, and our scrambled footsteps under a cloak of white. I stumbled, and Wierolf swung me up into his arms like I weighed nothing.

"They'll see you," I protested. "They'll —"

"Let them see me," he said, carrying me onward. "It's about time, don't you think? Here we go, up this step."

"But your wounds —"

We passed a knot of men in green, pressed together by guards in silver and black, marching them across the courtyard. I twisted in Wierolf's arms, trying to see. Nemair guards stood at every tower, muskets trained down on the men below.

"What — ? Where did they — ?"

"Do I have to *tell* you to shut up?"

An hour later I lay propped up in Meri's bed, under a ridiculous heap of blankets and feather beds that didn't really chase the chill away. Lyll and Antoch and Meri were all there, fawning over and coddling me, while the prince — who had refused to leave and apparently realized that no one could, in fact, make him — sprawled awkwardly on the bench by the window.

Lady Lyll tended to my hand properly, tsk-tsking as she did so, but it was still too early to tell how bad the damage was. Chilblains, she'd said, to start — frostbite, which had caused the numbness that kept me from noticing the blade slicing through my flesh. I had cut three fingers deeply, two to the bone, one very close to the fingertip. Lyll warned me I might lose that one, and that my hand might never fully heal. It seemed a small price to pay, she said, for saving her daughter and escaping with my life.

My life. I didn't try to explain how my fingertips *were* my life.

I couldn't stand them looking at me like that — like I was some kind of hero, when all I could think of was how *none* of this would have happened, if I'd just kept my fingers to myself. "I — I'm sorry. I didn't mean to lie to you —" I stopped, because of course I'd meant to. I hid my face behind my bandaged hand, but Lady Lyll slowly pulled it back down.

"You saved our daughter's life. That's not something you *apologize* for."

"What about Werne?" I said. "If he sees Meri, or the prince —"

"No," Wierolf said, crossing over toward me. "That's over now. No more hiding." He sounded strange and determined. "It's time to take a stand. Your lordships, I understand you have something in the works here at Bryn Shaer? I'd very much like to be a part of that. If you would acquaint me with your allies, I will gladly introduce you to mine."

"Your allies?" Lady Lyll said sharply. "Who?"

Wierolf looked at her evenly. "Tnor Reynart."

Lady Lyll's eyes narrowed, and I couldn't tell what she was thinking. But Meri cried out happily, "Stagne!"

Her mother wheeled her gaze toward Meri, who simply beamed. Lyll scowled and shook her head. "Why do I feel as though I've lost control of things here?"

"Enough," Antoch said. "We've got an injured girl here. No more politics in the sickroom."

But I was desperate to know more. I tried to get out of bed, with the half-formed plan that if we *left* my sickroom, we could keep talking — but strong arms held me down.

"You really won't rest until you know what's going on, will you?" Wierolf said. I shook my head, so in her low, even voice, Lyll explained everything I'd missed while scrabbling around in the snow.

Apparently the Inquisitor, unaccustomed to having his prisoners disappear out from under him, had been verging on hysteria, ready to dismiss the Greenmen he'd brought *and* tear Bryn Shaer apart stone by stone looking for Merista. While the guards were dispatched to retrieve the missing prisoner, Confessors checking the room for magic judged the situation altogether more dangerous than they were presently prepared to contain. They recommended that His Worship withdraw temporarily, despite the precautions of silver and scripture that were meant to protect the Holy Mother's servants.

"They had my books," Meri said. "*To Appear Without Form. To Cloud the Mind.* They must have really thought I just disappeared." She sounded a little frightened at the thought. "The things they accused me of . . ."

"And once they discovered that the girl claiming to be Werne's sister had disappeared as well, the Confessors packed up and dragged him out of here," Lyll said. "Apparently two young women with magic running loose is quite a different matter than one girl chained to a chair." Her voice was hard.

"And what about the Greenmen?" I asked.

"Gently encouraged to follow their master," she said. I nodded, remembering the group marched out of the courtyard by the Nemair guards.

"It won't last, though," Antoch said. "They're regrouping, and when they decide that being ejected from Bryn Shaer was an intolerable injury, they'll come at us in force."

"What about Phandre?" I asked.

"She confessed everything," Lady Lyll said. "If you can call it that. I had no idea she was so angry. I think —" She sighed. "I think she just wanted everyone to see how important she was, to finally prove that she was better than we, somehow."

"Sounds familiar, doesn't it?" Antoch said, and I tried to imagine what it must have been like for her, finding that message about her father's treachery hidden inside those damning books of Meri's. Strangely, the evidence she'd supplied to betray Meri had gone missing as well, though both the Cardom and Cwalo insisted they knew nothing about it.

I closed my eyes. Just like her father, Phandre had betrayed her friends. And for what?

"Where is she now?"

"We had to let her go," Lyll said tiredly. "She made her choice; she packed her things and left with the Inquisitor's men."

Stupid girl. I knew she didn't have any ideals, and now she would be deprived of the comforts she prized so much, as well. It would take the army weeks to get anywhere she could lodge in luxury. And more than that, I think the Nemair had genuinely been fond of her, as fond as anyone could be. I knew they felt responsible for her — and look how she'd paid them back.

"The guards also recovered Lord Daul's body," Wierolf put in gently. "He, uh — landed just outside their camp. There's no question he's dead."

I let out a sigh and felt my ruined hand unclench. "Berdal?"

Antoch answered. "The lad's fine. A little embarrassed, but unharmed. We found him tied up in the attic. Don't judge him too harshly — he took quite a knock on the head."

"But the Inquisition — Werne — the army?" They may have left the castle, but they were still camped, two-hundred-fifty strong, on our doorstep.

The prince darted a glance, full of meaning, toward Lyll, then back to me. "I have a plan for them," he said. "It will require the assistance of the Lady Merista, when she's feeling up to it."

Meri looked alarmed, but nodded. "Yes, Your Highness," she said.

Lyll cried, "Absolutely not! I forbid it!"

"You can't forbid me, Mother, I'm an adult now," Meri said reasonably, and all of us were shocked to silence.

Finally Antoch broke into a giant laugh that shook the room. "That's my girl." He leaned down and patted me on the head in an affectionate way I kind of loved him for. "Come now, ladies, Highness. Give the girl some room to rest." He ushered Lady Lyll and the prince toward the door, but Meri lingered.

"I'll stay with Celyn," she said. She'd had by far a worse day than mine, but here she was, moving smoothly through the room with a calm confidence that was oddly familiar.

As they filed out, Wierolf bent down to my level, though I saw him wincing, and whispered something in my ear. "If you were my sister, I'd have taken better care of you."

Meri stood beside the bed and poured me a shallow draught of warmed-over wine. Her pale face was whipped with red, her own fingertips spotted white — I'd forgotten she'd been out in the snow for as long as I had — and her wrists were raw from the silver chains.

"Was he really your brother?" she asked.

I took the wine she offered. "Say he's very like me, and I swear by Marau I'll kill you in your sleep."

She smiled a little, holding the goblet to my lips, then stood back and looked at me gravely. "Thank you," she said, almost whispering.

"Sweet little Meri." My voice sounded thick and — silly, and after a second I couldn't remember what I'd said. "Sly little Meri — you drugged me?"

"Poppy," she said, a note of quiet triumph in her voice. "Prince Wierolf said we'd have to trick you into taking it."

For a moment I couldn't fix her in my vision, and then I was too tired to try. I felt something thick and heavy at the end of my hand bounce softly against the bed, and then the warmth of Meri climbing into bed behind me. Warm arms wrapped around my body, legs tucked behind my own. A soft voice breathed against my ear, "Good night, Celyn."

I slept through that night, and they tried to keep me in bed the next morning too, but the poppy only brought me nightmares of snow and knives and men with blood in their beards. Besides, there was too much going on. I eased myself out of the bed, wincing as I rediscovered every one of my injuries. My hand hurt obscenely — burning and throbbing, and I gave it about ten seconds before I was seeking out a knife to strip the wretched bandages off again.

The door cracked open, and I started guiltily, spinning round to find the prince standing in Meri's doorway.

"Wierolf! I'm half naked!" My voice sounded rusty. I gave a cough.

"Fair's fair," he said cheerfully. "Leave that alone or *it will never heal.*" He strode across the room and threw open the lid to the clothes chest. He pulled out an ivory damask robe of Meri's and helped me slip my bulky arm through the sleeve.

"Have you eaten? Here —" He produced a roll from inside his own jerkin. It was flecked with wooly fluff.

"Whose clothes are those?"

Wierolf paused a moment to display a dun-brown coat and buckskin breeches. "Do you approve? It turns out there's a man-at-arms here who is very nearly of royal stature himself."

"Berdal."

The prince snapped his fingers. "That's the one. A good man."

*Prince Wierolf's man.* "Yesterday, in the courtyard —"

"Oh, yes. Everyone's talking about how Celyn just-a-maid was plucked from the snow by the gallant prince of Hanival. He's quite the hero, I understand."

"No, I mean —" I sounded impatient. "Why did you come back?"

He lowered himself to the window seat. "Why did you jump off the bailey? We're not runners, Digger, neither of us. The work was here. The danger was *here*."

"The Inquisitor is here," I added pointedly.

"Ah, yes. Your reunion with your brother sounded very . . . exciting."

I gave a snort. "Meri's *kernja-velde* was ruined."

"Oh, come now. I'm sure this is one birthday she won't soon forget."

"No, and she'll stop thanking me eventually too," I said. "I really should travel more — I spread such good fortune wherever I go."

"That's Tiboran's girl," he said, grinning and rumpling my hair. Nobs.

Instead of blasting us from the mountain and grinding us to dust, the commander of the Green Army agreed to meet with the Nemair and discuss terms by which we might all achieve a peaceable outcome to this situation. This would be the rebels' opportunity to present their documented grievances and demands to Bardolph's representative. I knew how much hope Lady Lyll had for this meeting, and I was concerned. I didn't believe Werne would listen, much less negotiate.

We gathered inside the east tower, overlooking the courtyard and the valley. We didn't have the Green Army's numbers, but we had the advantage of height — particularly Wierolf's. They'd found him a set of clothes that more or less fit, a nob's suit, all velvet and fur and damask, but it was Wierolf himself that made them look regal. All the Bryn Shaer Sarists were there — Wellyth, Sposa, Eptin Cwalo, and the Cardom, who were looking very pleased with themselves. And Meri, dressed in sober gray, her hair braided round her head and tucked beneath a caul, looking every inch Nemair: the grown-up, independent daughter of this house, though she'd had rather a different coming-of-age than anyone had planned. I saw that she'd left her necklaces off this morning.

Lyll and Antoch arrived last, leading with them a party I scarcely recognized, without their ragged bandits' clothes. Reynart stepped forward, absolutely splendid in brilliant violet robes, a silver star blazing at the breast, his longish hair billowing. He gave me a bow, and reached out for my good hand. A thrill went through me as my fingertips touched his, and his hand blazed up in a flash of glittering light. Following behind Reynart were Stagne, Kespa the healer, the Giant and his little daughter, even the *dog* — all in purple (the dog wore an improbable star-embroidered kerchief round its thick neck). They were twenty-one strong including Meri, who turned back the sleeves on her gown to reveal their purple silk lining. Suddenly, I was fiercely proud of her.

Were these all the wizards in Llyvraneth? Reynart had told me they weren't very strong without power like Meri's, Channeling the magic so the Casters could shape it into some useful form. The brief display I'd seen, of Meri and Stagne playing with light and fire, hadn't seemed that threatening — but Werne might think otherwise. Any magic provoked him, even my slight trace, and I doubted that the Confessors, much less the average Green Army soldier, had even a fraction of Reynart's understanding of Sar's gifts.

"It's almost midday," the prince said cheerfully. "Let's see if they've sent their men. Lady Nemair, if you'll lead the way?"

The thirty-odd of us climbed to the top of the tower. Below us, the two dozen liveried Nemair guards — including Berdal — were conspicuously stationed throughout the courtyard and armed with firearms instead of pikes. Among them, wearing makeshift black or gray sashes, were the men Berdal and Lord Antoch had recruited. Overnight, somehow, they had pulled out the artillery, pointing the cannon muzzles down on the ridge below, so it looked like we might well be hiding a much greater force.

I looked at the prince, tall and fierce behind those cannon, the Sarists a wall of violet behind him, the black-and-silver Nemair guards like a strong chain around the courtyard, and my pulse quickened. Lyll and Wierolf knew how to bluff.

The Nemair guards threw open the siege gates, their brisk boots making the first prints in the fresh snow. Waiting outside on the ledge stood a knot of soldiers and horsemen in green, Werne like a dark flame at their heart.

Lady Lyll's impassive face was turned down upon the soldiers marching on her home. The plan had changed, I realized — if the Nemair were up *here*, not down in the courtyard below, they must not be planning to parley after all.

Bardolph's men rode in, and a soldier riding beside Werne — their commander, I'd gathered, a man called Llars — looked around the courtyard, his expression growing dark. He leaned over in the saddle to speak to the Inquisitor.

Werne looked up at us, contempt briefly flashing across his composed face. "Celys commands us to be merciful in our correction of Her wayward children," he said. "But correct them we must. Residents of Bryn Shaer, the Goddess gives you this one chance to deliver unto Her servants the woman Merista Nemair and her waiting woman, called Celyn, and the rest of you will be spared. If you refuse, Celys's justice will be swift and —"

"I think we've heard enough." Wierolf's voice was soft, but it carried, halting Werne mid-sentence. Clearly not used to being interrupted, he just *stared*.

"Do you know who I am?" the prince asked, almost conversationally.

Werne squinted up at him. "The Holy Church does not recognize you or your authority in these proceedings!"

"Well, what about the army?"

"Your Highness," the commander said. He sounded grudging, as if he was trained to respect those who outranked him, and yet as a soldier in the king's army, he wasn't supposed to acknowledge Wierolf's existence or position.

"Good. Are you authorized to speak on behalf of Bardolph?"

Llars paused, and his men grew restless. The Nemair guard eased forward gently, almost imperceptibly. Lyll and Antoch, flanking Wierolf, watched the commander become more uneasy.

At last he said, "No."

Lyll was expressionless. They never meant to parley, then. The rebels' document would have been useless.

"I speak for the Goddess!" Werne said. "And I demand you produce the two heretics before we destroy you!" He kicked his mule forward, but Llars grabbed its reins.

"But you *don't* speak for this army," the commander said harshly. "Keep to your own purview, your Grace." Werne turned to him, a look of stunted hatred on his face.

"Gentlemen, please." Wierolf stepped forward, leaning lightly on the tower wall. "Your quarrel with me is so much more entertaining. Now. Let's discuss the situation in which we find ourselves. These good people" — he gestured toward Lady Lyll and her rebels — "came prepared for a civilized and productive negotiation, but as no one here seems able to represent His Majesty's views in this matter, you'll simply have to convey a message on our behalf instead. I presume you *are* authorized to do that."

Below the tower wall, Wierolf made a small movement with one arm, invisible to the men on the field below. Reynart stepped forward — with

*Meri*, who slipped into place beside the prince and gripped the battlement with her hands.

"Of course," Llars said, but Werne burst forward.

"*I* will speak for His Majesty!" he cried. "I will hear whatever outrageous claims —"

"Good," interrupted Wierolf. "The message is this."

And before I could blink, Reynart had thrown back his hand, and a ball of flame burst into the snow at Werne's feet. His mule reared up, spilling him to the ground. The soldiers scattered back, and I even saw a few of the Nemair men flinch. I had flinched myself. It happened so fast, so impossibly fast. Wierolf gave another nearly imperceptible nod, and Reynart flung his spread fingers toward the soldiers on the ridge.

A wagon exploded.

Then a tent.

A tree.

Someone screamed. A startled volley of arrows scattered into the air, falling to cinders, one by one. Below us, smoke and flame billowed up from the burning wagon, and another burst of magic blazed through the camp, ripping through tents, incinerating all but two of the remaining wagons. Horses and soldiers screamed, as Werne shrilled out from the ground, "Attack! Attack!" But the Green Army was in disarray, the men scattered and panicked, their supplies destroyed. Nobody was going to attack us anytime soon.

Meri stood, a picture of serenity, but she held fast to the stones and she was breathing hard. Magic streamed up all around her, bathing her in light. That kind of power came from our Meri?

Abruptly Wierolf put up his hand. Ribbons of red filled the sky from the skeleton of the ruined tree. Reynart eased smoothly back, just as the other Sarists stepped forward, forming a sort of guard around the prince. They linked their hands — a gesture that now seemed dangerous.

Llars was still struggling to calm his horse, which danced nervously around a patch of smoldering black on the white field of Bryn Shaer's courtyard. Werne had taken refuge below a stone trough, one green-clad arm flung up to protect his head, and a soldier reached down to pull him out.

Wierolf's face was set, but his voice rang out loudly. "Go back and tell your king that Prince Wierolf of Hanival is coming to Gerse. And I have a new weapon."

# CHAPTER THIRTY-SEVEN

The Green Army limped away from Bryn Shaer that day. Werne sent a messenger to us with one parting blow: a Writ of Expulsion, damning all the denizens of Bryn Shaer for heresy. Lady Lyll looked proud of it.

"What will we do now?" I asked her. She squeezed my arm and gave me a broad grin.

"Now we hold Meri's *kernja-velde!*"

It was not so simple as that, of course. Meri slept for two full days after her contribution to the battle on the tower, and when she woke, her magic was so weak and faint that even I couldn't see it. Reynart and Kespa assured us that this was to be expected, and that she would recover fully with rest and good food. But Meri fretted and Lady Lyll fussed, until Antoch brought in Stagne to separate them, and after that Meri's smile made more frequent appearances, and the sparkle she gave off may not have been magic alone.

As for Wierolf's brazen debut on the Llyvrin political scene, there was much to discuss, and debate, and dissect about what had just occurred, and what consequences might follow. The Sarists could not go to war immediately, of course; despite Wierolf's brashness and Lady Lyll's efforts to prepare for this eventuality, the plain fact was that these new rebels weren't ready. Even with the men Berdal had collected, the Nemair had nothing like an army, and although they had coaxed support from Corlesanne and Varenzia, those nations were unlikely to commit troops until their Llyvrin allies had some of their own. The prince felt he could count on assistance from a number of other key houses, but these names sometimes drew protest from Sposa or Lady Cardom or even the Nemair — until Wierolf had to give them what I was coming to call the Royal Eye, and declare, in his easy voice, that a particular matter was settled.

There was no question who was the leader here, and it was strange to watch, because it had seemed to me that no one could be more formidable than Lady Lyll. But of course Lyll had not done all this for her own benefit. It was always on behalf of a world with Wierolf on the throne. Some strange alignment of the moons had brought him here at this time, and it would be interesting to see how things shook out in truth. Would Wierolf be the leader these peoples' dreams had set him up to be? Or would he be his own man? I touched the little wooden sun lion he had given me, and wondered.

Reynart and his band joined these talks as well, to discuss how the prince's new weapon might best be wielded. Lady Lyll wasn't thrilled with the idea of her daughter becoming a permanent part of Wierolf's army of mages, but Meri was adamant.

"They *need* me," she kept saying. "And I don't know why we're having this discussion anyway. If I were a boy, you'd *expect* me to join the army!"

Lyll sat back, her lips pressed closed, and looked hard at Meri, as if she might never see her again — or as if she were really seeing her for the first time. "Yes," she finally said. "But I wouldn't *like* it."

Meri just snuggled up into Lyll's arms until her mother closed her eyes and rested her chin on Meri's dark head. Watching them, I felt a strange tightness in my chest, and I pulled away, feeling out of place and uncertain.

Wierolf spotted me hiding behind a column. He strode over, seeming lanky and comfortable in his new role.

"You look like you own the place," I said. "Maybe you should make Bryn Shaer your seat."

"After all the work the Nemair have put in? Hardly! No," he said, his grin vanishing. "I have another palace in mind. Come with us, Digger. You know you're welcome."

"And what would I do in an army?"

He burst out laughing. "I don't know, mount daring missions behind enemy lines, maybe? I think we could find a place for you." He touched my shoulder. "You have medical experience; you could work in the field hospitals. I can think of worse people to tend the wounded."

I looked at my bandaged hand. What would I be left with when my injuries healed? Didn't surgeons need ten good fingers? Didn't thieves? "No," I said. "I don't want to always wonder if the next patient I see will be you. Now that I know you, I kind of like you."

"Well, I'm glad we have that established," he said. "Don't worry. I plan to be around to antagonize you for a long while to come." He lifted me off the ground by the shoulders and kissed the top of my head.

"Gods!" I cried, pulling away. "Lady Lyll has *got* to find you a woman, Your Highness."

He grinned and darted a jab at me, which I blocked smoothly. And I took his ring again, because I *could*. He could have it back later. Maybe.

Antoch was the only one who seemed to share my sense of being unmoored. I'd find him sitting at the council table long after everyone else had left, staring at the maps but not quite seeing them. One evening I finally gathered up my nerve and went to him.

"I'm sorry," I said — wanting to elaborate, but not quite sure how to say everything I was feeling. That I was sorry not only for my role, but for what Daul had done, who he had been . . . things I wasn't remotely responsible for, but felt bad about anyway.

Antoch gave a sigh and gathered up the maps. "It's an old sadness," he said. "You haven't made it any worse. Daul, the Séthe. Some people let bitterness and envy fester until there's no curing it."

But I wondered. Maybe there could have been some reconciliation, or at least understanding between Antoch and Daul. Perhaps Daul hadn't crossed so far to the edge that he could not have been pulled back. But we'd never find out, because I'd helped shove him over the side.

We held Meri's *kernja-velde* exactly one week later than scheduled. The tables in the Round Court were pulled back for the whole room to be filled with dancing and merriment. Meri wore a beaded gown, yellow silk woven of threads that appeared soft green when looked at one way, and ever so faintly violet another. I wondered if there was some coded language of fabrics; could she send secret messages by the precise swishing of her skirts? But I kept my mouth clamped tight on that; no need to give Lyll or Lady Cardom any ideas.

Meri floated through the room, her hair loose down her back, her arms laden with treasures. All the girls and women of Bryn Shaer had a ceremonial role in guiding her along from childhood to adulthood. There weren't any family members younger than she, so the tiny red-headed Sarist and a girl from the kitchens took their places. Meri moved from the youngest girl to the eldest woman, passing off a doll and an outgrown kirtle to the younger girls, and accepting gifts from those older than she: a volume of poetry from Marlytt, a sewing kit from her mother, a heavy brooch from Lady Cardom. Lady Lyll had assigned me the traditional bottle of wine to give, handing it off to me with a grin.

Lady Lyll read out the benediction as Meri stepped forward. "May all the gods and goddesses smile upon our daughter, Merista, who this day leaves her childhood behind. By Celys and Sar, Tiboran and Mend-kaal, Zet, Marau, and the Nameless One, may she live a rich and blessed life."

Meri knelt on an embroidered cloth, a lively confection of flowers and animals at the center, blended artfully with celestial symbols radiating toward the edges. For a moment, it looked as though she were the center of the universe. With my hand bandaged, I couldn't help braid her hair for the ritual, so the job went to Lady Cardom, who glowed with pleasure as she and Marlytt did up the plaits and twists. But I stood by, holding a glass bowl of pearls and gold beads; and if one or two or a dozen vanished from the bowl before reaching Lady Merista's coiffure, I'm sure I couldn't explain it.

Once Meri's hair was in its complicated adult arrangement, Kespa and an older woman from Reynart's people rolled back Meri's sleeves and lifted her skirts, and spent the next half hour inking every inch of her exposed skin from feet to face with an elaborate pattern of deep violet stars and scrollwork that transformed her into an eldritch creature from some other realm. Even her fingernails were not spared, and though it was simply temporary ink, and not more tattoos, I thought Lady Lyll would have an apoplexy. But she controlled herself with typical steely calm.

Somehow the stately, dignified affair the Nemair had planned was dissolving into a strange ceremony that only Meri really understood, but that everyone else seemed to enjoy all the same. Reynart and his band mingled easily with the nobs, and I learned that some of them had been aristocrats once themselves. Stagne caught me, stroking a swirl of purple vine down the back of my hand with his brush.

"I'm no wizard," I warned him.

He shrugged and grinned. "If you say so." But after he floated off again, I found myself turning my hand back and forth in the light, until the inked leaves seemed to move on their own. Maybe Sar's fearsome gift had a playful side, as well. I had seen magic tear through the army camp, and Werne had every reason to fear it. But the only reason *I* had to be afraid of my magic was Werne.

I looked over the party, with rebel and wizard and prince and thief all consorting together, and wondered if everyone in this room was utterly mad. If only Werne had stayed for this, we'd have every lunacy in Llyvraneth represented here. Could any of this amity survive beyond this strange sheltered place in the mountains? I had my doubts; I had seen too well how the climate outside these walls warped and killed. But this — well, not perhaps this *exactly*, but something very like it — was what they were all fighting for.

Meri danced with her father, then Wierolf, and then Stagne, and as she and Stagne fumbled and laughed their way through a wild reel that grew faster and harder with every round, I realized that Lord Cardom was standing beside me, holding out a cup of sparkling Grisel and smiling faintly at the two of them.

"They look happy," he said, and he didn't sound the least bit wistful or disappointed. He was a nice man, and he would have treated Meri well, but Meri had chosen a penniless Sarist boy instead. Then Cardom was holding out his arm to me. We made a ridiculous couple, but I downed the Grisel in one draught and let him pull me into the dance.

"Mother wants to bring you home to Tratua with us," he said. "I thought I should warn you."

I choked out a laugh. "Tell her I'll consider it."

"Yes, that's probably wise."

As we danced, I glanced across the room, to where Marlytt sat in lively conversation with three of the Nemair guard. I had kept her complicity with Daul mostly out of the official story. She had enough black marks against her.

"Are you going back soon?" I asked Lord Cardom when the music ended, and he nodded.

"His Highness needs ships, and Mother wants to get started telling our neighbors which side they'll be on in the coming fight."

"May I ask a favor, milord? Will you take Marlytt to Tratua with you?"

He blinked at me. "Marlytt? Certainly, but why?"

Marlytt sat alone now, in a sea of ice-blue silk, a wine glass in her hand. The admirers had departed, and she looked tired. "Her family's there," I said.

Finally I found a place to hide, back in the shadows behind the fireplace. I had half a roast partridge I'd nicked off somebody's plate, and I was getting ready to enjoy wiping my hand on my gold skirts, when Meri found me. She said nothing, just settled beside me on the floor. I handed her a chunk of bird, and we sat there for ages, watching her party swirl on into the night. She spread her purple-or-green skirts out before her and stroked the cloth, which I'd been wanting to do *all day*. I reached out my hand, but paused an inch above the silk. I had, just for a moment, forgotten about the bandages.

"Does it still hurt?" she asked.

"Not so much," I said. "How about you?"

She fluttered her fingers, and a ripple of sparks spun through them. "Getting better. You were so brave," she added.

"*We* were brave," I corrected. Something slipped into my memory, and I murmured, "Just staying alive is brave these days."

Meri looked at me quizzically.

"Something your cousin said to me." At the time I had believed him, *wanted* to believe him. But was it really enough just to stay alive? I knew the answer.

Not for Meri, not for Lyll and Antoch, not for Wierolf.

Not for me.

Not anymore.

"Mother says you'll still be able to write, and sew, and play music, and work a stillroom," Meri said. There was an odd note in her voice, something final and bittersweet. "You won't stay, will you?"

Sweet Meri. I put my bandaged hand on hers. "Eptin Cwalo is leaving in a few days, and he's offered me a place in his caravan, as long as I let him make another case for Garod."

She bit her lip. "Where will you go?"

With a deep breath, I looked over the Round Court, at the great bloom of color displayed, the rich fabrics, the fancy dance steps, the food, and the fire and . . . and it felt too easy, too natural. I could stay here, make a life with these people, and be happy.

Or I could go home.

"Gerse," I said, closing my eyes. Like that, I was there again — the hard cobbled streets, the stench of sewage in the gutters, the long rainy winters and hot sticky summers. Lyll and Wierolf and the Sarists had their grand nob plans, but meanwhile Werne's Greenmen still menaced the common citizens of Gerse, and that would only get worse when the war started in earnest. That dark city had saved my life and made me welcome when the Celystra spat me out, and I'd run from it. My city deserved more from me. Tegen deserved more.

"I left a friend behind. I have to go back."

Meri nodded, a brightness in her eyes. "Well," she said. "Just don't forget you have friends here too."

I looked up then, and saw Lady Lyll and Wierolf crossing toward us. Meri hauled me to standing, and for a moment I looked at my hands in hers — one with the silver bracelet to seal my friendship with Meri and the house of Nemair, the other with the battered fingers of a thief who's made one too many mistakes. Somehow, by Tiboran's inscrutable design, they seemed to fit together.

I grinned at Meri. "Never."

*Digger will return in*
## Liar's Moon

# LEXICON

**Astilan of Hanival**: Prince of the realm. King Bardolph's nephew; cousin to Prince Wierolf.

**Acolyte Guard**: The Celystra's honor guard; once ceremonial, now King Bardolph's de facto secret police. Called "Greenmen," in slang for their entirely green uniforms.

**Bardolph of Hanival**: King of Llyvraneth.

**Berdal**: Guard and groom at Bryn Shaer.

**Breijarda Velde**: The Wide Pass through the Carskadon Mountains, connecting the provinces of Briddja Nul and Kellespau.

**Breijardarl**: Literally "broad valley," a settlement just beyond the Breijarda Velde. Formerly the center for the worship of Sar in Llyvraneth and home to a university for the study of magic (as well as medicine, astronomy, and other sciences). Its temple and university were closed by Bardolph early in his reign.

**Briddja Nul**: One of the three provinces that make up the nation of Llyvraneth. Briddja Nul occupies much of the northwest, and is home to the port city of Yeris Volbann.

**Bryn Shaer**: Literally "Bear's Keep," a castle fortress in the Carskadon Mountains, guarding the Breijarda Velde. Home to the Nemair.

**Caerellis**: Manor house north of Favom Court. Childhood home of Lyllace Nemair; now property of the Crown.

**Carskadon Mountains**: Literally "black mountains," mountain range bisecting the northern half of Llyvraneth, separating the provinces of Briddja Nul and Kellespau.

**Celys**: The great Mother Goddess, goddess of life and the harvest. Her symbols are the ash tree and the full moon.

**Celystra**: Temple complex in Gerse devoted to Celys. Seat of Celyst worship and power.

**Cardom, Lady**: Noblewoman staying at Bryn Shaer.

**Cardom, Lord**: Nobleman staying at Bryn Shaer. Son of Lady Cardom.

**Chavel**: Private secretary to the king.

**Contrare, Celyn**: Digger's alias.

**Confessor**: An investigator for the Inquisition, trained in the arts of torture.

**Corlesanne**: Nation to Llyvraneth's east. Traditionally tolerant of Sarism.

**Cwalo, Eptin**: Merchant from Yeris Volbann. Longtime friend of Lady Lyllace.

**Daul, Lord Remy**: Lunarist and Llyvrin nobleman staying at Bryn Shaer. Son of Senim; foster brother and childhood friend of Lord Antoch.

**Daul, Lord Senim**: Llyvrin nobleman and commander of Sarist forces during the war. Foster father of Lord Antoch. Deceased.

**Decath, Durrel**: Young nobleman from Gerse. Cousin to Merista Nemair.

**Decath, Lord Ragn**: Durrel's father.

**Digger**: Thief from Gerse.

**Favom Court**: Farm and manor house north of Gerse. Country residence of the House of Decath.

**Gairveyont**: Noble house on Llyvraneth's southeastern coast. Home to Lady Cardom's daughter.

**Gelnir**: One of the three provinces that make up the nation of Llyvraneth. A fertile region of farmland to the west and south, and home to Llyvraneth's capital city of Gerse.

**Gerse**: Capital city of Llyvraneth. Digger's home.

**Greenmen**: *see* Acolyte Guard.

**Inquisition**: Dedicated arm of the Celyst church charged with eradicating heresy. Led by a staff of inquisitors (specially ordained priests) under the command of the Lord High Inquisitor, Werne Nebraut. The Inquisition has wide-ranging powers and very little oversight.

**Kalorjn**: Battlefield in southeastern Kellespau; site of the Sarists' defeat in the war.

**Kellespau**: One of the three provinces that make up the nation of Llyvraneth. A hilly region covering the northeastern third of the island.

***Kernja-velde:*** Literally "third passage," the celebration of a young woman's reaching adulthood at age fourteen. The male equivalent is the *traese-velde*, or "fourth passage," at age twenty-one.

**Lieste**: Queen of Llyvraneth. Second and much younger wife of Bardolph.

**Llyvraneth**: Island nation consisting of three provinces: Gelnir, Briddja Nul, and Kellespau.

**Lunarism/lunarist**: A discipline equivalent to astrology, by which the future may be divined according to the movements of the moons. Lunarist: a practitioner of this art.

**Marau**: God of the dead and consort to Celys. Twin brother to Sar. His symbol is the crow.

**Mend-kaal**: God of the hearth, the home, and of labor. Twin brother to Tiboran; son of Celys and Marau. His symbol is the hammer.

**Morva**: Cook at Favom Court. Nurse to Lady Lyllace and Merista Nemair.

**Nameless One, The**: Goddess of justice and divine retribution. Daughter of Celys and Marau. Nicknamed "The Hound of Marau" because her moon follows Marau's closely in the heavens (the Nameless One's moon is speculated to be an asteroid captured by Marau's orbit).

**Nebraut, Werne**: *see* Werne.

**Nemair, Lady Lyllace**: Llyvrin noblewoman. Wife of Antoch.

**Nemair, Lord Antoch**: Llyvrin nobleman. Husband of Lyllace. Former Sarist rebel.

**Nemair, Merista**: Young noble girl. Daughter of Lyllace and Antoch; cousin to Durrel Decath.

**Reynart, Tnor**: A Sarist mage.

**Sar**: Goddess of magic and dreams. Twin sister to Marau. Her symbol is the seven-pointed star.

**Sarist**: Supporter of a rebellion against King Bardolph, favoring a more tolerant religious climate that would allow the worship of other gods in general and Sar in particular. Some openly worship Sar, while most simply support greater religious freedom in Llyvraneth. Not all Sarists are magical, but it is widely believed that everyone with magic must be a Sarist.

**Séthe, Lougre**: Former Sarist rebel. Deceased.

**Séthe, Phandre**: Young noblewoman. Daughter of Lougre; friend to Merista.

**Silver**: An elemental metal with antibiotic properties, used for thousands of years to treat infection in wounds and on burns. In Llyvraneth, silver also has anti-magical properties.

**Sposa, Lord**: Nobleman staying at Bryn Shaer.

**Stagne**: A young wizard. Friend to Merista.

**Talanca**: Nation to Llyvraneth's south.

**Taradyce, Lord Hron**: Llyrvin nobleman. Raffin's father; acquaintance of Digger from Gerse.

**Taradyce, Raffin**: Young nobleman from Gerse. Son of Lord Taradyce.

**Tegen**: Thief in Gerse. Digger's partner.

**Tiboran**: God of wine and theater. Twin brother to Mend-kaal. His symbol is the mask, and he has been adopted as a patron by those who must lie for a living, most notably thieves.

**Tigas or Tigas Wanderers**: A nomadic minority ethnic group in Llyvraneth, believed to have migrated north from Talanca hundreds of years ago.

**Tratua**: Port city in southeast Kellespau.

**Varenzia**: Nation bordering Corlesanne.

**Villatiere, Marlytt**: Courtesan from Gerse.

**Wellyth, Lord Petr**: Elderly nobleman staying at Bryn Shaer. Longtime friend of Lady Lyllace.

**Werne, Lord High Inquisitor**: Also called "Werne the Bloodletter."

**Wierolf of Hanival**: Prince of the realm. King Bardolph's nephew; cousin to Prince Astilan.

**Yeris Volbann**: Port city on Llyvraneth's northwest coast.

**Yselle**: Housekeeper at Bryn Shaer, native to Corlesanne.

**Zet**: Goddess of war and the hunt. Her symbol is the arrow. Patron of the nobility.

# CONFESSION OF ACKNOWLEDGMENTS

Under threat of torture, I am forced to reveal the names of the following individuals who provided aid, comfort, and material support at various times during the creation of this novel:

Rebel agent Erin Murphy, for never letting a client be left in the cold.

Handler extraordinaire Cheryl Klein, for heroic editing under the most harrowing conditions.

Local and long-distance allies Laura Manivong, Barb Stuber, Sarah Clark, Katie Speck, Jo Whittemore, and Rose Green. And particularly the Cleaner, Diane Bailey.

Scott McKuen, for information regarding the nature and behavior of moons.

Bruce Bradley of the Linda Hall Library of Science, Engineering & Technology Rare Books Room, for information on Renaissance-era bookbinding, blank books, and handwritten journals.

And my husband, Chris Bunce, who thankfully cannot be made to testify against me.

This book was edited by Cheryl Klein and designed by Phil Falco. The text was set in Alisal, a typeface designed by Matthew Carter in 2001. The display type was set in Angelo. The book was printed and bound at R. R. Donnelley in Crawfordsville, Indiana. The production was supervised by Cheryl Weisman. The manufacturing was supervised by Jess White.